TWISTED HATE

TWISTED BOOK THREE

ANA HUANG

PIATKUS

PIATKUS

First published in 2022 by Ana Huang
Published in Great Britain in 2022 by Piatkus
This paperback edition published in 2022

12

Copyright © 2022 by Ana Huang

Editor: Amy Briggs, Briggs Consulting LLC
Proofreader: Krista Burdine

The moral right of the author has been asserted

A CIP catalogue record for this book
is available from the British Library.

ISBN 978-0-349-43433-9

Printed and bound in Great Britain by Clays Ltd, Elcograf S.p.A.

Papers used by Piatkus are from well-managed forests
and other responsible sources.

MIX
Paper from
responsible sources
FSC® C104740

Piatkus
An imprint of
Little, Brown Book Group
Carmelite House
50 Victoria Embankment
London EC4Y 0DZ

An Hachette UK Company

www.hachette.co.uk

www.littlebrown.co.uk

Ana Huang is an author of primarily steamy New Adult and contemporary romance. Her books contain diverse characters and emotional, sometimes twisty roads toward HEAs (with plenty of banter and spice sprinkled in). Besides reading and writing, Ana loves traveling, is obsessed with hot chocolate, and has multiple relationships with fictional boyfriends.

To everyone who's ever felt like they weren't enough.

Playlist

Don't Blame Me
Taylor Swift
Talk
Salvatore Ganacci
Free
Broods
Daddy Issues
The Neighbourhood
You Make Me Sick
Pink
Animals
Maroon 5
Give You What You Like
Avril Lavigne
wRoNg
Zayn
Waves
Normani ft. 6LACK
50 Shades
Boy Epic
Only You
Ellie Goulding
One More Night
Maroon 5
I Hate U, I Love U
Gnash
Wanted
Hunter Hayes

CONTENT WARNINGS

This story contains explicit sexual content, profanity, mild violence, and topics that may be sensitive to some readers. For a detailed list, please visit *anahuang.com/content-warnings*.

1

JULES

Nothing good ever came from right-swiping on a guy holding a fish on a dating app. Double red flags if said guy's name was *Todd*.

I should've known better, yet there I was, sitting alone at The Bronze Gear, D.C.'s hottest bar, and drinking my hideously expensive vodka soda after being stood up.

That's right.

I'd been stood up for the very first time by a fish-wielding Todd. It was enough to make a girl say *fuck it* and throw away sixteen dollars on one drink even though she didn't have a full-time salary yet.

What was it with men and fish pictures, anyway? Couldn't they choose something more creative, like cage diving with sharks? Also marine animal-centric, but less mundane.

Maybe the fish was an odd thing to fixate on, but it prevented me from dwelling on the awfulness of my day and the hot, sticky embarrassment coating my skin.

Get caught in a sudden downpour halfway to campus with

nary an umbrella in sight? Check. (Five percent chance of rain, my ass. I should sue the weather app company).

Get trapped in an overcrowded metro train that stunk of body odor for forty minutes due to a power problem? Check.

Go on a three-hour apartment hunt which resulted in two blistered feet and zero leads? Check.

After such a hellish day, I wanted to cancel my date with Todd, but I'd already postponed twice—once for a rescheduled study group, the other when I was feeling under the weather—and I hadn't wanted to leave him hanging again. So I sucked it up and showed up, only to get stood up.

The universe had a sense of humor, all right, and it was a shitty one.

I finished the rest of my drink and flagged down the bartender. "Can I get the check please?" Happy hour had just started, but I couldn't wait to go home and curl up with the two real loves of my life. Netflix and Ben & Jerry's never let me down.

"It's already covered."

When my eyebrows shot up, the bartender tilted her head toward a table of preppy-looking twenty-something guys in the corner. Likely consultants, based on their outfits. One of them, a Clark Kent lookalike in a gingham shirt, raised his glass and smiled at me. "Courtesy of Clark the Consultant."

I stifled a laugh even as I raised my own glass and smiled back at him. So I wasn't the only one who thought he looked like Superman's alter ego.

"Clark the Consultant saved me from eating instant ramen for dinner, so cheers to him," I said.

That was sixteen dollars I could keep in my bank account, though I left a tip anyway. I used to work in the food service industry, and it made me obsessive about over tipping. No one dealt with more assholes on a consistent basis than service workers.

I finished my free drink and kept my eyes locked on Clark the Consultant, whose gaze swept appreciatively over my face, hair, and body.

I didn't believe in false humility—I knew I looked good. And I knew if I walked over to that table right now, I could soothe my bruised ego with more drinks, compliments, and maybe an orgasm or two later if he knew what he was doing.

Tempting...but no. I was too exhausted to go through the whole hookup song and dance.

I turned away, but not before catching the flash of disappointment on his face. To his credit, Clark the Consultant understood the implied message—*thank you for the drink, but I'm not interested in taking things further*—and didn't try to approach me, which was more than I could say for most men.

I slung my bag over my shoulder and was about to grab my coat from the hook beneath the bar when a deep, cocky drawl sent every hair on the back of my neck on end.

"Hey, JR."

Two words. That was all it took to trigger my fight or flight. Honestly, it was a Pavlovian response at this point. When I heard his voice, my blood pressure skyrocketed.

Every. Single. Time.

And the day just keeps getting better.

My fingers tightened around my bag strap before I forced them to relax. I would *not* give him the satisfaction of provoking any discernible reaction from me.

With that in mind, I took a deep breath, rearranged my features into a neutral expression, and slowly turned around, where I was greeted with the world's most unwelcome sight to go along with the world's most unwelcome sound.

Josh fucking Chen.

All six feet of him, clad in dark jeans and a white button-down shirt that was *just* fitted enough to show off his muscles. No doubt he planned it that way. He probably spent more time on his appearance than I did, and I wasn't exactly low maintenance. Merriam-Webster should stamp his face next to the word *vain*.

The worst part was, Josh was *technically* good-looking. Thick dark hair, high cheekbones, sculpted body. All the things I was a sucker for...if they weren't attached to an ego so large it required its own zip code.

"Hi, Joshy," I cooed, knowing how much he hated the nickname. I could thank Ava, my best friend and Josh's sister, for that gold nugget of information.

Annoyance sparked in his eyes, and I smiled. The day was looking up already.

To be fair, Josh was the one who'd insisted on calling me JR first. It was short for Jessica Rabbit, the cartoon character. Some people might take it as a compliment, but when you were a redhead with double Ds, the constant comparison got old fast, and he knew it.

"Drinking alone?" Josh shifted his attention to the empty bar stools on either side of me. It wasn't peak happy hour yet, and the most coveted seats were the booths lining the oak-paneled walls, not at the bar. "Or have you already scared off everyone within a twenty-foot radius?"

"Funny you should mention scaring people off." I eyed the woman standing next to Josh. She was beautiful, with brown hair, brown eyes, and a lithe body clad in an incredible graphic-print wrap dress. Too bad her good taste didn't extend to men, if she was on a date with *him*. "I see you've recovered from your bout of syphilis long enough to sucker another unsuspecting woman into a date." I directed my next words to the brunette.

"I don't know you, but I already know you could do way better. Trust me."

Did Josh actually have syphilis? Maybe. Maybe not. He slept around enough I wouldn't be surprised if he did, and I wouldn't be upholding girl code if I didn't warn Wrap Dress about the *possibility* of contracting an STD.

Instead of recoiling, she laughed. "Thanks for the warning, but I think I'll be okay."

"Making jokes about STDs. How original." If Josh was bothered by me insulting him in front of his date, he didn't show it. "I hope your oral arguments are more creative, or you'll have a tough time in the legal world. Assuming you pass the bar, of course."

His mouth curved into a smirk, revealing a tiny dimple in his left cheek.

I held back a snarl. I *hated* that dimple. Every time it popped up, it mocked me, and I wanted nothing more than to stab it with a knife.

"I'll pass," I said coolly, reining in my violent thoughts. Josh always brought out the worst in me. "Better hope you don't get sued for medical malpractice, Joshy, or I'll be the first to offer my services to the other party."

I'd busted my ass to get a spot at Thayer Law and a job offer from Silver & Klein, the prestigious law firm I interned for last summer. I wasn't about to let my dreams of becoming a lawyer slip away when I was so close.

No freaking way.

I was going to pass the bar exam, and Josh Chen was going to eat his words. Hopefully, he'd choke on them too.

"Big talk for someone who hasn't even graduated yet." Josh leaned against the bar and propped his forearm on the counter, looking irritatingly like a model posing for a *GQ* spread. He switched subjects before I could fire another retort. "You're awfully dressed up for a solo date."

His gaze swept from my curled hair to my made-up face before lingering on the gold pendant resting against my cleavage.

My spine turned to iron. Unlike Clark the Consultant, Josh's scrutiny seared into my flesh, hot and mocking. The metal from my necklace flamed against my skin, and it was all I could do not to yank it off and pelt it in his smug face.

And yet, for some reason, I remained still while he continued his perusal. It wasn't lecherous so much as it was assessing, like he was gathering all the puzzle pieces and arranging them into a complete picture in his mind.

Josh's eyes dipped to the green cashmere dress hugging my torso, skimmed over the expanse of my black-stockinged legs, and stopped at my black heeled boots before he dragged them back up to meet my own hazel ones. His smirk disappeared, leaving his expression unreadable.

A charged silence crackled between us before he spoke again. "You're dressed for an actual date." His pose remained casual, but his eyes sharpened into dark knives waiting to carve out my embarrassment. "But you were about to leave, and it's only five-thirty."

I lifted my chin even as the heat of embarrassment prickled my skin. Josh was many things—infuriating, cocky, the spawn of Satan—but he wasn't stupid, and he was the *last* person I wanted knowing I'd been stood up.

He would never let me live it down.

"Don't tell me he didn't show." There was a strange note in his voice.

The heat intensified. God, I shouldn't have worn cashmere. I was roasting in my stupid dress. "You should worry less about my love life and more about your date."

Josh hadn't looked at Wrap Dress since he showed up, but she didn't seem to mind. She was too busy chatting and laughing with the bartender.

"I assure you, of all the things on my to-do list, worrying about your love life isn't even in the top five thousand." Despite the snark, Josh continued staring at me with that indecipherable expression.

My stomach swooped for no obvious reason.

"Good." It was a lame retort, but my brain wasn't working properly. I blamed it on the exhaustion. Or the alcohol. Or a million other things that had nothing to do with the man standing in front of me.

I grabbed my coat and slid off my seat, intent on brushing past him without another word.

Unfortunately, I'd misjudged the distance between the bar stool rung and the floor. My foot slipped, and a small gasp rose in my throat when my body tilted backward of its own accord. I was two seconds away from falling on my ass when a hand shot out and gripped my wrist, pulling me back up into a standing position.

Josh and I froze at the same time, our eyes locked on where his hand encircled my wrist. I couldn't remember the last time we'd voluntarily touched. Maybe three summers ago, when he'd pushed me, fully clothed, into the pool during a party, and I'd retaliated by "accidentally" elbowing him in the groin?

The memory of him doubling over with pain still gave me great comfort in times of distress, but I wasn't thinking about that now.

Instead, I was focused on how disturbingly close he was—close enough for me to smell his cologne, which was nice and citrusy instead of fire and brimstone-y like I'd expected.

The adrenaline from my near fall pumped through my system, pushing my heart rate into unhealthy territory.

"You can let go now." I willed my breaths to come out steady despite the suffocating heat. "Before your touch gives me hives."

Josh's grip tightened for a millisecond before he dropped my arm like it was a hot potato. Annoyance wiped away his previously unreadable expression. "You're welcome for making sure you don't break your tailbone, *JR*."

"Don't be dramatic, *Joshy*. I would've caught myself."

"Sure. God forbid the words *thank you* leave your mouth." His sarcasm deepened. "You're such a pain in the ass, you know that?"

"It's better than being an ass, period."

Everyone else looked at Josh and saw a handsome, charming doctor. I looked at him and saw a judgmental, self-righteous jerk.

You can make other friends, Ava. She's bad news. You don't need someone like that in your life.

My cheeks flushed. It'd been seven years since I overheard Josh talking to Ava about me, right when she and I were becoming friends, and the memory still stung. Not that I'd ever told them I'd heard them. It would just make Ava feel bad, and Josh didn't deserve to know how much his words hurt.

He wasn't the first person to think I wasn't good enough, but he was the first to try and ruin one of my budding friendships because of it.

I flashed a brittle smile. "If you'll excuse me, I've exceeded my daily tolerance for your presence." I slipped on my coat and gloves and readjusted my bag. "Give your date my condolences."

Before he could respond, I pushed past him and quickened my steps until I hit the chilly March air. Only then did I allow myself to relax, though my pulse maintained its frantic speed.

Of all the people I could've run into at the bar, I *had* to run into Josh Chen. Could the day get any worse?

I could already imagine the taunts he'll pepper me with the next time I saw him.

Remember when you got stood up, JR?

Remember when you sat at the bar for an hour by yourself like a loser?

Remember when you got all dressed up and used up the last of your favorite eyeshadow for a dude named Todd?

Okay, he didn't know about the last two things, but I wouldn't put it past him to find out.

I tucked my hands deeper in my pockets and turned the corner, eager to put as much distance between myself and Satan's spawn as possible.

The Bronze Gear had been located on a lively street of restaurants, with music wafting in the air and people spilling onto the sidewalk even in wintertime. The one I was walking on now, while only one street over, was eerily quiet. Shuttered shops lined both sidewalks, and scraggly bunches of weeds sprouted from cracks in the ground. The sun hadn't quite set yet, but the lengthening shadows lent an ominous air to the surroundings.

I walked faster out of instinct, though I was distracted not only by my run-in with Josh but also the dozens of items on my to-do list. When I was alone, my worries and tasks crowded my brain like children clamoring for their parents' attention.

Graduation, bar prep, possibly reaming Todd out over text (no, not worth it), more apartment searching online, Ava's surprise birthday party this weekend...

Wait a minute.

Birthday. March.

I came to a dead halt.

Oh my God.

Besides Ava, I knew someone else with a birthday in early March, but...

I fished my phone out of my pocket with a shaking hand, and my stomach plummeted when I saw the date. *March 2*.

It was *her* birthday today. I completely forgot.

Tendrils of guilt squeezed my insides, and I wondered, as I did every year, whether I should call her. I never did, but...*this year could be different*.

I told myself that every year, too.

I *shouldn't* feel guilty. She never called me on my birthday, either. Or Christmas. Or any other holiday. I hadn't seen or spoken to Adeline in seven years.

Call. Don't call. Call. Don't call.

I worried my bottom lip between my teeth.

It was her forty-fifth birthday. That was a big one, right? Big enough to warrant a *Happy Birthday* from her daughter...if she cared about getting anything from me.

I was so busy debating myself I didn't notice anyone approach until the hard barrel of a gun pressed against my back and a raspy voice barked out, "Give me your phone and wallet. Now."

My heart jolted, and I almost dropped my phone. Disbelief hardened my limbs into stone.

*You've **got** to be kidding me.*

Never ask the universe questions you don't want answered because it turns out the day could, in fact, get a lot fucking worse.

2

JOSH

"Don't say it." I cracked open my beer, ignoring Clara's amused expression. The cute female bartender she'd been flirting with had left to deal with the happy hour rush, and she'd been watching me with a knowing smile ever since.

"Fine. I won't." Clara crossed her legs and took a demure sip of her drink.

She was an ER nurse at Thayer University Hospital, where I was a third-year resident specializing in Emergency Medicine, so our paths crossed often. We'd been friends since my first year of residency, when we bonded over our mutual love for action sports and cheesy nineties movies, but she had as much sexual interest in me, or any member of the male species, as she did a rock.

Clara certainly wasn't my date, at least not in the romantic sense, but I hadn't corrected Jules's assumption. My personal life wasn't any of her business. Hell, sometimes I wished it wasn't *my* business.

"Good." I caught the eye of a pretty blonde at the other end of the bar and flashed a flirtatious smile. She returned it with a suggestive one of her own.

This was what I needed tonight. Alcohol, watching the Wizards game with Clara, and some harmless flirting. Anything to take my mind off the letter waiting for me at home.

Correction: letters. As in plural.

December 24. January 16. February 20. March 2. The dates of the most recent letters from Michael flashed through my mind.

I received one every month like clockwork, and I hated myself for not throwing them out the instant I saw them.

I took a long swig of my beer, trying to forget the stack of unopened mail sitting in my desk drawer. It was my second beer in less than ten minutes, but fuck it, I'd had a long day at work. I needed to take the edge off.

"I've always liked redheads," Clara said, drawing me back to a conversation I didn't want to have. "Maybe because *The Little Mermaid* was my favorite Disney movie growing up."

Her face creased into a smile at my long-suffering sigh.

"Your lack of subtlety is astonishing."

"I like to have at least one trait that's astonishing." Clara's smile widened. "So, who was she?"

There was no use trying to sidestep her question. Once she sniffed out something she *thought* was juicy, she was worse than a Pitbull with a bone.

"My sister's best friend and a pain in my ass." Tension knotted my shoulders at the memory of my encounter with Jules.

It was *just* like her to be prickly even when I tried to help her. Forget an olive branch. I should hand her a bouquet of thorns and hope it pricked the fuck out of her.

Every time I tried to make nice—which, to be fair, wasn't often—she reminded me of why we would never be friends. We were both too stubborn, our personalities too similar. It was like pitting fire against fire.

Unfortunately, Jules and my sister Ava had been thick as thieves since they roomed together their freshman year of college, which meant I was stuck with Jules in my life no matter how much we got on each other's nerves.

I didn't know what her issue with me was, but I knew she had a penchant for getting Ava into trouble.

In the seven years they'd known each other, I'd watched Ava trip out on Jules's pot brownies and almost streak naked at a party, consoled her after she drunkenly dyed her hair semi-permanent orange at Jules's twentieth birthday party, and rescued them from the side of a road in Bumfuck, Maryland after Jules had the brilliant idea to join some strangers they met at a bar on a last-minute road trip to New York. The car broke down on their way there and, luckily, the strangers turned out to be harmless, but still. It could've gone so very wrong.

Those were just some of the highlights. There were a thousand other instances when Jules had convinced my sister to go along with one harebrained scheme or another.

Ava was an adult and capable of making her own decisions, but she was also too damn trusting. As her older brother, it was my job to protect her, especially after our mom died and our father turned out to be a fucking psycho.

And there was no doubt in my mind that Jules was a bad influence. Period.

Clara's mouth twitched. "Does the pain in your ass have a name?"

I took another swig of beer before answering with a curt, "Jules."

"Hmm. Jules is very pretty."

"Most flesh-eating succubi are. It's how they rope you in." Aggravation crept into my voice.

Yes, Jules was beautiful, but so were wolfsbane and blue-ringed octopi. Pretty exteriors hiding deadly poison which, in Jules's case, came in the form of her viperous tongue.

Most men were blinded by all those curves and big hazel eyes, but not me. I knew better than to fall for her trap. The poor sods whose hearts she broke at Thayer were further proof I needed to stay far away from her for my personal sanity.

"I've never seen you so worked up over a woman." Clara's face was now a mask of delight. "Wait till I tell the other nurses."

Oh, Jesus.

Gossip Girl had nothing on the nurses' station. Once news reached their ears, it spread through the hospital like wildfire.

"I am not *worked up,* and there's nothing to tell." I switched the subject before she could press further. I had no desire to discuss Jules Ambrose a second longer than necessary. "If you want real news, here's something: I finally decided where I'm going for vacation."

She rolled her eyes. "That's nowhere near as interesting as your love life. Half the nurses are in love with you. I don't get it."

"It's because I'm a catch."

It wasn't arrogance if it was true. I would never hook up with anyone at the hospital, though. I didn't shit where I ate.

"Humble, too." Clara finally gave up trying to pull more information about Jules out of me and went along with my obvious deflection. "Okay, I'll bite. Where are you going for vacation?"

My grin was real this time. "New Zealand."

I'd been torn between New Zealand for bungee jumping and South Africa for cage diving with sharks, but I finally decided on the former and bought my tickets last night.

Medical residents had crap schedules, but those of us in

emergency medicine had it better than surgeons, for example. I worked a mix of eight and twelve-hour shifts with one mandated day off every six days and four stretches of five days off annually. The tradeoff was we worked nonstop during our shifts, but I didn't mind. Busy was good. Busy kept my mind off other things.

I was, however, pumped for my first vacation this year. I'd been approved for a week off in the spring, and I could already picture my time in New Zealand: crisp blue skies, snow-capped mountains, the sensation of weightlessness as I free fell and the adrenaline rush that set my body alive whenever I indulged in one of my favorite adventure sports.

"Shut up." Clara groaned. "I'm so jealous. Which hikes are you going to do?"

I'd done extensive research on the best hikes in the country, and I regaled her with my plans until the bartender returned and she got distracted. Since I didn't want to cockblock—or pussyblock, in this case—I focused on my drink and the Wizards vs. Raptors basketball game on TV.

I was about to order another beer when a soft female voice interrupted me.

"Is this seat taken?"

I turned, taking in the cute blonde I'd made eye contact with earlier. I hadn't noticed her leave her spot at the bar, but now she stood so close I could see the faint smattering of freckles across her nose.

Habit kicked in, and I flashed a lazy smile that caused the blonde to blush. "It's all yours."

The whole hookup song and dance was so familiar by now I barely had to try. Everything was muscle memory. Buy her a drink, ask her about herself, listen attentively—or appear to do so—with the occasional nod and appropriate interjection, brush my hand against hers to establish physical contact.

It used to be thrilling, but now I did it because...well, I wasn't sure. Because it was what I'd always done, I guess.

"...want to be a vet..."

I nodded again, struggling not to yawn. What the hell was wrong with me?

Robin, the blonde, was hot and willing to take this somewhere private, if her hand on my upper thigh was any indication. Her childhood adventures in horseback riding weren't exactly riveting, but I was usually good at finding at least *one* interesting tidbit in every conversation.

Maybe it was me. Boredom was my constant companion these days, and I didn't know how to get rid of the bastard.

The parties I went to were the same old, same old. My hookups were unsatisfying. My dates were chores. The only time I felt anything was when I was in the ER.

I glanced at Clara. She was still flirting with the bartender, who was actively ignoring her customers and staring at Clara with an enamored expression.

"...can't decide if I want a Pomeranian or Chihuahua..." Robin droned on.

"Pomeranians sound nice." I made a show of checking my watch before saying, "Hey, I'm sorry to cut this short, but I have to pick up my cousin from the airport." It wasn't the best excuse, but it was the first one I could think of.

Robin's face fell. "Oh, okay. Maybe we can meet up sometime." She scribbled her number on a napkin and pushed it into my hand. "Call me."

I responded with a noncommittal smile. I didn't like promising things I couldn't fulfill.

Have fun, I mouthed at Clara on my way out. She shook her head and gave me a small smirk before shifting her attention back to the bartender.

It was my quickest exit from a bar in a while. I wasn't upset about how the night turned out. Clara and I often went drinking together and split when we got...distracted, but now I had to figure out where to go.

It was still early, and I didn't want to return home yet. I also didn't want to hit up one of the other bars lining the street in case Robin went bar hopping later.

Fuck it. I'll finish watching the game at the dive spot near my house. Beer and TV were beer and TV, no matter where they were located. Hopefully, the metro was running on time so I wouldn't miss the rest of the game.

I turned the corner onto the quiet street leading to the metro station. I made it halfway when I spotted a flash of red hair and a familiar purple coat in the alleyway next to an out-of-business shoe store.

My steps slowed. What the *hell* was Jules still doing here? She'd left a good twenty minutes before me.

Then I noticed the glint of metal in her hand. A gun— pointed straight at the scraggly, bearded man in front of her.

"What the fuck?" My words echoed in the empty street and bounced off the shuttered storefronts in disbelief.

Maybe I fell asleep at the bar and entered the *Twilight Zone,* because the scene in front of me didn't make any fucking sense.

Where the hell did Jules get a *gun?*

Jules shifted positions so she could look at me without taking her eyes off the man. A threadbare beanie sat on top of his longish brown hair, and a black coat that was two sizes too big hung on his skinny frame.

"He tried to mug me," she said matter-of-factly.

Beanie glared at her resentfully but was smart enough to keep his mouth shut.

I pinched my temple, hoping it would jolt me out of whatever alternate reality I'd stepped into. *Nope. Still fucking here.* "And I assume that's his gun?"

I was somehow not surprised Jules had turned the tables on her would-be mugger. If she got kidnapped, the kidnapper would probably return her within the hour due to sheer irritation.

"Yes, Sherlock." Jules's hand tightened on the weapon. "I called the police. They're on the way."

As if on cue, the wail of sirens sliced through the air.

Beanie stiffened, his eyes darting around with wild panic.

"Don't even think about it," Jules warned. "Or I'll shoot. I don't bluff."

"She'll do it," I told him. "One time I saw her nail a guy in the ass with a Smith & Wesson because he stole a bag of chips from her." I lowered my voice to a conspiratorial stage whisper. "She takes *hangry* to another level."

The situation was already absurd enough. I might as well play into it.

Like I said, I was bored.

Jules's mouth twitched at my fabrication before her face resettled into a stern frown.

Beanie's eyes widened. "You serious?" His gaze ping-ponged between us. "How do you two know each other? You banging?"

Jules and I recoiled in unison.

Either Beanie asked such a stupid, out-of-place question to distract us, or he wanted to make me throw up. If it was the latter, he was close to succeeding. My stomach churned like a cement mixer on overdrive.

"I would *never*. Look at him." Jules gestured at me with her free hand. "Like I would ever touch *that*."

Beanie squinted at me. "What's wrong with him?"

"I wouldn't let you touch me if you offered to pay off all my med school loans," I growled.

I didn't care if Jules Ambrose was the last woman in the world. She was one person I'd never sleep with. Ever.

She ignored me. "You ever hear the saying, the bigger the ego, the smaller the penis?" she asked Beanie. "Applies to him."

"Oh. That sucks." Beanie glanced at me with sympathy. "Sorry, dude."

A vein throbbed in my temple. I opened my mouth to inform her I would rather douse myself in bleach than allow her anywhere near my penis, but the slam of a car door interrupted me.

A cop the size of the Hulk got out with his gun drawn. "Freeze! Drop your weapon."

I groaned and almost pinched my temple again before I caught myself.

For fuck's sake.

I should've left when I had the chance.

Now, I was *definitely* going to miss the rest of the game.

3
___

JOSH

Forty-five minutes and dozens of questions later, the cops finally let us go.

Beanie had been taken into custody, and Jules and I walked in silence toward the metro station on the next street. Most people would freak out after being the victim of a mugging attempt, but she acted like she'd just finished grocery shopping.

I was less serene. Not only had I wasted an hour being grilled by the police, but I'd also missed the rest of the game.

"Tell me why every time I run into trouble, *you're* involved," I said through gritted teeth as the metro came into view.

"It's not my fault *you* chose to walk down that street and *you* chose to stay for a merry interlude instead of going on your way," Jules retorted. "I had it handled."

I snorted, my shoes pounding a furious rhythm on the steps. I could've taken the escalator, but I needed to work off my aggravation. Jules must've felt the same way, because she was right there next to me, pissing me off.

"*Merry interlude*? Who talks like that? And there was

nothing *merry* about it, I promise." I reached the turnstiles and yanked out my wallet. "Too bad the police didn't take *you* into custody too. You're a menace to society."

"According to who? You?" She looked me over with disdain.

"Yes." I gave her a cold smile. "Me and every person who's had the misfortune of running into you."

It was a horrible thing to say, but between the letters, a long shift at the hospital, and my general existential crisis, I wasn't feeling particularly charitable.

"God, you. Are," Jules slammed her metro card on the reader with unnecessary force, "The. *Worst.*"

I passed through the turnstile behind her. "No, that would be your sense of self-preservation. It's common sense to give muggers what they want." The more I thought about it, the more her actions baffled and infuriated me. "What if you couldn't disarm him? What if he had another weapon you didn't know about? You could've fucking *died!*"

Jules's face flushed. "*Stop* yelling at me. You're not my father."

"I'm not yelling!"

We stopped beneath the schedule board announcing the arrival of the next train in eight minutes. The station was empty save for a couple making out on one of the benches and a suited business type at the far end of the platform, and it was quiet enough for me to hear the furious rush of blood in my ears.

We glared at each other, our chests heaving with emotion. I wanted to shake her for being so stupid as to put her life in danger over a fucking phone and wallet.

Just because I didn't like her didn't mean I wanted her dead.

Not all the time, anyway.

I expected another snarky retort, but Jules turned away and lapsed into silence.

It was completely out of character and goddamn unnerving. I couldn't remember the last time she let me have the last word.

I exhaled sharply through my nose, forcing myself to calm down and think clearly about the situation.

No matter how I felt about her, Jules was Ava's friend, and she'd just survived an armed mugging attempt. Unless she was a damn robot, she couldn't be as unaffected by what happened as she appeared.

I examined her out of the corner of my eye, taking in her tight jaw and ramrod-straight back. Her expression was blank— a little too much so.

My anger cooled, and I rubbed a hand over my jaw, torn. Jules and I didn't comfort each other. We didn't so much as say *bless you* when the other sneezed. But...

Dammit.

"You okay?" I asked gruffly. I couldn't *not* check on someone after they almost died, no matter who they were. It went against everything I believed in as a doctor and a human being.

"I'm fine." Jules tucked her hair behind her ear, her voice flat, but I detected a slight shake in her hand.

Adrenaline rushes were crazy things. They made you stronger, more focused. They made you feel invincible. But once the high disappeared and you crashed back to earth, you had to deal with the aftermath—the shaky hands, the weak legs, the worries you'd staved off for a brief moment in time only to all come rushing back in one giant flood.

I would bet my last dollar Jules was in the midst of a post-rush crash.

"Are you hurt?"

"No. I got the gun away from him before he could do anything." Jules stared straight ahead, so intense I half-expected her to burn a hole in the station wall.

"Didn't realize you were a secret super soldier." I attempted to lighten the air, though I was curious as hell as to what happened. We'd talked to the police separately, so I hadn't heard her recount how she'd disarmed Beanie.

"You don't have to be a super soldier to disarm someone." She wrinkled her nose. *Finally*. A sign of normality. "I took self-defense classes when I was younger. They included learning how to handle a mugger."

Huh. I wouldn't have figured her for someone who took self-defense classes.

The train pulled into the station before I could respond. There were no empty seats since the stop before this one was a popular hub, so we stood shoulder-to-shoulder near the doors until we reached Hazelburg, the Maryland suburb that housed Thayer's campus.

Jules and I used to be next door neighbors when she and Ava lived together their senior year, but Ava had since moved to the city and I'd rented a new place. There were too many unwanted memories in my old house.

Still, Hazelburg was a small town, and my and Jules's houses were only a twenty-minute walk from each other.

We unconsciously fell into step beside each other after exiting the station.

"Don't tell Ava or anyone else what happened," Jules said when we reached the corner where we had to split—her to the left, me to the right. "I don't want them to worry."

"I won't." She was right. Ava *would* worry, and there was no point in getting her worked up over something that had already happened. "You sure you're okay?"

I almost offered to walk Jules home, but that might be too

much. We'd reached our limits of civility with each other, as evidenced by the next words out of her mouth.

"Yes." She rubbed her thumb and forefinger over the opposite sleeve of her coat, her expression distracted. "Don't be late to Ava's party on Saturday. I realize punctuality is not one of your few virtues, but it's important you're on time."

My sympathy evaporated in a gust of annoyance. "I won't be late," I said through clenched teeth. "Don't worry about me."

I walked away before she could respond, not bothering to say goodbye. Jules had to ruin it every. Single. Fucking. Time.

Maybe her prickliness was a defense mechanism, but that was none of my business. I wasn't here to peel back her layers like we were in one of those damned romance novels Ava liked so much.

If Jules wanted to be insufferable, I had every right to save myself from suffering by removing myself from her presence.

The wind nipped at my face and howled through the trees, underscoring how quiet the streets were. Hazelberg was one of the safest towns in the U.S. but...

The way Jules's hand shook while we were waiting for the metro. The tension in her shoulders. The paleness of her skin.

My brisk walk slowed to a meander.

You're reading too much into one movement. Just go home, man.

So what if it was dark and she was alone? The chances of anything happening to her were slim, even if she *was* a magnet for trouble.

I closed my eyes, unable to believe I was even contemplating doing what I was about to do.

"God motherfucking dammit." I bit out the words before I stopped and double backed in the direction Jules had gone in. I set my jaw, growing angrier with each step.

Angry at my conscience, which reared its head at the worst

times. Angry at Jules, for existing; at Ava, for being friends with her, and at Thayer's housing coordinator, for placing them in the same room and therefore making their friendship an inevitability all those years ago.

Fate liked to screw with me, and it'd never screwed me over harder than when it'd introduced a certain redhead into my life.

It didn't take me long to catch up with Jules. I stayed far enough behind her so she wouldn't notice me but close enough I could see her. The bright colors of her hair and coat made it easy, even in the dark.

I felt like a total creep, but if she saw me following her, we'd get into another argument, and I was too tired for that shit.

Luckily, we arrived at her house in less than ten minutes, and I relaxed when I saw the glow of lights behind the curtains. Stella, another college friend of Ava's and Jules's roommate, must be home already.

Jules walked onto the porch, reached into her bag...and paused.

I tensed again and edged behind a tree on the opposite sidewalk in case she turned around, but she didn't. She just stood there, frozen, for a full minute.

What the hell was she doing?

I was about to cross the street in case she was in shock or something when she finally moved again. She took the keys out of her bag, unlocked the door, and disappeared inside.

I released my breath in one long, slow sigh. It formed a tiny white puff in the wintry air, and I waited another minute, my eyes lingering on the spot where Jules had stood, before I turned and walked home.

4

JULES

"How was your date?" Stella looked up from her phone when I entered the living room.

"He didn't show." I unbuttoned my coat and hung it on the brass tree by the front door. It took me two tries, thanks to the tremble in my hand.

It's the cold. Not the attempted mugging or the brief moment of paralysis I'd experienced on the porch when I—

Stop. Don't think about it.

Stella's eyes widened. "No way. What an asshole."

I cracked a smile. Stella rarely cursed, so it always amused me when she let a bad word slip.

"It's okay. I dodged a bullet. I mean, have you *seen* his dating app picture? That freakin' fish. I honestly don't know what I was thinking." I peeled off my gloves and took off my shoes, avoiding my friend's eyes while I tried to suck enough oxygen into my lungs.

It hadn't taken me long to disarm the mugger, but the sensation of being helpless, even for a few minutes, resurfaced memories better left buried.

Wood digging into my back. Sour breath on my neck. Hands on—

"Jules."

I startled and almost knocked over the coat tree.

I'd held onto my calm during the aftermath of the attempted mugging, but now that I was safely home, my body finally started to process what happened.

It wasn't pretty.

My heart was a frantic drumbeat in my chest, my stomach a storm of nausea. Stella's presence was the only thing keeping me upright.

Her brow creased. "Are you okay? You've been staring into space for the past five minutes. I called your name twice."

"Yep." I pasted on a bright smile. "I just spaced. Thinking of ways to get back at Todd."

I wasn't going to waste another drop of energy on the asshole, but Stella didn't know that.

She tilted her head, her catlike green eyes narrowing. As a fashion blogger and influencer, she was glued to her phone ninety percent of the time, but she was also more observant than people gave her credit for.

"You wouldn't waste more energy on that guy," she said.

Okay, there was observant and there was creepy. Maybe those gross wheatgrass smoothies she loved so much gave her superpowers, like reading minds.

"Seriously, I'm fine." I upped the wattage of my smile. I had no qualms about turning to my friends for advice, but only when they could *do* something about it. Otherwise, there was no point making them worry. "I just want to watch a movie, eat ice cream, and forget about Todd the Toad."

A spark of suspicion remained in Stella's eyes, but thankfully, she didn't press the issue. "We have a pint of salted caramel ice cream left," she said. "*Legally Blonde* rewatch while we finish it?"

"Always." I never got tired of watching a perfectly coiffed Elle Woods kick ass. "I'm gonna shower first. You do whatever you have to do."

"Going through my DMs." She sighed. "Not that I'll ever get through them all."

"You don't have to reply to all of them, you know."

Stella had hundreds of thousands of followers, and I couldn't imagine how many messages flooded her inbox on a daily basis.

"I want to. Unless they're creeps." She waved a hand in the air. "Go do your thing. I'll be here."

While Stella returned to her phone, I entered our shared bathroom and turned on the shower, my smile fading.

I waited until the air thickened with steam before I stepped into the tub and rested my forehead against the slick tile wall, letting the drum of the water wash away my unwanted memories.

My senior year of high school. Alastair and Max and Adeline—

Stop.

"Get yourself together, Jules," I whispered fiercely.

I wasn't a young, helpless girl trapped in Ohio anymore.

I was in a whole other state, about to gain everything I had ever dreamed of.

Money. Freedom. *Security*.

And I'd be damned if I let anyone take that away from me.

5
———

JULES

By the time Ava's surprise party rolled around, I'd shoved the mugging attempt into the dim recesses of my mind. Distraction was the key to repressing memories, and luckily, I had enough distractions to keep me busy for the next five years.

"I can't believe you guys did this." Ava turned slowly, taking in the restaurant that had been transformed into a veritable party hall with wide eyes. And by party hall, I meant a seven-foot ice sculpture, multiple gourmet food stations, a live DJ, a chocolate fountain, and a temporary dance floor, all courtesy of her richer-than-God boyfriend. "You absolutely didn't have to."

"No, but we wanted to." I flashed a mischievous grin. "Plus, it was a good excuse to get a chocolate fountain. I've always wanted to see one in real life." I hugged her and breathed in her familiar perfume. The scent triggered a wave of nostalgia.

Ava had been the first person I'd met at Thayer. We'd hit it off right away, and I would never forget how she stuck by me when Josh insisted she end our friendship. She and Josh were extremely close, so the fact she stood up to him *for me* meant more than she would ever know.

We still hung out after graduation, but not as often as I would like. Part of me wished we could go back to the days when Ava, Stella, Bridget, and I would stay up all night, binge-eating cheese puffs and listening to the girls in the dorm room next to ours scream at each other because one of them hooked up with the other's boyfriend.

"Happy birthday, babe." I smiled, not wanting to be a downer despite the melancholy gripping me. "Surprised?"

"Definitely." Ava turned to her boyfriend and swatted him on the arm, though her eyes sparkled with delight. "You told me we were going to lunch!"

"We *are* at lunch." A shadow of a smile graced Alex Volkov's lips. Ava was probably the only person who could pull so much emotion out of him—yes, that was sarcasm—and the only one who could hit him, even playfully, without losing a limb. "Technically."

I gasped. "Was that a joke?" I looked around at Ava and Stella and purposefully skipped over Josh, who stood on the other side of Ava. "Alex made a joke. Quick, someone mark down the date and time."

"Hilarious," he said flatly.

He radiated CEO vibes even in a button-down shirt and jeans, which was as casual as Alex ever got. His eyes glinted like jade-colored ice chips in a face that could've been carved by Michelangelo himself, and his expression was cold enough to give someone freezer burn.

Whatever. He could glare all he wanted, but as Ava's friend, I was immune to his wrath, and he knew it.

"You surprised me with a birthday party once," he told Ava, his voice softening a smidge. "I figured it was past time I returned the favor."

I could practically see Ava melt.

"I think I just got a toothache from the sweetness," Stella said as Alex whispered something else in Ava's ear that made her blush.

"We need to book a dentist appointment, stat," I agreed.

Despite our jokes, we were grinning like idiots. Alex and Ava had been through a lot, and it was nice seeing them so happy, though the word was relative where Alex was concerned.

Meanwhile, Josh lounged against the dessert table, his expression darker than his black shirt.

He used to be best friends with Alex until their falling out, which was a whole other story unto itself. They were civil now, but there was a big difference between *civil* and *friends*.

"Wipe the sour expression off your face, Dr. Killjoy," I said. "You're bringing down the vibes."

"If my face bothers you so much, don't look at it," he drawled. "Unless you can't help yourself, which is understandable."

I scowled. I'd planned the party with help from Stella and Alex, and while I'd been tempted to exclude Josh from the guest list, he *was* Ava's brother. His presence was expected, like E. coli on undercooked chicken.

Before I could respond to his conceited statement, an excited squeal punctured the air, followed by a loud clatter and two dozen heads swiveling toward the entrance.

I followed their wide-eyed stares to the couple that had just entered, flanked by two suited bodyguards the size of mountains.

My face lit up. "Bridget!"

She grinned and waved. "Surprise."

"Oh my God!" I rushed over to her at the same time as Ava and Stella, and we collided in a messy, laughing group hug that would've ended with us on the floor had Bridget's fiancé Rhys and bodyguard Booth not steadied us. "I thought you couldn't make it!"

"My scheduler found an event at the embassy that coincidentally 'required' my presence this weekend." Bridget's blue eyes glowed with mischief. "My meeting with the ambassador ran long, or I would've gotten here sooner." She gave Ava a one-on-one hug after we untangled ourselves. "Happy birthday, sweetie."

"I can't believe you're here." Ava squeezed her tight. "You must be so busy..."

Bridget von Ascheberg may have attended Thayer University with us, but that was where our similarities ended because she was an honest to God, real-life queen.

She'd been a princess when we met her, but after her older brother abdicated, Bridget became first in line to the throne of Eldorra, a small European kingdom. Her grandfather, the former King Edvard, recently stepped down due to health issues and Bridget had been coronated queen two months ago.

"I wouldn't miss this for the world. Plus, it's a good break." Bridget brushed a strand of golden hair out of her eyes. With her blue eyes, classic features, and cool elegance, she bore a striking resemblance to Grace Kelly. "Parliament is being difficult. Again."

"I got her out of the palace just in time, or she would've ruptured an artery," Rhys added, his dry tone at odds with the affection in his eyes as he looked at Bridget.

Standing at a tattooed, muscled six foot five, Rhys Larsen was one of the most dangerously good-looking men I'd ever met, but beneath his rough exterior was a heart of gold. He used to be Bridget's bodyguard until they fell in love, and now he was the future Prince Consort, since the King Consort title didn't exist in Eldorra. They'd had to overcome a lot of obstacles to be together considering she was royalty and he wasn't, but they were now one of the most beloved couples in the world.

The loud snap of a camera shutter interrupted our reunion, and I suddenly remembered we weren't alone. The rest of the guests were still staring, slack-jawed, at Bridget and Rhys.

Having a literal queen waltz into a birthday party without warning *could* be a bit of a shock.

No one approached us though, except for Josh, who greeted Bridget with a normal hug and Rhys with one of those handshake hugs guys loved so much. I guess Booth and Rhys's bodyguard looked intimidating enough to scare off people from approaching.

"So." Bridget linked her arm with Ava's and walked to the nearest table. "Tell me what I missed."

For the next half hour, we caught each other up on our lives while Josh hit the bar and Alex and Rhys sat quietly across the table. They occasionally said something to each other but spent most of the time watching Ava and Bridget with infatuated expressions. Well, as infatuated as someone as cold as Alex and as gruff as Rhys could look anyway.

I ignored the pang in my heart at their obvious love for my friends and refocused on the conversation.

I'd given up on love a long time ago. There was no use longing for it.

"Jules and I are looking for a new place after our current lease is up," Stella said. We still lived in Hazelburg since I was attending Thayer Law, but our lease ended in April, and I would be graduating in late May. After that, we'd both be working in the city, so it made sense for us to find something in D.C. "No luck yet though."

Everything we found was either too far from our offices, too expensive, or too gross. I was pretty sure one of the apartments we'd looked at used to be a drug den.

Gotta love house hunting in the city.

"Where are you looking to move?" Rhys asked.

"Ideally downtown, anywhere close to the red line," I said. The red line dropped me off right at Thayer, and the fewer metro transfers I had to endure, the better.

A thoughtful expression crossed his face. "I know someone who owns a building downtown. He may be able to help. Don't know if he has any openings, but I'll ask."

Stella's eyebrows shot up. "He owns the *entire* building?"

Rhys shrugged. His shoulders were so massive the movement was akin to mountains shaking. "He's into real estate investment."

"That would be great." I gave Alex a pointed stare. "At least *someone* in real estate can help us."

Alex was CEO of The Archer Group, the largest real estate development company in the country.

I was joking about him helping us, but he actually responded instead of ignoring me. "My properties are full, unless you want to sleep in a shopping center or office building."

"Hmm." I tapped a finger on my chin. "The shopping center has potential. I love clothes."

"Me too," Stella agreed.

Alex looked unamused.

"Speaking of real estate development..." Ava said as Josh reappeared with a drink in hand. He slid into the empty chair next to Alex's, taking great care not to look at his ex-best friend. "One of Alex's business associates has a new ski resort in Vermont, and we bought tickets for the grand opening to support him. Four tickets, to be exact, so we can bring two guests. Bridget and Rhys, I know you guys won't be here, and Stella, you mentioned you have a big event in New York the last weekend of March..."

Stella was always getting invited to fancy fashion events because of her blog, but if she couldn't make it, and Bridget and Rhys couldn't make it, that left...

Oh no.

"Josh, Jules, what do you think? We can all go together." Ava beamed. "It'll be so much fun!"

A weekend trip with Josh? I'd have more fun getting a root canal without Novocain, but Ava looked so excited I couldn't bear to say no, especially on her birthday.

"Yay." I tried to summon as much enthusiasm as I could. "Can't wait."

"I would love to, but..." Josh grimaced, doing the worst job of faking remorse I'd ever seen. "I'm working that weekend."

Thank God. I could handle third wheeling it if it meant I wouldn't have to—

"Too bad." Ava didn't blink an eye at her brother's response. "The resort has a triple black diamond."

Josh's glass froze halfway to his lips. "You're shitting me."

My stomach sank. Josh was a notorious adrenaline junkie, and there were few things more adrenaline-inducing than the most dangerous type of ski trail in the world. It was like waving premium powder under a cocaine addict's nose.

"Nope." Ava sipped her drink while Stella stared at her phone, barely hiding her grin, and Rhys and Bridget exchanged amused glances. Alex was the only one who showed no visible reaction. "I know you've always wanted to ski on one, but since you have to work..."

"I think I can trade shifts," Josh said after a long pause.

"Great!" Ava's eyes sparkled in a way that set off my inner

alarm bells. "It's settled then. You, me, Alex, and Jules are going to Vermont."

Josh's strained smile mirrored my own. We didn't agree on much, but he didn't have to say it for me to know we agreed on at least one thing.

The trip wouldn't end well. At all.

6

JOSH

THE LIST OF THINGS I'D RATHER DO BESIDES GO ON A weekend trip with my ex-best friend and the redheaded menace included, but was not limited to, feeding my hand through a woodchipper, eating a pound of raw maggots, and watching *Glitter* on repeat with my eyes taped open.

But—and this was a big but—it was Ava's birthday, and the resort had a triple black diamond. I'd never skied a triple black diamond before.

The prospect of the challenge sent a rush through my blood. I would be an idiot to turn the opportunity down.

"Josh."

My spine stiffened when Alex appeared, the glass of Coke and whiskey in his hand matching mine.

"Alex."

I kept my eyes on the dance floor where Ava and her friends were partying like it was 1999. We'd long dispersed from our table, and the rest of the guests had stopped gawking at Bridget and transitioned to sneaking peeks in between songs. Her security had temporarily confiscated everyone's phones, but I bet a few people had snapped pictures of her when she arrived and said pictures would be splashed all over the gossip sites by tomorrow morning.

"Surprised you're not out there with everyone else." Alex leaned against the wall, his eyes also on the party, though they were trained only on Ava. "You used to be the first person on the dance floor."

"Yes, well." I drained my drink in one long gulp. "A lot has changed since college."

The unspoken meaning hung sharp and heavy between us, like a guillotine waiting to drop.

Once, Alex and I had been best friends.

Now, we were strangers with only one commonality tying us together.

If it weren't for Ava, I would happily never see or speak to Alex again.

At least, that was what I told myself.

"Vermont wasn't my idea," Alex said, sidestepping the elephant in the room.

"I know. Ava isn't as sneaky as she thinks she is."

She'd been trying to get me and Alex to make up for over a year. She may have forgiven him for lying to us to get closer to my father, whom Alex thought had been the one behind his family's murder, but the betrayal ran deeper for me.

Ava and Alex had only been dating for a few months when he discovered his uncle was the real culprit and he revealed the truth behind his revenge plan. But he and I had been friends for eight *years*.

I'd invited Alex into my home. Treated him like a brother. Shared secrets and advice and things I'd never told my own family. And all that time, he'd been lying to me. *Using* me.

The whiskey aftertaste turned bitter on my tongue.

"She misses you," Alex said quietly.

"I'm right here." I glanced at the bar. "We text all the time."

"You know what I mean."

"I don't, actually."

His mouth flattened into a tight line. "You've been acting different lately. Ava is worried—"

"Dude, stop." I held up my hand. "If Ava is worried about me, she can tell me herself. But don't act like we're going to be best friends again. We're not. Because you know what's required in a friendship? Trust. And you lost mine a long time ago."

I stepped around Alex before he could respond and went straight to the bar, my throat and chest tight. He didn't follow me, and I didn't expect him to. He didn't chase after anyone except Ava. It was the only reason I hadn't put up more of a fight when they got back together.

For all his faults and fuckups, Alex really did love my sister. I wanted her to be safe and happy, and if she was safe and happy with him, then I could suck it up and act civil.

That didn't mean I had to have heartfelt conversations with him on the sidelines of the dance floor though.

"Hey, man." I nodded at the bartender. "Tequila shot. Make it a double."

I needed something stronger than whiskey to get through the rest of the party.

"You got it."

I'd just tucked a couple of dollars in the tip jar when I was interrupted, yet again, by a wholly unwelcome interloper.

"Trouble in bromanceland?" The silky purr sent a ripple of irritation and something else I couldn't name down my spine.

"Beat it, JR. I'm not in the mood." I didn't turn my head to look at Jules, but I could see the flash of distinctive red hair and the gold sparkles of her dress out of the corner of my eye.

"Your nicknaming skills leave a lot to be desired, Joshy."

Jules came up beside me and smiled at the bartender, who stopped making *my* drink to smile back at her. "I'll have a Sex on the Beach, if that's not too much to ask." She tapped her nail on the menu, which listed only basic drinks like screwdrivers and cranberry vodkas and certainly no fucking Sex on the Beach.

The bartender's eyes gleamed. "For a beautiful girl like you, nothing is too much to ask."

The line was so cliche I barely held back a snort.

"Thank you." Jules's smile widened.

If another group of guests hadn't come up to order, I was sure I would've witnessed more nauseating flirting. Thankfully, the bartender got distracted and quickly finished making our drinks before tending to the half dozen people vying for his attention.

"Slumming already?" I tsked in mock disappointment. "I expected better of you."

"Why? Because he's a bartender and not a *doctor*?" Jules arched an eyebrow. "Your snobbery is showing."

"No. Because his lines are as pathetic as your attempt to slander me." I tossed back my shot and didn't bother with a chaser. "But hey, whatever floats your boat."

"Don't try to deflect from your own failed relationship."

"I'm not in a relationship." And I had zero interest in entering one anytime soon. Sex was just that, sex. Not a prelude to dating or matching couples' outfits or whatever people were into. I made sure every woman I slept with knew the deal, because I didn't believe in leading people on or giving them false hope.

My residency took up most of my time, and even if I wasn't so busy, my desire for a long-term girlfriend hovered somewhere south of zero. I wasn't made for the commitment game. I always got bored after a few weeks, and the whole couple thing sounded exhausting. Constant dates, phone calls, checking in with the other person...

I shuddered at the thought.

Good for the people who were happy and in love, but I wasn't one of them and I never would be.

"I'm talking about Alex." Jules received her drink from the bartender with a flirty smile before turning back to me. "I remember when you two were practically joined at the hip."

A stone fist squeezed my chest, but I kept my tone light. "Didn't realize you were so interested in my personal life, JR."

"I'm not, unless it happens to affect *my* personal quality of life." Jules took a delicate sip of her cocktail. "And since we're all going on an overnight trip together, this stupid grudge you hold against Alex directly impacts me and Ava."

I tightened my grip around my glass and imagined it was Jules's throat. "Stupid?" A sharp edge bled through and colored the word with venom. "*Stupid* is a fight over which movie to watch. *Stupid* describes whatever poor schmuck ends up marrying you. But I assure you, it does *not* apply to what happened with Alex. Don't talk about things you know nothing about."

Jules didn't back down from my glare. "I may not have been personally involved in your...situation," she said with more tact than I thought her capable of. "But I *am* best friends with Ava. I know what happened, and it happened almost two years ago. She's forgiven Alex. He's apologized. It's time to grow up and move on."

For once, I didn't detect any snark, just straightforward advice, but that didn't stop my muscles from bunching with tension. "Easy for you to say." God, I needed another drink. "Come back to me when you've been betrayed by someone close to you."

Something dark flickered in Jules's eyes. "How do you know I haven't already?"

I stilled.

How do you know I haven't already?

I didn't know much about Jules's past. Hell, I didn't know much about her at all beyond what she showed people—the brash attitude, the brazen flirtatiousness, the strange mix of ruthless ambition and reckless partying.

But I did know that one sentence she'd just uttered rang truer than anything else I'd heard in years.

My gaze locked onto Jules, whose wide eyes and slightly parted lips revealed her surprise at the words that'd just left her mouth.

I swallowed the urge to ask her what happened while the air between us thickened with...not camaraderie, exactly, but a hint of understanding that eased some of the pressure in my chest.

We didn't have the type of relationship where we discussed our problems with each other. Even if we did, I doubted Jules would answer my question. It wasn't in her nature to display vulnerability.

She straightened, a shutter falling over her face and erasing all traces of her previous softness. "Whether you forgive Alex or not is up to you. Just don't ruin everyone else's fun with your sulking...though your mere presence may be enough to achieve that goal."

With that, she swanned off, her hips swaying and her head held high.

A low growl rose in my throat before I caught myself. There was no use wasting energy fuming over her. I needed to save every ounce for ensuring I didn't kill her in Vermont. As satisfying as it would be, I wasn't throwing away my future for a moment of *extreme* satisfaction.

I shifted my attention back to the bartender, eager to order another shot, only to find him staring at a certain spot on the dance floor with a besotted expression.

No, not spot. *Person.*

Jules raised her arms over her head and rolled her hips to the music in a way that had every man around her drooling. She looked over her shoulder and winked at the bartender before shooting me a smug stare.

I did the most mature thing I could think of: I flipped her off.

She laughed, her expression growing smugger, before she turned her back on me.

"She's so hot." The bartender's eyes glinted in a way that sharpened my already raised hackles. "Please tell me she's single."

I masked my irritation with a tight smile. "You know what a succubus is?"

He scratched his chin. The group from earlier had rejoined the party, leaving just us at the bar. "Are those the little plants? My sister loves those things. Got a whole windowsill full of 'em."

"No, man. Those are *succulents.*" I lowered my voice. "A succubus is a demon that appears in the form of a beautiful woman to seduce men and suck the life force out of them. They're supposed to be mythical, but..." I gestured in Jules's direction. "She's a real-life succubus. Don't fall for her trap. There's a vicious demon lurking beneath that pretty face."

It was impossible for an actual human being to have hair that red, eyes that fierce, and curves that lush. Supernatural hijinks were the only thing that made sense.

"Oh." The bartender's eyes widened. "Does that mean she'll sleep with me?"

Oh, for fuck's sake.

"You'll have to ask her." I leaned closer like I was telling him a secret. "Here's a tip. She *loves* when people compare her to Jessica Rabbit. Tell her how much you've always wanted to bang a real-life JR and you're in. Bonus points if you *call* her JR. It's her favorite nickname."

He frowned. "Really?"

"Trust me." I rubbed a hand over my mouth to hide my shit-eating grin. This was like taking candy from a baby. "I've known her for years. The comparison really gets her going."

"Sweet." The bartender's skeptical expression cleared, replaced with a delighted smile. "Thanks, man." He clapped me on the shoulder and poured me another shot. "On the house."

It was a free open bar so *all* the drinks were technically on the house, but I didn't point that out. Instead, I lifted my glass in thanks and grinned harder when I pictured Jules's reaction to being called JR by the bartender.

She was so predictable. She might as well mark all the buttons I could push with giant, glowing X's.

And yet...

How do you know I haven't already?

My glass paused at my lips for a fraction of a second before I shook my head and welcomed the fiery burn of tequila down my throat.

Still, her words echoed in my mind and drove me crazy with their ambiguity.

Who could've betrayed Jules? She'd never had a big fallout with Ava, Bridget, or Stella, nor had she had a real boyfriend in the years I've known her. Our aversion to committed relationships was one of the few things we had in common.

Was it a high school boyfriend who broke her heart? A family member who fucked her over?

My eyes drifted to the dance floor again. Jules was still

dancing with abandon to a remix of the latest pop hit. Ava said something to her, and she threw her head back, her throaty laugh carrying over the music.

Sparkling dress. Sparkling eyes. Looking for all the world like any beautiful, carefree girl with the world at her feet.

How do you know I haven't already?

I wondered what secrets Jules was hiding beneath that party girl exterior.

And, more importantly, I wondered why I cared.

7

JULES

Ava's birthday marked a reversal in fortune, because after several shitty weeks, everything ran smoothly again. A more superstitious person might have said *too* smoothly, but I never looked a gift horse in the mouth. I was going to milk every second of perfect weather, professor's praises, and random good luck while they lasted.

Case in point: my apartment search, which might finally yield results thanks to Rhys.

The weekend after Ava's party, I found myself in the lobby of The Mirage, the luxury apartment building Rhys's friend owned. Rhys had secured a coveted showing for me and Stella, and I'd arrived early not only because I was paranoid about running late—D.C.'s metro was notoriously unreliable—but also because I needed a quiet spot to take my interview with the Legal Health Alliance Clinic (LHAC).

Although I'd received a job offer from Silver & Klein last summer, I couldn't join as a practicing attorney until I passed the bar exam. Most firms allowed graduates to join before results were out, but not Silver & Klein.

I needed a short-term job to tide me over between graduation and the release of the results in October. The temporary research associate position at LHAC, a medical-legal partnership where doctors and lawyers worked together to provide care to underserved communities, was perfect.

"That's all the questions I have today," I said after Lisa, the clinic's legal director, finished describing what a typical workday looked like. I sank deeper into the lobby's velvet couch, glad no one else was around except for the receptionist. I didn't want to be one of those people who took obnoxious business calls in public. Unfortunately, I had nowhere else to take the interview without risking missing the showing. "Thank you so much for taking the time to speak with me."

"Of course," Lisa said, her voice warm. "I'll be honest since you're the last candidate we're interviewing. You're the *best* candidate I've spoken to. Great work experience, great grades, and I think you'll fit in wonderfully with the rest of the staff." She hesitated for two beats before adding, "I don't usually do this right after an interview, but I'd like to extend an unofficial offer for you to join the clinic. I'm happy to send an official email later, and you can think it—"

"I accept!" My cheeks flushed at my eagerness, but fuck it. Getting the job would be a *huge* burden off my shoulders. I could stop the job search and focus on bar prep, which was going to take up all my free time.

Lisa laughed. "Great! Any chance you can start Monday? Eight a.m.?"

"Absolutely." I'd stacked my classes so they were all on Tuesday and Thursday, and I had the rest of the week free.

"Perfect. I'll send an email with details later. I look forward to working with you, Jules."

"I look forward to working with you too." I hung up with a

grin. It was all I could do not to break out into a little dance in the middle of the lobby.

Whatever pixie dust had been sprinkled at Ava's party, I needed a gallon of it ASAP. I'd never had such consistent good luck.

Then again, maybe the universe was reimbursing me for the way the bartender had hit on me after the party ended. He'd called me *JR* and told me how much he loved my resemblance to Jessica fucking Rabbit. I'd almost thrown my drink in his face.

I *bet* Josh had something to do with it. He probably fed the bartender some bullshit about how I liked being called JR.

What an asshole.

But no. I wouldn't let thoughts of Josh ruin what had otherwise been an incredible week.

I took a deep breath and tried to return to my happy place when I heard the guy manning the front desk make a strangled noise.

I lifted my head in time to see Stella rush through the revolving doors.

"Sorry, I got held up at work and left as soon as I could," she said breathlessly, oblivious to the way the receptionist was ogling her. Her legs were so long it only took her a few strides to reach me. "Am I late?"

"Nope. The leasing director hasn't—"

I didn't finish my sentence before a well-groomed woman in a sleek gray suit approached us, her expression as brisk as her stride.

"Ms. Ambrose, Ms. Alonso. I'm Pam, the Director of Leasing for The Mirage."

"Nice to meet you, Pam," I drawled, amused by how she spoke like she was the director of the NSA instead of an apartment building. That was a feature in D.C., not a bug. Everyone pretended they were more important than they actually were, which wasn't surprising in a city where the first question someone asked after meeting you was always, *What do you do?*

It was a town of walking resumes and career climbers, and I wasn't ashamed to say I was one of them. A good career meant good money, and good money meant security, shelter, and food on the table. If someone wanted to shame me for wanting those things, they could fuck right off.

I flinched when Stella jabbed her elbow in my side.

"Get your pointy elbows away from me," I whispered.

"Don't ruin our chances of getting this apartment," she whispered back.

"All I said was *nice to meet you.*"

"It's your tone." Stella shot me a warning stare as we followed Pam toward the elevator.

"*My* tone?" I placed a hand over my chest. "My tone is always impeccable."

Stella sighed, and I stifled a grin. She was the most unflappable of all my friends, so I considered it an achievement when I riled her up. Then again, she'd been a little *less* unflappable these past few months. Our house was always sparkling clean, which was a sure sign she was stressed.

I didn't blame her. From what she told me, her boss at *D.C. Style* gave Miranda Priestly a run for her money.

While we rode the elevator up to the tenth floor, Pam rambled on about the building's amenities. They included a rooftop lounge and pool, a state-of-the-art gym, and a twenty-four-seven doorman and concierge.

The more she spoke, the more my anticipation and worry spiked. The Mirage's website hadn't listed rent prices, but I'd bet my impending law degree it was expensive as hell. Rhys said his friend would give us a generous discount, but he hadn't specified how much.

God, I hoped we could afford it. I would kill for a rooftop pool, though I didn't care much for the gym. The only workouts I liked were the ones in bed, and even then, it'd been a while. Nothing killed one's love life like law school.

We stopped in front of a dark wood door with 1022 inscribed in gold.

"Here we are. The last available unit at The Mirage," Pam said proudly. She opened the door, and Stella and I let out simultaneous gasps.

Oh. My. God.

It was like someone took my dream apartment and 3D-printed it into reality. Floor-to-ceiling windows, a balcony, gleaming parquet floors, a brand-new kitchen with marble counters, and a cooking island. I'd always wanted one of those.

I didn't cook, but that was only because I'd never had an island. I could only imagine how good my food deliveries—I mean, my home-cooked meals—would look sprawled across that beautiful expanse of granite.

And while I shouldn't spend so much money on food deliveries when I was trying to save money, it was better than wasting money on groceries that went bad because I didn't know how to properly cook them. Right?

"Gorgeous, isn't it?" Pam beamed with the enthusiasm of a pet owner showing off her prized poodle at Westminster.

I managed a nod. I might've also been drooling; I wasn't sure.

Then Pam showed us the bedrooms, and I was positive I *was* drooling, because the bedrooms had walk-in closets. Small ones, but still. *Walk-in closets.*

A strangled noise slipped from Stella's throat.

As a fashion blogger, she owned more clothes and accessories than any human should own, and I could already see her mentally color-coordinating her clothes.

On the list of things Stella would give up her left arm for, a walk-in closet ranked number three, after a collaboration with Delamonte, her favorite fashion brand, and an extended trip through Italy filled with pasta, shopping, and sunsets over wine.

I wasn't making it up. She had a written list pinned to the bulletin board in her bedroom.

"The apartment is okay." I attempted to sound as casual as possible. "How much is the rent again?"

Pam told us, and I almost choked on my spit. Even Stella flinched at the number.

Seventy-five hundred dollars. *Per month.* Not including utilities.

That wasn't rent. That was highway robbery.

"Oh," Stella said faintly. "Um, I think our friend mentioned we were eligible for a special discount. How much is rent then?"

Pam arched one penciled-in brow, her smile wilting. "That *is* the price of rent with the discount, dear." Condescension dripped from the last word, and Stella flinched again.

I placed a protective hand on her arm and glared at Pam. Who did she think she was? She had no right to look down on us. Just because we weren't obscenely rich didn't mean we were any less than the residents at The Mirage.

"She is not your *dear,*" I said coldly. "And how is it legal to charge that much for *one* apartment?"

Pam's nostrils flared. She drew herself up to her full height, her voice quivering with outrage. "*Ms. Ambrose,* I assure you, everything we do here at The Mirage is aboveboard. If the pricing is outside your budget, might I suggest you look somewhere more—"

"Is everything all right, Pam?" A smooth, deep voice sliced through the air like a freshly sharpened knife.

"Mr. Harper." Pam's patronizing tone disappeared with the suddenness of a blown-out candle flame. Breathless deference replaced it. "I thought you were in New York."

I turned, curious to see who had the snobby leasing director so worked up, and the air whooshed out of my lungs in one strong gust.

Holy mother of God.

Thick, wavy, dark brown hair. Cheekbones that could chisel ice. Eyes the color of whiskey and broad shoulders that filled out his expensive Italian wool suit like it was custommade for him, which it probably was. Everything about him screamed wealth and power, and his sex appeal was so potent I could practically taste it.

I'd met my fair share of good-looking guys, but the man before me...wow.

"My business in the city wrapped up earlier than expected." The godlike man smiled at me. "Christian Harper. Owner of The Mirage."

Harper. Why did that name sound so familiar?

"Jules Ambrose. Future owner of a penthouse at The Mirage," I quipped.

After I became a partner at Silver & Klein, that is. It *will* happen. Stella was the woo-woo one with her crystals and horoscopes, but I low-key believed in manifestation as long as I mixed it with a healthy dose of hard work. It'd gotten me out of Ohio and into Thayer Law after all.

Amusement glowed in Christian's eyes. "Nice to meet you, Jules. I expect you'll be buying the penthouse from me sometime in the future then."

My eyebrows rose. So he actually lived at The Mirage. I'd expected him to reign over a mansion in the suburbs, but on second glance, Christian Harper did not look like a man who would live in the suburbs. He screamed city vibes through and through.

Black coffee. Expensive watches. Fast cars.

Christian turned to Stella. His face remained relaxed, but something flared in his eyes, hot and bright enough to drown out his earlier amusement.

He held out his hand. After a brief hesitation, she took it.

"I'm Stella."

"Stella," he repeated, softly and slowly, like he was savoring the syllables. He didn't move an inch, but the intensity of his stare was so strong it pulsed in the air. Time seemed to slow, and I wondered if that was a superpower of the rich—manipulating reality until it bent to their will.

A pink flush rose on Stella's cheeks. She opened her mouth, then closed it and glanced down at where his hand still gripped hers.

Another long second stretched by before Christian released her hand and stepped back with an indecipherable expression etched on his perfect features.

The movement pressed *play* on the scene, and time returned to normal. Pam stirred, the faint honks of cars ten floors below filtered through the glass windows, and my breath rushed out in an exhale.

Christian's gaze lingered on an uncharacteristically wary-looking Stella for a fraction of a second longer before he shifted his attention back to me. The intensity disappeared, replaced with a portrait of easy charm and hospitality once again.

"How do you like the apartment?" he asked.

"It's beautiful but out of our budget," I admitted. "We appreciate you setting up this tour for us though. Thank you."

"Well." Pam cleared her throat. "Mr. Harper, I can take it from here. I'm sure you have plenty of—"

"What's your budget?" Christian asked, ignoring his leasing

director completely.

Stella and I exchanged glances before I responded.

"Twenty-five hundred a month. Total." I was almost embarrassed to say it out loud. It was a pathetic fraction of the regular rent.

I'd expected Christian to laugh in our faces and throw us out. Instead, he rubbed a thumb over his bottom lip, his expression speculative.

Silence descended again, but this time it was filled with breathless anticipation—mostly mine, though a glimmer of hope shone in Stella's eyes as well.

I tried to tamp down my expectations. There was *no way* he'd agree to that price. Christian was a businessman, and businessmen did not—

"Done," he said.

Pam's mouth fell open in shock.

I hated to admit it, but my face likely matched hers. "Excuse me?"

There was a difference between not looking a gift horse in the mouth and questioning something that was *completely insane*. Sure, Christian was friends with Rhys and Rhys was future royalty, so it didn't hurt to be in his good graces, but we weren't Rhys's family or anything. The Mirage would be taking a huge financial hit if Christian rented the apartment to us for such a low price.

Or maybe it wouldn't. I didn't know. There was a reason I studied law and not business or economics.

"Twenty-five hundred a month. Done," Christian said as casually as if he were buying a Starbucks coffee. "Pam, draw up the papers."

A vein pulsed in her temple. "Mr. Harper, I think we need to discuss—"

Those whiskey eyes sharpened and lanced into her.

Pam fell silent, though her expression remained mutinous.

"I'll wait here." A razored edge ran beneath Christian's otherwise genial tone.

Another warning, this one less subtle.

"Of course." Pam's mouth stretched into a forced smile. "I'll be right back."

I waited until she left before I crossed my arms over my chest and narrowed my eyes at Christian. "What's the catch?"

He straightened his suit sleeve. "Elaborate."

"Twenty-five hundred a month would barely cover the utilities, much less the rent. I know we're friends of a friend and all, but it doesn't make financial sense."

If something seemed to good to be true, it probably was. There *had* to be a catch.

The corner of Christian's mouth tugged up. "Unless you install an indoor water park and keep it running twenty-four-seven, I doubt your utilities will cost that much each month. And there is no catch. Rhys is an old friend, and I owe him a favor."

"How do you know him?" Stella asked.

Christian paused, that indecipherable expression flickering across his face again before he responded with a smooth, "We used to work together."

Suddenly, it clicked.

"Harper Security," I said, naming the elite private security firm Rhys worked for when he was Bridget's bodyguard. "You're the CEO."

"At your service," he drawled.

"I hope not." Any situation that required me or Stella to get a bodyguard wouldn't be a good one. "So, there's really no catch?"

"No. My only stipulation is you sign today. I doubt members of The Mirage's waiting list would be happy I let you skip the line, and I can't guarantee this offer will be available if you wait until tomorrow or even tonight."

Stella and I exchanged another glance. I hated rushing into things, but this was our dream apartment. What if Christian *did* change his mind later? I would never forgive myself for letting the opportunity slip through my fingers.

Pam returned with the papers, her face screwed into a sour frown.

Too bad. If she had a problem with what was happening, she could take it up with her boss, though I doubted she would. Christian did not look like the type who tolerated insubordination.

"Here." She practically shoved the papers into my hand.

"Thank you, Pam." I bestowed her with a gracious smile. "I'm *so excited* we're going to be your tenants." I paused. "Sorry, I mean Christian's tenants."

Her mouth tightened further, but she was smart enough not to respond.

Half an hour later, after Stella and I painstakingly reviewed every line of the lease, searching for red flag phrases like *tenants must provide sexual services to the building's owner every month to make up for their ridiculously cheap rent* and finding none, we signed on the dotted line.

Pam signed after us, and it was done.

We were officially tenants of The Mirage, effective in five weeks.

Unreal.

"I'm glad we could make it work." A half-smile touched Christian's mouth. "I have a meeting I'm running late for, so I'll leave you in Pam's capable hands. I'm sure I'll see you both around." He slid a brief glance in Stella's direction before leaving.

After his tall, lean frame disappeared into the hall, Pam

released a sharp sigh. "Congratulations," she said tightly. "You just secured one of the city's most coveted apartments for pennies."

"Lady Luck has always smiled on me." It wasn't true, but it was worth seeing her eye twitch.

We exited the apartment and rode the elevator down to the lobby in silence. Once we hit the ground floor, Pam left us with the world's most tepid goodbye, but I didn't care.

"We did it!" I waited until Stella and I stepped outside The Mirage before I threw my arms around her in an impromptu hug. I couldn't hold back my giddiness anymore. Between the lease and LHAC, today was the best day ever. Period.

"We got our dream apartment!" I sighed, starry-eyed at the possibilities.

Late night drinks on the rooftop. Morning swims in the pool. Diving into a pile of clothes in my walk-in closet just because I could.

"Pinch me," I said. "I think I'm dream—ow!"

"You said to pinch you," Stella said innocently. She broke into a laugh and dodged my playful attempt to swat her. "Seriously, though, I'm so happy it worked out, but..."

"But?"

"You don't think it was too easy? The way he just agreed to our price?" Her bottom lip disappeared between her teeth while a small crease formed between her brows.

"It *was* too easy," I admitted. "But we both looked over the lease twice. There was nothing out of the ordinary. Maybe Christian was just being nice because we're Rhys's friends."

"Maybe." Doubt lingered in Stella's eyes.

"We'll be fine." I linked my arm through hers and guided her to the Crumble & Bake a few streets over for celebratory cupcakes. "And if we aren't, I happen to know plenty of lawyers."

8

JOSH

As an ER resident, I saw some crazy shit, and the last week was no exception.

A man whose car collided with a fence and arrived at the hospital *with* the fence post stuck through him? Check. (He was currently in the ICU, but chances were, he'll survive).

A patient who stripped off all their clothes and ran around the ER naked before two nurses finally caught them? Check.

Someone with a broken-off cucumber stuck in their rectum? Check.

Total insanity, but that was why I'd chosen emergency medicine over surgery, which my father had pushed for. He wanted to brag about having a heart surgeon for a son, but I thrived on chaos. On the thrill of coming into work every day and not knowing what challenges lay ahead. It kept me on my toes, though I could do without removing vegetables from other people's orifices for a long, long while.

"Get some rest," Clara said as I clocked out after another grueling night shift. "You look like a zombie."

"False. I always look perfect. Right, Luce?" I winked at

Lucy, another nurse. She giggled in agreement while Clara rolled her eyes.

"See you tomorrow. Try not to miss me too much." I rapped my knuckles against the counter on my way out the door.

"We won't," Clara said.

At the same time Lucy chirped, "We'll try!"

A chuckle rose in my throat, but by the time I stepped outside, it'd already faded, crushed by bone-deep exhaustion. However, instead of heading home for some much-needed shuteye, I made a left toward the north side of the hospital campus, where the Legal Health Alliance Clinic was located.

I'd somehow misplaced my charger before my shift and my phone was at eight percent, so the backup charger I kept at LHAC was my only hope of keeping my all-important cell alive.

When I arrived at the clinic, Barbs's car was the only one in the tiny parking lot squished next to the building. Most of the staff didn't trickle in until half past eight, but she opened and closed the office every day, so she kept longer hours.

"Hey, beautiful," I quipped when I entered the reception area.

"Hey, handsome," she said with a wink.

When I'd volunteered at LHAC as a med student, Barbs kept me supplied with home-cooked pastries and sage advice like *when life gives you lemons, make lemonade and hang out with someone whose life gave them vodka.* She was one of the reasons I'd continued volunteering despite my crazy residency schedule. The clinic staff had become my surrogate family over the years, and even though I only had time to drop by once or twice a week in between shifts, they kept me grounded.

"Wasn't expecting to see you today." Barbs tucked her pen behind her ear. "A little birdie told me you just came off a night shift."

I didn't ask how she knew. Barbs was the most plugged-in person in the Thayer Hospital system. She knew things about people before *they* did.

"Trust me, I'm going home and crashing soon." I scrubbed a hand over my face, trying to keep my eyes open. "I just need to grab my charger."

I'd volunteered at LHAC so long I had my own desk. The bulk of my work involved staffing its free health clinic for uninsured health patients, but I also consulted on various legal cases that required a medical opinion.

"Before you do, you should say hi to our new research associate." Barbs nodded at the kitchen door down the hall. "You'll like her. She's feisty."

I raised my eyebrows. "New associate already?"

LHAC had been inundated with new cases recently. Lisa, the legal director, had been talking about hiring a short-term associate to help out until the rush was over, but I hadn't expected it to happen so soon.

"Yep. Third year at Thayer Law." Barbs's eyes gleamed in a way that sent my guard shooting straight up. "Smart girl. Pretty too, if a bit eager. She started on Monday, and I found her waiting outside fifteen minutes before the clinic opened."

"Congrats, you just described half the girls at Thayer." A majority of the university's students were Type A to a fault. "Don't even think about it," I added when Barbs opened her mouth. "I don't do office romances."

I had a reputation as a player, but I would never hook up with someone I worked with, not even in a volunteer setting.

Barbs didn't bat an eye at my foul language—she'd said and heard much worse at the clinic—though her face did pucker in disappointment. She fancied herself the hospital matchmaker, and she'd been trying to matchmake me for years.

"Besides, if I did date anyone from the clinic, it'd be you," I added teasingly.

She maintained her frown for ten seconds before it melted into a smile. "You're a terrible liar."

"Me, lie?" I placed a hand over my chest. "Never."

She shook her head. "Go. Take that charm elsewhere. You're too young for me. And come back to me after you've seen her," she called after me, laughing when I tossed her an exasperated look over my shoulder.

I grabbed my charger from my desk and pocketed it. Then, curious despite myself, I headed to the kitchen to meet the new associate. I might as well see what all the fuss was about.

I pushed open the kitchen door, my mouth curving into a welcoming—*What. The. Fuck.*

My smile disappeared faster than candy at a kid's birthday party.

Because sitting in the middle of the room, drinking coffee out of *my* favorite mug and examining a stack of papers, was none other than Jules Ambrose.

My blood pressure spiked.

No. *Fuck* no. I must've fallen asleep after my shift and entered a vivid nightmare because there was *no way* Jules was the new research associate. The universe wouldn't be so cruel.

She glanced up at the sound of the door opening, and I would've taken great pleasure in the way her face paled had I not been equally thunderstruck.

"What the hell are you doing here?" Our voices mingled in a discordant melody—her words pitched high with stress, mine low with horror.

A muscle jumped in my jaw. "I work here." I released the doorknob and crossed my arms over my chest. "What's your excuse?"

"*I* work here. *You* work in the ER." Jules arched an

eyebrow. "I see you're going senile already. That's what happens when your brain uses all its limited faculties on basic upkeep."

Goddammit. I didn't have time for this. I came here to pick up my charger, and now I was stuck arguing with the she-devil when all I wanted was sleep.

But it was too late. There was no backing down unless I wanted her to rub getting the last word in my face until the end of time.

"Don't project, it's unbecoming. Just because you have lower than average mental capacity doesn't mean everyone else does." A smirk touched my mouth when her eye twitched. "As for the clinic, I've been volunteering here since I was in med school."

Translation: it was *my* space. I'd claimed it first.

Was that a juvenile way to look at things? Perhaps. But there were so few places I felt truly at home. The clinic was one of them, and Jules's presence would smash that peace to smithereens.

"It's not too late to quit." I leaned against the wall, keeping my eyes locked to hers in a silent challenge. "You'd have more fun spending your free time elsewhere. I'm sure there's a poor sap who's willing to fill in the gaps in your schedule if you're bored."

"I could say the same for you, Judgy McJosh." Jules sipped her coffee out of my fucking mug. "Or have you run out of women who'll fall for your bullshit? Unless you're using the volunteer excuse to pick up women, which is just sad."

I closed the distance between us in three strides and slammed my hands on the table hard enough to rattle the high-lighters lined up next to her papers. I leaned forward until our faces were only inches apart and our breaths mingled in a cloud of animosity.

"Quit." The word vibrated, taut and furious, between us.

Jules's eyes glowed with challenge. "No."

Her slow, precise enunciation ratcheted my blood pressure up another notch.

My knuckles dug into the hard wood as I fisted my hands on the table. My heart pounded so hard its drumbeat echoed in my head, taunting me.

I didn't know why *this* one thing bothered me so much. Jules was the new research associate. So what? I didn't come into the clinic often, and I didn't have to talk to her if I didn't want to. Plus, hers was a temporary position. She'd be gone in a few months.

But the mere idea of her here, in my haven, drinking out of my mug and laughing with my friends and filling every molecule of air with her presence, made it really fucking hard to breathe.

One. Two. Three. I forced oxygen into my lungs with each count.

A few feet away, the fridge hummed, oblivious to the battle playing out in the kitchen. Meanwhile, the clock ticked its way toward the half hour, reminding me I should be long gone by now.

Shower. Bed. Blissful sleep.

They called my name, yet here I was, face to face with Jules, unwilling to wave the white flag in our silent war.

Even at this close proximity, I couldn't spot a single flaw in her creamy skin. I could, however, count the individual lashes framing her hazel eyes and spot the teeny tiny mole above her upper lip.

The fact I noticed those things pissed me off even more.

"I thought you were all about corporate law. Big bucks. Prestige." Each syllable came out cold and sharp enough to sting. "The clinic may not be as fancy as Silver & Klein, but we do important work here. It's not a playground for you to mess around in until you leave for the 'big leagues.'"

It was a low blow. I knew it even as I said it.

Jules probably needed a job to tide her over until she passed the bar exam, and there was nothing wrong with that.

But my frustration—over my father, over Alex, over the empty, gnawing feeling in my chest that had plagued me for more nights than I cared to admit—turned me into someone I didn't recognize and didn't particularly like. Normally, I could pretend I was the same carefree guy I'd been in school, but for some reason, my mask never lasted long with Jules.

Perhaps it was because I didn't care whether she saw the worst of me. There was a certain liberation in not giving a shit about what other people thought.

"How like you to assume the worst of me." If my voice was cold, Jules's was an inferno, incinerating the sharp edges of my irritation until only the ashes of shame remained.

"What, you think I'm going to swan in here every week, push a few papers around, and *pretend* to work just because I'm a temp? Newsflash, asshole, when I commit to doing something, I do it *well*. I don't care if it's a big law firm, a nonprofit, or a fucking lemonade stand at the end of a dead-end road. You're not better than me just because you're a doctor, and I'm not the devil just because I want a high-paying career. So you can take your sanctimonious attitude and shove it up your ass, Josh Chen, because *I'm over it*."

Silence blanketed the room, broken only by Jules's ragged breaths. Her earlier cool had evaporated, replaced with flushed cheeks and blazing eyes, but for once, I didn't take pleasure in riling her up.

I opened my mouth to say something, anything, but I was too stunned to formulate an appropriate response.

Jules and I had exchanged more barbs than I could count

over the years. She always gave as good as she got, but what happened just now...if I didn't know better, I could've sworn she was actually hurt.

A hot poker of guilt stabbed at my chest.

I straightened and rubbed a hand over my face, wondering when the hell my life had gotten so complicated. I missed the days when Jules and I insulted each other with zero guilt or remorse, when my sister wasn't in love with my ex-best friend, and when my best friend had still been my friend.

I missed the days when I was *me*.

Now here I was, about to do something old Josh would've rather cut off his arm than do.

"I shouldn't have said that," I finally conceded. "It was a low blow, and I..." A muscle worked in my jaw. *Dammit*. "I'm sorry."

I spit out the words. It was the first time I'd ever apologized to Jules, and I wanted to get it over as quickly as possible.

Just because I did the right thing didn't mean I had to like it.

I braced myself for Jules's gloating, but none came. Instead, she just stared at me like I hadn't spoken.

I forged ahead. "However, the clinic *is* important to me, and I don't want our...differences to get in the way of our work. So I propose a truce."

Proposing a truce might as well be surrendering, but I refused to let our animosity poison my time at the clinic. Everywhere else, fine. But not here.

Her brow wrinkled. "A truce."

"Only when we're in the clinic." I wasn't naive enough to think we could uphold any semblance of peace outside a work environment. "No insults, no snarky comments. We keep it professional. Deal?" I held out my hand.

Jules eyed it like it was a coiled-up cobra waiting to strike.

"Unless, of course, you don't think you can do it."

Satisfaction trickled through me when her lips thinned. I'd touched on a competitive nerve, as I knew I would.

She didn't take her eyes off mine as she grasped my hand and squeezed. Hard.

Jesus. For someone so small, she was fucking strong.

"Deal," she said with a smile.

I smiled back through gritted teeth and squeezed even harder, relishing the way her nostrils flared at the pressure.

"Excellent."

Forget what I said about being bored.

This was going to be an interesting few months.

9

JULES

IF SOMEONE HAD TOLD ME A MONTH AGO THAT I WOULD willingly agree to a truce with Josh Chen, I would've laughed in their face and asked what they were smoking. Josh and I were as capable of acting civil toward each other as a tiger was of changing its stripes.

But, as much as I hated to admit it, his reasoning made sense. I took pride in my work, and the last thing I wanted was for my personal feelings to affect the workplace. Plus, I'd been so caught off guard by his apology my brain spazzed. I hadn't been able to think straight, much less wade through what the consequences of a ceasefire with Josh Chen might look like.

Surprisingly, they haven't been terrible...though that might be because I haven't *seen* Josh since the truce. According to Barbs, he only came in on his days off or when he wasn't wiped from a shift.

I had no issue with that. The less I had to see him, the better. Part of me was still embarrassed by how I'd lost my cool when he accused me of not taking my job seriously. We'd hurled much worse insults at each other over the years, yet that one thing had made me snap.

It wasn't the first time I'd been judged—for my looks and my family, the career I chose and the clothes I wore, the way I laughed too loudly when I was supposed to be demure and asserted myself too boldly when I was supposed to be invisible. I was used to shaking off criticism, but the sneers and side eyes accumulated over time, and I'd gotten to the point where I was just *tired*.

Tired of working twice as hard as everyone else to be taken seriously and fighting even harder to prove my worth.

I shook my head and tried to refocus on the documents before me. I didn't have time for a pity party. I needed to finish fact checking a case today, and the clinic closed in three hours.

I'd gotten through half the papers when the door swung open and Josh waltzed in, carrying a small box from Crumble & Bake.

"Oh look, if it isn't—" *My favorite devil's spawn.* I bit off the rest of my words when Josh raised a challenging brow. "My best friend's brother."

It would take some adjusting before I curbed my knee-jerk instinct to insult him the second I saw his face.

"Astute observation." He set the box on the table and took the seat next to me. A whiff of his cologne floated over, mingling with the sweet scent wafting from the box. "Let me guess. You've annoyed the rest of the staff so much they banished you to the kitchen?"

"If you had a modicum of observational skill, you'd notice there isn't a desk for me yet." I forced myself not to stare at the pastries. *Don't give in to the temptation of sweets.* "I'm working out of the kitchen until it comes in. *And*," I pointed my pen at him, triumph filling my veins, "you broke the truce."

"No, I didn't." Josh rolled up his sleeves, revealing tanned, lightly veined forearms. A heavy watch glinted on his wrist, and as someone with an odd thing for men and watches, I would've found the sight hot had he not been, well, him. "Sarcasm isn't the same as an insult. I'm sarcastic with my friends all the time. It's how I show my love."

I rolled my eyes so hard I was surprised I didn't enter another dimension. "Yes, you obviously meant to show your love for me with your statement."

"No, I meant to show my *love* for you with this." Josh lengthened his drawl with exaggerated slowness, like he was speaking to a child. He opened the box, and my eyes zeroed in on the cupcake sitting smack dab in the middle.

Salted caramel. My favorite.

My stomach emitted a low rumble of approval. I'd been so caught up in work I hadn't eaten since my paltry lunch of a salad and smoothie a few hours ago.

Josh's mouth lifted into a smirk while I shuffled my papers loudly to hide the sound. I wouldn't give him the satisfaction of salivating over anything he bought.

"Consider it my official olive branch." He pushed the box toward me. "Along with me not mentioning how *you* broke the truce by insulting my observational skills, which are excellent, by the way."

Only Josh could claim credit for not doing something he *just* did.

Instead of arguing with him, I poked at the cupcake with suspicion. "Did you poison it?" There was a difference between being civil and buying someone their favorite cupcake unprompted.

"Nah, I was in a rush. Maybe next time."

"Hilarious. Netflix should give you a standup special." I plucked the cupcake from the box and examined it more closely for signs of tampering.

"I know." Josh oozed cockiness. "It's one of my many wonderful attributes."

I fought another eye roll. There were probably a hundred poor souls walking around with low self-esteem so Josh Chen could sail through life with an ego the size of Jupiter. Satan must've been distracted the day he created his hellspawn and poured a little too much obnoxiousness into Josh's beaker.

"How did you know salted caramel is my favorite?" I squinted at a tiny black mark on the cupcake wrapper.

A mere scratch from an errant marker, or proof of poison? Hmmm...

"It doesn't take a genius to figure it out." Josh nodded at the venti drink on the table. "Every time I see you, you're inhaling a caramel mocha the size of your head."

Okay, fair point. My love for all things caramel-flavored wasn't exactly a secret.

"Keep it up and you'll get diabetes," he added. "All that sugar isn't good for you."

"So you're feeding me more sugar in the hopes I'll become diabetic." I tapped my pen against the table with my free hand. "I *knew* you had nefarious intentions."

Josh sighed and pinched his brow. "Jules, eat the damn cupcake."

I stifled a grin. I was mostly fucking with him at this point, and I really was starving. If I was going to die, I might as well die eating something I loved.

I peeled back the wrapper and took a small bite. Warm, delicious sweetness burst onto my tongue, and I couldn't hold back a soft moan of appreciation.

Nothing beat a salted caramel cupcake after hours of work.

Josh watched while I ate, his exasperated expression giving way to something I couldn't identify.

Uncharacteristic self-consciousness pricked at my skin. "What?"

He opened his mouth, then closed it and leaned back in his chair, lacing his fingers behind his head. "I like you a lot better when you aren't talking. I should bring you food more often."

"Good thing I don't give two damns whether you like me or not." My words dripped with honey. "But if you want to buy me food, go ahead. Just know I'll inspect every inch before it goes into my mouth."

I realized my mistake before the sentence fully left my mouth.

Shit. That came out dirtier than I'd intended.

Josh's face split into a devilish grin.

"Don't." I held up one hand, my cheeks warming. "Save yourself from whatever juvenile joke you were about to spew."

To my surprise, he did.

Josh tapped a finger on the pile of papers in front of me. "You know there are other places you could work besides the kitchen."

"Like where, the bathroom?" LHAC was tiny, and I didn't want to impose on anyone else's workspace. "It's fine. It's comfortable in here."

If you overlooked the ice-cold temperature, rickety table, and stiff wooden chairs, that is. Still, it beat working from the toilet seat.

"Yeah, if you compare it to the Siberian wild."

I released an annoyed sigh. "Are you here to work, or are you here to pester me?"

"I can do both. I'm a great multitasker," Josh quipped before his eyes turned serious. "Heard we got a new case today."

"Yep." I slid the papers toward him, snapping into work mode. "The Bowers. The mother, Laura Bower, fell down the stairs and can't work for the next two months. No insurance, so they have a crazy amount of medical bills, and she's the family's sole breadwinner. Her husband Terence got out of jail a few years ago but hasn't been able to find work because of his criminal record. They have two kids, Daisy and Tommy, ages six and nine."

"They're facing eviction." Josh scanned the files.

I nodded. "Laura needs a stable place to recover from her fall, to say nothing of the issues that accompany homelessness."

Murky, unwanted memories crowded my brain at the last word.

Cold nights. Empty stomach. The incessant itch of anxiety crawling over my skin.

My situation had been different from the Bowers, but I remembered all too well what it was like to wake up every morning and wonder if that was the last day I'd have a roof over my head and food on the table.

My mother had been a cocktail waitress, but she'd been more interested in blowing her meager income on shopping than paying the bills. Sometimes, the lights would cut out in the middle of me doing homework because she forgot to pay the electric bill. Eventually, I figured out how to siphon electricity from our neighbor at the ripe old age of ten. Not the most ethical solution, but I did what I had to do.

A shiver rolled through me.

You're fine. You're not that little girl anymore.

"I know her." Josh rapped his knuckle against the paper with Laura's picture stapled to it, yanking me back into the present. "I treated her when she came in. Multiple broken bones, heavy bruising, twisted ankle. Still, she was in good spirits and making jokes, trying to keep her kids from panicking." His face softened. "The ER can be a blur, but I remember her."

"Yeah," I said quietly. "She seems really nice."

I'd never met Laura, but I could tell she was the type of mother I would've killed to have.

I cleared my throat in an attempt to ease the knot of emotion that had taken residence there. "Legally speaking, the obvious solution is to clear Terence's criminal record so he can find a job," I said. As the clinic's practicing attorney, Lisa needed to sign off on everything I did, and she'd agreed clearing his record was the best solution. "He was charged for marijuana possession. One ounce, and he spent a year in jail for it."

Heat crept over my neck the way it had when I first learned the case details. Few things pissed me off more than the inequity of draconian drug laws. "How stupid is that? Some rapists only get a few months in jail, but have a little marijuana on you and your record is stained forever. That's such *bullshit*. You have weed farmers in Colorado raking in the cash from the sale of marijuana while people like Terence are vilified for it. Tell me where the justice is in that. I—what?" I stopped when I noticed Josh staring at me with a tiny, almost fascinated smile.

"I've never seen you so worked up over something that wasn't me."

"Once again, you've proved your self-absorption knows no bounds." My flush of anger cooled, though my indignation at the injustice of it all remained. "That's not me breaking the truce," I added. "That's a fact."

"Sure it is," Josh said dryly. "But you're right. There is no justice in what happened to Terence."

I cocked my head, sure I'd heard wrong. "Repeat that. The middle sentence."

First the apology, then the admission I was right. Was that *really* Josh sitting across from me, or had aliens abducted him and switched him out with a more agreeable body swap?

"No."

"Do it." I nudged his foot with mine, earning myself a scowl. "I want to hear you say it again."

"Which is exactly why I won't."

"Come on." I gave him my best puppy dog face. "It's Friday."

"That has nothing to do with anything." Josh heaved a long, put-upon sigh when I deepened my puppy eyes. "I *said*, you're right." He sounded so disgruntled I almost laughed. "*Only* about this one thing, though. Not anything else."

"See. That wasn't so hard." I folded the cupcake wrapper neatly into a square and pushed it to the side for future disposal. "You have a decent smile when you're not being an ass," I added generously, since we were being nice.

"Thanks."

I ignored Josh's sarcasm and switched back to the case. I wanted to finish all my work before I left so I didn't have to spend the weekend worrying about it. Our Vermont trip was tomorrow, and while I wasn't looking forward to two days in a cabin with Josh, I *was* looking forward to my first vacation of the year.

I didn't count my trip to Eldorra for Bridget's coronation. I'd only been there for a weekend, and it'd been so crazy I barely had time to sleep, much less sightsee.

"Now, about the Bowers." I tapped my pen against the paper. "Lisa mentioned we could provide free medical checkups for Laura while she's healing."

"Yes. Usually, we have them come into the free clinic." Josh waved in the general direction of the exit, and it only occurred to me now that he must've been staffing the clinic all day. The pop-up tent was set up outside LHAC, so I wouldn't have seen him arrive. "But given Laura's situation, we can make home visits. We just have to fill out the appropriate paperwork..."

For the next hour, Josh and I worked on the Bower case

together. He created a checkup schedule and handled the medical paperwork while I finished fact checking the details and gathered the information we needed to clear Terence's record.

I snuck a glance at Josh while he scribbled something on a blank sheet of paper. His brow etched with a frown of concentration, and I realized it was the first time I'd seen him work.

"Like what you see?" he asked without looking up from his paper.

Heat crawled up my neck again, this time from embarrassment. "Only if the thesaurus changed *like* to be a synonym for *loathe*."

The corner of his mouth curved up a fraction of an inch. "*Truce*, JR."

I couldn't tell whether the soft reminder was mocking or not, but it made my stomach flip. Maybe he *had* poisoned the cupcake.

I highlighted a passage in the case with more aggression than necessary. Josh and I made a surprisingly good team, but I didn't fool myself into thinking our truce was a precursor to an actual friendship.

Only a few things in life were certain: death, taxes, and the fact that Josh Chen and I would never be friends.

10

JOSH

THE BRIEF CAMARADERIE JULES AND I EXPERIENCED AT the clinic fizzled less than twenty-four hours later, when I arrived at the airport's private jet terminal to find her looking bright-eyed, bushy-tailed, and all too smug about beating me to the airport.

"You're late." Jules sipped her coffee. No doubt it was a caramel mocha with extra crunch and oat milk because she was lactose intolerant and hated the taste of almond milk.

So predictable.

"We haven't boarded yet, which means I'm not late." I dropped into the seat opposite hers and frowned at her outfit. Yoga pants and boots, topped with a fuzzy purple jacket and giant sunglasses she'd propped on top of her head. "Where the hell did you get your jacket? Barneys R Us?"

"I wouldn't expect someone who showed up to the airport in *sweatpants* to understand fashion." Jules's eyes flicked toward the sweatpants in question, and my irritation melted into smug satisfaction when she lingered a second too long on a certain area.

"Take a picture. It lasts longer," I drawled.

Her eyes snapped up to mine. "Thanks for the offer, but I'm just thinking about how easy it would be to cut your prized possession off." She smiled. "Sleep tight this weekend, Joshy. You never know what goes bump in the night."

I didn't bother responding to her ridiculous threat, but my eyebrows popped up when she picked up the small white paper bag next to her and tossed it at me without warning.

I caught it easily, my reflexes honed from years of sports.

I opened the bag, and my eyebrows rose higher when I saw the blueberry muffin sitting at the bottom.

"In return for the cupcake." Maybe the lighting was playing tricks on me, but I thought I spotted the faintest pink tint on Jules's cheeks. "I don't like owing people."

"It was a cupcake, JR, not a loan." I shook the bag. "Did you poison this?" I asked, mirroring her question from yesterday. "Ava will be upset if her beloved brother drops dead during her birthday trip, which means Alex will be upset, which means you'll be dead."

Her sigh contained the weariness of a thousand ages. "Josh, eat the damn muffin."

I debated for all of two seconds before I shrugged.

What the hell. There were worse ways to go than death by blueberry.

"Thank you," I said grudgingly.

I ripped off a piece of the pastry and popped it in my mouth while my eyes roved the terminal. "Where's the happy couple?"

"Probably whispering sweet nothings to each other over breakfast." Jules tilted her head toward the fancy-looking restaurant further down the terminal.

I snorted at the thought of Alex whispering sweet anythings to anyone, even my sister. "You didn't join them?"

"Didn't feel like third wheeling."

"That's never stopped you before."

Instead of responding, she eyed me over the rim of her cup, a small notch forming between her brows. "Is it weird for you?" she asked. "Going on a trip with Alex."

I paused, my jaw tensing for a second before I resumed chewing. "It is what it is. Ava asked, so I'm here. The end," I said after I finished eating.

A taut silence stretched between us, ripe with unspoken words.

Jules lowered her drink before raising it to her mouth again, like she wanted to shield herself from what she was about to say next. "You're a good brother."

No snark, only sincerity, but the words hit me somewhere south of my gut.

"Your sister's in the hospital..."

"Almost drowned..."

"I'm sorry son, but your mom...she overdosed..."

"He lied to us." Tears streaked Ava's cheeks. *"He lied to both of us."*

"Join us for the holidays." I clapped a hand on Alex's shoulder. *"Spending Christmas alone is just wrong."*

"I'd feel better if I had someone I trusted looking after her, ya know?"

"You're the only person I trust, period, outside of my family. And you know how worried I am about Ava..."

Disjointed memories crowded my brain.

Was I a good brother?

I hadn't been there when Ava almost died, *twice*. I'd been too blind to see the truth about our father all those years. I'd *looked up* to the man, did everything I could to make him proud. And I'd all but pushed Ava into Alex's arms because, once again, I'd trusted someone who ended up betraying me.

In the end, Alex and Ava's relationship worked out, but I would never forget the months when she walked around like a shell of herself. Quiet, withdrawn, and devoid of the spark that made her *her*. Every day, I woke up fearing I would find her the way I'd found our mom—with too many pills in her stomach and not enough will to live.

All because I was too goddamned stupid and placed my trust in people I shouldn't have.

I knew it technically wasn't my fault that Michael tried to kill Ava, or that my mom committed suicide, or that Ava fell in love with Alex. But that was the thing about guilt. It didn't give a damn about facts or reason. It sprouted from the tiniest seeds of doubt, slipped through the cracks of your psyche, and by the time you realized what the ugly darkness oozing through your veins was, it'd already burrowed itself so deep you couldn't dig it out without losing a part of yourself.

"Josh." Jules's voice sounded muffled and far away. "Josh!"

It was louder and clearer this time, enough so it yanked me out of my thoughts and back into the sun-drenched terminal.

I blinked, my heart slamming against my ribcage with such force it rattled my bones. "Yeah."

The notch between her brows deepened, and something akin to concern passed through her eyes. "I've been calling your name for the past five minutes. Are you...okay?"

"Yeah," I repeated. I raked a hand through my hair and forced myself to take deep breaths until my heartbeat slowed to a normal rate. "Just thinking about some things."

It was the lamest reply I could've given, but Jules didn't call me out on it. Instead, she stared at me for a minute longer before she flicked her eyes over my shoulder and said, "Alex and Ava are here."

I twisted my head in time to see the couple in question come into view.

"Hey!" Ava broke away from Alex and hugged me. "You're on time."

"Why does everyone think I'm not punctual? I am," I grumbled.

I swear, you're late to *one* party and suddenly everyone thinks you make a habit out of it.

"Sure." My sister patted me on the arm before she addressed the group at large. "You guys ready to board?"

"Yep." Jules stood and tossed her empty drink into a nearby trash can. "Let's do this."

She and Ava fell into step ahead of me and left me with Alex, who I greeted with a stiff nod. "Alex."

"Josh." His face was blank, per usual, but the tense set of his shoulders suggested I wasn't the only one who had qualms about this weekend.

I could only hope we all made it out intact.

———

By the time we landed in Vermont an hour and a half later, I'd drowned my anxieties about the weekend with two mimosas, hold the orange juice, courtesy of the private jet service.

A black Range Rover waited for us outside the airport, which was only a thirty-minute ride to the resort, and Ava spent most of the drive detailing the resort's luxury amenities: a world-class spa, two gourmet restaurants, the famed triple black diamond, and a bunch of other things I tuned out.

All I cared about was the ski trail. *My first triple black diamond.* It was going to be epic.

I was itching to drop off my luggage and hit the slopes, but unfortunately, we hit our first snag before we even checked in.

"What do you mean, the lodge is occupied?" Icicles

dripped from each word as Alex glared at the poor front desk assistant. Henry, according to his name tag.

"I'm terribly sorry, Mr. Volkov, but it appears there was a mix-up in the system, and we double-booked this weekend." Henry gulped. "The other guests arrived last night and checked in."

"I see." Alex's voice dropped another ten degrees. "So where, exactly, are we supposed to stay, considering I already shelled out a *considerable* sum of money for the Presidential Lodge?"

Henry gulped again and tapped furiously on his computer.

Ava tugged on Alex's hand and whispered something in his ear that caused his shoulders to relax, though he kept his glare pinned to Henry.

I leaned against the counter, not dumb enough to open my mouth while Alex was on the warpath. Even Jules was silent, though that might be because she was too busy eye fucking some guy across the lobby.

I gave the guy a quick once-over. Blond hair, unnaturally white smile, the same pale blue shirt and khakis as the rest of the resort staff. I'd bet my last dollar he was a ski instructor. He just had that annoying, eager look.

"Put your tongue back in your mouth, JR. You're drooling."

"I don't drool." Jules smiled at Ski Bro, who smiled back.

Irritation curled in my stomach. It was the resort's grand opening weekend, and he was loitering in the lobby, flirting with guests. Didn't he have a job to do?

"There's one VIP lodge left," Henry said. "The Eagle Lodge isn't as big as the Presidential Lodge, but it has the best view and the same amenities. Of course, we're happy to refund you for the difference in pricing as well as include a complimentary meal and spa gift card to make up for the inconvenience."

If Ava weren't here, I was sure Alex would've ripped the guy a new one, but all he said was, "How much smaller is the Eagle Lodge?"

"It has two bedrooms instead of four. *But* the couch in the living room can be converted into a bed," Henry hastened to add when Alex's brows lowered.

"It's fine." Ava placed a hand on Alex's forearm. "It's just for the weekend."

Alex's nostrils flared before he acquiesced with a short nod. "The Eagle Lodge is fine."

"Great." Henry's relief was palpable. "Here are the key cards..."

I shifted my attention back to Jules while he gave instructions on how to get to the lodge.

"You done having sex in the lobby?"

Jules was *still* silently flirting with Ski Bro, but she tore her eyes away from him at my comment. "If you think I'm having sex right now, it's no wonder women leave your room unsatisfied."

Touché.

A small smile played on my lips. If adventure sports were my physical release, sparring with Jules was my mental one. Nothing else gave me quite the same rush.

"Women leave my room feeling all sorts of things, but I guarantee unsatisfied isn't one of them."

"That's what men always think," she scoffed. "I regret to inform you they're probably faking it."

"I can tell the difference between a fake orgasm and a real one, JR."

"So you're saying women *have* faked orgasms with you." Her voice was all sugar and arsenic.

"My first few times." I wasn't embarrassed by the fact.

Everyone started at zero. "But practice makes perfect. Maybe you'll find out for yourself one day, if you're lucky."

Jules gagged as we followed Alex and Ava out of the lobby to our lodge. "Don't make me throw up. We just got here, and I despise vomit."

A laugh rumbled in my throat. She was so fucking easy to rile up.

But when we arrived at the lodge, my laugh died in the face of hiccup number two: the pullout couch was not, in fact, a pullout. It was just a damn couch, which meant there were only two rooms for the four of us, and every possible pairing sounded worse than the last.

"I can room with Jules." Ava slanted an apologetic glance in Alex's direction. "You and Josh can share."

"No." I would rather swim naked in the icy river bordering the resort than room with Alex.

"What's the alternative?" she argued. "I don't want to spend all day debating room assignments."

There were only two other options. I could room with Ava or Jules. If I roomed with Ava, Alex and Jules would have to be roommates, and that was fucking weird.

"I'll share with JR." I jerked my head in Jules's direction. "You and Alex take the master. The guest bedroom has two beds, so we'll make it work."

It wasn't ideal, but it was the least terrible choice.

Jules echoed my sentiment with as much enthusiasm as a mouse entering a snake's cage.

"You sure?" Ava was fully aware of the animosity between us, and she was probably picturing us murdering each other in our sleep.

It wasn't out of the realm of possibility.

"Yep. Let's just get this over with so we can hit the slopes."

We wouldn't be in our rooms much, anyway. I could just turn in for the night and pretend Jules wasn't there.

Unfortunately, the universe and its fucked up sense of humor had different plans.

When we opened the door to the guest bedroom, we were greeted with hiccup number three, AKA the worst thing I'd ever seen in my entire life.

"No *fucking* way," Jules said at the same time I growled, "You've *got* to be shitting me."

Because sitting smack dab in the middle of an otherwise beautiful room, piled high with fluffy pillows and a luxurious navy comforter, was a four-poster bed.

Bed. Singular. As in, there was only one.

And I had to share it with Jules Ambrose.

Kill me now.

11

JULES

God was punishing me for wrongs I'd committed in my past life. That was the only explanation I could think of for why I'd been subjected to my predicament.

Josh and I both refused to back down and take the couch, so we were stuck in the same room, the same *bed*, for the next two nights. A gentleman would've offered to sleep elsewhere, but Josh wasn't a gentleman. He was the spawn of Satan...one who was currently staring at me with narrowed eyes as I tried to finesse my way out of skiing.

"You guys go ahead," I told Ava, making a pointed effort to ignore Josh's suspicious gaze. "I just remembered I left something at the cabin."

"You sure? I can go with you."

"Nah. We already wasted enough time with the room situation, and I might hang in the lodge for a bit first." I waved a breezy hand in the air. "You go ahead. I'll be fine."

"Okay." Ava sounded doubtful. "We'll be here."

I held my breath and waited until Alex and Ava disappeared on the ski lifts before releasing it. A prickle of anxiety wormed in its way into my system as I eyed the vast expanse of snow before me.

I didn't think I would be this affected, considering it'd been seven years since my last ski weekend, but that trip had spawned so many awful memories. Plus, there was the tape—

Don't go there.

"What the hell did you leave at the cabin?" Josh interrupted my reverie. For someone who'd been so excited about skiing, he didn't seem in much of a hurry to hit the slopes.

He was fully decked out in top-of-the-line ski gear—black pants, a blue jacket that stretched across his broad shoulders, and ski goggles he'd pushed up so they sat on top of his gray cap. The outfit lent him a rugged, athletic charm that had half the woman in the vicinity eyeing him with interest.

"I left my phone." I shoved my hands in my pockets and gripped the phone nestled at the bottom of the right pocket.

"You had it in your hand on our walk here."

Dammit. "Why are you so concerned with what I left behind?" I deflected. "Don't you have a black diamond to attend to?"

"*Triple* black diamond," Josh corrected. "And I'm working my way up to it."

"Well, don't let me stop you."

His gaze turned assessing. "Wait," he said slowly, his eyes raking over my form in a way that made my skin itch. "Do you know *how* to ski?"

"Of *course* I do." Josh's eyebrows rose further as monuments to his skepticism, and I added grudgingly, "Depending on how you define *know*."

My ex-boyfriend Max taught me during *that* weekend when I was eighteen. I hadn't touched a pair of skis since.

The anxiety expanded and ate at my nerves, but that didn't stop me from glaring at Josh when he burst into laughter.

Instead of dignifying his mockery with a response, I turned and stalked away the best I could in my stupid ski boots. Angry puffs of snow sprayed up with each step.

"*C'mon Jules. You love me, right?*" *Max kissed me and squeezed my ass.* "*If you loved me, you'd do this for me. For us.*"

"*It's for security reasons, babe. In case he decides to press charges.*"

"*I promise I'll never show anyone.*"

Sweat trickled down my spine at the memories, but I forced them back into the box where they belonged before they could replay further. I'd already lived them once; I didn't need to do so again.

"Wait." Josh caught up with me, still laughing. The sound chased off the vestiges of my unwanted trip down memory lane, and for once, it didn't make me want to slap him, though the next words out of his mouth did. "You're telling me you dressed up in a ski outfit, rented skis, and came all the way down here...but you *can't ski*? Why the hell didn't you say anything earlier? You could've signed up for lessons or something."

"I thought I could wing it." It wasn't the best plan, but it was a plan. Sort of.

"You thought you could *wing skiing*?"

My cheeks blazed. "Obviously, I changed my mind."

"Yeah, good thing you did, or you would've probably died." Josh's laugh finally tapered off, but amusement lingered at the corners of his mouth and teased the dimple making a half appearance.

My stomach dipped. I'd never faced genuine amusement from Josh before. His smile, absent of sarcasm and maliciousness, was...disconcerting, even when it was only a quarter of a smile.

"I'm spending the rest of the day in the lodge, so don't

worry about me dying." I crossed my arms over my chest. "Maybe I'll find a guy who can teach me how to ski."

"Like the one you were eye fucking in the lobby?" he asked, his tone dry.

"Perhaps." I didn't deign to acknowledge the *eye fucking* part of Josh's statement. He seemed strangely fixated on my brief interaction with a stranger, though the guy *had* been cute. Maybe I could track him down later. Flirting always perked me up, and I could use some action that didn't come courtesy of my hand or battery-operated friends.

Josh rubbed a hand over his jaw, his brows tight and his cheekbones like slashes against the snowy background. "I'll teach you how to ski."

"Right."

"I'm serious."

I paused, waiting for him to crack and gloat about how he'd fooled me, and how I didn't *really* think he'd teach me, did I?

But the moment never came.

"Why would you do that?" My stomach swooped low again for no reason. "What about your beloved triple black diamond?"

Josh offering to help me made *no sense,* especially since he'd been going on about that freaking ski run all morning. If he taught me how to ski, we'd have to stick to the beginner's bunny slope.

"I'm doing it because I'm a nice person. I love helping my sister's friends," Josh said smoothly. *Right.* And I was the Queen of fucking England. "Besides, skiing is skiing. Doesn't matter the slope."

"I'm pretty sure that's not true." Even I, a novice, knew that.

Josh let out a long-suffering sigh. "Look, do you want to learn or not?"

"I'll teach you how to ski." Max's teeth flashed white against his face. *"Trust me. I won't let you fall."*

My chest knotted. I hated that Max still plagued me in the present when he should be rotting in the past, where he belonged.

Because of him, I hadn't gone skiing in seven years. It'd been an unconscious choice, but I hadn't realized how deep the scars ran until now. Everything that reminded me of Max made me want to hurl, but maybe it was time to replace those bad memories with new ones.

I didn't *want* ski lessons from Josh, but I needed them. They would be a distraction, and when I got like this—when my mind couldn't stop obsessing over the past to the point where I drove myself crazy—distractions were the only lifeline I had.

"Fine." I rubbed the sleeve of my jacket between my thumb and forefinger, taking comfort in the sensation of thick, sturdy material against my skin. "But if I die, I'll come back as a ghost and haunt you until the day you die."

"Noted. I'm surprised you don't know how to ski," he said as we walked toward the bunny slope. "Thought you grew up near Blue Mills."

Blue Mills was Ohio's most famous ski resort, and it was located less than an hour's drive from Whittlesburg, the Columbus suburb where I grew up.

"My family wasn't big on skiing." I zipped and unzipped the top of my jacket to release some of the restless energy pouring through my veins. "We didn't have the money for it even if we were."

I wanted to snatch back the accidental admission the second it left my mouth, but it was too late.

A frown carved itself into Josh's forehead.

He knew I'd attended Thayer undergrad on a need-based

scholarship, but what he and even my closest friends *didn't* know was how bad it'd been in the early years, before my mother married Alastair. And they sure as hell didn't know how much worse it got *after* she married him, even though Alastair had been the richest man in town.

"You don't talk much about your family." Josh skipped over the part about us not being able to afford skiing—a tiny kindness I hadn't expected but was nonetheless grateful for.

"There's not much to talk about." I bit the inside of my cheek until a faint coppery taste filled my mouth. "Family is family. You know how it is."

A shadow crossed his face, dimming the light in his eyes and erasing any trace of his dimple. "I don't think my family situation is a common one."

I suppressed a wince.

Right. Psycho father who tried to kill Ava *twice* and who was now serving life behind bars. Not common indeed.

Michael Chen had seemed so normal, but the biggest monsters always lurked beneath the most unsuspecting guises.

Josh and I didn't speak again until we arrived at the bunny slope.

"We'll run through the basics first before going up the hill," he said. "Don't need you crashing into a poor child and traumatizing them. Lucky for you, I'm an awesome teacher, so this shouldn't take too long."

"Your hilarity is only matched by your modesty," I deadpanned. "Okay, *awesome teacher,* let's see what you got. And remember." I pointed at him. "If I die, I'm haunting your ass for eternity."

Josh placed a hand over his heart, a scandalized expression spreading across his face. Any hints of his earlier brooding had disappeared. "JR, I'm shocked. There are *children* around. Try to keep your obsession with my ass under wraps until we return to our room."

I mimed gagging. "Unless you want my vomit decorating your fancy ski suit, I suggest you stop talking and start teaching."

"I can't teach without talking, genius."

"Oh, shut up. You know what I mean."

After another few minutes of bickering, we strapped on our skis and got down to business. I wasn't a total novice, so I picked up the basics quickly. In theory, anyway.

I had the etiquette down pat, but we hit a *tiny* bump when Josh ran me through a series of exercises designed to make me more comfortable on skis.

"Shit!" Frustration welled in my stomach when my ass hit the ground for what must've been the dozenth time.

I didn't remember it being so hard the first time around. I prided myself on being a fast learner, but we'd been at it for the better part of the morning and I'd only marginally improved.

"Let's try again."

To my surprise, Josh had remained calm during our entire lesson, never yelling or teasing me for not picking up what eleven-year-olds around us were accomplishing so spectacularly. Every time I messed up, he repeated the same three words. *Let's try again.*

For the first time, I saw what he must be like in the emergency room: cool, level-headed, patient. It was strangely comforting, though I'd never admit it.

"I don't think I'm built for skiing." I pushed myself off the ground with a wince. "I propose we ditch the slopes for hot chocolate and people watching. We can guess who's here with their mistress and who'll be the first to hook up with a staff member."

The *we* slipped out without thinking. Since when did I

voluntarily include Josh in my activities? But people watching was no fun without someone to appreciate my insights, and since Ava was preoccupied, her brother was my only option.

Josh walked toward me, his steps slow and precise, until he was so close I could smell the faint, delicious scent of his cologne.

I forced myself not to shift beneath the weight of his scrutiny.

"We could do that," he said. "But that would be quitting. Are you a quitter, Jules?"

My pulse kicked up at the sound of my name in that deep, slightly husky voice. Had he always sounded like that, or was I going crazy? His voice used to pierce my eardrums like nails dragging across a chalkboard. Now, it was...

Nope. Not going there.

"No." I held his stare even as another bead of sweat rolled down my spine, leaving a trail of heat and electricity in its wake. "I'm not."

The mere suggestion I was a quitter made my teeth clench.

"Good," Josh said, still in that calm, even voice. "Try again."

I did, again and again, until my muscles screamed and exhaustion clawed at my bones. But I *would* get the hang of this. I'd mastered harder things than skiing, and failure wasn't an option. I *needed* to prove to myself I could do this. My pride wouldn't allow anything else.

All the torture finally paid off an hour later when I completed all the exercises without falling and Josh proclaimed me ready for the bunny slope.

"Good job." The corners of his mouth pulled up just the tiniest bit. "You caught on faster than most people."

I narrowed my eyes, trying to detect any hint of sarcasm, but he sounded sincere.

Huh.

We walked to the top of the hill, where Josh gestured toward a spot in the distance.

"We'll take it easy," he said. "I'm going to stand there, and I want you to ski down and stop in front of me using the snow-plow. Do you need me to go over how to do it again?"

"No. I got it."

My stomach jumped with nerves and anticipation as Josh took his spot and motioned for me to join him.

Here goes nothing.

I took a deep breath and started my descent. I was going a *little* faster than I should, given the short distance to Josh, but that was fine. I could just snowplow early.

Honestly, this wasn't so bad. It was actually kind of exhila-rating—the wind in my face, the fresh mountain air, the smooth glide of my skis against the snow. It was nothing like my weekend with Max. I might even—

"Stop!"

Josh's shout yanked me out of my rambling thoughts, and alarm kicked me in the gut when I realized how fast I was speeding toward him.

Shit. I pushed the backs of my skis out to form an inverted V, the way he'd taught me, but it was too late. Velocity propelled me faster and faster down the hill until—

"Fuck!" I crashed into Josh with enough force to knock both of us to the ground.

My breath whooshed out of my lungs in a painful rush, and he let out an audible grunt as I landed on top of him, our limbs akimbo, snow spraying up and sprinkling us with tiny white crystals.

"What part of *stop* don't you understand?" he growled, annoyance stamped on every inch of his face.

"I *tried* to stop," I said defensively. "It didn't work."

"Obviously." Josh let out a small cough. "Christ, I think you bruised my ribs."

"Stop being dramatic. You're fine." Nevertheless, I glanced down to make sure we weren't bleeding and that our arms and legs weren't bent at unnatural angles. I couldn't *see* bruised ribs, but his face wasn't scrunched in pain or anything, so I assumed he wasn't dying.

"You could've killed me."

I rolled my eyes. And people said *I* was a drama queen.

"It was a fall, Chen. You could've moved out of the way."

"Somehow, I'm not surprised you're blaming me for something *you* did wrong. You're something else, JR."

"Stop calling me JR." It was an inane argument to have while we were plastered together on the snow, but I was so freaking sick of that nickname. Every time I heard it, I lost a fraction of my sanity.

"Fine." The annoyance evaporated from Josh's expression and gave way to lazy mischief. "You're something else, Red."

"Red. How creative," I said flatly. "I'm baffled by how you come up with such unique and totally not obvious nicknames."

"Didn't realize you spent so much time thinking about my nicknames for you." Josh tugged on a lock of my hair, a wicked gleam entering his eyes. "And I'm not calling you Red because of your hair color. I'm calling you Red because you make me *see* red half the time. Plus, it rolls off the tongue better than JR."

My answering smile contained enough sugar to give him diabetes on the spot. "I can see how two syllables might be too much for your puny brain to handle."

"Babe, nothing about me is puny." Josh lowered his hand and let it drift to my shoulder, where it lingered long enough to sear through layers of fabric and into my bones.

My breath caught in my throat. An unwitting mental image of his *nothing* flashed through my mind, and a hum of electricity surged through my blood, so swift and unexpected I lost my words.

For the first time in my life, I couldn't think of a single comeback.

Instead, I was suddenly, painfully aware of how close we were. I still lay on top of him from our fall, and our torsos pressed so tight against each other I could feel his heartbeat—fast, erratic, and completely at odds with his languorous drawl. The white plumes of our breaths mingled in the tiny distance between our faces, and a brief zing of surprise traveled through me at the sight.

Considering the tightness in my chest, I hadn't thought I was breathing at all.

Josh's smile faded, but his hand remained on my shoulder—a whisper-light touch compared to his earlier hair tug, yet enough for me to feel it from the top of my head to the tips of my toes.

I licked my parched lips, and his eyes darkened before dipping to my mouth.

The hum of electricity transformed into a bolt of lightning, lighting me up from the inside.

I should get off him. I *needed* to get off him before my thoughts wandered down even more disturbing paths, but there was something so reassuring about the solid weight of his body beneath mine. He smelled like winter and heat all wrapped into one, and it was making me light-headed.

It's just the mountain air. Get yourself together.

"Jules," he said softly.

"Yeah?" The word stuck in my throat before it came out all wrong. Weird and raspy and not at all like my normal voice.

"On a scale of one to ten, how badly do you want to fuck me right now?"

The moment shattered into a thousand pieces.

My skin flamed as I shoved myself off him, making sure to jab my elbow into his face as I did so.

"Negative one thousand," I hissed. "Times infinity."

Josh's laugh erased any goodwill he'd accrued during our ski lessons.

I couldn't believe I thought he might be somewhat tolerable. One semi-decent morning didn't change the fact he was the same *insufferable*, cocky ass he'd always been.

The worst part was, he wasn't entirely wrong. There had been a moment, just the briefest one, when I'd imagined what his hands would feel like on my skin. What his mouth would taste like, whether he liked it long and slow or fast and hard.

A ball of angry embarrassment formed in my throat. Clearly, I needed to get laid, and fast, if I was fantasizing about freaking Josh Chen.

"Methinks the lady doth protest too much." Josh pushed himself up, his mouth curved into a smug grin even as his eyes simmered with banked heat. The sight made me feel somewhat better. At least I wasn't the only one affected by our proximity. "We can make it happen, you know. I'm no longer opposed to the idea. Our relationship is progressing."

"The only *relationship* we have is in your dreams." I yanked my cap off and ran a hand through my tousled hair. "We're done with lessons."

"Quitter." The soft mockery prickled against my skin, but I didn't take the bait again.

"I'm not quitting. I'm postponing." I jutted out my chin. "I'll sign up for *real* lessons with the resort tomorrow. Maybe I'll get the guy from the lobby as my instructor." Blond hair, eager smile, muscled body. Lobby Guy might as well have *Ski Bro* stamped on his forehead. "I'm sure I'll actually enjoy my time with him."

Josh's grin took on a hard edge. "Whatever you need to tell yourself, Red."

Instead of responding, I turned on my heels and stormed away as gracefully as I could in skis. I should've taken them off before my grand exit, but it was too late now.

The dull ache of irritation throbbed in my stomach and intensified the closer I got to the lodge. God, I was an idiot. I should've known better than to—

Out of nowhere, the ache escalated into blinding pain. It ripped through me like a serrated blade and forced me to double over with a small gasp.

No. No, no, no.

My pulse roared in my ears.

It was too early. It wasn't supposed to happen until next week.

But when another spike of pain caused tears to form in my eyes, it was clear Mother Nature didn't give a damn about my schedules.

It was happening *now,* and there was nothing I could do about it.

12

JOSH

AFTER JULES STORMED OFF, I SQUEEZED IN ONE RUN DOWN the advanced ski slope before I met up with Alex and Ava for lunch.

I assumed Jules had returned to the lodge after our failed ski lesson, but the fourth spot at the table was conspicuously empty.

I eyed it, distractedly answering Ava's questions about how my morning went, before I asked, "Where's the redheaded menace? Off sticking pins in a voodoo doll somewhere?"

Considering the way she'd stomped off, I wouldn't be surprised if the voodoo doll was of me.

I didn't know what possessed me to offer her ski lessons in the first place. I blamed it on the mountain air and the champagne I'd imbibed on the flight, but spending a morning with Jules hadn't been as terrible as I'd expected. Plus, it'd been worth it for her reaction alone when I asked how badly she wanted to fuck me.

My mouth tugged up at the memory of Jules's crimson cheeks. She could deny it all she wanted, but she'd thought about it. I'd seen it in her eyes, felt in the shallow rise and fall of her chest against mine.

She hadn't been the only one thinking impure thoughts.

Our fall had been an accident, but the way her curves molded to my body had been a revelation. We'd both been bundled up in winter clothing, but in my mind, we might as well have been naked. I could picture it so vividly—her silky skin, her lush curves, her aggravating snark melting into a moan as I fucked her senseless...

Fuck.

I snapped open my napkin and placed it over my lap. My cock strained against my zipper, and I prayed neither Alex nor Ava noticed my uneven breaths as I reached for my glass again.

I didn't know what was in the air that made me fantasize about Jules so much today, but it was fucking with my head. I'd been *this* close to doing something crazy earlier, like—

"She texted and said she's not feeling well." Ava sipped her water, her expression cagey. "She's resting at the cabin."

My arousal cooled at the new information. "She was fine an hour ago."

Alex arched an eyebrow. "How do you know?"

Shit. "I, uh, ran into her on the slopes."

"Jules said she didn't go skiing." Suspicion flared in Ava's eyes. "She stayed at the lodge after she picked up her phone from the cabin."

Double shit. "Maybe she went to the ski run first, then changed her mind." I lifted my shoulders in what I hoped was a casual shrug. "Who knows? Her mind works in strange ways."

A tiny smirk touched Alex's mouth.

Luckily, the waiter arrived and saved me from further interrogation. After we placed our orders, I shifted the conversation to Ava's latest assignment at *World Geographic* magazine, where she worked as a junior photographer. Nothing animated her more than talking about photography.

I half-listened as my sister rambled on about her project documenting the city's street art scene. I loved her, but I gave zero shits about photography.

My eyes strayed again to Jules's empty seat. Knowing her, she had a minor headache and was claiming near-death symptoms.

Probably.

Maybe.

She's fine. I cut into my chicken with unnecessary force.

Whether Jules was being her usual dramatic self by forgoing lunch or *actually* dying, I didn't care. It had absolutely nothing to do with me.

BY THE TIME LUNCH ENDED, I'D PUSHED JULES OUT OF MY mind...for the most part. I didn't blink when Ava left to check on Jules and bring her lunch, but my muscles knotted when she insisted Alex and I hit the slopes without her.

I'd avoided one-on-one interactions with Alex all morning. It seemed my luck had run out.

I fixed my eyes on the horizon as we walked toward the triple black diamond, our conversation consisting of nothing more than the soft crunch of our boots in the snow.

We'd exchanged a few sentences here and there at lunch, but Ava and I had dominated the discussion while Alex ate quietly.

That had always been our dynamic, even before our falling out. I talked, he listened. I was the extrovert, and he was the introvert. Ava used to jokingly call us yin and yang.

I could say the same for her relationship with Alex. Her

sunny optimism was as far removed from Alex's icy cynicism as the sun was from the moon, but they somehow made it work.

"Fifty bucks says Ava stays with Jules and doesn't join us," Alex said as we approached the ski run.

I snorted. "No bet. Jules always drags her into shit. I wouldn't be surprised if we returned to the cabin and found the place on fire."

Unless, of course, Jules really was incapacitated. Ava hadn't elaborated on what she'd meant when she said Jules "wasn't feeling well."

Was it a migraine? A stomachache? Was she hurt after she'd crashed into me earlier?

Worry clawed up my throat before I forced it back down. She'd stomped off well enough after my joke. She was *fine*. If she wasn't, Ava would've freaked out more.

Before Alex could answer, our phones emitted simultaneous pings. We checked our messages, and I shook my head when I read the texts.

Ava: I'm staying with Jules for a bit. Don't wait up for me. I'll see you at dinner.

Ava: Have fun! xx

"You called it." I pocketed my cell. I wasn't sure whether Jules needed Ava to stay with her, or if this was another one of Ava's attempts to force me and Alex to make up. Probably both. "What's up with Jules, anyway? Ava didn't say." I kept my tone as casual as possible.

"I didn't ask."

Of course he didn't. Alex only cared about two people, and both their names started with an *A*.

"Well, I'm sure she's okay." I slid my goggles off my head and over my eyes.

"You seem unusually concerned with her well-being. I thought you hated her."

My spine turned rigid at the implication. "I'm not, and I do."

"Right."

I ignored his knowing glance and angled my head down the hill. "Race you to the bottom."

It was part olive branch, part distraction. I'd been handing out a lot of those lately. But if I could thaw my relationship with Jules—only a little bit, for short bursts of time—perhaps I could do the same with Alex.

It didn't mean I forgave him. I had no trouble holding onto a grudge, but actively hating someone was exhausting, especially when you were stuck in close proximity to them for an extended period of time. And these days, I was just so damn tired all the time. Even when I was physically fine, I was mentally exhausted.

Life chipped away at me, bit by bit, and I didn't know how to reclaim any of the pieces I lost.

Surprise passed through Alex's face before the tiniest of smiles graced his lips. "Loser buys drinks for the rest of the weekend."

"Considering I'm a struggling medical resident and you're a fucking millionaire, I'm getting the short end of the stick," I grumbled.

"Don't insult me. I'm a billionaire," he said. "But if you have that little faith in your skiing ability..." He shrugged. "We can call it off."

I scowled. I hated his reverse psychology bullshit, yet I always fell for it. "I have plenty of faith in my athleticism, desk jockey." I held out my hand. "It's a deal."

Alex let out a soft laugh, unperturbed by the desk jockey insult. He made a shit ton of money sitting behind his desk, so I guess I wouldn't be bothered either if I were him.

He shook my hand with a competitive glint in his eyes. "Deal."

And just like that, we were off.

We were both pros at skiing, so it didn't take us long before we were flying down the hill.

We weren't supposed to ski such a difficult run at such high speed, but neither of us had ever given a damn about such rules.

My stress from work, my tension with Alex, my disturbing new fixation with Jules....they all melted away as I entered my element.

Adrenaline pumped in my veins, fueled by the wind whipping against my face and the cold air stealing into my lungs. My heart was a wild animal uncaged, my senses sharpened blades that picked up on every detail of the world around me—the flecks of snow spraying up at me, the whistle of the wind and the quiet roar of my heart, every bump and ridge as I tore down my first triple black diamond.

A black-clad figure whizzed by me.

Alex.

My face split into a grin as my competitiveness kicked up another notch. I drove pressure onto the tip of my outside ski and blew past him.

I thought I heard Alex laugh behind me, but the wind carried the sound away before it fully reached my ears.

I made a tight turn around a jutting rock, then another hairpin turn to follow the path of the run. Most people would freak out going this fast on a triple black, but for me, nothing beat the rush of escaping death by the skin of my teeth.

Between Ava's near-drowning, my mom's suicide, and the people I saved—and couldn't save—in the emergency room, Death and I were old acquaintances. I hated the bastard, and every time I survived one of my escapades, it was a metaphorical fuck you to the reaper.

One of these days, he would catch me as he did everyone else. But not today.

More turns. More obstacles that, if I were a less experienced skier, would've landed me in the ER as a patient instead of a doctor. I took each one as they came, never slowing down, though I didn't go quite as fast as I would on a normal slope.

Alex and I kept roughly the same pace until the end, when I beat him to the bottom of the trail by less than five seconds.

Satisfaction filled my lungs. "Looks like drinks are on you this weekend." I pushed my goggles back up my head, my chest heaving with exertion. "Good thing you're a billionaire with a *b*, because I'm asking the bartender for the most expensive drink they serve. Every time."

"Not yet." Alex narrowed his eyes. It was always hilarious seeing his reaction when he lost because it happened so infrequently. "Best out of three."

"Changing the rules after the fact." I tsked in disappointment. "You're a sore fucking loser, Volkov."

"I don't lose."

"What do you call what just happened?" I gestured at the steep, winding trail behind us.

Rare mischief gleamed in his eyes. "Alternative winning."

"Oh, fuck off with that bullshit." But I couldn't help laughing.

Since I wasn't one to ever turn down a challenge, I agreed to the best of three, though I regretted it when Alex beat me by a minute on the second run.

The third run was even closer than our first. We were literally neck to neck until the last second, when I pulled ahead by a hair.

A smug grin bloomed on my face, and I opened my mouth before Alex cut me off.

"Don't say a word," he warned.

"Wasn't going to." My expression said it all.

"Don't feel bad." I clapped him on the back as we walked back to the lodge for dinner. "There's no shame in alternative winning. Just ask any silver medalist."

"I don't feel bad. If I do, I'll just buy myself a gold medal. Twenty-four karats, Cartier."

"You're an asshole."

"Always."

I shook my head with a laugh. I hadn't hung out with Alex in so long I'd forgotten how fucked up his sense of humor was, though I was one of the few people who even considered it humor. Most people chalked his deadpan deliveries up to him being a dick, which...well, fair enough. Ava used to call him a robot—

My smile disappeared.

Ava. Michael. Kidnapping and secrets and thousands of lies that tainted every memory of our friendship.

That afternoon had been our closest to normal in a long time, and I'd almost forgotten why Alex and I were no longer friends.

Almost.

Alex must've picked up on the shift in atmosphere because his smile faded alongside mine and his jaw visibly tightened.

Tension descended like an iron curtain between us.

I wished I could forget what happened and start over. I had plenty of friends, but I'd only ever had one best friend, and sometimes I missed him so damn much it hurt.

But I wasn't the same person I was two years ago, and neither was Alex. I didn't know *how* to move on no matter how much I wanted to. Every time I made progress, the yoke of the past yanked me back like a jealous mistress.

And yet, our ski competition proved Alex and I could act normal around each other even when Ava wasn't there. It wasn't enough, but it was a start.

"I had a good time today," I said stiffly, testing the waters for myself as much as for Alex.

A beat passed before he responded. I'd surprised him again. Twice in one day—that had to be a record. "I did too."

We didn't speak again after that.

13

JOSH

Jules was absent again at dinner, but since I didn't want to invite any further questions from Alex about why I was so concerned about Jules—which I *wasn't*; I was merely curious —I waited until we returned to our cabin before grilling Ava.

"What's wrong with JR?" I kept my voice low.

Alex had disappeared into their bathroom for a shower, but I wouldn't be surprised if he had supersonic hearing.

Ava chewed on her lower lip

"Ava." I pinned her with a stern stare. "If she's going to die on me in the middle of the night, I need to know so I can plan my sleep accordingly."

"Funny." She glanced at the closed door. "Okay, I'm only telling you because you're a doctor. Also, because it got worse this afternoon but she's too stubborn to ask for help."

My earlier seed of worry blossomed into a full fucking tree, leaves and all. "What got worse?"

My sister hesitated before saying, "Jules has really...painful periods. Beyond regular cramps. The pain usually goes away after a day or so, but during that day..."

"It's unbearable," I finished. A hard knot formed in my chest. "Endometriosis?"

Most women experienced primary dysmenorrhea, or common menstrual cramps. Secondary dysmenorrhea, such as endometriosis, was the result of reproductive organ issues and was usually far more excruciating.

Ava shook her head. "I don't think so, but I don't want to speak for Jules. She doesn't like talking about it."

"Understood."

There was a societal stigma regarding periods, and a lot of people, men and women alike, were uncomfortable discussing them.

After years of med school and residency, I had no problem discussing any bodily function, but I wouldn't bring something up if the other person didn't want to talk about it.

"Lay off the insults tonight, all right?" Ava gave me a pointed stare. "She's not in the mood."

"I'm not a monster, little sis." I ruffled her hair, earning myself a scowl. "Don't worry."

After Ava turned in for the night, I stopped outside my room and rapped my knuckles against the door in case Jules was indecent. No answer.

I waited another beat before I opened the door with a quiet creak. The lamp was on, and I immediately zeroed in on Jules's curled-up form. She lay in a fetal position on her side, hugging a pillow to her stomach. I couldn't see her face, but I saw her stiffen at my entrance.

Still awake.

"Hey," I said softly. "How are you feeling?"

"Fine. Just a stomachache," she mumbled.

I closed the distance between us until we were face to face, and my chest pinched again when I noticed her shallow breaths and the white-knuckled grip strangling her pillow.

"Did you take any ibuprofen? I have some." I always carried a mini first aid kit with bandages, painkillers, and other essentials.

"Yep." Jules peered up at me with a scrunched brow. "Ava told you, didn't she?"

"Yeah." There was no point in lying.

She groaned. "I should've told her not to say anything."

"Pretty sure I would've noticed something was wrong when I saw you curled up like a deformed shrimp."

It didn't count as an insult if I was trying to make her feel better. It gave her the perfect opportunity to snark back, and arguing with me always perked her up.

My smile faded when she didn't respond.

Okay, maybe the deformed shrimp comment wasn't as helpful as I thought.

Should I try to help her, or should I leave her alone? There wasn't a foolproof method for alleviating severe cramps, and she'd already taken ibuprofen, but there were other remedies that might help.

The question was whether or not she wanted my help.

I made up my mind when Jules winced and clutched her pillow closer to her abdomen, her face screwed with pain.

Fuck it. I was helping her whether she liked it or not. It wasn't like I could sleep next to her knowing she was in agony. I wasn't *that* much of an asshole.

I walked into the bathroom and scanned the amenities lined up on the marble counter. When we dropped off our luggage, I could've sworn I saw—*aha*. I picked up the tiny bottle of lavender oil and returned to Jules's side.

"I might be able to help with the cramps," I said. "Turn over."

"Why?"

"Trust me." I held up my free hand when she opened her

mouth. "Yes, I know. You *don't* trust me. But I am a trained medical professional, and I promise I don't have nefarious intentions. So unless you want to toss and turn all night..."

"Trained medical professional, yet your bedside manner could use major work." Nevertheless, she did as I asked and shifted positions so she lay on her back.

"I've never had any complaints before." I sat next to her on the bed and placed the pillow to the side. I nodded toward the hem of her shirt. "May I?"

Wariness etched onto Jules's face, but she acquiesced with a short nod.

I lifted her shirt, baring her stomach, before I uncapped the oil and warmed a few drops in my hands. It was made for baths, but it'd serve as a massage oil in a pinch.

I swept my palms over her abdomen and rubbed gentle circles before easing into more targeted kneading. I wasn't a licensed massage therapist, but I'd picked up on the basics and a few tricks over the years.

Jules's muscles tensed at my initial touch, but as the minutes passed, they gradually relaxed.

"That's it," I murmured. "Deep breaths. How do you feel?"

"Better." Her eyes fluttered shut. "You're good at this." It came out equal parts grudging and admiring.

"I'm good at everything." A smile ghosted my mouth at her scoff.

We fell into a comfortable silence as I continued my massage. Jules's skin was soft and warm beneath my touch, and her breathing evened out into a steady rhythm.

I stole a glance at her face. Her eyes were still closed, so I allowed myself to linger on the sweep of the dark lashes against her cheeks, the lush curve of her bottom lip, and the silken fan of her coppery hair splayed out on her pillow. Her brow was no longer scrunched with pain, and the knot in my chest loosened.

It was my first time seeing Jules so unguarded. It was... unnerving. I was so used to our bickering I'd never given much thought to what she was like behind all the fire and brashness.

How do you know I haven't already?

My family wasn't big on skiing. We didn't have the money for it even if we were.

Jules has really...painful periods. Beyond regular cramps.

I'd known Jules for years, yet I knew so little about her. Her family, her history, her secrets, and her demons. What was she hiding beneath that fiery exterior? Something told me it wasn't all sunshine and rainbows.

I shifted my attention back to the task at hand and tried to reign in my wandering thoughts. "Feel better?" The words came out strangely husky.

"Mmhmm." Jules's drowsy affirmation elicited another smile.

My gaze drifted upward again, and heat curled low in my stomach when I saw her staring at me with a lazy, slumberous expression.

Her lips parted slightly as our eyes locked. Held. Burned.

Electricity charged the previously tranquil air and danced over my skin, which suddenly stretched too tight over my bones and thundering heartbeat.

Jules's breathing turned erratic again. Not only could I hear her rapid inhales and exhales, I could *feel* them beneath my hands, and they matched the uneven rhythm of my own breaths.

She licked her lips, and God himself wouldn't have been able to stop the X-rated images flooding my brain. Those full, pouty lips wrapped around the head of my cock, that delicate pink tongue licking up and down my length while she stared up at me with her big hazel eyes...

My hands stilled and curled into loose fists. There was no

use pretending I was still giving her a massage. The only thing I could focus on was the erection straining against my zipper and hiding said erection from Jules.

It was so fucked up. She was in pain, and here I was, hard as a rock. Proof that the body and mind were incompatible more often than not.

But Jules didn't quite look like she was in pain anymore. Instead, she was looking at me like...

Don't go there.

"You should be good for now." I cleared my throat of its rasp before speaking again. "I'll bring out a warm compress so you can use it through the night."

I stood and walked into the bathroom before she could respond, angling my body so she couldn't see the severely ill-timed tent in my pants. By the time I came back out with the towel compress, Jules was already fast asleep.

Relief and disappointment coursed through me in equal measure.

I placed the folded towel gently on her stomach and moved her hands on top of it to prevent it from sliding off. I pulled the comforter up, turned off the lamp, and stepped into the bathroom once again, where I turned the water on full blast and let it pound the tension out of my muscles.

I rubbed my hands over my face, trying to make sense of the events of the past fourteen hours.

That morning, Jules and I had traded insults like normal, but over the course of the day, I'd willingly taught her how to ski, worried over her well-being, and given her a fucking aromatherapy massage. Not to mention, I was still harder than a steel pipe.

What the hell is happening to me?

Instead of giving in to the urge to take care of my situation downstairs, I finished my shower and changed into sweatpants.

I couldn't jerk off to Jules, not when she was sleeping in the other room and I didn't even *like* her. Then again, lust and like weren't always a package deal.

I climbed into bed, making sure to stay as far away from her as I could, and tried to fall asleep, but my damn brain wouldn't shut off.

Jules. Alex. Michael's letters. Jules. My fucking erection that won't fucking go away. Jules.

My cock pulsed harder, and a low groan rose in my throat.

This was going to be a long night.

14

JULES

I woke up to the faint scent of lavender and the heavy weight of a muscled arm draped over my waist. I couldn't remember the last time I woke up with a guy in my bed. I usually didn't do sleepovers.

The arm was nice, though. Strong, solid, and comforting, like it could protect me from anything, and it belonged to someone who smelled *amazing*.

I issued a soft sigh of contentment and snuggled closer to the owner of the arm. I kept my eyes closed. I wasn't quite ready to leave my comfy nest and face reality yet.

The arm tightened around my waist and pulled me closer to him until my back pressed flush against his torso. My lips curved of their own accord when he let out a drowsy masculine rumble and buried his face in my neck. Meanwhile, heat bloomed low in my stomach at the way the hard, sculpted lines of his body molded against my softer ones.

Who was he? Did we have sex last night?

My brain wasn't firing on all cylinders yet, and sifting

through my memories of the past twenty-four hours seemed too daunting of a task this early in the morning.

I stretched and grazed something soft and fluffy. I cracked one eye open out of curiosity and spotted a folded hand towel on the bed next to me.

What was I doing with a towel in—

Vermont. Room mix-up. Ski lessons. Period. Josh. Massage.

My brain finally woke up, and the highlights from yesterday bombarded me at breakneck speed.

My eyes fully popped open. If Josh and I had to share a room, that meant the arm...

"Aaaah!" I threw him off and scrambled out of bed, banging my shin against the nightstand in my haste.

One day, I would look back and wince at my undignified scream, but all I could focus on right now was the fact that I'd *slept* with Josh Chen. Only literally, thank God, but still.

"Jesus." He groaned and covered his eyes with his forearm. The sheets slipped down, revealing his bare, muscled chest. "It's too early for your banshee impressions, Red."

My breaths puffed out in rapid indignation. "You were *cuddling* me," I accused. "And you don't have a shirt on."

I forced my eyes to stay on his face instead of the way his muscles flexed with each movement. Lean and powerful, they were the muscles of someone who honed them through sports and the outdoors, not the gym.

Broad shoulders, defined pecs, a sliver of his six-pack abs peeking out from the rumpled sheet around his waist...

Stop it.

"You were warm and *there*. It was instinct." Josh yawned and stretched his arms over his head. "It's nice to see you alive, I guess. You were barely functioning yesterday."

Despite his blasé tone, he scanned me with sharp eyes, like he was searching for traces of my discomfort from last night.

Thankfully, my periods were excruciating only for twenty-four hours or so. After that, the pain subsided to normal cramps. I'd dealt with them since I was eleven, and I'd learned how to fit my schedule around my estimated period start dates. This month's had started four days early, though, which was why I'd been so caught off guard.

"Yes, well, you can't get rid of me that easily." Some of the aggravation left my voice when I remembered what he did for me last night. I didn't know whether it was his technique or the mere fact of having someone comfort me, since I usually hated being around people the first day of my period, but his massage had eased my pain more than anything else I'd tried over the years. He must've also made the hot towel compress after I passed out.

He didn't have to do any of those things, but for some reason, he had.

"Thank you." My gratitude came out equal parts grudging and sincere. "For...you know." I gestured at my stomach.

I waited for Josh to gloat over my thanks—the first I'd ever given him—but he responded with a simple, "You're welcome."

Silence hummed between us. I pushed a lock of hair behind my ear, suddenly self-conscious. I was bloated as hell from my period, and I must look like a mess with my face all groggy and my hair mussed from sleep.

Instead of looking away, Josh stared at me with an intensity that burrowed beneath my skin and kindled a fire low in my stomach, similar to the one that'd burned through me before I fell asleep last night.

I'd been floating on the verge of unconsciousness, but the combination of his strong hands, warm eyes, and the relief over my eased pain had sent my fantasies traveling down untrodden paths. Fantasies of what his touch would feel like on other parts of my body and whether his tongue was as talented as his hands...

A knock startled me out of my inappropriate musings.

Josh and I tore our eyes away from each other. The visible tension in his shoulders matched the rigidity of my muscles. We weren't doing anything inappropriate, but that didn't stop me from feeling like a kid whose hand was caught in the cookie jar when Ava's voice floated through the thick oak door.

"You guys up? Breakfast ends in half an hour."

My gaze shot to the clock on the wall. *Shit.* We'd slept in later than I thought.

"Yeah," I said. "We'll be right out."

Josh and I didn't speak again while we got ready. There was no way I was skiing today, so I pulled on a pair of soft yoga pants and an oversized sweater. When I was on my period, my desire to dress up plummeted to zero.

"How are you feeling?" Ava asked as we walked to breakfast.

"Much better." *Thanks to your brother.* "Thanks, babe."

She looped her arm through mine. "How do you feel about hitting the spa after breakfast instead of skiing? We have that gift card we still need to use."

Oh, thank fucking God. "Ava," I said. "Don't tell Alex, but you're the real genius in the relationship."

She laughed.

The rest of the morning passed in a blur, with Alex and Josh skiing and me and Ava enjoying the spa's massage and facial services. But even though my massage therapist was professionally trained, she didn't hit the spot the way Josh had.

"A little to the left, please...to the right...just a bit harder..." I tried my best to pinpoint what was off about my session.

"Like this?" The therapist followed my instructions to a tee, but it still didn't compare to Josh's touch. "How does this feel?"

"Great," I mumbled, giving up. "Thank you."

Maybe it was the oil Josh used. It smelled better than the floral ones at the spa.

By the time Ava and I met up with the guys for lunch, I was more irritated than relaxed by my constant thoughts of a certain doctor.

I wouldn't put it past him to mix some sort of sex potion with the massage oil before he used it on me. That was the only plausible explanation for why I kept thinking about him.

There *had* to be a catch for why he'd been so nice.

"How was the spa?" Alex rested his hand on the back of Ava's chair and brushed his lips over her cheek.

"It was great." She smiled, her face glowing with so much love it made my chest ache. "How was skiing? Did you guys do the triple black again?"

"Yes," Josh said at the same time Alex replied, "No. I went snowboarding."

"Oh." Ava's eyes darted between them. "Okay."

Awkward as fuck.

We settled into silence as we flipped through our menus. Josh sat next to me, and every time either of us moved, our legs brushed against each other.

Signature burger, pan-roasted salmon...

His pants wisped over my calves. I set my jaw and tried to focus. *Pan-roasted salmon with fennel salad...*

He reached for his glass, his shirt sleeve grazing my hand as he did so.

I yanked my arm back and stared determinedly at the list of entrees. *Pan-roasted salmon with fennel salad...*

When our server appeared, bright-eyed and perky, I'd read the same dish description a dozen times.

"I'll have the salmon," I muttered after everyone placed their orders. "Thanks."

I hated salmon.

I glared at Josh. This was all his fault. If he hadn't distracted me, I would've been able to get through the rest of the menu and order something I wanted.

His eyebrows rose. "Back in fighting form, I see," he said while Alex and Ava talked quietly across from us. "I missed that look of irritation on your face. It's like a balm to my soul."

"That's because you're used to seeing it on everyone who comes into contact with you."

Slipping into an argument with Josh was like slipping into old pair of jeans, comforting and familiar.

Josh's cheek dimpled. "Nah. Just you, Red. Everyone else loves me."

"I guarantee that's not true."

My phone lit up with a new text. I picked it up, eager for a distraction, but my brows pulled together when I read the message.

Unknown: Hey Jules

The area code indicated an Ohio phone number.

Everything around me disappeared while a loud buzzing filled my ears. I typed out my answer with shaking fingers.

Me: Who is this?

Hope, fear, and anticipation curdled in my stomach. *Maybe it's my mom...*

An eternity passed in the ten seconds it took for the reply to pop up, but when it did, I almost dropped my phone in shock.

Unknown: It's Max

Max. My ex-boyfriend. How did he get my number? Why was he contacting me now after seven years of radio silence?

There was only one reason, and the prospect made bile rise in my throat.

Max: We need to talk.

I shoved my phone in my bag. Cold sweat slicked my palms, and I wiped them against my thighs in an attempt to gather myself.

"Hey."

My head jerked up at the sound of Josh's voice.

He leaned forward, his brow puckered with what would've passed for concern had it been anyone else.

"Who was that? You look like you've just seen a ghost." His eyes flitted to my bag, where my phone burned a hole through the leather.

I wasn't answering Max. I didn't know what to say, and I didn't want to know what *he* had to say. Maybe if I ignored him, he'd disappear for another seven years.

Forget diamonds; denial was a girl's best friend.

"No one. Just spam," I lied.

Josh didn't bring up the issue again, but the weight of his stare pressed down on me for the rest of the meal.

I lifted a forkful of salmon to my mouth and chewed. It tasted like cardboard.

I bet Max still had the tape. He'd been sitting on it for years. What if he decided it was finally time for him to cash in on the blackmail material? What if I couldn't meet his demands?

If he released the tape, it would ruin my career before it began. Everything I'd worked so hard for, down the drain in an instant.

My stomach ached, and it wasn't just from my cramps.

I'm going to be sick.

I shoved my chair back and ran to the bathroom, ignoring my friends' startled glances. I made it into a stall just in time for my lunch to reappear. Even after I threw up everything I ate, I dry heaved until my throat was raw.

I thought I'd escaped my past, but at the end of the day, our demons always caught up with us.

15

JULES

Max didn't contact me again after his initial texts. I was the one who'd ignored him first, but his silence festered until I was a mess of anxiety by the time I boarded my flight back to D.C.

I'd used my period as an excuse for why I ran out of lunch so suddenly, and no one questioned it, though Josh's skepticism had been so thick it was tangible. I'd ignored it; I had bigger issues to worry about than whatever he thought of me.

I tapped my pen against my desk and stared at the screen before me. I was finally working on LHAC's main floor after my desk arrived yesterday, and I could hear the shuffling of papers from Ellie's desk behind me, the faint flush of the toilet from the bathroom down the hall, and the jangle of the bells above the front door every time it opened. It was more chaotic than working alone in the kitchen, but I thrived with background noise.

Unless, of course, I was distracted by other things.

My eyes strayed to my phone. It sat dark and silent next to my mug of pens, but that didn't stop me from holding my breath like it was going to light up with a new message from Max any minute.

I should just call him and get it over with, but I couldn't bring myself to leave my cycle of half miserable, half blissful ignorance.

Focus.

I took a deep breath and straightened my shoulders. I'd just started typing again when Ellie squealed behind me.

"Josh! I didn't know you were coming in today."

"Hey, El." Josh's deep, flirtatious drawl raised my hackles. "New haircut?"

Surprised flattery filled her giggle. "Yep. I can't believe you noticed."

My grimace reflected back at me from my computer screen. Ellie was sweet, but her crush on Josh was so obvious it was painful.

"It looks good," Josh said. "Short hair suits you."

"Thank you." Another giggle.

I typed faster, the *click-clack* of my keyboard adopting a furious tempo as the sound of footsteps neared. They stopped next to me.

Clack. Clack. Clack—

"Jules."

I waited several beats before I lifted my head to meet Josh's eyes. The first thing I noticed were his scrubs. It was my first time seeing him in his doctor's clothes, since he usually changed out of them before arriving at the clinic. The blue uniform was too shapeless to be objectively flattering, and yet...

Something in my chest stumbled.

Oh no. Oh no, no, no.

My stomach knotted with horror. I couldn't possibly feel... attraction toward Josh Chen. Not here, in D.C. I could chalk up my momentary loss of good judgment in Vermont to the mountain air, but here I had no excuse.

Any butterflies, flutters, and skipped heartbeats were unacceptable. Unthinkable. Downright disgusting.

"I see your desk has arrived." Josh's gaze flitted from my face to my favorite fluffy pink pen. A hint of a smile filled the corners of his mouth. "Looks like we're neighbors. Lucky you."

He angled his head toward the desk across the aisle from mine. I'd wondered who it belonged to, since its sparse decorations provided no clue as to its owner's identity.

"I'm thrilled," I said flatly. I leaned back in my chair and narrowed my eyes. "I didn't realize volunteers had their own desks."

"They don't. Only I do." His voice took on a familiar cocky lilt. "I'm beloved around here, Red."

Sadly, it was true. The rest of the clinic staff fawned over him like he was the second coming of the messiah. It was enough to make a girl want to hurl.

"I can't imagine why." *Keep to the truce.* "Well, as lovely as this conversation is, I have to get back to work. Lots to do," I chirped with false pep.

Josh's eyes glinted with amusement. "Of course."

He settled in at his desk, and we didn't speak again for the rest of the afternoon.

By the time the clock ticked toward five, I was bleary-eyed from staring at the screen so long, and my wrists ached from typing. I might've been a *little* aggressive with my keyboard, but it was a good release for my pent-up tension.

"What a day." Ellie yawned. "I could use a drink. Anyone else down? The Black Fox has a great happy hour special."

The Black Fox was the bar across the street and a popular watering hole for hospital staff.

"I am." Marshall was the picture of eagerness. Like Ellie,

he was a full-time research associate, and if Ellie's interest in Josh was a flashing neon sign, Marshall's interest in Ellie was a full-blown billboard complete with floodlights and ten-foot-high letters spelling out I LOVE ELLIE. "I mean, I'll go with you."

"Great," Ellie said. "Josh?"

"Sure. I'll never turn down a cheap drink." His dimple made a quick appearance. "You in, Red?"

I hesitated. I had to study for finals and pack for my upcoming move, but I *could* use a de-stresser. "Sure, why not?"

No one else at the clinic could join us, so half an hour later, it was just the four of us who crowded around a table at The Black Fox, nursing watered down but insanely cheap drinks.

"I propose we play a game." Ellie was technically speaking to the whole table, but her eyes were fixed on Josh.

His lips quirked. "What kind of game?"

He sat beside me, one arm draped over the back of the chair next to him while his other hand held a half-empty glass of Coke and whiskey. He'd changed out of his scrubs, and his pose, combined with his tousled dark hair and new outfit—navy blue cashmere sweater with the sleeves pushed up, watch glinting on his wrist—made him look like he was posing for a men's fashion magazine.

I drained the rest of my drink in an attempt to douse the heat blooming in my stomach.

"Truth or Dare," Ellie decided.

"El, I don't know if that's a good idea." Marshall shifted in his seat. "We work together. It's inappropriate."

I suppressed a wince. Marshall was only a few years older than Ellie, but lecturing someone on propriety in the middle of happy hour wasn't the best way to spark a girl's interest.

"It's just us. It's not like Lisa's here." Ellie waved a dismissive hand in the air. "So? What do you think?"

Josh lifted his glass to his lips, his eyes dancing with amusement. "Let's do it."

"Great." She beamed and turned to me. "Jules?"

"Sure." In normal times, I would've been the one who suggested a game first, but all my worrying over the past week had drained me of energy and the best I could do was go with the flow.

"Marshall?" Ellie nudged him, causing his cheeks to flush red.

"Okay." He sounded resigned.

To no one's surprise, Ellie chose Josh for the first round. "Truth or Dare?" she asked.

"Truth."

Huh. I tamped down my surprise. I'd expected him to choose Dare.

Ellie leaned forward so he had an unimpeded view of her cleavage. She'd tossed her blazer long ago, and her breasts practically spilled out of her tank top.

I glanced at Josh, whose gaze remained fixed on Ellie's face. His expression didn't so much as flicker.

The same couldn't be said for Marshall, who looked like he was about to burst into flames.

"Are you interested in anyone at the clinic?" Ellie asked.

Subtle.

Josh's eyebrows winged upward. "A volunteer or staff member?"

I shifted in my seat, and the vinyl released an embarrassing squeak when my thighs unstuck from the material. Josh flicked his eyes in my direction, his amusement visibly deepening. I lifted my chin defiantly in reply.

"Either or," Ellie said, bringing his attention back to her. "But let's say it's a staff member."

"I'm interested in everyone at the clinic," Josh said. "You're all great."

She deflated, obviously realizing she should've been more specific.

"Jules." Josh shifted his gaze to me, and I straightened in anticipation. "Truth or Dare?"

"Dare." I answered without hesitation.

A slow smile spread across his face. "I dare you to kiss someone at this table for thirty seconds."

I recognized the satisfied gleam in his eyes; he expected me to back down.

Too bad for him, I'd never backed down from a dare in my life.

I kept my gaze fixed on his as I leaned forward, closing the distance between us inch by agonizing inch until his smile slipped and heat flared in his eyes.

I waited until our faces were only inches apart before I swerved abruptly and kissed a startled Marshall instead.

"Mmmphng," he squeaked.

"You okay with this?" I whispered against his lips.

"Mmmphng," he repeated, higher pitched this time. He didn't move away, so I took that as a yes.

I guided him through the kiss and let it linger for the requisite thirty seconds before I pulled back. A self-satisfied smile bloomed on my mouth at the reactions around me. Ellie's jaw grazed the table while Josh stared at me, his amusement from earlier locked away behind a stone-faced mask. Marshall, meanwhile, sat frozen in his chair with glassy eyes and his mouth agape.

"Sorry for springing that on you," I said. "But you're a great kisser. A-plus."

"N-n-no problem," he stuttered. "I, um, I..." His eyes darted toward Ellie, who eyed him with a smidge more interest than before.

I hid a smile. The best way to spark a woman's interest was to introduce a little competition. "I believe that was thirty seconds?"

I directed my question at Josh, who responded with a cool, "More than thirty. You must've been really into it."

"Like I said..." I toyed with my now-empty glass. "Marshall's a great kisser."

"I'll take your word for it." He flicked his eyes toward Marshall. "Marshall, my man. Your turn."

We played another three rounds before Ellie reluctantly excused herself, citing an early flight tomorrow. Apparently, it was her grandmother's eighty-fifth birthday, so she was flying home to Milwaukee for the celebration.

She eyed Josh like she wanted him to leave with her, but he merely wished her a good night and a safe flight home. Marshall, of course, offered to split an Uber with her since they had to go in the same direction.

And then there were two.

"Ellie has a crush on you," I said after our coworkers left. I stole the last fry from the basket and popped it in my mouth. I wasn't breaking girl code because I was one hundred percent sure Josh knew. Hell, he was so arrogant he probably thought every straight woman crushed on him even when they didn't.

His lips curved. "I'm aware."

"You interested?"

"You care?"

I chewed slowly and swallowed before I responded with a deliberate, "Not even a little bit."

Animosity crackled between us, masking something else beneath the surface.

"Of course you don't," Josh said softly. He finished his

drink without taking his eyes off me. "Nice show you put on with Marshall earlier."

"I have no idea what you're talking about."

"Don't play dumb. It's unbecoming."

"I'm not. You think I wouldn't have kissed Marshall of my own accord, just because he doesn't have a perfect face and six-pack abs?" I shot Josh a pointed stare. "Looks aren't everything. At least Marshall is sweet."

His smile took on a hard slant. "You don't want or need sweet, Red. It would bore you to death."

"Oh, really?" My voice dripped with poisonous honey. "Then please, pray tell, what do I want and need? Since you know me so well."

Josh leaned forward until his mouth hovered near my ear, and it was all I could do not to pull back. My heart rumbled so loud in my chest I would've missed his reply had his voice not poured into me like dark silk, dangerous yet seductive.

"You *want* someone who can challenge you. Excite you. Keep you on your toes. And as for what you need..." His whiskey-scented breath gusted across my skin, peppering it with a thousand goosebumps. "You *need* someone to bend you over and fuck that attitude right out of you."

My reaction was instantaneous.

My nipples pebbled into hard, painful points, and a rush of hot moisture soaked my panties. Every gust of air against my sensitized skin added to the need pulsing low in my belly.

"You think Marshall can do that?" Josh's voice wrapped around me like a velvet embrace. "Fuck you the way you need?"

"And you can?" I managed. *Oxygen.* I needed oxygen. "Keep dreaming."

"I wasn't offering." Josh's hand grazed my knee for a

millisecond, just long enough to set my body aflame. "But it's nice to know that's where your mind went."

I was saved from having to formulate a witty response in my current lightheaded state when someone cut into our conversation.

"Jules?"

The unfamiliar voice had the same effect as a bucket of cold water.

I jerked back, heart pounding, while Josh took his time resettling in his seat with a dark, satisfied smile.

That fucking bastard.

After our interloper left, I would pay him back. Somehow.

In the meantime, I had someone else to deal with.

My eyes fell on the preppy, somewhat familiar-looking guy who'd interrupted us. He wore the unofficial D.C. men's uniform of a blue-and-white gingham shirt and khakis, and he'd slicked back his hair in a way that did nothing for his features.

He fixed me with an expectant stare, which I returned with a blank one of my own until my memory pieces slotted into place and recognition dawned.

It was Todd...the guy who'd stood me up weeks ago.

16

JOSH

I'D MET MY FAIR SHARE OF DOUCHEBAGS, BUT I COULD SAY with utmost confidence the guy standing before me was the douchiest of them all.

Maybe it was his oily smile and the way he slicked back his hair, like he was a smarmy politician running for office. Or maybe it was the way he leered at Jules, like she was a juicy steak and he hadn't eaten in days.

Irrational loathing replaced my earlier satisfaction at successfully working Jules up.

*You **need** someone to bend you over and fuck that attitude right out of you.*

Whiskey had loosened my tongue, and Jules and Marshall's kiss had given me the final push to say what I'd been thinking. To say what we'd *both* been thinking since Vermont.

Jules could hiss and snarl all she wanted, but she couldn't hide her desire. She wanted me as much as I wanted her, and we both hated ourselves for it.

"Todd." Jules packed a gallon of disdain into one word.

My mouth ticked up into an involuntary smile before it flattened again.

She *knew* this guy?

"I thought that was you, but I wasn't sure. You look even better in person," he told her chest.

My jaw tightened. I appreciated breasts as much as the next guy, but that was just damn rude. He hadn't looked her in the eye since he arrived.

Part of me was grateful for the interruption, which came right as I was about to do something I would regret. Another, darker part of me wanted to gouge his eyes out for looking at her that way.

I rolled my glass between my fingers, disturbed by my violent, unwanted thoughts. Where the hell had they come from? Since when did I care whether other men looked at Jules?

I don't. Todd has a punchable face. That's all.

"*You* don't." Jules's voice oozed enough sweet venom to fell an elephant. "I guess pictures *can* be deceiving."

This time, I couldn't hold back a grin despite my irritation.

She was savage. I fucking loved it.

If Todd was offended, he didn't show it. I wasn't even sure he heard her; he was too busy ogling her breasts, which strained against the buttons of her shirt.

"I'm sorry about our date the other day," he said, and just like that, my grin disappeared again. "My car broke down and my phone died. I texted you a few times after, but you never responded."

I pieced together the puzzle before Jules responded. *This* was the guy who'd stood her up at The Bronze Gear?

Jesus. I thought she had better taste than that.

"If by the other day, you mean almost a month ago, then apology not accepted," Jules said coolly. "You also never texted me, but it's okay. I suffered a massive lapse in judgment when I swiped right on you. I'm back to normal now, so you can run along." She shooed him away with a wave of her hand. "Also, my face is up here, asshole."

Todd's face flushed an angry shade of purple. "I was trying to be nice because I felt bad about what happened. You don't have to be such a bitch about it."

A low growl rose in my throat.

I opened my mouth, but Jules beat me to it. "As far as I can tell, you're the only one bitching here. I'm just enjoying my drink." She arched one brow. "Keep bothering me, and I'll have security throw you out on your ass for harassment. So if you don't want to be humiliated in front of all these people..." She gestured at the crowd around us. "I suggest you take my earlier advice and leave. Immediately."

Todd's lips thinned, but he was smart enough not to test the validity of Jules's threat.

"Don't say a word," Jules said after Todd stormed off. She tossed back the rest of her cocktail without looking at me.

I raised my hands in surrender. The coiled tension in my muscles eased with Todd's departure, though traces of aggravation simmered in my veins. "Not a peep." After a long pause, I added, "You swiped right on *that* guy?"

Pink tinted her cheeks. "I'm busy with law school," she snapped. "My options are limited, and I have needs, so..."

"You lowered your standards to hell?"

"Perhaps, but at least I haven't reached *you* yet," she said sweetly. "Speaking of which, I haven't seen you with anyone lately. What happened, Joshy? Ran out of women who'll fall for your bullshit?"

"It's a choice, Red. I can get any girl I want at any time."

"False. You can't get me."

"I haven't tried."

We stared at each other, our implied challenge hanging thick in the air.

If I tried...would she succumb to what her eyes told me she wanted? Would she let me bend her over and take her like I'd said earlier, or would she fight me for control every step of the way?

My lips curved.

Something told me I already knew the answer. Jules never made things easy. It was one of the things I secretly liked about her.

"You're an arrogant ass." Calculation entered her eyes. "Since you're so confident in your abilities with women, let's play another game."

Intrigue bloomed. "What kind of game?"

"It's simple. We see which one of us can get the most phone numbers in an hour." Jules cocked her head, her hair spilling in waves of coppery silk over her shoulder. "Winner gets bragging rights."

It might seem low stakes to an outside observer, but bragging rights for us held the same cachet as a Rolex or Lamborghini. Maybe more.

Nothing mattered more than our pride.

"Deal." Cockiness filled my smile. Jules was good, but I was going to win.

I always did.

"Good." She glanced at the giant clock hanging on the wall. "We reconvene at ten to seven."

I was gone by the time she finished her sentence. I'd been scanning the room since she brought up the game rules, formulating a plan, so I didn't hesitate in beelining toward a group of twenty-something women in the corner.

Lucky for me, the bar's female to male ratio was about two

to one, giving me the upper hand even if I stayed away from women who were with their significant other.

I kept my conversations brief and flirtatious. I never promised more than I could give, and I made the women I talked to feel good enough they had no qualms about parting with their numbers after only a few minutes. I suspected a few knew I was up to something, considering how quickly I was moving through the crowd, but that didn't stop them from flirting back.

By the time six-thirty rolled around, I'd secured well over a dozen numbers. I should've been thrilled, but suspicion trickled through me when I noticed Jules hadn't moved from her seat. She sipped her drink, her face serene as she watched me work the room.

What was she up to?

Unable to take it anymore, I ended my conversation with the woman I was currently talking to and stalked over to Jules. I planted my hands on the wooden tabletop and narrowed my eyes. "Okay, what's your game?"

"What do you mean?" Jules asked, innocent as a newborn lamb.

"We have..." I checked the time again. "...ten minutes left and you haven't even *tried* to talk to a guy. Don't tell me you're banking on them approaching you first."

A few had, but Jules wasn't the passive type. She liked to go in guns blazing, no matter the situation.

"I'm not."

"Forfeiting, then? If you're scared of losing, just say so. No need to go through this whole song and dance."

"Oh, I'm not forfeiting." Jules finally set her drink down and unfolded herself from her chair. She slipped out of her jacket, her movements like honey gliding against the gentle curves of a glass bottle.

Slow, smooth, sensual.

Fucking hell.

My throat dried at the sight before me.

Jules wore a standard professional uniform—a white button-down shirt tucked into a gray skirt, black heels, and a discreet gold necklace that peeked out from beneath her collar. But with her body and confidence, she might as well have been wearing the world's sexiest lace lingerie.

No matter how hard I tried, I couldn't stop my eyes from devouring her flash of cleavage and the way her outfit hugged her ample curves. Her voluptuous figure wasn't toned and lean like so many of the women in my gym, but it was soft. Lush. And entirely too appealing.

Heat scorched my blood as an image of me pushing her up against a wall, yanking up that tight little skirt, and fucking her until she screamed flashed through my head.

I shoved it aside the minute it popped up, but it was too late. My cock was already hardening, and arousal thrummed low in my gut.

Tension hardened my jaw. I *hated* this newfound effect she had on me. I'd gone years without being turned on by her, and now, I couldn't stop fantasizing about her. I didn't know what changed, but it was pissing me the fuck off.

"I'm winning this bet. Watch and learn, Chen," Jules purred before sashaying over to the DJ.

The view of her walking away did nothing to ease the ache in my groin.

Of all the horrible things that could happen to me, being sexually attracted to Jules Ambrose topped the list. No question.

Need, frustration, and curiosity battled for dominance as she said something to the DJ. He nodded, his face creasing with sympathy.

A burst of suspicion entered the mix when he cut off the music. Why would he...

I shot up when I realized what she had up her sleeve.

She *wouldn't*. No fucking way.

"I'm sorry for interrupting your happy hour, but I'll keep this quick." Jules's voice rang through the now silent bar, clear and strong but with a touch of vulnerability that had everyone leaning in to hear more.

"Long story short, I just got out of a *long*, terrible relationship, and my friend"—she gestured toward me, causing dozens of heads to swivel in my direction—"reminded me the best way to get over someone is to get under someone else. So I'm looking for a rebound." The mix of studied hesitation and suggestiveness in her voice was enough to drive any red-blooded male crazy. Goddammit, she was *good*. "If you're interested in a no strings attached night or two, give me your number. Thank you."

Straight to the point, even if the point was a false one. Classic Jules.

The bar reverberated with stunned silence for one, two, three beats before pandemonium broke out. Cheers and applause rang through the space while dozens of men rushed toward her, nearly tripping over themselves in their haste to be her "rebound."

I shook my head, unable to process what was happening. I felt like I'd just been dropped into the middle of a farfetched movie scene. I wouldn't have believed it had I not witnessed it with my own eyes.

Of *course* that was Jules's plan. She was the *only* person I knew who could pull off such a move.

She caught my eye over the crowd, her face glowing with triumph. *Sucks to lose,* she mouthed.

It did. I hated losing. But I couldn't even be mad because what she just did? Fucking genius.

I rubbed a hand over my mouth, unable to hold back a laugh of grudging admiration.

Jules Ambrose was something else.

17

JULES

THE FINAL SCORE IN OUR GAME? SIXTEEN NUMBERS FOR Josh, twenty-seven for me.

"You cheated." Despite his declaration, the gleam in Josh's eye told me he was more upset he hadn't thought of my idea first than by my unconventional strategy.

"Can't cheat if there were no rules." The thrill of victory added an extra bounce to my step.

We'd left the bar after tallying our numbers and were currently walking home from the Hazelburg metro station. Maybe it was the alcohol or the body heat radiating off Josh as he walked beside me, but I was roasting in my coat even though the early evening temperature hovered in the low fifties. I didn't feel like carrying it though, so I kept the coat on.

"Should've known you'd find a loophole." Josh angled his chin toward my bag, where I'd stuffed the dozens of napkins with men's numbers scribbled on them. "You gonna call any of them?"

"Maybe. Couldn't be worse than trying to find someone on a dating app." My smile dimmed when I remembered my encounter with Todd. He had some nerve, approaching me like that. Then again, men possessed nothing if not audacity.

"Hmm."

The disgruntled sound settled into my bones and caused my pulse to spike. Was Josh...*jealous?*

No. That was ridiculous. To be jealous, he had to like me, and while we'd developed a grudging mutual respect, we didn't *like* each other. I still wanted to punch the cocky smirk off his face every time I saw him.

"And you? Are you going to call any of the numbers you got?" I asked casually.

"Maybe," Josh said. "Haven't thought about it."

"Hmm."

Shit. The sound slipped out without thinking. Now it sounded like *I* was jealous.

"What's the deal with you lately, anyway?" I added quickly in an attempt to draw attention away from my slipup. "You used to go through a different girl every week, but I haven't seen you with someone in months."

"You're exaggerating, and I didn't *go through* them. I made my intentions clear from the start. I wasn't interested in a committed relationship, and they all knew it before we did anything." He slid a glance in my direction. "You understand."

I did. Our approach to sex and relationships was one of the few things we had in common. Like Josh, I'd never been interested in long-term dating. There were too many goals to reach, too much of the world to see, and too much of life to live without being tied down to one person.

Besides, after my only experience with a serious relationship, I wasn't in any hurry to jump into another one.

"You want to attend law school?" Max grimaced. "Why?"

"I think I'd make a good lawyer." I twisted the hem of my shirt

around my finger. It was a new piece I'd bought with my allowance from Alastair, my stepfather. After years of threadbare clothing, I couldn't stop touching it to make sure it was real, that I was really wearing a designer shirt that cost more than my old monthly budget for food. "It pays well if I go into corporate law, and I can help—"

A loud laugh cut me off. "Oh, come on, Jules."

"What?" *My brow creased with confusion and a touch of hurt.*

"You're so cute." *He gave me an indulgent smile, like I was a child who announced I would be running for president.* But let's be real, babe, you don't want to be a lawyer."

I twisted my shirt harder around my finger. "I'm serious."

"Then be serious." *Max ran his hand over my shoulder and rubbed my arm soothingly before he squeezed my breast, his eyes taking on a familiar lusty gleam.* "You're way too hot to be stuck in some musty courtroom all day. You should be a model. Capitalize on that face and body. Not everyone is lucky enough to be born with your looks."

*I forced a smile. Yes, I'd been blessed with above average looks, but I didn't **feel** lucky. Not when that was the only thing people saw when they looked at me, and not when my own mother viewed me as competition instead of family.*

But maybe Max was right. Maybe I was getting ahead of myself. What made me think I could be a lawyer? I did well in my classes, but there was a difference between getting a 4.0 at a small high school in Ohio and succeeding at a top-tier law school.

"Come on. Enough boring talk." *Max's breath roughened as he popped open the buttons of my shirt.* "I can think of something better we can do with our mouths..."

A sour taste filled my mouth. I'd been so young and naive. I wasn't the same person I'd been at seventeen, but sometimes, the whispers from my past reasserted themselves, making me question everything I'd achieved and strived for.

Max's recent texts didn't help, either. He was like the ex that wouldn't die. Figuratively, not literally.

The alcohol-induced buzz in my head grew louder. Maybe I should call him to see what he wanted. Then I could put him behind me once and—

"Jules!"

Josh's panicked shout pierced my ear at the same time squealing tires screeched through the night. I lifted my head, my eyes widening at the sight of headlights barreling toward me.

I'd been so caught up in my thoughts I'd wandered into the middle of the street without looking.

Move! my brain screamed, but my body wouldn't obey. I just stood there, frozen, until an iron grip closed around my arm and yanked me back onto the sidewalk a millisecond before a truck sped past, horn blaring.

Momentum took over and my face collided with Josh's chest. It was like slamming into a brick wall. The force of the action, combined with the spike of adrenaline from my brush with death, robbed me of words and breath. All I could do was stand there, face pressed against Josh's torso, while he engulfed me in a tight embrace.

"Are you okay?" His heart thundered beneath my cheek.

"I'm fine," I said hoarsely, too stunned to form a better response.

I raised my head and gulped when I saw his expression. Concern lined his brow, but his eyes blazed and a vein visibly pulsed in his temple.

"Good." His arms tightened around me until I lost my breath all over again. "Now what the *hell* were you thinking, walking out into the middle of the street like that?" His low voice vibrated with anger. "You almost got killed!"

"I..." I didn't have a good answer.

What was I supposed to say? *I was too caught up in memories of my shitty ex to pay attention to where I was going?*

I had a feeling that wouldn't fly.

God, if Max was the last person I thought of before I died, I would be pissed.

"I called your name twice and you didn't even react." The pale glow from the streetlights slashed across Josh's face, throwing his razor-sharp cheekbones and the hard, chiseled line of his jaw into sharp relief. "What the fuck happened?"

"Nothing. I just got distracted." Technically true. Still, my stomach twisted at what would've happened had Josh not been there.

"Thank you for saving me, though I'm surprised you did." I attempted to lighten the tension blanketing the air. "I thought you'd be more liable to push me into traffic than save me from it."

"That's not funny."

"It's kind of funny."

"Not. Funny," Josh repeated. He bit out each word like it was a bitter pill. "Do you think death is funny? Do you think it's *fun* for me to watch someone almost die?"

My smile waned. "No," I said softly.

I had a feeling we weren't talking about me anymore.

As an ER doctor, he worked closer with life and death than anyone else I knew. I couldn't imagine the things he saw at the hospital, the calls he had to make and the people he couldn't save. But he was so sarcastic and light-hearted all the time I'd never thought about how it affected him.

Josh released me and stepped back, his expression like granite.

"I'm walking you home," he said flatly. "Who knows what trouble you'll stumble into if I left you alone?"

We were only two blocks away, so I didn't bother protesting. I knew when to pick my battles.

We walked in silence to my house, which was dark when we arrived. Stella was probably still at the office or at an event. Between the magazine and her blog, she basically worked two jobs.

I stepped onto the porch and fished my keys out of my bag with a shaking hand. "You've delivered me home safe and sound. Five stars for service, two stars for conversation," I quipped, inserting the key into the lock. "I'd give you one star on the latter, but since you saved my life, I'm being generous."

Perhaps I should've been more serious, considering Josh's mood, but when in doubt, I defaulted to sarcasm. I couldn't help it.

A muscle pulsed in his jaw. "Is everything a joke to you, or are you really that oblivious?" he demanded. "You got into Thayer Law, so I assume you have some awareness of the world around you. So stop with the fucking act, Red. It's a play no one wants to see."

My spine hardened into iron. I recognized that tone of voice. It was the same tone he'd used when he told Ava to stop being friends with me. The same one he *always* used when he saw me doing something he considered a *bad influence*, like I wasn't good enough for him or his friends.

Sharp. Judgmental. Self-righteous.

An angry flush scalded my face.

"What's that supposed to mean?" The front door clicked open while a hard, defensive note crept into my voice.

"It *means* you act all tough and unbothered when it's just that. An act." Josh took a step toward me. A tiny one, just enough for the tips of his shoes to kiss mine. The point of contact acted as a channel for his anger, which funneled into me and stoked the embers of indignation burning in my stomach.

"I wouldn't care, except your recklessness doesn't affect just you. It also affects the people around you. But you never thought about that, did you?" Dull red burned on his cheekbones. "You only think about yourself. I don't know what the fuck happened in your past, but it doesn't take a genius to figure you out. You're a scared little girl who chases highs to run from your demons, never caring about the destruction you leave in your wake. Classic fucking Jules Ambrose."

Deep, bone-rattling hurt stole the breath from my lungs and stung my eyes.

Any camaraderie Josh and I developed over the past few weeks evaporated, incinerated into ash by the firestorm of emotions whipping around us.

It wasn't just about tonight, and it wasn't just about us. It was about the past seven years—every insult, every sneer, every argument and frustration in our lives, even if it had nothing to do with the other. It all boiled over until a crimson haze passed before my eyes and the only thing I could focus on was how *angry* I was.

Instead of trying to calm down, I reveled in it.

Anger was good. Anger prevented me from dwelling on the truth behind his statement, and anger coated my words with venom when I spoke again.

"You're one to talk." I tilted my chin up, my eyes searing into his endless midnight ones. "Josh Chen, the golden boy. The adrenaline junkie. You want to talk about chasing highs? How about you putting your life on the line every time you pursue some stupidly reckless new activity even though you're Ava's *only* family left? How about the fucking moral high horse you ride around on because you're a *doctor* and everything you do is for the supposed greater good?"

My nails dug tiny crescents in my palms. "You're the one who can't let go of shit that happened years ago. *He lied to me, he betrayed me.*" I mimicked his voice. "Tough shit. That's the way the world works. You survive and get over it, or you get stuck in your own martyrdom. You say I hide behind my act? I say you hold onto your grudge because that's *all* you have left to hold onto. It's the only thing keeping you alive, and you don't give a damn if it hurts the people you supposedly love."

It was a low blow to match a low blow until we were both in hell, caught in the culmination of years of animosity and words we would've never uttered to anyone except each other. Lies stripped away, truths uncovered only to be disguised as insults.

Part of me was disgusted. Another part sang with exhilaration.

In a world that expected politeness and praised restraint, there was nothing more freeing than finally letting it all out. No holds barred.

Fury carved savage lines into Josh's face. "Fuck. You."

"You. Wish."

The white plumes of our breaths mingled in the cold. The air around us fell unnaturally still, like it was waiting with bated breath for our next move.

"I don't need to wish, Red." His voice turned dark. Smoky. It slithered past my defenses and kindled a heat in my lower belly that had both nothing and everything to do with my anger. "I could fuck your brains out right now. Make you take back every word you said and have you begging for more by the end of it."

It was a warning, not seduction. And it made the fire burn even hotter in my veins.

"You know what they say about men who talk a big game." Anticipation climbed up my spine at the danger swirling in the air. We were one step away from crossing a line we couldn't come back from, and I was riding high enough I didn't care. "They're overcompensating for the smallest packages."

A smile slashed across Josh's face, vicious enough it introduced a seed of trepidation.

"Oh, Red. You're about to find out just how untrue that is," he said softly.

He moved so fast I didn't get the chance to draw another breath before he yanked me against him and crushed his mouth against mine.

And my world as I knew it shattered into a million pieces.

18

JULES

Shock glued my feet to the floor. I'd suspected this would happen, that I would push Josh past his breaking point. I'd goaded him into it, after all.

But now that it *was* happening, I couldn't formulate a response. No words, no movement, just utter disbelief and dark, disturbing heat that raced through my veins like wildfire.

The warmth from earlier had erupted into a full-blown volcano, dripping lava until every nerve ending blazed with sensation. My heart thundered with the force of a thousand galloping horses, and the pounding spread until it throbbed in every part of me—my head, my throat, the suddenly, agonizingly sensitive spot between my legs.

Josh curled his hand around the back of my neck, holding me captive while he plundered my mouth.

He kissed the way we fought. Hard. Rough. Explosive.

I hated how much I loved it.

I regained control of my limbs and raised my hands to push him away, but to my surprise, I fisted his shirt instead. I gathered handfuls of the white cotton and yanking him closer until we were pressed so tight against each other I wasn't sure where I ended and he began.

A small moan escaped when Josh shifted his hips just enough so his hardness rubbed against my core.

"Can't get enough of me, can you?" His mocking whisper ghosted over my lips, its softness a sharp contrast to the force with which he tugged on my hair.

Tears sprang to my eyes at the flash of pain. The throbbing in my lower belly intensified. "Fuck you," I hissed.

"I already know that's what you want, Red." He closed his teeth around my bottom lip and tugged hard enough to send another twin frisson of pain and pleasure spiraling through my body. "No need to beg for it."

A low growl rose in my throat. I finally shoved him off me, my heart racing and my lips and pussy throbbing in equal measure. "I will *never* beg you for anything."

Josh wiped his mouth with the back of his hand, the movement so slow and deliberate it became more sexual than it should've been. A flush of arousal colored his high cheekbones, and the intensity of his gaze as he dragged it over my face to where my coat gaped open seared into my flesh.

"Don't be too sure about that." The embers in his eyes burned brighter. "Let's make another bet, Red. I bet if I bent you over and yanked up that little skirt of yours, I'd find you soaking for me. And I bet I could have you begging for my cock, for me to make you come so hard you'll see fucking stars before the night is over."

My teeth clenched in aggravation. I hated his ego, his arrogant smirk, his *everything*. And yet, I was so wet I could feel myself dripping at the images his filthy words conjured.

"Nice try, *Joshy*, But I'm not taking the bait."

It was the coward's way out, but I was one touch away from

detonating, and I refused to give Josh the satisfaction of being the one to press the button.

"Didn't think you would," he taunted. "Scared, Jules?"

"Can't take a hint, Josh?"

We glared at each other, our anger tangible in the cold night air, before the gap between us disappeared and our mouths crashed against each other again. Harder, more desperate than the first time, our tongues fighting for dominance while our hands roamed over every inch of skin.

Josh pushed me through the half-open door and kicked it shut behind us without breaking the kiss.

Our fingers flew over our clothes in a frantic rush to remove them.

My coat. His shirt. My skirt. His pants. They all fell to the living room floor until we were naked, our skin heated with the hum of electricity surging through my blood and in the air.

"Get on your hands and knees."

My skin pebbled with goosebumps at Josh's rough command, but instead of obeying, I lifted my chin in defiance. "Make me."

The words barely left my mouth before he closed the distance between us in two strides and twisted me around. He drove his knee into the back of mine, forcing me to the ground. I struggled half-heartedly, but I was no match for Josh's strength.

One hand locked my wrists together behind my back in a steel grip while the other slipped between my legs and rubbed my swollen clit.

The jolt of pleasure wrenched a half gasp, half moan from my throat.

"What was that you were saying?" Josh mocked. He pushed a finger inside me while keeping his thumb on my clit. I was so wet I didn't feel any friction even when he was knuckles deep in me. "Just like I'd guessed. You're fucking soaking."

My hands curled into fists. I was already panting, so turned on I could barely think straight, and we'd barely started.

"Beg for it, Red." He curled his finger and hit my most sensitive spot, eliciting another moan, before he slowly dragged it out and shoved it back in. His breathing harshened. "Beg me to fuck you. To make you come all over my cock like you so desperately crave."

"You wish." My nails dug into my palms. "My vibrator does a better job than you. *On its lowest speed.*"

Josh let out a soft laugh. "You have to make things difficult." He released my wrists and fisted my hair, jerking my head back until his mouth hovered near my ear. "But I love a good fight."

My response died on my tongue when he thrust another finger inside me. In, out, in, out, faster and faster until the tell-tale tingles of an impending orgasm gathered at the base of my spine. He reached around and pinched my nipple, and a full-body shudder rolled through me right as the—

He yanked his hands away.

No!

My body slumped forward on all fours without his support, and I let out a small scream of frustration at the ruined orgasm. I twisted my head around to glare at him. "You fucking *bastard.*"

My only solace was that I wasn't the only one suffering. Josh's chest heaved with deep, ragged breaths, and his cock jutted straight up, so hard it looked painful. A blade of moonlight sliced through the windows and cast sharp shadows across his face, highlighting the stony set of his jaw and the blaze of lust in his eyes.

"You know what to do if you want to come." His mouth

curved as he pushed my legs further apart. "Look at you. You're a mess."

I didn't have to see myself to know he was right. Wetness slicked my thighs, and every brush of air against my bare pussy triggered another needy shudder.

Still, I clung on to enough of my rational brain to twist the situation back on him.

Two could play his mind games.

"Scared you can't live up to your promise, Chen?" I purred. "What happened to fucking the attitude out of me? You talk a big game, but it looks like you're *lacking* in follow-through." I dropped a pointed glance to his arousal.

Despite my taunt, my core clenched at the sight before me.

Josh's body could serve as the mold for a Greek god statue. Broad shoulders, perfectly carved abs, sculpted arms...and a long, thick cock that looked like it could wreck me with little effort.

Fuck. My mouth dried.

He leaned forward and, without taking his eyes off mine, slowly wrapped one hand around my throat. He squeezed hard enough to cut off my breath for several beats before he loosened his grip. I gasped in a lungful of air, my head swimming from the brief deprivation of oxygen.

"One of these days," he said. "That mouth of yours is going to get you into trouble."

I didn't get a chance to respond before he slammed into me from behind with a vicious thrust. A scream ripped from my throat at the painful stretch of his size and the roughness with which he fucked me. Tears sprung to my eyes, but my scream eventually faded into a string of mindless whimpers and squeals as he pounded into me.

"What was that?" Josh's breath grazed my cheek. "You

always have so much to say. Where are your words now, hmm?"

"Go. To. Hell," I panted. It was the only sentence I could manage before another sharp thrust scrambled my thoughts.

His dark chuckle reverberated through me. "You're my personal hell, Red." He gave my hair another sharp tug. "And God help me, I don't want to fucking leave."

Before I could untangle the meaning behind his words, he flipped me around so I was on my back. He kept his hand on my throat, pressing me into the ground while he propped my leg on his shoulder. At this angle, he hit spots I didn't even know existed.

My nails dug into his skin, partly out of instinct and partly as payback for his mindfuckery. Satisfaction bloomed on my lips at his pained hiss when I raked them down his back. In retaliation, he fucked me even harder until our groans and the furious slap of our bodies against each other were the only sounds in the dark space.

I deliberately clenched around him until Josh let out a low hiss. Sweat beaded on his brow; tension lined his face and turned it into granite.

"Seems like I'm not the only one who needs to come," I taunted.

I clenched again, and his hiss morphed into a curse.

"I was going to take it easy on you. But now..." He pressed harder against my throat until faint spots danced across my vision and the heat blazed hotter in my body. "We'll have to do it the hard way."

His next thrust was so savage I lost whatever breath I had left.

Nothing about what we were doing was sweet or sensual. It wasn't about emotional connection. It wasn't even about physical attraction, no matter how wet I was or how much he ruined me.

No, we fucked like it was our catharsis, a purge of everything dark and ugly that'd festered over the years. There was a certain liberation in not giving a fuck what the other person thought about you. We could be the worst, most untamed versions of ourselves, and in a world where everyone tried to fit everything into neat little boxes, it was as exhilarating as it was painful.

But as good as it felt, my orgasm remained out of reach. Every time I grazed it, Josh would slow down, drawing out our session of furious, exquisite torture.

"Beg me, Red." Josh reached between us and stroked my clit, sending another sharp burst of pleasure through my body. "Tell me how much you need to come." He scraped his teeth against my neck and sucked hard. "How much you need *me* to make you come."

Normally, I would make a joke about self-esteem issues, but I was too gone to think clearly.

"No." My refusal sounded weak to my own ears. I was too desperate for relief. It was only a matter of time before I caved, but I sure as hell could put up a fight before I did.

"No?" Josh eased his thrusts, and another scream of frustration welled in my throat.

Fucking sadistic *asshole*.

"I hate you," I moaned. I rolled my hips, seeking the friction I needed to no avail.

"I'm counting on it." His eyes glittered down at me. "Use your words, Red, or we'll be here all night."

Don't say it.

He slid into me with torturous slowness again.

I couldn't hold back my pathetic whimpers as he played

with me, edging me over and over until I was about to lose my damn mind.

Don't say it, don't say it, dontsayit—

"Please." I choked out the word.

"Please what?"

"Please let me come." The words faded into a moan as Josh increased his speed.

"You can do better than that." Sweat gleamed on his skin, and taut muscles corded his neck. Holding back tortured him as much as it did me, but I couldn't take much satisfaction from that when I was on the knife's edge of insanity.

An electric spike of sensation speared through me when he hit *that* spot.

"Josh, please," I sobbed, not caring anymore. "I can't—I need—*please*..."

Me saying his name must've snapped something inside him, because he finally stopped teasing and started fucking me with full force again.

"You feel so fucking good," he growled. "You love my cock wrecking that tight little pussy, don't you?"

"*Yes.*" I gasped. "Yes, God, please. I'm going to...I'm...Oh God, oh *fuck!*"

I screamed as white-hot pleasure blazed through me. Every thought and memory incinerated, leaving only mind-numbing pleasure in their wake.

Josh kept fucking me, and another orgasm chased the first one, followed by another. They rolled on and on, wringing me out until I was little more than a boneless heap on the floor.

After my third or fourth orgasm, Josh finally came, and we lay there, our breaths heavy in the sudden quiet, before he pushed himself off me and tossed his condom in the nearby trashcan. I hadn't even noticed him put one on.

The lust-fueled fog cleared from my brain. I *always* made sure the guy used protection, even though I was on birth control. Thank God Josh had, but the fact I hadn't even thought to ask...

Fuck.

I watched him dress in silence, the import of what we did hitting me.

I'd had sex with *Josh Chen*. My best friend's brother and one of the people I despised most.

And not just any sex. Angry, toe-curling, brain-melting sex. Sex where I'd begged for more and came so hard I still felt the aftereffects.

Oh my God. My stomach lurched. *What have I done?*

19

JOSH

THERE WERE AT LEAST A DOZEN DIFFERENT KINDS OF SEX.

There was sweet, sensual lovemaking. Rough, hard fucking. There were casual quickies and emotional interludes and every shade of intimacy in between. After twenty-nine years on earth, I thought I'd experienced every type of sex possible.

Until Jules.

I didn't even know what to call what we did. *Sex* seemed too bland and generic a description. It'd been something rawer, more primal. Something that dug deep into the nest of thorns hidden in the pits of my consciousness and yanked them out for the world to see. Every shadow and jagged piece of me, laid bare.

Jules had unlocked a darker version of me than I thought myself capable of, and now that it was out, I wasn't sure I could ever put it back in.

It should've been terrifying, but it was liberating. The greatest high I'd ever experienced.

Greater than BASE jumping. Greater than mountain

biking Bolivia's infamous Death Road. And a million times greater than any night I'd spent with any woman in the past.

Jules and I hadn't spoken a word to each other before I left the other night, but days later, my need for another hit consumed me.

"Earth to Josh." Ava snapped her fingers in front of my face. "You there? Or are you already in New Zealand?" she teased.

I forced myself back into the present. It was one of the rare days we both had off, so we'd scheduled a catchup over lunch.

"Yeah." I sipped my water, wishing it were something stronger. Was it too early to start drinking? It was five o'clock somewhere, right? "I wish I was in New Zealand. I can't fucking wait."

T-minus seven weeks until my trip. I *was* pumped, but I couldn't summon the desire to talk about it. I was too distracted by thoughts of Jules.

Maybe I'd been right when I called her a succubus. That was the only explanation I could think of for the way she'd infiltrated my every waking *and* sleeping second.

"It'll be fun." Ava ripped off a piece of her bread and popped it in her mouth. "Just make sure to bring me back a *Lord of the Rings* souvenir or I'll never forgive you."

"You don't even *like Lord of the Rings.* You fell asleep halfway through the first movie."

"Yes, but you can't go to New Zealand without bringing back a LOTR souvenir. It's inhumane."

"Inhumane. I don't think that word means what you think it means," I said, citing one of our favorite movies.

The Princess Bride was one of my favorite movies. I wasn't ashamed to admit it. It was a fucking classic.

Ava made a face. "Whatever. Speaking of, where were you Wednesday night? You didn't answer any of your texts."

Shit. I'd answered her texts the next morning, but I'd hoped she wouldn't ask why I'd been MIA since we'd had tentative plans to watch the latest Marvel movie together.

"Sorry. Something came up that I needed to take care of right away."

What would Ava say if she knew I'd slept with her best friend? Nothing good, I bet. She was fiercely protective of her friends, and she knew Jules and I mixed as well as oil and water.

Except for in bed, apparently.

"And the award for Vaguest Answer goes to..." Ava's phone alarm went off, and she winced. "Shoot. I have to go. I'm meeting Alex for a show at the Renwick Gallery, but it was great catching up." She stood and gave me a quick hug. "Get some rest, okay? You look exhausted."

"What? No, I don't." I checked my reflection in the plate-glass window and relaxed. No pale skin, no purple smudges or bags beneath my eyes. I looked perfect.

"Made you look." Ava grinned at my scowl. "You are so vain."

"That's a Carly Simon song, not an accurate descriptor of me." Just because I cared about my appearance didn't make me vain. The world traded in appearances, so it made sense for me to look as good as I could. "I thought you had to go," I added pointedly.

I loved Ava, but like all little sisters, she could be a major pain in my ass.

No wonder she and Jules were friends.

"Fine, I can take a hint. But I'm serious," she threw over her shoulder on her way out. "Get some rest. You can't run on coffee forever."

"I can try!" I called after her, earning myself an odd look from nearby diners.

Ava always fussed about my sleep schedule, but I was a medical resident. The only regular sleep schedule I had was a nonexistent one.

I closed out my check and left soon after my sister did. We had a great lunch, but I wished we could talk about more than our jobs and plans for the weekend. We used to be each other's sounding boards, but now she had Alex and I had a crap ton of things I couldn't tell her about. Namely, what happened with Jules, and Michael's letters, of which I received another one yesterday.

Two years, and I couldn't bring myself to cut him out of my life. I never visited him in prison, but I kept his correspondence as a proxy for...hell, I didn't know. But every day, my curiosity intensified. It was only a matter of time before I opened one of his letters, and I hated my future self for it. It felt like a betrayal.

Michael tried to kill my sister and framed my mother, and I was still holding onto a remnant of the man he used to be. The one who taught me how to ride a bike and brought me to my first basketball game when I was seven. Not a felon, but my father.

I swallowed the bitter lump in my throat as I entered the metro station just in time to catch the next train to Hazelburg. I pushed thoughts of Michael aside, choosing to focus on my plans for the rest of the afternoon instead. I spiraled every time I thought about my father, and I wasn't wasting a precious day off agonizing over him.

I tapped my fingers against my thigh, restless. It was too late to go hiking. Maybe I could ring up some old college friends, see if they were free to hang out that night.

Or you can see Jules again.

My teeth clenched. Christ, what was wrong with me? It'd

been a fuck. A great one, but a fuck nonetheless. I shouldn't be this obsessive about it after *one* night together.

I took out my phone and pulled up a travel guide for New Zealand, determined to erase a certain redhead from my mind.

It didn't work.

Every time I saw a waterfall, I pictured fucking Jules under it.

Every time I saw a restaurant, I pictured us eating there together like a goddamn couple.

Every time I saw a hike, I pictured...well, you got the idea.

"Fuck." I was going insane.

The woman seated next to me with her young daughter pinned me with a glare before she moved them both farther down the train.

Normally, I would've apologized, but I was too annoyed to offer more than an apologetic grimace.

There was only one way to get Jules off my mind. I didn't like it, but it was the only solution I had.

When I arrived in Hazelburg, I headed straight to Jules's house. Was what I was about to do a bad idea? Probably. But I'd take a bad idea over having her live rent-free in my head for God knew how long.

I knocked on the door. It opened a minute later, revealing dark curls and surprised green eyes.

"Hey, Josh," Stella said. "What are you doing here?"

Shit. I'd forgotten about Jules's roommate. Like everyone else, Stella thought Jules and I hated each other—which we *did* —so it would be weird if I said I showed up to see Jules. Unless...

"I need to talk to Jules about a case at the clinic," I lied. "It's urgent. Is she here?"

If Stella suspected I was lying, she didn't show it. Then

again, she was one of the most trusting people I knew, so it probably didn't occur to her that I wasn't telling the truth.

"Yep. Come in." She opened the door wider and motioned me inside. "Jules is upstairs in her room."

"Thanks." I took the stairs two at a time until I reached Jules's room.

I rapped my knuckles against the door and waited for her "Come in!" before I stepped inside and closed the door behind me.

Jules sat at her desk, looking more dressed down than I'd ever seen her. Sweats, oversized T-shirt, no makeup, hair tossed up in a bun. While I appreciated a skimpy outfit as much as the next guy, I kinda liked this version of her. It was more authentic. More human.

Shock passed over her face at my appearance before she turned back to her computer and resumed typing.

"What are you doing here?" she asked casually, like her nail marks weren't etched into my back from when I'd fucked her brains out a few days ago.

I tamped down my annoyance and leaned against the dresser, folding my arms over my chest.

I had work to do, trips to plan, and sleep to catch up on. But it'd been four days, eleven hours, and thirty-two minutes since we'd had sex, and all of them had been consumed by memories of cinnamon and heat and the silky slide of her skin beneath my hands.

I didn't know what kind of voodoo spell Jules cast on me, but I needed to get it out of my system. If one night wasn't enough, then I would indulge in as many nights as necessary to rid myself of my disturbing obsession with her.

"I have a proposition for you," I said.

"No." She didn't look up from her screen.

"I propose we form a mutually beneficial arrangement," I

continued, ignoring her flat rejection. "As much as it pains me to admit, you weren't terrible in bed, and I know *I'm* not terrible in bed. We're both too busy to date or deal with the online dating scene. Therefore, we should enter a friends with benefits agreement. Minus the friends part."

It was genius, if I did say so myself. The physical chemistry was there, and neither of us had to worry about the other catching feelings. We could just fuck until we got tired of it.

Honestly, Mensa should offer me membership for such a brilliant plan.

"Josh." Jules closed her laptop and twisted to face me. "I would rather burn in the fiery depths of hell than sleep with you again."

I smirked. "We won't be doing much sleeping, Red. Or have you forgotten?"

I spotted the instant she remembered our night together.

Her pupils dilated, her chest rose and fell faster, and her cheeks flushed the faintest shade of pink. The average person wouldn't have noticed such minor changes, but I wasn't average. I noticed everything about her, whether I wanted to or not.

Self-satisfaction bloomed on my lips.

"We won't be doing much of *anything* except tolerate each other's presence for Ava's sake," she said through gritted teeth. "You're lucky I didn't bite your dick off."

"But then you wouldn't have been able to come so hard around it. Multiple times," I said silkily. "That would've been a damn shame. Your screams are so sweet."

I smiled at her snarl.

"You're a logical person. Think about it," I reasoned. "We both have needs, and this is the perfect way to fulfill those needs *without* the headache that comes up with finding someone to hook up with. Less Todds, more orgasms. It's a win-win situation."

Jules remained silent. She was thinking about it.

I pounced on the opening and went in for the kill. "But if you're afraid you'll fall for me in the process, I don't blame you." I offered a casual shrug. "I'm pretty irresistible."

My smile widened when her eyes sparked. Challenges were as much her weakness as they were mine.

"Not even in your wildest dreams." Jules leaned back in her chair. "Remember the last game we played? I won, you lost."

"I don't have dreams about you, Red. Only nightmares."

"Could've fooled me, considering how hard *you* came the other night." Jules released her hair from her bun and let it cascade over her shoulders. The movement stretched her shirt across her chest, and my eyes involuntarily dipped to where her nipples poked through the thin material in hard, pebbled points.

When I lifted them again, my jeans had tightened, and Jules wore a smug smile. "If we're going to do this, we need to set some ground rules."

Bingo. Mission accomplished.

I savored the triumph for a minute before I inclined my head. "Agreed. Ladies first."

I'd learned my lesson from our wager at The Black Fox. Always set rules.

"This is a strictly physical arrangement," Jules said. "We don't have claims on each other's time outside of sex, so don't ask me where I am or what I'm doing when we're not together."

"Fine." I had no plans to do either of those things. "We keep this between us. Don't tell anyone—not your friends, people at the clinic, and *especially* not Ava."

"Of course I won't tell anyone." Jules wrinkled her nose. "I hardly want people to know I'm involved with you."

"You could only be so lucky."

We ran through the rest of our rules in rapid succession.

"Always use protection."

"No sleeping over."

"No getting jealous if the other person goes on a date with someone else."

Fine with me. An *exclusive* friends-but-not-friends-with-benefits situation was too close to an actual relationship for comfort.

"If you want to end the arrangement, be upfront about it. No ghosting or beating around the bush. That's fucking immature."

"No falling in love."

I scoffed. "Red, you'll fall in love with me before I ever fall in love with you." The mere idea was absurd.

Jules was the most difficult woman I'd ever encountered. God help whichever poor bastard ended up falling for her.

"As if." She sniffed. "You think *far* too highly of your dick, Chen. It gets the job done, but it's not a magical rod."

"Last rule. Never refer to my cock as a *rod* again."

Some slang should be banned from the English language.

"Whatever, Joshy McRod." Jules offered a deceivingly sweet smile. "Do we have a deal?"

"Deal." I grasped her outstretched hand and squeezed. She squeezed back twice as hard. It reminded me of when we shook on our clinic truce. We were making an awful lot of deals lately, for some reason. "Only fucking, no feelings."

I didn't doubt for a second I could hold up my end of the deal. Most people caught feelings in these types of arrangements, which was why they never lasted long.

But if there was one thing I was sure of, it was that I would never, ever fall in love with Jules Ambrose.

20

JULES

THE TEXTBOOK DEFINITION OF INSANITY WAS DOING THE same thing over and over and expecting different results.

My definition of insanity was entering into a sexual arrangement with Josh Chen.

I blamed my hormones and law school. If I weren't so busy, I wouldn't have to resort to sleeping with the enemy. Literally.

We hadn't had sex since our pact last week, but it would happen eventually. I was already getting antsy thinking about it. My vibrators were *fine* when they were all I had, but now that regular and, as much as I hated to admit it, great sex was an option, my body was screaming at me to make up for years of orgasms lost during law school.

I tried to ignore the persistent buzz beneath my skin as Alex, Ava, Stella, and I entered Hyacinth, a hot new club on 14th Street.

I would *not* think about him tonight, not around Ava. That was just wrong.

Plus, I was paranoid she'd developed mutant mind reading

powers and could tell whenever I was thinking about her brother.

I snuck a glance at her, but she was too busy talking to Alex to notice my guilty expression.

"This place is insane." Stella tilted her head up to examine the giant waterfall chandelier hanging above us. Strands of crystals dripped over three tiers and reflected the lights flashing through the club. Music pulsed through the room and reverberated in my bones, adding to the contagious energy climbing up my spine.

I'd missed this, the feeling of being *alive* and out in the world instead of cooped up in a library. Ava and Stella liked their alone time, but I thrived on a crowd's energy. It gave me more buzz than any caffeine or adrenaline hit.

"Only the best to celebrate our new home." I bumped my hip against hers. "Can you believe it? I thought Pam would have a heart attack."

After weeks of waiting, Stella and I had finally moved into The Mirage. We'd picked up our keys from an irritated Pam that morning and spent the rest of the day unpacking with help from our friends. Now, we were celebrating with a well-deserved night of drinks and dancing at the hottest new club in town.

Stella shook her head. "Only you would sound so happy about that."

"Can't help it. She makes it so easy." I flashed a mischievous smile. "I promise we'll be the *best* tenants ever."

"J, I swear to God, if you get us kicked out of the building..."

"I won't. Have more faith in me. But if seeing us around raises her blood pressure..." I shrugged. "That's not our fault."

Stella sighed and shook her head again.

Ava touched my arm. "Alex and I are going to grab a table.

You guys coming?" Only the roped-off VIP area contained tables, but I wasn't surprised Alex could finagle us access.

I *was* surprised he'd helped us unpack, though that was one hundred percent Ava's doing. He'd worn the same grumpy look he was wearing now all day.

"Later. I'm scoping out the floor first." I appreciated a good VIP area as much as anybody, but I wasn't sequestering myself on my first night out in months. "You go ahead. I'll meet up with you guys in a bit." I patted Alex's shoulder. "Smile. It's not illegal."

His stony expression didn't budge.

Oh, well. I tried.

While Alex, Ava, and Stella made their way to the VIP area, I pushed my way to the bar. I'll do a lap of the dance floor later, see if anything interesting was happening, then join them.

I was the one who'd suggested we go clubbing tonight, even though we were all tired from unpacking, so I didn't blame them if they wanted to chill. Honestly, we should've stayed in, but it was my last semi-free night before graduation. I had to do *something* before bar prep took over my life, and our new apartment was as good an excuse for a celebration as any.

I placed my order for a whiskey sour and scanned the club while I waited. Gold outline sketches of hyacinths snaked over the black walls while fresh bouquets of the actual flower dotted the modular tables scattered throughout the room. A green-haired DJ pumped out remixes from his platform overlooking the dance floor, and servers in skimpy black uniforms circulated with trays of shots. It was leagues above what other D.C. nightspots had to offer, and I could see why Hyacinth was so pop—

My phone buzzed with a new text.

Annoyance and anticipation swirled in my chest when I saw who it was.

Josh: Tonight, midnight.

We'd agreed to keep our communications short, to the point, and vague enough that if anyone saw them, we could explain them away with a creative excuse. His text met all three criteria, but still.

What happened to a good old-fashioned *hey, how are you* first?

Me: Can't. I'm busy.

Josh: Too busy for an orgasm?

Me: Your fragile ego can't take a postponement? If that's the case, this isn't going to work...

For once, Josh ignored the bait.

Josh: Tomorrow, 10pm. My place.

Josh: P.S. You're going to pay for the fragile ego comment...

My breath hitched, and I was in the middle of typing out a reply when I heard my name, loud and clear, over the pounding music.

"Jules."

I froze, ice trickling through my veins at the sound of *that* voice.

It couldn't be him. I was in D.C. How could he have possibly found me, in this club on this night?

My mind was playing tricks on me. It had to be.

But when I raised my head, my eyes confirmed what my brain desperately wanted to deny.

Light brown hair. Blue eyes. Cleft chin.

No. Panic clawed up my throat, rendering me mute.

"Hey, J." Max smiled, the sight more menacing than reassuring. "Long time no see."

21

JULES

"What...you..." My ability to form a coherent sentence died an undignified death as I stared at my ex-boyfriend.

He was here. In D.C. Standing less than two feet away and wearing an alarmingly calm expression.

"Surprise." He stuffed his hands in his pockets and rocked back on his heels. His pants were more faded than he typically liked, his shirt more wrinkled. His face had lost the fullness of youth and taken on a gaunter shape.

Other than that, he was the same Max.

Handsome, charming, manipulative as hell.

Some people were capable of change, but Max was as set in his ways as concrete. If he was here, he wanted something from me, and he wouldn't leave until he got it.

"Jules Miller, speechless. Never thought I'd see the day." His chuckle set off a dozen alarm bells in my mind. "Or should I say, Jules Ambrose? Nice name change, though I'm surprised you didn't change it all the way."

My muscles turned rigid.

"It was a legal name change." I'd changed it after I moved to Maryland, and given I'd only been eighteen at the time with no mortgage, no credit cards, and no debts, it didn't take long to erase Jules Miller and replace her with Jules Ambrose.

Perhaps I should've changed my first name too, but I loved the name Jules, and I couldn't bring myself to get rid of my old identity completely.

"One of the few legal things you did," Max joked, but the words lacked humor.

The club's energy, so exhilarating minutes ago, morphed into something more sinister, like it was one discordant beat away from exploding into chaos. Walls of sound and body heat pressed against me, trapping me in an invisible cage.

Max was one of the few people who knew about my past. One tiny push, and he could topple my world like it was a Jenga tower.

"You're supposed to be..." Once again, I grasped for words that never came.

"In Ohio?" Max's smile hardened. "Yeah. We have a lot to talk about." He flicked a glance around us, but everyone was too busy battling for the bartender's attention to pay us much mind. Nevertheless, he angled his head toward a dark corner of the club. "Over there."

I followed him to a quiet hallway near the back exit. It was only steps away from the main club, but it was so dark and hushed it might as well be another world.

I tucked my phone back into my purse, Josh temporarily forgotten, and wiped my palms against my dress.

If I were smart, I would run and never look back, but Max had already tracked me down. Running would only delay the inevitable.

"I'm hurt you didn't answer my texts," Max said, never

losing his affable expression. "With our history, I expected at least a reply."

"I have nothing to say to you." I kept my voice as even as possible despite the shake in my hand. "How did you even find me? How did you get my number?"

He tsked. "Those aren't the right questions. Ask me why I haven't reached out until now. Ask where I've been the past seven years." When I didn't, his face darkened. "Ask me."

A sick feeling rose in my stomach. "Where have you been the past seven years?"

"Jail, Jules." His smile didn't reach the cold, flat plains of his eyes. "I was in jail for what *you* did. I only got out a few months ago."

"That's not possible." Disbelief constricted my throat. "We got away."

"*You* got away. You ran off to Maryland and created a perfect little life for yourself with the money we stole." A shadow of a snarl rose on Max's mouth before his expression smoothed again. "You left with no warning and left me to deal with the mess you made."

I bit back a stinging retort. I didn't want to provoke him until I figured out what he wanted, but while it was true I'd run off without leaving him so much as a note, we'd hatched the idea to steal from Alastair together. Max was the one who got greedy and deviated from the plan.

"They'll be back soon." I glanced around my stepfather's office, my anxiety a tight knot in my chest. "We have to go **now.***"*

We already had what we came for. Fifty thousand dollars in cash, which Alastair kept in his "secret" safe. He thought no one knew about it, but I'd made a point of exploring every nook and cranny of the mansion when I lived here. That included any places where Alastair may have stashed his secrets. I even figured out his safe combination—0495, the month and year he founded his textile company.

Cracking his safe wasn't rocket science, and fifty grand wasn't a secret, but it was a helluva lot of money, even after Max and I split it in half.

That was, if we stayed out of jail. We'd yet to get caught after seven months of pulling jobs in Columbus, but lingering here was just asking for trouble.

"Hold on. I...almost...got it." Max grunted as he pried open the custom-made lock of the small metal box attached to the safe's interior. It served as a second layer of security for Alastair's most prized item: an antique diamond necklace he'd won at an auction several years ago after bidding over a hundred thousand dollars for it.

I already regretted telling Max about the necklace. I should've known fifty grand wouldn't be enough for him. **Nothing** was enough for him. He always wanted more money, more clout. More, more, more, even if it got him into trouble.

"Leave it," I hissed. "We can't even pawn it without leading the authorities right to us. We have to—"

The bright beam of headlights filled the windows and threw a spotlight on our frozen forms. It was followed by the slam of a car door and Alastair's deep, distinctive voice.

He and my mom went to dinner in the city every Friday, but they usually didn't return home until ten. It was only nine-thirty.

"Shit!" Panic climbed up my throat. "Leave the fucking necklace, Max. We need to go!"

"I'm almost done. This baby will have us set for years." Max wrenched the lock off with a triumphant smile and snatched the diamonds out. "Got it!"

I didn't bother responding. I was already halfway out the door, adrenaline propelling me down the hall and toward the back exit. The duffel bag of cash banged against my hip with each step.

However, I skidded to a stop when I heard the front door open, causing Max to nearly crash into me.

"That was a terrible restaurant, Alastair." My mom sniffed. "The duck was cold, and the wine was awful. We need to choose a better option next week."

My fingers tightened around my bag strap at the sound of Adeline's voice.

I hadn't spoken to her since she kicked me out a year ago, right after my seventeenth birthday. Despite the awful way we'd parted, her familiar dulcet tones caused tears to sting my eyes.

My stepfather murmured something I couldn't hear.

They were close. Too close. Just a wall separated the foyer from the hallway, and Max and I had to pass through the open arch connecting the two spaces to reach the exit. If my mom or Alastair turned into the hall instead of walking straight toward the living room, we were screwed.

My mom continued complaining about the restaurant, but her voice gradually faded.

They'd gone to the living room.

Instead of relief, old hurt crowded my chest. I was her only daughter, yet she'd chosen her new husband over me and never looked for me once after she threw me out for something **he** did.

Adeline had never been the warmest or most empathetic mother, but the callousness of her actions stung harder than I thought possible. No matter how harsh her words, it was supposed to be me and her at the end of the day.

Turned out, it was her and money. Or her and her ego. It didn't matter. All that mattered was, I wasn't and had never been first in her eyes.

"What are you doing?" Max passed me. "Let's go!"

I shook myself out of my trance and followed him. Now

wasn't the time to engage in self-pity. It was only a matter of time before Alastair discovered his money and prized jewels were missing, and we wanted to be long gone by then.

My stomach flipped when the exit came into sight. We were going to make it. Just a few more steps—

Crash!

My eyes widened in horror when Max bumped into a side table in his haste. The porcelain vase sitting on it toppled to the floor and shattered with enough force to wake the dead.

He stumbled and landed on the broken pieces with a curse.

"What was that?" Alastair shouted, his voice carrying through the house. "Who's there?"

"Fuck!" I grabbed Max's hand and dragged him up and down the hall. "We have to get out of here!"

He resisted. "The necklace!"

I glanced over my shoulder and spotted the glittering diamonds lying amongst the jagged white shards.

"We don't have time. Alastair's almost here," I hissed.

My stepfather's angry footsteps grew louder. In less than a minute, he would catch us, and we could kiss our freedom goodbye unless he was in a forgiving mood.

Bile rose in my throat at the prospect of being at that creep's mercy.

Max was greedy, but he wasn't an idiot. He took my advice and abandoned his quest for the necklace.

I spotted a glimpse of Alastair's thinning blond hair and furious face right as we flew through the back door, but I didn't stop running until Max and I passed through the forest bordering the property and reached the side road where we'd parked our getaway car.

It was only then that I noticed the blood staining Max's sleeve.

"They tracked me down using the blood I left behind from

nicking myself on that stupid vase." Bitterness crept into Max's voice. "A few fucking bloodstains, and I lost years of my life. The judge happened to be a good friend of Alastair's, so he handed down a heavy fucking sentence. Of course, you were long gone by the time the police came. There was no evidence you were involved—they couldn't catch your face on the security cameras—and Alastair didn't want to drag the case out when he already had me as the fall guy. Bad publicity, you see. So you got away scot-free."

I hated the twinge of guilt in my gut. We'd both been in the wrong, and he was the only one who paid for it.

I understood why he was angry, but I also didn't regret running when I had the chance.

I'd only fallen into the con life because of Max. I'd needed money, and it'd been impossible for me to get a job in town after people found out my own mother kicked me out. She never told anyone why she did so, and the rumors ran wild—everything from me selling drugs to me getting knocked up and losing the baby because of my supposed coke habit. Either way, no one wanted to touch me with a ten-foot pole.

Luckily, I had enough cash saved up to tide me over until I met Max two weeks after being kicked out. I'd been sucked in by his looks, charm, and flashy car, and it hadn't been long before he roped me into running cons with him in Columbus.

But our ski weekend had shattered his spell, and I'd only stayed with him until I had the resources to leave Ohio for good. My acceptance to Thayer and Alastair's cash gave me what I needed, and I snuck away the night after we broke into my stepfather's mansion.

I hopped on a midnight bus to Columbus, bought the next flight to D.C., and never looked back.

"You might think I'm upset." Present Max smoothed a hand over his hair. "I'm not. I've had a lot of time to reflect over the years. Become a better person. I've learned how to let bygones be bygones. That being said..."

Here it was.

I curled my hands into fists and braced myself for what he had to say next.

"You owe me. I took the fall for you."

"What do you want, Max?" I didn't point out that he had, in fact, committed a crime and took the fall for himself. There was no point. "I'm sorry you got caught. Truly. But I can't give you those seven years back."

"No," he said, the picture of reason. "But you *can* do me a favor. It's only fair."

Needles of dread pricked at me. "What kind of favor?"

"It wouldn't be any fun if I told you now, would it?" Max smiled. "You'll see. I'll let you know when the time is right."

"I'm not having sex with you." The mere idea turned my stomach.

"Oh, no." His laugh bounced around the hallway and scraped against my skin like nails on chalkboard. "After how well-used you must be after all these years? No, thanks."

Heat rushed to my face, and I resisted the urge to stab him in the balls with one of my stiletto heels.

"Although you have always been enthusiastic in the sack, so you have that going for you." My stomach hollowed when he pulled out his phone. "I even have evidence."

He pressed a button, and my stomach churned when past me's moans filled the air.

"Right there," onscreen me gasped, sounding disgustingly sincere even though I'd hated every second of what I'd been doing. "That feels so good."

"Yeah, you like that?" The man's rough voice sent a wave of nausea crashing through me. "I knew you were a fucking slut the moment I saw you."

The video was grainy, but it was clear enough to see both our faces and his cock as he pumped in and out of me. I'd barely known the guy, but Max had convinced me to sleep with him *and* capture it on camera.

I'd been such a fucking idiot.

"Turn it off." I couldn't stand the sound of my fake moans. Each one drilled into my brain and dragged me back to the dark days when I'd craved approval so much I would've done anything for it, including have sex with a man twice my age just so I could steal from him.

"But we haven't gotten to the good part yet." Max's smile widened. "I love it when you let him fuck you in—"

"Turn it off!" Cold sweat drenched my skin. "I'll do your fucking favor."

The video finally, blessedly stopped.

"Good. I knew you were smart." Max pocketed his phone. I wasn't dumb enough to think stealing it would do anything except piss him off. He must have backups of the video stashed somewhere. "After all, you don't want to lose your job at Silver & Klein, do you? A fancy law firm like that probably wouldn't react well to one of their employees having a sex tape floating around online."

The bile churned harder. "How do you know about that? How did you even find me and get my number?"

Max shrugged. "It's not hard to track you down when pictures of you with a *queen* are splashed all over the internet, especially with the royal wedding is coming up. Once I discovered your new name, it took only a simple Google search to turn up what I needed. Jules Ambrose, member of the *Thayer Law Review*. Jules Ambrose, recipient a full-ride scholarship to Thayer Law." His smile turned bitter. "You're living a good life, J. As for your number...well, those things aren't exactly classified. Paid some cash to an online service and voila. Done."

Fuck. I'd never considered the consequences of having my connection with Bridget be so publicized. But I never expected Max would look for me after all these years. I'd feared it, but I hadn't *expected* it.

"And Hyacinth? How'd you know I would be here?"

Breathe, Jules. Breathe.

Max rolled his eyes. "I'm here to have fun, J. Plus I have... business in D.C. Not *everything* is about you. Running into you was a lucky coincidence, though I'd planned to text you again eventually. I was just...busy these past few weeks."

His casual annoyance was more sinister than any outright threats or violence, though he'd always disdained physical violence. It was too plebeian for him; he preferred mind games and manipulation, as evidenced by our current conversation.

I could only imagine what kind of "business" he was up to, though. I would bet my new apartment it was something illegal.

"And when do you plan on asking for this *favor*?" If I had to do it, I wanted to get it over with as soon as possible.

"Whenever I want. It could be a few days from now. Weeks. Months." Max offered a loose shrug. "Guess you'll have to keep a close eye on your phone. Don't want to miss a text from me or *poof,* you might wake up one day to find your video online."

My stomach hollowed. The idea of Max's threat hanging over my head for an indeterminate length of time made me want to hurl.

"If I do it, you'll erase the tape," I said.

It was worth a shot.

His expression hardened. "I'll erase the tape if and when I want to erase it." He brushed a strand of hair out of my eye, the action grotesquely tender considering the circumstances. "You don't have any leverage, babe. You've built this fancy life of yours on a foundation of lies, and you're just as helpless now as you were when you were seventeen." He trailed his hand down my neck and caressed my shoulder. A swarm of invisible spiders crawled over my skin. "You will do—"

A familiar voice cut in, deep and edged with hardness. "Am I interrupting something?"

22

JULES

My knees weakened with relief. I never thought I'd welcome the sound of that voice, but in that moment, I could build a shrine to it and worship at its altar.

I looked over Max's shoulder, oxygen creeping back into my lungs at the sight of Josh's tousled hair and lean, powerful frame.

"Josh." I breathed his name like it was my salvation.

In a way, it was.

Max's eyes sharpened before he dropped his hand and turned, giving Josh a polite nod that the other man didn't return. "Not interrupting. I was merely saying hi to an old friend." Curiosity touched his gaze as it flicked between us, but he didn't address Josh further. "Good seeing you, J. Remember..." He tapped his phone with a smug smile and walked away.

I waited until he disappeared around the corner before I slumped against the wall, my heart racing and my dinner threatening to make an ugly reappearance.

Josh crossed the distance between us and gripped my arms.

He swept his eyes over my face, concern etching tiny grooves in his brow. "You look like you're about to throw up."

I forced a smile. "That's my natural reaction whenever I see you."

The insult fell flat without the conviction to back it up. In truth, I wanted to bury myself in Josh's chest and pretend the past half hour never happened. He wasn't my friend, but he was a pillar of stability in a world that had suddenly flipped on its axis.

He didn't bother acknowledging my pitiful attempt at snark. "Was he hurting you?" A dark current rippled beneath his voice and warmed my icy skin.

"No." Not physically, anyway. "Like he said, he's...someone I used to know. We were catching up."

I couldn't let anyone know the truth about Max or my past. Josh already thought the worst of me. I didn't want to imagine his reaction if he found out I used to be a thief.

"In the biblical sense?" The current went from dark to pitch black.

"Careful, Josh," I warned, ignoring the small flutter in my chest despite everything that'd happened. "Or I'll think you're jealous."

A harsh smile carved his mouth. "I don't get jealous."

"There's a first time for everything." I straightened, basking in Josh's concern more than I should've. "What are you doing here, anyway?"

"For the same reason as you, I imagine," he said sardonically. "I wanted to check out the club, but I wasn't feeling it and was about to leave when I saw you."

"Right." We were near the exit, so that made sense.

Although Max had left, his presence lingered like a rotting smell, as did his ultimatum.

Did he already have a favor in mind, or would he make it

up as he went along? He said no sex, but it could be something illegal. What if he wanted me to steal for him again? That being said, why was Max asking for *only* one favor? He'd spent seven years in jail. I would've thought he'd ask for more. Did he really want a favor, or was he using it as a coverup for something else? If so, what?

My brain pounded with a thousand questions I didn't have the answer to.

Breathe. Focus.

I would deal with the Max situation later, when my shock wore off and my brain cleared. There wasn't much I could do about it now.

I blinked, forcing thoughts of my ex aside no matter how hard they tried to claw their way back to the forefront of my mind.

If the Olympics gave out gold medals for repression, I'd win one every four years.

"You said you were busy tonight." Josh leaned his forearm against the wall above my head. His eyes pierced mine.

"I am." I tossed my hair over my shoulder and pasted on an impudent smile. "Or maybe I just didn't want to meet up with you. I guess you'll never know."

"You trying to provoke me, Red?" His dark warning snaked through me.

Yes.

"I only provoke people I care about." I blinked up at him, the picture of innocence. "That doesn't include you, *Joshy.*"

Anticipation climbed in my chest when a soft snarl rose in his throat. "It's not *care* I want from you."

He claimed my lips in a punishing kiss. My blood burned at the onslaught, and when his tongue forced mine into submission, I yanked a fistful of his hair in retaliation until he hissed out a pained growl.

"Oops," I mocked. "Forgot how soft you were. I'll try to be gentler next time."

Josh straightened and licked the spot of blood on his lower lip. I'd nipped him so hard during our kiss I'd broken skin.

"Don't worry, Red," he said, his smile a vicious slash across his face. "I'll show you just how soft I can be."

He closed his hand around my wrist in an iron grip and yanked me toward an unmarked door across the hall. Surprisingly, it was unlocked.

Josh pushed me in.

It was some sort of supply closet slash overflow room. Paper goods and utensils crowded the black metal shelves, a fog machine sat in the corner between a rolled-up rug and a broken-down chandelier, and a mirror hung on the wall opposite the door above a small table.

The *click* of the door locking behind me brought my attention back to Josh. His presence filled every corner of the room, making the small space feel even smaller, and I could feel the heat radiating from his body across every inch of my skin.

Or maybe the heat was from the way he looked at me, like he wanted to devour me whole.

Sparks danced through me.

Blood pounding in my ears, electricity lighting up my veins. Thoughts of Max already fading into the nether where they belonged.

This was exactly what I needed.

"Are you just going to stand there, or are you going to do something?" I asked in as bored a tone as I could muster.

Josh's eyes glinted in the dim light. He walked toward me, each slow step sending another jolt of anticipation and fear down my spine.

It took him only a few strides to reach me, but by the time he did, my heart was ready to burst out of my chest.

He didn't take his eyes off me as he yanked my dress up and ripped my underwear off.

I hissed out a protest when the flimsy silk shredded without resistance.

"That was my good underwear, *asshole*."

Josh lowered his mouth to mine. "Ask me if I care." He swallowed my angry retort with another bruising kiss while his fingers delved between my legs to find me already wet and aching for him.

Such a fucking jerk. That didn't stop my body from craving his, but it also didn't mean I had to make it easy for him.

I pushed him off and slapped him. Not hard, but enough for the satisfying smack of my palm meeting flesh to echo through the tiny space.

Adrenaline lit up my blood when his brief flare of shock morphed into fury.

Pinpricks of fear fanned my arousal into a white-hot flame. It burned hotter when he forced me to my knees and undid his belt and pants.

The thinly carpeted floor dug into my skin, and my breaths came out in harsh rasps when his cock sprung out, thick and angry and already leaking pre-cum.

"Open your mouth."

Need pulsed through me like a living thing, but I met his blazing eyes with defiant ones of my own. I kept my lips firmly pressed together.

The message was clear.

Make me.

Josh's eyes blazed hotter. His hand closed around my throat, and he squeezed. Harder and harder, until darkness edged my vision and I couldn't take it anymore. I opened my mouth to gasp for air, managing to drag in one breath before he shoved his cock in.

Oh God.

I gagged horribly, my throat bulging around his girth as drool leaked from the corners of my mouth and dripped down my chin.

"Tuh mphfg." *Too big.* My whine of protest came out muffled. I pushed half-heartedly against his thighs even as my juices dripped down my own.

The hard floor, the pinch of pain when Josh fisted my hair with both hands, the sensation of having my throat completely filled...it was too much.

My nipples hardened into diamond points, and I resisted the urge to stroke my clit.

I was already close to orgasm, and he hadn't even touched me yet.

Josh tugged my head back until he stared straight down into my tear-filled eyes. "I'm going to fuck that smart mouth of yours until the only sound you'll be able to make is the one of you choking on my cock," he said calmly. He rubbed one of my tears away with his thumb.

An electric shiver ripped down my spine at the contrast between his lethally soft threat and his tender touch.

"The next time you want to insult me, I want you to think about this." He withdrew until just the tip of his cock remained in my mouth, paused, and plunged down in one sharp thrust. I gagged again, the tears flowing faster, the heat in my belly stoking hotter. "You on your knees, gagging on every inch of my cock while I ruin your tight little throat."

I whimpered. My nipples and pussy were so sensitive a strong gust of air could very well tip me over the edge.

"*Mphm yphf.*" *Fuck you.*

Josh smiled, and the pinpricks of fear intensified until my entire body was a live wire of sensation.

"This is going to be fun."

That was the last warning I got before he started fucking my mouth so mercilessly it was all I could do to try and suck in breaths through my nose before he bottomed out again.

My helpless gurgles mixed with his harsh groans and the obscene slap of his balls against my chin as he punished my throat exactly the way he'd promised.

Hard. Brutal. Unrelenting.

I squirmed and tried to ease the ache in my jaw, but he was too big and the fucking too furious. Eventually, however, my throat opened up, and he was able to slide even deeper with less resistance.

"That's it," Josh groaned. "Every inch, just like that. I knew you could take it."

I moaned at the praise. I couldn't see properly through the tears clouding my vision, but the buzz between my legs had grown too loud for me to ignore.

I reached down to rub my clit.

Before I could make contact, Josh yanked himself out of my mouth, lifted me up, and bent me over the table, ignoring my protest.

"You were enjoying your punishment a little too much, Red. We can't have that." He pushed my legs wider with his knee, his voice rough with lust. "Look at you. You're fucking soaked for me."

"It's not for you, asshole." My retort sounded breathless and unconvincing to my own ears. "I hate you."

The word *you* sharpened into a yelp when his palm landed on my ass with a sharp sting.

"That was for the fragile ego quip you made earlier. This..." *Slap.* "...is for the hallway. And this..." The hardest strike of all, one that made my body jerk on impact. "...is for driving me fucking insane."

A pleading sob fell out of my mouth when Josh yanked my

head back so his mouth hovered near my ear. "Tell me why I can't stop thinking about you. Hmm? What the fuck did you do to me?"

I shook my head, unable to form a response or make sense of the pain and pleasure ricocheting through me.

I was on fire. Skin blazing, tears and drool pooling on the table beneath me, but it all burned so exquisitely I never wanted it to stop.

Josh's low snarl rumbled down my spine and made my toes curl. "Hold on to the table."

I heard the faint tear of a foil wrapper. I just managed to curl my hands around the cool wood before he was inside me, driving deep and hard into my pussy with each upward thrust.

I cried out, my mind emptying of any thoughts except the sensation of his cock pounding into me and the slide of his skin against mine.

No Max. No secrets. No lies. Just ecstasy in its purest, most undiluted form.

"Still hate me?" Josh's fingers dug into my throat with just enough pressure to intensify the heartbeat between my legs.

"Always," I gasped. I was getting lightheaded, but when I gripped his wrist, I didn't know whether it was to push him off...or keep him there.

His mouth curved into a tiny smirk as he stared at me in the mirror above the table—his eyes glittering with lust, the skin over those knife-blade cheekbones stretched taut with anger.

"Good."

The table banged against the wall with each savage thrust. My eyes fluttered closed from the sheer overload of sensation, but they flew open again when Josh gave my hair another sharp tug.

"Open your eyes, Red." His other hand gripped my throat harder, and a fresh burst of arousal clouded my vision. The pressure, the ease with which his grip encompassed my throat, it all felt horrifyingly right, like I was made to wear his fingers around my neck. "I want you to see exactly whose cock you're taking."

My skin flushed hotter than it already was. I stared at our reflections, taking in my glazed eyes and swollen lips. Hands on the table, back arched, head pulled back by Josh's firm grip. I looked humiliatingly wanton, like I'd been fucked within an inch of my life and still wanted more.

Behind me, desire carved harsh lines into Josh's features, and his eyes burned into mine as he resumed his thrusts. Slowly this time, feeding his cock into me inch by inch until he was buried to the hilt.

He leaned down and tugged gently on my earlobe with his teeth. "Whose cock, Red?"

"Yours," I whimpered.

"That's right. Now tell me..." He pulled out and slammed back into me with so much force I would've slid across the counter had his hand not still gripped my throat. "Does this feel fragile to you?"

"Mmmph." I managed a garbled reply, but even that faded into a string of moans when Josh picked up speed and settled into a punishing rhythm.

My first orgasm hit me like a lightning bolt, so sudden and explosive I didn't get a chance to process it before the second one rolled in. Slower, then building up, up, up until it crashed over me and drowned me with mind-numbing pleasure.

When Josh finished with me, I'd come so hard so many times I was a boneless wreck. I collapsed on the table, my body quivering while he rubbed his palms over my ass and soothed the burn from his ruthless spanking earlier.

"You look so beautiful like this." His gentle voice was at complete odds with the feral way he'd fucked me, but it settled over my skin like a warm blanket. He continued rubbing me with soft strokes until the burn faded and my breaths returned to normal.

He turned me around, cleaned me up with one of the paper towels lining the shelves, and pulled my dress down around my thighs before sitting me on the table.

"Feel better?" he asked casually, like he hadn't just destroyed me in a club supply closet.

"Uh-huh." I was too dazed to come up with a more coherent response, though part of me realized Josh knew all along what this was—a distraction I'd goaded him into giving me, as hard as he could.

His mouth twitched with amusement, though his eyes remained heavy-lidded with desire. "Good. Now say goodbye to any friends you came with. I have plans for round two, and they require more space than we presently have."

Round two. Right.

My brain still wasn't functioning properly, but round two sounded good to me.

I *should* spend the first night in my new apartment, but the prospect of lying awake in my room, plagued with panic over what to do about Max, seemed less appealing than eating dirt.

My stomach twisted when thoughts of Max and his amorphous *favor* crept back in, erasing some of my high.

No. *Tomorrow*. I'll deal with him tomorrow.

I waited a few minutes after Josh left before I finally gathered the strength to stand on my own. I fixed my hair and makeup the best I could, but I wasn't a magician. There was no way I could go back into the club looking the way I did.

I sent my friends a quick text instead, telling them I'd met a guy and I would check in with them later. They were used to me doing this in our college days, so they didn't question me.

I snuck out of the supply closet and slipped out the back exit.

My stomach fluttered when I saw Josh waiting for me, his lean, muscled form silhouetted against the moonlight.

This was crazy. *I* was crazy for sneaking behind everyone's backs to hook up with him. I didn't even *like* the guy.

But like and need were different things, and right now, I needed what only he could give me.

I just hoped I didn't get too addicted in the process.

23

JOSH

Jules and I barely made it into my house before I was inside her again.

We'd already had sex once tonight. That should've taken the edge off my need, but I was addicted to this. To her. Her taste, her smell, the little breathy moans she let out every time I thrust into her and the way her pussy clamped around my cock like it was made for me. I wanted all of it, all the time.

I couldn't remember the last time I'd been this ravenous over a woman. It would've been concerning had I given a single fuck, but I subscribed to the philosophy that we should enjoy the good things while they lasted. And I was enjoying the fuck out of myself...with one notable thorn in our encounter.

"Who was the guy, Red?" I slowed my thrusts so I could reach between us and stroke her clit. A dark smile curled my mouth when her head fell back and her lips parted at the touch.

I'd been distracted by Jules's obvious provocation at Hyacinth. Now that I was home, something clawed at my chest when I remembered the way her *old friend* brushed her hair out of her face. It had been an intimate, knowing touch, the kind you only gave someone you'd slept with.

Given Jules's reaction when he left, she hadn't been thrilled to see him, but that didn't stop the irrational beast inside me from rearing its ugly head.

"What guy?" she gasped. She was a mess—hair tousled, lips swollen, skin slicked with sweat and marked from my teeth.

It was the most beautiful sight I'd ever seen.

I ignored the strange pang in my chest and lowered my head until my lips brushed hers. "Your friend from the club."

Jules hadn't provided any details other than the *old friend* line, and I thought that would be enough. But it was an hour later, and I still couldn't shake my irritation at seeing them together.

She stiffened. She had her limbs wrapped around me while I braced her against the living room wall, and I felt the tension in every part of her body.

"He's what you said. A friend." She cocked an eyebrow. "Are you really talking about another guy while you're still inside me?"

"I'll do whatever I like when I'm inside you." I pinched her nipple, hard, in punishment. "How close of a friend is he?"

Her eyes glittered with amusement even as her mouth parted at my rough touch. "Jealous?"

"Not even a little bit."

It mirrored our conversation at Hyacinth, and like at the club, I scoffed at the suggestion I was jealous. I didn't get jealous, especially not over women. People got jealous of *me*.

"One week into our pact and you're already breaking the rules," Jules purred. "I expected more of you."

"I'm. *Not*. Jealous," I snarled, emphasizing each word with a hard thrust inside her.

Her breath hitched. "Could've fooled—"

Jules let out a muffled whine of protest when I clamped my hand over her mouth.

"I only want to hear you when you're begging and coming, Red." I smiled at the indignation in her eyes, but the smile disappeared a second later when sharp pain lanced into my palm.

I yanked it away with a shocked hiss. She fucking *bit* me!

"My bad." A lazy gleam of satisfaction replaced her indignation. "Your hand was in my way."

A growl rose in my throat. I pinched her nipple again until she let out a sharp cry, her face screwed in pleasure and pain.

"*That's* what I want to hear," I said.

I picked up speed, my cock pistoning in and out of her in a punishing rhythm until she lost her words to a string of moans and came again.

Jules's head fell back, her mouth falling open in a breathy scream from the force of her orgasm. *Fuck.* The sensation of her cunt rippling around me was too much to take, and I came right after with a loud groan.

My blood pumped with a mixture of lust and anger, and I sank my teeth into the curve of her neck while the high from my orgasm faded. Her cinnamon and spice scent filled my nostrils, drugging me almost as much as the sound of her delicious cries.

"For someone who claims to hate me so much, you sure scream a lot for me." I lifted my head and rubbed my thumb over her blossoming hickey with satisfaction.

The primal, territorial part of me loved that I'd marked her. I wanted to shove it in her *old friend*'s face and declare her off-limits unless he wanted a highly unpleasant meeting with my fist.

Just because I didn't *like* Jules didn't mean I wanted anyone else to see her like this. Body languid, face drowsy with contentment as she stretched against me. None of the prickly armor she wore in public.

This was a side of her only a select few got to see, and no one else was invited to the fucking club.

"It's a scream of disgust, Chen," she drawled. "I'm sure you're used to those."

I withdrew from her and chuckled when she almost collapsed on the ground without me holding her up.

She glared at me, eyes spitting fire.

"Then it seems you have a disgust kink, because you can't get enough of me." I tossed my condom in the nearby trash can and pulled on my pants. "No more tonight, Red, or I'll have to start charging per orgasm. But if you want more of my cock, I could be persuaded, depending on how nicely you beg."

"Fuck you." She snatched her dress off the floor.

"Hmm, not your best work. You might want to practice the *nicely* part."

My chuckle morphed into a full laugh when she stormed past me toward the bathroom, her head held high.

She was so easy to rile up.

Since Jules was taking forever and a day in the shower, I used the opportunity to clean up the mess we'd made in the living room—a toppled coat tree, knocked-over picture frames.

I'd just finishing straightening up when a boom of thunder cracked the silence. My head jerked up, and I crossed to the window and pulled aside the curtains.

"*Fuck.*"

Somehow, the light drizzle from earlier had exploded into a full-blown storm. Another crack of thunder rattled the old wooden bones of the house, and rain lashed against the windows in such thick sheets it created tiny, fast-flowing river systems on the glass.

"What's going on?"

I turned to see Jules fresh out of the shower, her hair damp around her shoulders and her body wrapped in a tiny towel.

My cock perked with interest, but I ignored the horny bastard. It'd had enough for the night. It was time for my brain to take the wheel, and my brain told me the faster I got Jules out of here, the better.

Unfortunately, I couldn't let her leave when it was storming like this outside.

"The apocalypse started while we were fucking," I said.

She peered over my shoulder and rolled her eyes. "You're being dramatic. It's a little rain." She fished her phone from the table where she'd left it.

"What are you doing?"

"Calling a car." Her brow puckered. "The price surge when it rains is ridiculous—hey!"

I ignored her protest as I snatched the phone out of her hand. "Unless you have a death wish, you are not getting in a car in these conditions."

"It's *rain*, Josh. Water. I'll be fine."

"Water that cars can slide and get into accidents in," I growled. "I work in the ER. Do you know how many car accident cases I see from storms? A *lot*."

"You're being paranoid. I'm not—"

Our phones shrieked with emergency flash flood warning text alerts.

"That's it." I shoved her phone into my pocket. "You're staying until the rain lets up."

I wouldn't let anyone, not even my worst enemy, go home in these conditions. The chances were slim, but if anything happened to her...

My throat constricted.

I couldn't have another death on my hands.

Jules must've seen the conviction in my eyes, because she

sighed in resignation. "Can I at least borrow something to wear while I wait? I'm not spending the next God knows how many hours in my club dress."

Half an hour later, she'd changed into one of my old T-shirts and we'd settled on the couch, arguing over which movie to watch.

"Too boring."

"Too cheesy."

"No horror. I hate horror."

"That's a kid's movie, Red."

"So? Kid's movies can be good."

"Yeah. If you're a fucking kid."

Jules responded with a sweet smile. "Funny you should say that, considering how hard you cried watching *The Lion King*. Last year."

I scowled. *Ava.* How many times did I have to tell her not to share every single fucking thing about me with her friends?

"Mufasa didn't deserve to die, okay?" I snapped. "At least I'm not such a wuss I hide behind my hands every time the poster for a horror movie pops up."

"I'm not a *wuss*. I just dislike ugly things, which is why I try not to look at you—don't you *dare* put *The Ring* on!"

"Try and stop me."

After more useless bickering, we finally settled on the fairest way to choose—by closing our eyes and scrolling until we hit the lucky selection.

It was...*Finding Nemo*.

You've gotta be shitting me.

I kept my expression neutral, but my muscles locked with tension as the movie's opening scene unfurled.

"Why are you so quiet?" Jules slid a sidelong glance in my direction. "Don't tell me you don't like this movie either. It's a classic."

A dozen excuses sat on the tip of my tongue, but the truth swept past all of them and spilled out before I could stop it. "This was me and my dad's favorite movie," I said shortly. "We watched it every year on my birthday. Tradition."

Jules's face softened for the first time that night. "We can watch something else."

"Nah, we're good. It's just a movie."

Onscreen, Marlin the clownfish pursued the boat that had captured his son Nemo to no avail.

It was ironic that a movie about a role model parent was the one that reminded me most of Michael, considering he was the exact opposite of a good parent.

"*Finding Nemo* is fish propaganda," Jules said out of nowhere. "Did you know real-life fish are terrible parents? Most fish species are happy to abandon their newborns to fend for themselves. It's not worth the energy and risk for them to try and protect their offspring."

A startled laugh escaped me. "How do you know that?"

"I did a report on it in high school. I got an A," Jules added with pride.

I suppressed another smile. "Of course you did." My leg brushed against hers when I shifted positions, and a tiny electric zing shot up my thigh before I yanked it away. "What does your dad do?" I asked, trying to cover up my knee-jerk reaction.

Part of me was also genuinely curious. Jules never talked about her family.

She shrugged. "No idea. He left when I was a baby."

"Shit. I'm sorry." *Way to step into it, Chen.*

"It's fine. From what I hear, he was an asshole anyway."

"Children of asshole fathers unite," I quipped, earning myself a small laugh.

We fell into a comfortable silence as we watched the movie. I only half paid attention to what was happening onscreen; the other half was busy gauging Jules's reactions to my favorite scenes. Her laugh when Marlin met Dory, her gasp when the shark started chasing the pair, her humming along to Dory's famous *just keep swimming* mantra.

She must've seen the movie already, but she reacted like it was her first time. It was oddly charming.

I dragged my eyes back to the screen. *Focus.*

It was only when we neared the end of the film that I realized the rain had stopped. I checked on Jules to find her passed out with her head nestled against the throw pillow on her other side.

One of our rules was no sleepovers, but she looked so peaceful I couldn't bring myself to wake her up.

It was only one night, and the weather had *forced* her to stay over. It wasn't like we were going to make a habit of staying over each other's places.

Just one night. That's it.

24

JULES

I woke to the scent of bacon and coffee, my favorite smell in the world. Individually, they were amazing, but combined? Utter perfection.

I was surprised Stella was cooking bacon, though. She only ate meat once in a blue moon. Now that I thought about it, she didn't drink coffee, either, just tea and her criminally grassy green smoothies.

Weird. Maybe she was entering a new coffee and meat phase.

I opened my eyes and stretched, ready to bask in the glory of my beautiful new room at The Mirage. Instead, I was greeted with the world's most hideous painting. The mess of brown and green looked like a herd of cats had vomited on it.

What the hell?

I shot up straight, my heart pounding with panic until bits and pieces from last night slowly came back to me.

Hyacinth. Max. Josh. Storm.

I must've fallen asleep during the movie, and Josh must've moved me into his room sometime during the night.

My heart rate slowed. Thank God I wasn't in some psycho murderer's sex dungeon, though I wasn't sure sleeping over Josh's place was much better.

I looked around his room, taking in the simple wooden furniture, navy comforter, and light gray walls. Atrocious art aside, it looked like a regular guy's room, though the faint scent of citrus and soap lingering in the air was so delicious I wanted to bottle it up for future enjoyment.

My eyes landed on the digital clock on the nightstand. 9:32 a.m. *Shit.* I should've been long gone by now.

I climbed out of bed and quickly washed my face and rinsed my mouth in the bathroom across the hall before I walked into the kitchen. I opened my mouth, ready to bid Josh a hasty goodbye, but my words died at the sight before me.

Josh was cooking. Shirtless.

Holy hell.

I think I just unlocked a new kink, because I suddenly couldn't imagine anything sexier than watching a man cook bare-chested.

The sculpted muscles of his back flexed as he reached for the salt next to the stove. His hair was even more tousled than usual, and the sunlight streaming through the windows gilded his skin with a deep bronze glow. A sliver of black sweats peeked over the kitchen island blocking the bottom half of his body. The pants rode just low enough to send my imagination spiraling in all sorts of X-rated directions.

I watched him in silence, fascinated by the easy grace with which he moved. I'd pictured him subsisting on pizza and beer like he had in school, but judging by the gleaming pots and pans hanging on hooks over the island and the neatly labeled spices lined up on the counter, he knew his way around the kitchen.

It was strangely attractive.

I knocked into one of the island stools in my trance, and Josh turned at the sharp scrape of wood against tile. His gaze skimmed over me before he looked away.

"You're awake."

"I've never slept in so late." I slid onto the stool and tried to keep my eyes above his waist. *Don't think about sex. Don't think about sex.* "Thanks for letting me stay over," I added awkwardly.

Sleepovers hadn't been part of our pact, and I wasn't sure how to deal with it, especially after how, ahem, aggressive our nighttime activities had been.

It wasn't like we'd made long, sweet love and I woke to him cooking me breakfast. It was more like...well, like he fucked my brains out and a thunderstorm trapped me in his house.

"I wasn't going to throw you out in the rain, Red." Josh slid a plate piled high with eggs, bacon, toast, and crispy hash browns onto the island.

My stomach rumbled, and I peeked over his shoulder at the stove. "Any chance you have a second plate?" I asked hopefully. "I'm starving."

"Nope." He popped a piece of bacon in his mouth. "Only made enough for one. Cooking breakfast for you would be too much like dating, and you already broke the rules by sleeping over. I had to sleep on the couch last night because of you. You can have my leftovers though."

My jaw unhinged. "Are you serious?"

Disbelief erased the last bits of my grogginess. Obviously, I wasn't *entitled* to breakfast, but it was pretty rude to eat right in front of me without offering me a plate.

"Does it look like I'm joking?"

"It looks like you're two seconds away from a slow, painful death," I growled. "There are plenty of knives in here, and I know how to use them."

"Then use them to cook something for yourself." Josh continued eating like he didn't have a care in the world.

My eye twitched. Gah, he was so...so...*ugh!*

"You are *such* an asshole."

"I remember you calling me the same thing last night." He sipped his coffee. "Right before I fucked your brains out. Seems you have a thing for assholes, Red."

Heat scalded my face and neck. "That was last night. This is now. And I didn't mean to sleep over," I snapped, hating how right he was. "I just fell asleep."

"Yes, that's what sleeping over means," Josh said slowly. "With those reasoning skills, you'll be winning court cases in no time." He straightened and wiped his mouth with a napkin before tossing it in the trash. "I'm taking a shower. I have a shift in an hour." He tipped his chin toward his plate. "Have at it if you want."

I scowled at his retreating back.

My pride demanded I leave, but as always, my hunger overrode all.

I pulled the plate toward me and realized it was near full. He'd only eaten a few pieces of bacon. *Weird.* Josh usually ate like a horse. I once saw him mow down a double decker burger, large fries, two hot dogs, and a chocolate milkshake in less than twenty minutes.

For a doctor, he ate like crap.

I finished half the plate and returned to Josh's room to change back into my clothes from last night. My dress was horribly uncomfortable compared to the softness of Josh's shirt, but I resisted the urge to steal his clothes for myself. That was girlfriend behavior, and God knew I wasn't his girlfriend.

By the time I was ready to leave, Josh still hadn't gotten out of the shower.

I debated waiting for him so I could say bye, but that felt

too awkward, so I sent him a quick text and slipped out quietly instead.

I'd just climbed into my Uber when a new message popped up on my screen.

No text, just an image. A still image from the tape, to be exact. I was on my knees while—

I quickly deleted it, but the bacon and eggs I ate earlier resurfaced in my throat.

Max.

I'd pushed him to the back of my mind while I was with Josh, but now, my anxiety from last night rushed back in a wave of nausea.

I knew exactly why he sent that picture. To fuck with my head and remind me of his dark, looming presence in my life. That was his M.O. He liked to toy with people until they drove themselves insane and did all the hard work for him.

I closed my eyes, trying to relax, but the car smelled like overly sweet air freshener and it made me gag even more.

I wished I could rewind time and freeze it so I stayed in the comforting oblivion of Josh's house forever, but there was no hiding from the truth in the harsh light of day.

I could only hope that whatever "favor" Max asked of me was doable...or my life as I knew it would be over.

25

JOSH

Did I wait until Jules left before I stepped out of the shower like a coward? Possibly.

But I'd rather be a coward than deal with the awkward morning after goodbye. Our arrangement was supposed to eliminate that awkwardness by setting clear boundaries and expectations, but of course, the weather had to fuck it all up on our first night.

If I ever made it to heaven, I was going to have a long, hard talk with God about timing.

I was still irritated with myself for letting Jules sleep over when I arrived at the hospital, but the chaos in the ER quickly wiped away any thoughts of my personal life.

Strokes. Knife wounds. Broken arms and legs and noses and everything in between. They flooded the emergency room in an unceasing, back-to-back wave, and the work week following Hyacinth was so insane I had zero time to agonize over my sex pact with my little sister's best friend.

Jules and I did squeeze in a few quickies, none of which

ended in a sleepover or cuddling, thank God. But for the most part, it was all work, all the time.

Most people would hate working such long hours, but I craved the stimulation—until I hit one of Those Days.

I had good days, bad days, and Those Days—capital T, capital D—in the ER. The good days were when I walked away knowing I'd made the right interventions at the right time to save someone's life. The bad days ranged from patients trying to assault me to a mass casualty incident when only me, my attending physician, and a few nurses were on duty.

Then there were Those Days. They were few and far in between, but when they happened?

They were devastating.

The unending flatline of the monitor drilled into my skull and mixed with the roar in my ears as I stared down at my patient's closed eyes and pale skin.

Tanya, seventeen years old. She'd been driving home when a drunk driver T-boned her car.

I'd done all I could, but it wasn't enough.

She was dead.

One minute she was alive, the next she was gone. Just like that.

My breaths rushed out in ragged pants. After what felt like an eternity but was, in reality, a minute at most, I lifted my head to find Clara and the techs staring back at me, their expressions grim. A faint sheen shone in Clara's eyes, and one of the techs audibly swallowed.

No one spoke.

"Time of death: 3:16 p.m." That was my voice, but it sounded strange, like it was coming from someone else.

After a moment of silence, I walked out. Down the hall, around the corner, and toward the designated relatives' room where Tanya's parents waited.

Thud. Thud. Thud.

Everything sounded muffled except for the echo of my foot-steps against the linoleum floors.

Thud. Thud. Thud.

I'd lost someone in the ER before. During my first year of residency, I treated a patient who'd been shot in the chest during a random drive-by. He'd succumbed to his injuries within minutes of arriving at the hospital.

There was nothing I could've done; he'd been too far gone. But that didn't stop me from walking out of the trauma bay, into a bathroom, and throwing up.

Every doctor lost a patient eventually, and every death hit hard, but Tanya's socked me right in the gut.

Maybe it was because I'd been so confident she would pull through. Or maybe it was because she barely had the chance to live life before death snatched it so cruelly from her.

Whatever it was, I couldn't stop a destructive swarm of *what ifs* from crowding my brain.

What if I'd made a different call during the treatment process? What if I'd reached her earlier? What if I were a better doctor?

What if, what if, what if.

Thud. Thud. Thud.

My steps faltered for a second outside the relatives' room before my hand closed around the doorknob and twisted. It was like I was watching a movie of myself—I was here, but not really.

Tanya's parents jumped up when they saw me, their faces drawn tight with worry. A minute later, the worry exploded into horror.

"I'm sorry...did everything we could..."

I kept talking, trying to sound sympathetic and profes-sional, to sound anything but numb, but I barely heard my own words. I only heard the mother's keening wail and the father's angry shouts of denial, which collapsed into shuddering cries of grief as he gathered his wife into his arms.

Each sound drove a phantom spike through my chest until I was so littered with them I couldn't breathe.

"My baby. Not my baby," Tanya's mom sobbed. "She's here. She's still here. I *know she is*."

"I'm so sorry," I repeated.

Thud. Thud. Thud.

Not my footsteps, but the thundering of a broken heart.

I maintained my stoic mask until I ran out of useless words and left the family to their grief. I had a dozen other patients to treat, but I needed a minute, just *one minute*, to myself.

I quickened my steps until I reached the nearest bathroom. The numbness spread from my chest to my limbs, but when I closed the door behind me, the soft click of the lock sliding into place unleashed a sharp sob that ripped through the air.

It took me several seconds to realize it came from me.

The pressure building behind my ribcage finally exploded, and I doubled over the sink, dry heaving until my ears rang and my throat was raw.

Tanya's lifeless body on the stretcher. Ava in the emergency room after she almost drowned. My mom's open, empty eyes after she overdosed on pills.

The memories ran together in a macabre stream.

I gagged again, but I hadn't eaten since I started my shift eight hours ago and nothing came out.

By the time my dry heaves faded, sweat clung to my skin and my head pounded with tension.

I turned on the faucet and splashed my face with cold water before paper toweling off the moisture. The rough brown material scratched against my skin, and when I caught my reflection in the mirror, I saw a faint reddish mark from where I'd rubbed it against my cheek.

Faint purple smudges beneath my eyes, sallow complexion, white lines of tension bracketing my mouth. I looked like hell.

God, I needed a strong drink. Or, better yet, a vacation with several strong drinks.

I set my jaw and tossed the crumpled paper towel into the trash. By the time I returned to the main floor, I'd fixed my professional mask back in place.

I didn't have the luxury of wallowing in grief or self-pity. I had a job to do.

"Hi there." I smiled at my next patient and held out my hand. "I'm Dr. Chen..."

The rest of my shift passed without any major incidents, but I couldn't shake my clammy skin or erratic heartbeat.

"Are you okay?" Clara asked when I clocked out.

"Yep." I avoided her sympathetic gaze. "See you tomorrow."

I didn't give her a chance to respond before I headed to the locker room. I usually showered at home, but I was desperate to wash the blood off. It stuck to my skin, thick and cloying, invisible to everyone except me.

I squeezed my eyes shut and stayed beneath the water until it ran cold and a deep chill settled into my bones. Normally, I couldn't wait to leave the building after a shift, but right now, nothing sounded worse than being alone.

My friends were all working, and it was too early to go to a bar, which left me with one remaining option.

I toweled off, got dressed, and fished my phone out of my jeans pocket to text Jules only to find a message already waiting from her, sent twenty minutes ago.

Jules: You off work yet?
Me: Just got out.

Me: *Where are you?*

It was Tuesday, so she wasn't working at the clinic today.

Jules: *SciLi, in the back.*

Relief rattled my lungs. That was within walking distance.

Me: *Don't move. Be there in fifteen.*

26

JOSH

THE HOSPITAL WAS RIGHT NEXT TO THAYER'S CAMPUS, so it didn't take me long to reach the science library, formally christened the George Hancock Library after a long-dead donor and informally known as SciLi. It was a hidden gem tucked on the third floor of the biology building. Whereas Fulton, the school's main library, was always packed during exam time, SciLi was quiet year-round.

The walk gave me time to push lingering thoughts of Tanya's death to the back of my mind. Being outside the hospital and surrounded by smiling, chattering students made it easier. It was like I'd stepped onto a movie set where I could pretend to be the person I wanted to be instead of the person I was.

When I arrived at SciLi, there were only a handful of students scattered throughout the space. Walls of books stretched two stories toward the double-height ceiling, interrupted only by massive stained-glass windows set at regular intervals. The glow from the green glass desk lamps mingled with the sunlight to cast a warm, hazy glow over the hushed sanctum.

The thick emerald carpet muffled my footsteps as I walked toward the back, where Jules sat by herself.

"Working hard, I see," I said when I reached her. A tall stack of textbooks sat next to her ever-present caramel mocha, and loose sheets of notes and index cards covered every inch of the oak surface.

"Someone has to." She raised her head, and alarm pinched my chest when I noticed her puffy, red eyes.

"Were you crying?"

What the fuck were they doing over at the law school? I was pretty sure study materials weren't supposed to make someone cry unless they were tears of frustration, and Jules wasn't the type to lose it over academic stress.

"No." She tapped her highlighter against her notebook. "I have allergies."

"That's bullshit."

We kept our voices low since we were in a library, but everyone was so zoned out and we were so far from the nearest person it didn't matter much.

Jules's tapping picked up speed. "Why do you care? I called you for sex, not a heart-to-heart."

"I *don't* care." I dropped into the chair next to her and lowered my voice further. "But I'd rather not fuck a crying woman unless you're crying from pleasure. Any other kind of tears is a turnoff."

"Charming."

"Would you rather I get turned on by others' distress?" I slipped into our banter with shocking ease, considering my day in the ER, but when I was around Jules, everything else ceased to exist.

For better or for worse.

"I don't have the energy to argue with you today, okay?" she snapped, her voice lacking some of its usual fire. "Either fuck me or leave."

My brief flare of good humor evaporated. Normally, I wouldn't hesitate to take her up on her offer of sex, but today wasn't normal.

"Newsflash, Red, you're not the only one who has shitty weeks, so stop acting like you're so fucking special," I said coldly. "This is a *mutually* beneficial arrangement. It doesn't mean you can call me and expect me to come running to service your needs like a fucking gigolo."

"That's not what I'm doing."

"Could've fooled me."

We glared at each other, the air between us crackling with thinly veiled frustration before Jules's shoulders slumped and she dropped her highlighter to rub her face.

My irritation fizzled at the simple action. I blew out a long breath, unable to keep up with the day's wild rollercoaster of emotions.

"Bad day at work?" she asked.

My laugh lacked humor. "You could say that."

I didn't talk about the downsides of my work unless it was with someone else in the field. Nothing brought down the mood faster than saying *hey, so someone died on my watch today*.

But the pressure from earlier was building in my chest again, and I needed to relieve it before it drove me crazy.

"I lost someone today." I leaned back in my chair and stared at the ceiling, unable to face Jules as I admitted my failure. "She was seventeen. Got hit by a drunk driver."

It felt weird saying the words out loud. *I lost someone*. It sounded so generic. People lost toys and house keys; they didn't lose lives. They had lives wrenched from them, stolen by the cruel hands of an unforgiving god.

But that didn't roll off the tongue quite as nicely, I supposed.

A soft hand covered my own. I stiffened and kept my eyes on the ceiling, but the knot in my chest loosened a smidge.

"I'm so sorry," Jules said softly. "I didn't—I can't imagine..."

"It's fine. I'm a doctor. It happens."

"Josh—"

"And you?" I interrupted, twisting my head to look at her. "What happened? Don't give me that bull about allergies again, either."

"I *do* have allergies." Several beats passed before she admitted, "It's possible I'll have to...do something I'm not proud of. I promised myself I would never do it again, but I might not have a choice. I just..." A hard swallow shifted the delicate lines of her throat. "I don't want to be that person."

It was vague as hell, but her distress was palpable and seeped through my skin into places it had no business touching.

"I'm sure it's not as bad as you think it is," I said. "As long as you didn't murder anyone or set anything on fire."

"Wow. The bar really is in hell."

A small smile touched my lips for the first time that day. "At least it's warm down there."

Jules snorted out a laugh. "If only I had your optimism."

"You can only wish." I angled my head toward the small reference library located off the main library. "So, still want to fuck?"

Nothing turned a crappy day around like a good fuck.

Plus, between her inadvertent sleepover and the brief lowering of our guards just now, we were edging too far from the rules of our pact. It was time to bring it back to what it was supposed to be about: sex. Quick, transactional, and mutually satisfying.

Judging by the rigid lines of Jules's neck and shoulders, she needed a physical release as much as I did.

She responded by gathering her notes and stuffing them in her backpack. We left her textbooks on the table—I highly doubted anyone would want to steal a tome on corporate law —and walked as casually as we could into the reference section.

I led us to one of the stacks that didn't fall under the gaze of the security cameras before I pinned her to the shelves and molded my mouth to hers. It started chaste, almost clinical—a way for us to forget our troubles and nothing else.

But I couldn't stop thinking about how exhausted she'd looked, or how comforting her hand had been over mine, and before I knew it, the kiss softened into something more...not tender, exactly. But understanding.

It was our first non-angry kiss, and it felt nicer than I expected.

I cupped her face and traced my tongue over the seam of Jules's lips until she opened for me. God, she tasted incredible, like heat and spice and sugar all rolled into one.

I'd always been a chocolate guy, but cinnamon was fast becoming my new favorite flavor.

Her arms snaked around my neck, and her soft sigh whispered down my spine and settled somewhere low in my stomach.

"Think we can forget about our shitty week for a while?" she whispered.

Fierce protectiveness welled in my chest at the touch of vulnerability in her voice, but I forced it back down.

We were only together for sex. Anything else was off the table.

"Sweetheart, in a few minutes, you'll forget your own name."

I sank to my knees, my mouth tipping up at the surprise in her eyes. Our last few times had been rough and deliciously filthy, but today, I was in the mood for a different kind of feast.

I hooked my fingers in the waistband of her underwear and pulled them down beneath her skirt. "Might want to cover your mouth, Red."

That was the only warning I gave before I spread her thighs and dived in, alternating between gentle licks and long, hard pulls on her sweet little clit.

I groaned. She tasted even better down here. Most women thought men wanted them to taste like berries or lavender or whatever, but if we were eating pussy, we wanted to taste pussy. That was the whole fucking point.

Jules fisted my hair with one hand when I pushed two fingers inside her. I pumped them in and out slowly while I continued teasing her clit. It was swollen and tender, and when I grazed my teeth against it, her soft cry arrowed straight to my cock.

I forced myself to keep the rhythm soft for a while longer before I increased the pace and intensity, sucking and finger fucking her until her arousal dripped down my hand and her thighs. I lapped it all up, drunk from the taste of her. Forget food and water. I could subsist on Jules forever.

I pulled my fingers out replaced them with my tongue, eager for more.

Jules shook around me. She fisted my hair harder with a muffled cry, and a second later, her juices flooded my tongue.

Fuck.

My senses swam with her scent, and when she squirmed, trying to inch away from me, I gripped her hips and forced her to remain still.

"Josh..." My name fell out as a whimper, also muffled.

My blood surged when I lifted my head and saw she'd clamped her free hand over her mouth to soften her moans. The prettiest rose shaded her cheeks, and tears glittered in her eyes from the suppressed force of her orgasm.

My cock threatened to punch a hole through my jeans. I loved hearing her sweet screams, but there was also something so fucking hot about seeing someone hold back when you knew all they wanted was to explode.

"I'm not done yet, Red." I gave her clit another languorous lick. "You don't want to interrupt a man before he's finished eating, do you?"

Jules responded with another moan.

I returned to my meal, licking and sucking and tongue fucking her with abandon. By the time I was done, I had to hold her up with one arm as I rose to my feet.

I wiped my mouth with the back of my hand and savored the lingering taste of her. My blood pounded with arousal.

I wished we had time for another round, but we were already pushing our luck. No one had stumbled on us, but the smell of sex permeated the air, and it wouldn't take an errant passerby to piece two and two together.

"I've always wanted to defile the library," Jules mumbled, clinging to me in a way she never would've outside sex.

A laugh bubbled in my throat. "*Defile* might be too strong a word, though I suspect they'd revoke my library access if anyone finds out what happened."

My cock pulsed, eager for its turn, but when she reached for my belt buckle, I grasped her wrist and placed it back by her side.

Confusion creased her brow. "But—"

"I'll take care of it later. Don't worry about it."

"Josh, that looks painful."

It *was* painful. I was so hard it was fucking excruciating. But a sick part of me reveled in it.

The pain reminded me I was still alive.

"You need a release too," Jules pointed out, and I knew she wasn't just talking about an orgasm.

"I'll take care of it," I repeated. Walking out with a boner the size of the Washington Memorial would be awkward as fuck, but the other people in the library had looked so zoned out I wasn't sure they'd notice. "Don't want to push our luck."

"Right." She closed her eyes, her breaths slowing.

Lazy silence swirled in the air.

Today was a complete one-eighty from the type of sex we usually had, but sometimes you needed hard and fast; other times you needed long and languid.

Besides, I could eat Jules out for days and not get tired of it.

My eyes lingered on her delicate features and rosy flush for a second longer than they should've.

On impulse, I said, "You want to go with me somewhere next Saturday? It's not a date," I clarified when her eyes popped open. "The hospital is having its annual all-staff picnic and I *know* the nurses will try to set me up like they do every year. Figured I'd preempt it by bringing a fake date." I emphasized the word *fake*.

Jules's brows rose. "That's against the rules of our arrangement."

Yeah, I fucking knew. I wasn't sure what possessed me to ask her when I could've brought any number of casual female acquaintances, but reason flew out the window whenever Jules Ambrose was involved.

It was damn infuriating, but since I couldn't do anything about it, I might as well lean into it.

"Rules are meant to be bent." I shrugged. "Look, if you ever need someone to pretend to be your date, I'm game. It's easier than asking some random person."

When Jules continued to hesitate, I added, "There'll be free food."

A beat passed before she said, "I could make it work."

"Good. I'll text you the details later." I turned to leave, but her soft, tentative voice stopped me.

"Josh. Are you going to be okay?"

I stilled. A strange lump formed in my throat at her unexpected concern before I swallowed it. "Yeah. I'll be fine." I threw her a quick smile over my shoulder. "See you next Saturday, Red."

After I left the library—where no one noticed my hard-on, thank God—I went straight home and poured myself a glass of Macallan. The shit was expensive, but it'd been a birthday gift from Alex. I'd rationed it out over the years, saving it for my biggest celebrations and shittiest days.

I finished my first glass and poured myself a second one. I didn't touch my erection. Instead, I sat in my living room and leaned my head back against the couch, listening to the silence.

Seeing Jules had provided a surprising measure of comfort, but the momentary lightness I'd experienced in the library had already drained away.

I tossed back the rest of my drink and savored the burn of whiskey sliding down my throat.

In that moment, it was the only thing keeping me warm.

27

JULES

I couldn't stop thinking about Josh or what happened in the library. Not only the part where he went down on me—though I'd replayed *that* particular experience more times than I could count—but the look on his face when he told me his patient died. The way he'd kissed me, soft yet desperate, like he craved comfort but couldn't bring himself to ask for it. And the way he'd looked when he left, like he bore the weight of the world on his shoulders.

They were thoughts I shouldn't have. There was no room for them in our arrangement, but that didn't stop them from occupying space in my head rent-free.

"Stop it, Jules," I ordered as I walked toward the park where the hospital's all-staff picnic took place. "Get it together."

A nearby family gave me a strange look and quickened their steps until they passed me.

Great. Now I was talking to myself and scaring off parents and children.

I released a deep sigh and tried to tame the flutter of nerves in my stomach when I neared the park entrance.

It was a picnic, for God's sake. I only agreed to come because there was free food, and I never turned down free food. It wasn't like it was a real date.

A breeze swept past and blew my dress up around my waist.

"Shit!" I hastily pushed down the billowing cotton, already regretting my outfit choice. It was finally warm enough for dresses again, but my weather app had fucked me over once again and failed to mention how *windy* it was. I'll have to spend the entire day holding down my skirt unless I wanted everyone at Thayer Hospital to find out what color underwear I wore.

"Flashing people already? We haven't even gotten you drunk yet." Josh's lazy drawl drifted into my ears.

I looked up to find him leaning against the entrance, arms folded across his chest. There was no trace of the tension and grief that lined his face in the library. Instead, a sly grin dimpled his cheeks, and a faint glow of amusement lit his eyes as they skimmed over me from head to toe.

Relief kindled in my chest. Cocky Josh was a pain in my ass, but for reasons I'd rather not examine, I preferred him being a pain to being *in* pain.

"This is a family picnic, Chen," I said as I approached him. "No alcohol allowed."

"Since when did you become such a prude?" He gave my braid a light tug and laughed when I swatted his hand away. "Braid, flats, white dress." His second, slower perusal triggered another cascade of flutters that filled my chest and tickled the base of my throat. Maybe one of the kind doctors at the picnic could perform an impromptu checkup, because my internal organs were clearly malfunctioning. "Who are you and what have you done to Red?"

"It's called a versatile wardrobe. You'd know if you had taste." I returned his scrutiny with a pointed one of my own, though in hindsight, that was a bad idea.

A short-sleeved green shirt stretched across the muscled ridge of Josh's shoulders and offset his tan. His jeans weren't tight, but they were fitted enough to show off the long, powerful lines of his legs, and he'd tamed his normally tousled hair into a neat coif. That, combined with his aviators, exuded an *Old Hollywood movie star during a casual day out on town* vibe that was more appealing than it had any right to be.

"Versatility doesn't equal taste." Josh placed a hand on the small of my lower back and guided me into the park. Tingles gathered at the base of my spine and radiated outward until they blanketed every inch of my skin. "Even I know that."

"Whatever." I was too distracted by the traitorous tingles to formulate a better comeback. "You're one to talk about taste. Look at the painting in your bedroom."

"What's wrong with the painting?"

"It's hideous."

"It's not hideous. It's *unusual*. The guy I bought it from said it used to belong to a famous collector."

I rolled my eyes. "It belonged to a famous collector and somehow ended up in your hands? Okay, sure. On that note, I have something I'd like to sell you. It's called the Brooklyn Bridge."

"Don't be a hater. Not everyone can have the same discerning eye for art."

"Someone call Roget's Thesaurus. Apparently, *discerning* is now a synonym for *appalling*."

Josh laughed, unfazed by my insults. "Glad to see you're feeling better, Red. Missed that poisonous tongue of yours."

My smile faded at the reminder of why I'd been in such a terrible mood at the library. I'd received yet another "reminder" text from Max that morning. I could call him out on his bluff, but I didn't think he was bluffing. Max loved toying with people, but when push came to shove, he had no qualms about throwing anyone under the bus.

When added to the stress from school, bar prep, and Bridget's upcoming wedding, it was too much. I'd cried over my textbooks in the library like an idiot and messaged Josh in the heat of the moment for a distraction.

I'd gathered myself by the time he arrived, but I didn't regret texting him. His presence had been oddly therapeutic, and what he did in the stacks...

My toes curled.

"What about you?" I asked. I hadn't been the only one in a shitty mood. "How are you feeling?"

A shadow crossed his face before it melted into another flippant smile. "I'm great. Why?"

"It's okay to grieve," I said, not fooled by his insouciance. I didn't want to poke at his wounds, but I knew how destructive bottled-up emotions could be. "Even if it's over something that's part of your job."

Josh's smile dimmed, and his throat flexed with a hard swallow before he looked away.

"Let's grab something to eat," he said. "I'm starving."

I took the hint and dropped the issue. Everyone handled grief differently. I wasn't going to force him to talk about something he wasn't ready or willing to discuss.

"So, who's staffing the hospital while everyone is here?" I changed the subject to something lighter.

Josh's rigid shoulders relaxed. "Essential staff is still there, but they're rotating shifts so everyone has a chance to swing by the picnic," he said. "This is the only all-staff event we have besides our holiday party, so it's a big deal."

"Jules!" A beautiful, familiar-looking brunette beamed

when we arrived at the food table. "So nice to see you. I didn't realize Josh was bringing a date."

"It's not a date," Josh and I chorused.

A short pause followed, during which the brunette's already wide grin broadened.

"Of course. My bad." She held out her hand, her eyes twinkling with humor. "I'm Clara. We sort of met at The Bronze Gear."

Recognition slammed into me. "You were Josh's date."

They worked together? And they were apparently on good terms, judging by the ease with which they greeted each other.

A horrifying tendril of jealousy snaked around my gut and squeezed.

Oh no. Oh no, no, no. I could *not* be jealous over Josh.

Scratch that. I *wasn't* jealous over Josh. I probably ate expired yogurt for breakfast or something. That was the problem with lemon-flavored foods—they tasted tart whether they were supposed to or not.

Clara burst into laughter. "Oh no, I wasn't his date. Just his coworker. I'm a nurse in the ER."

"She has a girlfriend." Josh assembled a hot dog on a plate. "The bartender from The Bronze Gear. Speaking of, where's Tinsley?"

"She's *not* my girlfriend. We're just dating, and she's working, so she couldn't make it." Clara eyed me with a speculative gleam in her eyes. "If you're not his date..."

"She's my *fake* date," Josh said before I could answer. "Remember last year's picnic? I could barely breathe with all the people shoving their daughters in my face. I wanted to avoid a repeat."

"It must've been traumatizing," Clara said.

I smirked at her dry sarcasm. I liked her already. Any woman who called Josh out earned an A-plus in my book.

"It was. Here." Josh finished assembling his food and handed it to me before replicating his efforts on a fresh plate.

A hot dog with ketchup, mustard, and relish. A side of salad. A handful of chips and a chocolate chip cookie to top it all off.

"Do you really need *two* plates?" I gestured at the one in my hand. "That's excessive, even for you."

He stared at me like I was dumb. "That plate is for you," he said. "*This* is mine." He added a hamburger and coleslaw to his bounty.

Thank God he didn't do that for mine. I hated coleslaw. The texture grossed me out.

"Oh." I shifted my weight and tried to ignore the buzz of warmth beneath my skin. "Thanks."

Instead of responding, Josh turned his back on me to greet another coworker.

Trust him to do something semi-nice and act like a jerk again immediately after.

I took an annoyed bite out of my hot dog and caught Clara watching us. She turned away when she noticed me staring, but her shoulders shook with what looked suspiciously like laughter.

Since LHAC wasn't officially part of Thayer Hospital, no one else from the clinic was here, which saved me and Josh from having to explain our fake date to Barbs and company. I also wasn't worried about my friends finding out. None of them knew anyone who worked at the hospital except Josh.

For the next few hours, I accompanied Josh as we circulated the park and played the dutiful part of his date whenever someone tried to introduce him to their sister, daughter, or granddaughter. He hadn't been lying when he said everyone wanted to set him up—I counted a dozen matchmaking attempts, even with me by his side, before I gave up.

"I don't understand the appeal," I grumbled after a nurse and her daughter walked away, looking disappointed. "You're not even that great a catch. A trout, at most. Maybe a large-mouth bass, emphasis on the largemouth."

"You liked my mouth just fine in the library." Josh's silky response sent flames licking over my skin.

"It was *okay*."

I sucked in a gasp when he tugged me to his side, his whisper a dark warning in my ear. "Don't provoke me, Red, or I'll spread you out on the picnic table and tongue fuck you until you have to fucking crawl home because your legs don't work anymore."

He released me and smiled at the man approaching us. "Hey, Micah," he said, like he hadn't just threatened to make me come my brains out in front of a thousand people a mere second ago. "How's it going?"

After they greeted each other, Josh introduced me to Micah, who offered me a perfunctory smile.

"So, Jules, what do you do? Are you a student?" The other resident was around Josh's age, but he oozed pretentiousness in a way that was completely at odds with Josh's easy charm. Josh may be arrogant, but at least he was self-deprecating about it. Micah looked like he believed his own hype a little too much.

"Yes, at Thayer Law. I graduate in a few weeks."

Micah's eyebrows popped up. "Law? *Really?*"

I stiffened at his obvious skepticism.

"Yes, really." I dropped my polite tone and adopted one so icy I hoped it froze his balls off. Some people might give Micah the benefit of the doubt, but I recognized judgment when I saw it, and I had zero obligation to be nice to someone who didn't bother hiding his condescension. "Surprised?"

"A little. You don't look like a law student." Micah's eyes

dropped to my chest, and tiny prickles of humiliation stabbed at me.

Beside me, Josh stilled, his easygoing manner giving way to a dark, volatile tension that roiled the air around us.

"I didn't realize law students had a universal *look*." I resisted the urge to cross my arms over my chest. I wouldn't give Micah that satisfaction. "How are they *supposed* to look?"

He laughed, not even having the decency to look embarrassed by my callout. "You know what I mean."

"I don't." Josh spoke up before I could respond, his tone deceptively light. "What do you mean, Micah?"

Discomfort crossed his coworker's face for the first time as Micah finally realized the conversation wasn't heading in the direction he'd intended.

"You know." He waved a hand in the air, trying to play it off. "It was a joke."

Josh's smile didn't reach his eyes. "Jokes are supposed to be funny."

"Lighten up, man." Micah's frown of discomfort morphed into annoyance. "Look, all I'm saying is, I was surprised, okay?"

"That's not what you're saying. What you're saying is you made assumptions about her intelligence based on her appearance, which is quite unfair, don't you think?" A lethal edge ran beneath Josh's otherwise pleasant voice. "For example, if I were to make an assumption about *you*, I would think you were a pompous jackass based on the Harvard-branded clothing you wear at any opportunity despite the fact you only got in because your last name is engraved on their newest science building. But I'm sure that's not true. You *did* graduate from Harvard Med—near the bottom of the class, but you graduated. That counts for something."

Micah's mouth fell open while a ball of emotion curled up in my throat and refused to budge.

I couldn't think of the last time someone stood up for me. It was a strange feeling—warm and thick, like honey sliding through my veins.

"Regardless, I do not appreciate your rudeness toward my date." Josh's voice hardened.

"This is a work event, so apologize, walk away, and we'll leave it at that. But disrespect Jules again, and I'll put you in the emergency room myself."

Micah's nostrils flared, but he wasn't dumb enough to argue. Not when Josh looked like he was actively *hoping* the other man would step out of line so he could deck him.

"I'm sorry." Micah's stiff apology contained as much sincerity as a crocodile's tears. He spun on his heels and stalked away, his reedy body quivering with outrage.

A heavy silence descended in his wake.

Some of the tension drained from Josh's body, but the line of his jaw remained a hard slash.

I tried and failed to swallow the persistent lump in my throat. "You didn't have to do that."

"Do what?" He unscrewed the cap of his water bottle and took a sip.

"Defend me."

"I didn't defend you. I called out an asshole for being an asshole." He slid a sidelong glance at me. "Besides, I'm the only one who gets to be a jerk to you."

I huffed out an embarrassingly watery laugh. I was so used to fighting my own battles I wasn't sure how to handle having someone by my side.

Josh was supposed to be my nemesis, but he turned out to be my ally. In this particular instance, anyway.

"Well, if there's one thing you excel at, it's being a jerk." I rubbed my skirt between my fingers. The smooth cotton calmed my racing nerves.

"I excel at everything, Red." Josh's languid drawl settled over me like a warm blanket.

Our eyes locked and held. An electric charge flared in the air between us and buzzed down my spine.

I'd known Josh for years, but this was the first time I saw him in such bold, painstaking detail.

The sharp curve of his cheekbones tapering down to a strong jaw. The rich, dark eyes like melting chocolate, fringed by lashes so long it should be illegal for men to have them. The arch of his brows and the firm, sensual curve of his lips.

How had I never noticed how incredibly, devastatingly gorgeous Josh Chen was?

I'd known it on an intellectual level, of course, the way I knew the earth was round and the oceans were deep. It was impossible for someone with those features, arranged in that way, to be anything except beautiful.

But this was the first time I'd *experienced* it. It was like peeling back the transparent sheet cover on a famous art piece and finally seeing it in its full glory.

Josh's hands curled into loose fists by his side before he unclenched them.

"Last call soon." The words came out rough and scratchy, like it hurt him to speak. "If you want more food, we should grab it now before the picnic ends."

The electric charge dissipated, but its effects lingered as a film of tingles on my skin.

"Right. More food." I cleared my throat. "I'm always down for more food."

We fixed our plates in silence before settling beneath one of the large oak trees bordering the park. Most of the food had been picked clean, but we'd managed to snag the last of the burgers and a chocolate cupcake to share.

"Your coworkers seem to like you a lot, Micah the Dickhead

notwithstanding." I sliced the cupcake into neat halves with a plastic knife and handed Josh his portion.

He took it, his mouth quirking. "Don't sound so surprised. I'm a likable person, Red."

"Hmmm." I snuck a glance at him while we ate. We'd fought, we'd fucked, but there was still so much I didn't know about him.

How was it possible to know so little about someone after seven years?

"Did you always want to be a doctor? Don't bother making a joke about playing doctor as a kid," I added when I noticed the gleam in his eyes. "If I can preempt it before you say it, it's lame."

A deep laugh rumbled from Josh's chest. "Fair enough." He leaned against the tree trunk and stretched out his legs. A thoughtful expression crossed his face. "I'm not sure when I decided to become a doctor. Part of it was expectations, I guess. Doctor, lawyer, engineer. The stereotypical careers for a Chinese-American kid. But there was another part that..." He hesitated. "This is going to sound cheesy, but I want to help people, you know? I remember waiting in the hospital when Ava almost drowned. It was the first time I realized the people around me wouldn't live forever. I was fucking terrified. And I kept thinking...what if I'd been with her by the lake that day? Could I have saved her? Would the drowning have even happened? And my mom. What if I'd noticed something was wrong earlier and gotten her help..."

A deep ache spread through me at the tiny crack in his voice.

I placed a tentative hand on his knee, wishing I was better at comforting people. "You were just a kid," I said gently. "What happened wasn't your fault."

"I know." Josh stared at where my hand rested against the

blue denim of his jeans. His throat bobbed with a hard swallow. "But that doesn't stop me from feeling like it was."

The ache intensified.

How long had he lived with his guilt and kept it to himself? I doubted he'd told Ava, not when it was guilt over her. Perhaps he'd told Alex when they were friends, but I couldn't picture stiff, icy Alex being particularly reassuring.

"You're a good brother, and you're a good doctor. If you weren't, I would've heard about it. Trust me." I imbued my smile with mischief. "I'm plugged into all the gossip."

That earned me a small laugh. "Oh, I know. You and Ava wouldn't shut up whenever you got into one of your rants."

My heart jumped into my throat when he covered my hand with his and twined our fingers together. He squeezed, that one action saying more than words ever could.

Three months ago, I would've never willingly touched him, and he would've never willingly turned to me for comfort.

Yet here we were, existing in the strangest iteration of what our relationship could be. Not quite friends, not quite enemies. Just us.

"And you? Why'd you become a lawyer?" Josh asked.

"I'm not a lawyer yet." I remained still, afraid any movement would shatter the fragile, therapeutic peace between us. "But, um, *Legally Blonde* is one of my favorite movies."

I laughed when his eyebrows shot toward his hairline. "Hear me out, okay? The movie was the jumping-off point. I looked up law schools out of curiosity, and I fell into a rabbit hole. The more I learned about the field, the more I liked the idea of..." I searched for the right word. "Purpose, I guess. Helping people solve their problems. Plus certain types of law pay well." Warmth suffused my cheeks. "That sounds shallow, but financial security is important to me."

"That's not shallow. Money isn't everything, but we need it to survive. Anyone who says they don't care about it is lying."

"I guess."

We fell into companionable silence again. The golden spring afternoon cast a soft haze over the scene, and I felt like I was living in a dream where the rest of the world didn't exist. No past, no future, no Max, exams, or money worries.

If only.

"So, what you said earlier." Josh twisted his head to look at me. "Good brother and doctor, huh?" He removed his hand from mine. I mourned the loss of his touch for a brief moment before he tugged on my braid again, a crooked smile forming on his mouth. "Was that a compliment, Red?"

"My first and last for you, so savor it while you can."

"Oh, I will. Every morsel." The velvety suggestion in his voice bypassed my brain and went straight to my core.

"Good," I managed.

What was happening to me? Maybe someone spiked the food with aphrodisiacs because I shouldn't be this flustered over Josh.

What started as a fake date was quickly turning into an existential crisis. Hating Josh was one of the core pillars of my lifestyle, along with my love for caramel mochas, my aversion to cardio, and my rainy-day pastime of browsing obscure book-stores. Take my hate for him away, and what was I left with?

My heartbeat quickened. *Don't go there*.

Josh's smile faded, leaving behind an intensity that sent shivers from my head to my toes.

An endless second stretched between us, suspended by the same electric charge from earlier before a shriek of nearby laughter snapped it in half.

Josh and I jerked apart at the same time.

"We should go—"

"I have to leave—"

Our voices tangled in a rush of excuses.

"I have to pack for Eldorra," I said, even though our flight wasn't for another five days.

As Bridget's bridesmaids, Ava, Stella, and I were flying in early for pre-wedding prep, courtesy of Alex's private jet. Josh wasn't in the wedding party, but he was joining us because why fly commercial when you could fly private?

"Right. I'm gonna stick around, help clean up." Josh raked a hand through his hair. "Thanks for coming. We successfully warded off all matchmaking attempts."

"Thanks for inviting me. Glad I could help."

An awkward beat passed.

Given our arrangement, we should be heading to his place for sex because that was supposed to be the cornerstone of our relationship, but after our conversation just now, that felt...wrong.

Josh must've thought the same, because he didn't say anything else except, "See you soon, Red."

"See you."

I quickened my steps until I reached the park exit, too afraid to look back lest Josh see the confusion scrawled over my face.

He was working all week, so I wouldn't see him until our Eldorra trip. I could take the time to reset and return to our equilibrium, AKA attracted to but barely tolerating him.

But I had a sinking feeling that whatever knocked our world off its axis had done so irrevocably. Not in one afternoon, but in all the moments that led up to it—our truce at the clinic, our ski lessons, our night in Vermont, our sex-only pact. Hyacinth and the library and the hundreds of small moments in which I thought about Josh and didn't experience the same visceral irritation I used to when he crossed my mind.

Disrespect Jules again, and I'll put you in the emergency room myself.

That's not shallow.

Was that a compliment, Red?

I didn't know what to make of my strange new feelings toward Josh, but I knew one thing: there was no going back to whatever we used to be.

28

JOSH

In hindsight, taking Jules to the picnic was the worst idea I'd ever had. The short-term gain of outsmarting the hospital's matchmakers wasn't worth the long-term pain of replaying the afternoon over and over in my head like a broken record I couldn't bear to toss.

You were just a kid. What happened wasn't your fault.

You're a good brother, and you're a good doctor.

Every time I thought about our conversation beneath the tree, I wanted to rewind and freeze time so we could stay in that moment forever.

Sun shining, food in our laps, the emptiness in my chest a little less empty with Jules's presence filling it up.

It was unacceptable.

Wanting to fuck her was fine. Wanting to call her when I had a crappy day was not.

It didn't matter if she was the only person I could talk to without fearing judgment. There would be no more quasi-dates from now on, not even fake ones. And *definitely* no more sleepovers or letting her borrow my shirt.

I still hadn't washed the one I'd lent her after Hyacinth. I'd get around to it eventually, but it didn't smell bad. It smelled faintly like her—warm and cinnamony with a hint of amber.

The same scent enveloped my senses now as I buried my face in her neck and drove deeper into her, trying to ease the ceaseless, unquenchable *need* in my stomach. But every thrust and kiss only magnified it, and my frustration spilled into the speed and force of my fucking.

The headboard banged against the wall in rhythmic response to my thrusts as I pounded into Jules, my muscles taut and slicked with sweat from the past half hour.

We'd landed in Athenberg that afternoon, and Jules and I must be on the same wavelength because she showed up to my suite twenty minutes after we checked in with nothing more than a, "Wanna fuck?"

No mention of the picnic, library, or any other rule we'd broken, thank God. We were both eager to return to the status quo, and I'd happily obliged.

Now, if only I could fuck the hunger for Jules out of my system, I'd be a happy man.

"*Josh.*" Her sharp cry ricocheted through the hotel room as she clawed at my back and exploded around me.

Jules fucked the way she fought—fierce and fiery, no holds barred. It was addictive.

The exquisite burn from her nails matched the fire in my veins as I clamped a hand over her mouth, cutting off her cry.

"Shh. You'll wake everyone up." My jaw clenched with the effort to hold back my own orgasm as her pussy rippled around me. *Christ.* It should be illegal for someone to feel that damn good. "You don't want our friends to hear, do you?"

My suite was across the hall from Jules and Stella's and only two doors down from Alex and Ava's. Alex was taking a video call in the hotel's conference room downstairs, and Ava and Stella were napping ahead of Bridget's bachelorette party tonight, but I didn't want to risk it.

We were already risking enough sneaking around right under Ava's nose.

The headboard banging might give me away, but I could easily play that off as coming from another room on the floor.

Jules whimpered, but when I removed my hand from her mouth, she successfully kept her cries down even as she came a second time.

She pressed her face against my shoulder, her body shaking with her silent release.

"Good girl," I whispered. "Keep those screams in, Red. I'm the only person who gets to hear how much you love my cock in that tight little cunt."

Another, louder whimper.

Her pussy clamped around me even tighter than the first time, and a blinding orgasm ripped through me with such sudden, unexpected force it rendered me speechless for a second.

When the aftershocks finally faded, I sank against her, reveling in the sensation of her soft curves melting into my body. She felt so damn perfect I was tempted to stay there forever and lose myself in her warmth.

I allowed myself to savor the moment for another second before I reluctantly pulled away. I handed Jules a bottle of water from the hotel's mini bar, my mouth curving at her content, slightly dazed expression.

"Thanks." She took a sip of the drink, her voice slumberous with post-coital bliss. "I'll leave soon. Just..." A yawn split her face. "Give me a second."

Disappointment spiked in my chest at the thought of her leaving before I forced it down. *This is just sex,* I reminded myself.

"As long as it's only one second. Don't want you accidentally sleeping over." I settled next to her in the bed. I itched to draw her closer, but I propped my hands behind my head instead.

She glared at me, her contentedness giving way to irritation. "I see the asshole is back."

"He never left."

"Obviously." Jules climbed out of bed and shrugged into her shirt.

"I'm *kidding*, Red." I leaned over and grasped her wrist before she could button her top. "Stay a bit longer if you want. It's not like Ava and Stella are awake to hang out."

I pulled her back into bed. She resisted for a second before relaxing next to me. She knew I was right. If she left now, she had nothing to do except wander the hotel.

"What are you guys doing tonight, anyway?" I asked.

"Dinner and clubbing." Jules wrinkled her nose. "I wish we could throw Bridget a full-blown bachelorette party, but tonight is the only night she has even a little free time, so we're keeping it simple."

My eyebrows reached my hairline. "You're taking the Queen of Eldorra *clubbing? In* Eldorra?"

"We'll be in disguise."

I stared at Jules, unsure if she was joking. She stared back with one hundred percent seriousness.

"Disguise," I repeated. "I hate to break it to you, Red, but a wig and sunglasses aren't gonna be enough to disguise the most famous woman in the country."

"We're not wearing sunglasses," she scoffed. "No one wears sunglasses at night except douchebags. No, we hired a makeup artist to transform our faces."

"Are you fucking with me? How the fuck is a makeup artist supposed to transform your face?"

"A skilled MUA can do a *lot*," Jules said primly. "Clearly, you've never watched any before and after makeup transformations on YouTube."

I rubbed my face. The conversation was getting more surreal by the minute. "No, I haven't, because I *don't wear makeup*."

"So? You're not an astronaut but that doesn't stop you from watching videos about rocket launches."

"Yeah, because rockets are cool."

"So's makeup."

"Not to me."

She rolled her shoulders in a shrug. "You've always lacked taste."

"I'm fucking you, aren't I? What does that say about you?"

Jules stretched her arms over her head and yawned. "That I'm a lovely, generous human being who'll throw you a pity fuck when no one else will—"

A squeal cut off her words when I lifted her and delivered a sharp smack on her ass before sitting her on my lap. Her back pressed against my torso, and I reached around to spread her thighs.

"Don't make me spank your pussy next, Red." I rubbed my thumb over her still-swollen clit in warning. "I won't be as gentle."

A shiver rolled through Jules's body, but she sank against me and fell quiet as I caressed her.

Yes, this was supposed to be sex only, but I would be an asshole if I kicked her out without *some* post-sex downtime, right?

I smoothed my palm up her thighs, over her stomach and to her breasts. It was more comforting than it was sexual, and I loved how fucking soft she was. Soft and warm and perfectly tailored for me, her curves fitting my hands like pieces of a puzzle I never wanted to finish solving.

"What are you doing tonight while we're out?" She made a small, contented noise as I gently squeezed and kneaded her breasts.

"Grab a drink. Explore the city." I had no clue. "I'll figure something out."

"Alex will be staying behind too."

My hand stilled before I dropped it to my side. "Don't see what that has to do with me." The lightness of my tone contrasted with the sudden stiffness in my shoulders.

A sigh floated from Jules's throat to my ears. "All I'm saying is, it's painful watching you guys avoid each other. I can't imagine it's fun for you to hold onto your grudge either. Being angry at someone is exhausting, and it's been almost two years. Maybe..." Her voice softened, taking on a far-off quality, and I wondered if she was talking about herself as much as she was me. "Maybe it's time to forgive, even if you don't forget."

I leaned my head against the headboard and closed my eyes. "Maybe."

It wasn't that I didn't want to. It was that I didn't know *how* to. Every time I tried, the past reared its ugly head and dragged me back.

How could I let go of something that refused to let go of me?

"It would be—"

A knock on the door cut her off. "Josh?" Ava's voice drifted into my room.

Jules shot up straight and twisted her head to look at me. We stared at each other with wide eyes.

"Can I come in? I think you have my backpack," Ava said. "It has my laptop."

Fuck. My gaze strayed to my black backpack. We'd bought the same one during a holiday sale a few years ago.

I gently extricated myself from Jules, climbed off the bed and unzipped it. Yep, there was Ava's laptop sitting snug in between her notebook and a blue folder. *Double fuck.*

I must've grabbed hers by mistake at the airport.

I gestured at Jules to get into the bathroom, but she sat frozen on my bed, looking like a wax mannequin of herself.

"Can you get it later?" I called out. My heart slammed against my chest. "I'm, uh, busy."

I would open the door and hand Ava's backpack to her, but there was no way to do so without her seeing the bed.

"I need my laptop. I have to get some work done before the bachelorette tonight."

Double fuck.

I stepped toward the bed, but Jules finally moved. She wrapped the sheet around herself and darted into the bathroom so fast she was almost a blur. I waited until the door closed behind her before I picked up the backpack and cracked open my door.

"Hey." I shoved the bag at my sister. "Here ya go. See you later." I tried to close the door, but Ava pushed it back open with narrowed eyes.

"Why are you being so shifty?"

"I'm not being shifty." Sweat beaded on my brow. "I'm irritated because you interrupted me."

"Doing what?"

"Uh, exercising." Technically true. Sex was the best form of cardio. "I thought you were napping."

She gave me a strange look. "I woke up." Her eyes drifted from my sex-tousled hair to my tense shoulders. A faint green tint colored her skin. "Wait...do you have a girl in there? Was that banging sound *you*? That was what woke me up."

Heat climbed on my face.

"How is that possible? We literally *just* arrived an hour ago." Ava clapped a hand over her mouth. "I think I'm going to be sick. You are not allowed to have sex when I can hear you. I'm scarred for life."

"You're being dramatic, and what can I say? I'm a legend." I pasted on my cockiest smile. "Now please leave before she comes out of the bathroom. Nothing kills the vibe like a little sister sticking her nose where it doesn't belong."

"Trust me, I don't want to..." Ava's eyes fell on something behind me. "Oh, weird. Jules has those exact shoes."

Shit! I'd accidentally let the door drift open while we were talking.

Jules's clothes were out of sight, but her shoes were right there, front and center, at the foot of the bed.

It was a testament to how much we used to dislike each other that Ava didn't think the shoes could belong to her.

"They must be popular." I forced a laugh and resisted the urge to wipe the sweat from my forehead. "Wish you hadn't told me that. The second thing that kills the vibe fast is any mention of the she-devil. Anyway." I pushed Ava further into the hallway. "Great to see you, don't come back. Unless you want a firsthand look at the symphony."

We both gagged at the same time.

If the vibe wasn't already dead, it was six feet under and rotting now at the prospect of my sister being in the room while I had sex.

"I'm going to wash my eyes and ears out with bleach." Ava shuddered.

I waited until she returned to her room before I closed the door and leaned my forehead against it. Relief cooled the sweat on my skin, but my heart still raced like it was competing in the fucking Indy 500.

"That was a close call."

I lifted my head and saw Jules peek out of the bathroom, her eyes wide.

"These fuckers almost got us in trouble." I nudged her shoes with my foot.

"Those are my favorite shoes, Josh. It's not their fault." She stepped fully into the bedroom and fished her clothes off the floor. "We shouldn't have done this in the hotel. It was stupid. If she caught us..."

I grimaced. Jules was right. It *was* stupid to hook up in the hotel when our friends were literally down the hall. We could get caught any minute.

Normally, I'd never be that reckless, but...

I watched Jules get dressed, my heart rate not slowing down one bit despite the fact the danger had passed.

For some reason, logic always flew out the window where Jules was concerned.

Jules snuck out after making sure the hallway was clear and left me to my own devices.

Restless, I showered, hit the gym, showered again, and watched *Fast Five* in my room while the girls got ready and left for the palace. Only royal relatives were allowed to stay at the palace for the wedding, so even though the girls were Bridget's bridesmaids, we were camped out in a five-star hotel, courtesy of the crown.

I usually had no issues entertaining myself while traveling, but the crowd of paparazzi outside the hotel deterred me from venturing out.

Unfortunately, our hotel, as luxurious as it was, lacked stimulating activities. Michelin-starred restaurants and a world-renowned spa were *fine,* but I needed more excitement.

Alex will be staying behind too.

Jules's words echoed in my head. What *was* he doing? Eating babies and ruining lives, probably.

By the time night descended, I was bored enough to join him.

Temptation snaked around my spine, but instead of knocking on his door, I headed downstairs to the bar. It'd been closed earlier, but when I arrived, the telltale glow of lights sent relief coasting through my lungs.

I stepped inside, taking in the two-story ceiling, plush blue velvet couches, and the massive wall of glittering bottles behind the polished mahogany bar. It blew the fanciest bar in D.C. out of the water, times ten.

I slid onto a blue leather stool and waited for the bartender to finish setting up. It must've just opened, because we were the only people present, and the space was eerily quiet save for the soft jazz piping through invisible speakers.

Part of me craved the buzz of a crowd; another part relished the silence.

Like in most areas of my life right now, I didn't know what the hell I wanted.

I drummed my fingers against the counter and scanned the bottle display, searching for a good drink to start the night, when a familiar voice sliced through the silence.

"This seat taken?"

The drumming stopped. Tension locked my muscles in place.

I turned to face the newcomer, already wishing I'd ordered room service instead of braving a common space when Alex was also roaming the grounds.

My former best friend stood a few feet away, dressed in the same black turtleneck and pants he wore on the plane. Fatigue lined his face, and a pinch of concern squeezed my chest.

According to Ava, his insomnia had improved over the years, but there were still times when he went days without sleeping, only to crash afterward.

I remembered several instances during undergrad when he would pass out in the middle of a conversation or study session.

Not that it was my concern anymore.

"Obviously, it isn't." I flicked my eyes at the empty stool next to me.

"That's not what I meant," Alex said coolly.

A muscle ticked in my jaw. The bastard never made things easy.

*In that case, it **is** taken.*

The words hovered on the tip of my tongue, but Jules's voice floated through my head again.

Being angry at someone is exhausting, and it's been almost two years. Maybe it's time to forgive, even if you don't forget.

Two years.

They'd stretched for an eternity and passed in the blink of an eye all at once.

In that time, Alex and I had only one moment when things between us seemed semi-normal—our ski afternoon in Vermont.

I blamed my twinge of nostalgia for what I said next. "All yours."

A flicker of surprise crossed his face before it smoothed into its usual impassive mask.

Alex took his seat right as the bartender finished setting up and approached us. "Thanks for waiting," he said in lightly accented English. "What can I get you?"

"I'll have a Macallan neat." Alex didn't look at the menu before ordering. There was no doubt a bar as fancy as this one served Macallan.

The bartender nodded and shifted his attention to me.

"A Stella is fine, thanks." The only Macallan I drank was from my bottle at home, though it now sat empty after I drowned my sorrows over Tanya's death in it.

Otherwise, the whiskey was too rich for my med school loan-riddled wallet.

"Still haven't graduated to real alcohol, huh?" Alex drawled after the bartender left to fix our drinks.

"Still haven't developed taste, huh?" I volleyed back. "It's okay, man. They'll still let you into your billionaires' club if you admit to liking beer."

"Beer tastes like carbonated urine." He delivered each word with his trademark icy precision, but a tinge of amusement lurked beneath the surface. "I'm also not discussing taste with someone who once dressed as a rat for Halloween." He paused before adding, "A rat who wore a red bandanna."

"Oh, for fuck's sake, that was *one time*." I'd been a gladiator, Superman, a doctor (not my most inspired costume, I admit), Waldo from *Where's Waldo,* and a thousand other personas for Halloween, yet everyone always brought up the fucking rat. "I did it to prove I could pull anyone I wanted even if I was dressed as a rat. And I did."

The Morgenstern twins. That had been a good night.

The memory of one of my favorite threesomes usually got me going, but tonight, it did nothing for me. Not even a flicker of excitement or desire.

Weird.

"That's what you always say." Alex sounded unimpressed.

"Because it's true. Ask the Morgensterns."

"Whatever makes you feel better."

A scowl knotted my brow. "You're such a goddamn asshole. I don't know how I was ever friends with you," I grumbled, accepting my drink from the bartender with a nod of thanks.

Alex's lips curved, but the air between us suddenly weighed heavy with ghosts from the past—pickup basketball games, late-night study sessions, parties and guys' trips and random memes we sent each other throughout the day.

Well, l sent him memes and he replied with frowning or

eye roll emojis, but Alex had a shit sense of humor, so I didn't expect him to appreciate my excellent meme selection.

Jules's advice may have pushed me to extend a tentative olive branch, but the truth was, I missed having a best friend. I missed having *Alex* as my best friend. He was cold, rude, and grumpy as fuck, but he'd always had my back. Every fight I got into, every bad day I had, he'd been there to bail me out and talk me down.

I took a swig of beer to wash down the sudden tightness in my throat while Alex quietly sipped his drink.

The bar was starting to fill up, and soon, the room buzzed with enough activity to drown out the silence roaring between us.

I finished my beer and was about to order another one when Alex interjected.

"Two more Macallans." He slid his black Amex across the counter and flicked a glance in my direction. "On me."

My first instinct was to turn it down, but I wasn't dumb enough to say no to a free premium drink.

"Thanks."

"You're welcome."

More silence. God, this was fucking painful.

"How are things going between you and Ava?" I finally asked.

Ava always gushed about their relationship, but she was Alex's first real girlfriend, and I was curious as hell about his perspective. If I hadn't witnessed it with my own eyes, I wouldn't have thought him capable of a long-term relationship.

Alex's face softened. "We're good."

"*Good.* That's high praise coming from you." I wasn't joking. The strongest positive term I'd ever heard him use was *fine*.

Gourmet steak cooked by a world-famous chef? Fine.

Flying in a private jet? Fine.

Graduating top of his class from Thayer? Fine.

For someone so smart, he had a limited vocabulary.

"I love your sister," Alex said simply.

My glass froze halfway to my lips. Of course, I knew he loved Ava, but I never in a million years would've guessed he'd admit it to anyone except her.

The Alex I knew had zero tolerance for sentimentality. Make it *verbal* sentimentality and his tolerance dropped into the negatives.

"Good." I regained motor control. My glass touched my mouth and whiskey flowed into my stomach, but the shock from Alex's statement lingered. "Because if you hurt her again, I'll take that stick out of your ass and stab you with it."

"If I hurt her again, I'll let you."

A tense beat passed before I let out a short laugh. "You've changed."

Part of me appreciated the growth, while another part mourned how much time had passed since our friendship ended. Enough that we were funhouse mirror versions of ourselves—the same people at our core but distorted by the changes wrought over time.

"Everyone changes. Without change, we might as well be dead." It would've been an inspiring quote had Alex not delivered it with all the emotion of a block of ice.

"Speaking of Ava..." He rolled his empty glass between his finger, his expression even broodier than usual. "I'd hoped we could talk before the girls came back."

"What do you think we're doing right now? Chopping liver?"

"I mean *talk*."

My smile fell.

There it was. The giant, trumpeting elephant in the room.

Alex and I had avoided talking about what happened since our confrontation after he broke up with Ava.

How he became my friend only to get closer to my father.

How he'd used Ava and broke her heart.

How he'd lied to me for seven fucking years.

He'd tried reaching out after he and Ava got back together, but I'd ignored him and we'd never had a real, honest conversation about it.

It was long past due, but that didn't stop my stomach from knotting with dread at the prospect of digging up bones from the past.

"I understand why you're still upset with me. It was...a betrayal of trust, what I did. But I..." Alex paused, clearly searching for the right words. A speechless Alex Volkov was a rare sight, and I would've reveled in it more had I not been so distracted by the burn in my chest.

"I've never had many friends," he finally said. "People flocked to me because I was rich, smart, and I could help them get what they wanted." He listed the qualities in a detached manner, so self-assured he came off more analytical than arrogant. "They were transactional relationships, and I was fine with that. But you were my first real friend. Even if my intentions weren't true at the start of our friendship, everything that came after was."

The burn intensified. "What you did was fucked up."

"I know."

I rubbed a hand over my face, trying to quiet the debate raging in my head.

We'd reached a fork in the road. I could either stay on the circular path I'd walked for the past two years, or I could take the only exit available to me.

The first option was comfortable and familiar, the latter

unknown and scary as fuck. I didn't want to end up betrayed and lied to again.

But Jules was right. Holding onto anger *was* exhausting, and I was already so fucking tired these days. Physically, mentally, emotionally.

Sometimes, it was a struggle just to breathe.

"It's been almost two years." I was halfway to the exit, but I couldn't bring myself to take the leap just yet. "Why bring this up now?"

"Because you're the most stubborn person I've ever met. If someone tries to push you in one direction, you'll do your best to go in the other." Dry humor laced his words. "But what I did was wrong, and I am...sorry. For the most part."

What the fuck? "That's the worst damn apology I've ever heard."

"I don't aspire to be the type of person who apologizes so much that they're good at it."

Typical Alex logic.

"But if I hadn't done what I did, we would've never been friends, and my life..." Another, longer pause. "My life would be half of what it is today," he finished softly.

The burn in my chest spread, and my throat flexed. "You're becoming sentimental, Volkov. Don't let your business opponents know or they'll eat you alive."

"Au contraire. More sentimentality in my personal life means more steam I need to let off elsewhere. It's been very lucrative for business." Alex oozed satisfaction.

"I'm sure it has." I passed my hand over my face again, trying to figure out where to go from here. This was not how I'd envisioned the day going when I woke up. "You know we can't just go back to being best friends again and pretend like the past didn't happen, right?"

The line of his jaw turned rigid. "I know."

"But...if you want to catch a Nats game or something when we're back in D.C., I wouldn't be opposed," I added gruffly.

Alex relaxed, and a smile flickered over his mouth. "You miss the box seats, don't you?"

"Hell yeah. I'm open to bribery if you would like to get back into my good graces."

"I'll keep that in mind."

I finished my second drink before I asked, "How did you know Ava was the one?"

I'd never been in love. I didn't particularly want to be, but I wanted to know what cracked Alex's stony heart. Before Ava, I could imagine a robot more capable of feeling than the man sitting next to me.

"I like being with her."

"No shit. Be more specific."

He sighed. "It's easy being with her," he said after a long moment. "She understands me in a way no one else does, even if our worldviews are fundamentally different. When I'm not with her, I wish she were there. When I *am* with her, I want that moment to last forever. She makes me want to be a better person, and when I think about a world where she doesn't exist..." His jaw flexed. "I want to burn every inch of it to the ground."

I stared at him. "Holy fuck. Who are you and what the fuck have you done to Alex Volkov?" I clapped him on the back. "Whoever you are, you should write for the murderous edition of Hallmark."

Alex glared at me. "Tell anyone I said that, and I will skin you alive with a rusted knife to prolong the pain."

"Exactly. Just like that. So murderously romantic."

"Your box seats are skating on thin ice, Chen."

"Hey, remember. *I'm* the one who has to forgive *you*. Be nice." I motioned the bartender for another drink.

Despite my jokes, my brain couldn't stop replaying Alex's words.

*When I'm not with her, I wish she were there. When I **am** with her, I want that moment to last forever.*

I'd never felt that way toward a woman...except for one.

Unbidden images from the past two months ran through my head. Me and Jules beneath the tree at the picnic. Me telling her about Tanya's death in the library. The adorable way her brow scrunched when she was concentrating and the proud smile that lit up her face when I finally proclaimed her ready for the bunny slope in Vermont.

The way she laughed, the way she tasted, and the way I felt when I was with her, like I never wanted her to leave.

I'd chalked all that up to a mixture of lust and blossoming friendship, but what if...

No. Fuck no.

Sweat misted my palms. I tossed back my drink without tasting it.

I did not *like* Jules. Half our fucks were hate fucks. They were hot, but just because I liked fucking her didn't mean I wanted anything else from her.

So what if she wasn't as terrible as I originally envisioned? She was still *her*.

Infuriating, snarky, a pain in my fucking ass...and loyal. Passionate. So beautiful sometimes it hurt to look at her.

What would I do in a world where Jules didn't exist? I wouldn't *burn it down*, but...

Fuck, why was it so hot in here?

My phone vibrated with an incoming call. I answered it, relieved for the distraction. I would take a hundred telemarketers over my wildly disturbing thoughts.

"Hello?" I didn't recognize the number, but it contained Eldorra's country code. Maybe it was the palace or something.

"Hey, it's me," Ava said. She sounded subdued.

"What's up? Aren't you supposed to be at the club right now?"

My short-lived relief at the distraction faded when she explained her situation. *God motherfucking dammit.* I'd wanted more excitement earlier, but I should've fucking clarified, because this was *not* what I had in mind. "Okay. I'll be right there...no. We'll talk about it later."

Alex's brows formed a deep V as he listened to my end of the call.

"What's wrong?" he asked after I hung up.

"It's Ava and the girls." I stood and shrugged on my jacket, already halfway out the door. "They got arrested."

30

JULES

In my defense, I had a good reason for breaking a guy's nose and inadvertently starting a club fight. The dickhead had grabbed Ava's ass and started grinding on her even after she said no and tried to push him off. When my and Stella's attempts at intervention also failed, I did what I had to do. I tapped his shoulder, waited for him to turn around, and sucker punched him in the face.

His friends had jumped into the fray, and, well, you can guess where it went from there.

In the US, the incident would've ended with us thrown out of the club, but Eldorra's strict public disturbance laws landed all of us, Dickhead and friends included, in the lovely county jail.

"At least Br—our other friend wasn't with us," I said, opting for optimism. "*That* would've been a mess."

Ava and Stella murmured in agreement.

Bridget was a common Eldorran name, but I erred on the side of caution in case the officer leading us toward the exit pieced two and two together. Then again, we'd had to provide our real names when we were booked. If anyone on staff paid attention to the tabloids, they would recognize us as Bridget's bridesmaids, no matter how good a job the makeup artist had done in disguising us.

I adjusted my brunette wig. Between the wig, my colored contacts, and the makeup artist's mind-blowing skills, I barely recognized myself *or* my friends. It'd allowed us to enjoy the club in peace until Bridget left early because she had a morning interview with *Vogue Eldorra*. However, she'd insisted we stay and party given it was our last night of "freedom" before the wedding insanity.

At the time, it'd seemed like a good idea. Now, after three hours of detainment and the prospect of facing a furious Josh, it seemed like a monumental mistake.

Anxiety speared my stomach as we stepped into the reception area.

We'd used our one phone call on Josh, asking him to bail us out. Well, Ava had. She could've called Alex, but she was worried he'd freak out, so she'd phoned her brother instead while she figured out how to explain the situation to her boyfriend. Josh would also freak out, but to a lesser extent than Alex.

As it turned out, we needn't have gone through the trouble.

Alex and Josh *both* waited in the exit area, their faces carved with tension.

"Are you okay?" Alex crossed the room in two long strides and gripped Ava's arms. Worry blazed in his eyes as he searched her for injuries.

Luckily, other than my swollen knuckles, Dickhead's broken nose, and a couple of bruised egos, we'd escaped unscathed.

"I'm fine," Ava reassured him. "Really."

Alex's lips pressed together, but he didn't say anything else as we exited the building and climbed into the town car waiting outside.

Thick silence muffled the luxurious interior while Ava, Stella, and I removed our disguises and wiped off our makeup using the baby wipes I'd stashed in my clutch. The makeup artist had contoured my nose into a different shape, added an alarmingly realistic mole on my upper lip, and drawn thicker, darker eyebrows that matched my wig. Watching the mask melt away in the car's window reflection as I scrubbed a wipe over my face was a bit surreal.

Josh and Alex hadn't said a word about our disguises when they saw us, and they didn't say anything now as we took them off.

Alarm prickled my stomach. Usually, Josh would be the first to make a smartass comment, so his silence didn't bode well.

Alex spoke again halfway to our hotel. "What," he said, his voice so chilly it triggered a rash of goosebumps on my arms, "the hell happened?"

My friends and I exchanged glances. Ava gave Josh a brief rundown earlier, but he didn't know the details, and we couldn't tell Alex the truth.

"Some guy groped me, and I punched him," I said, taking creative liberty with the truth. "It escalated from there. Who knew Eldorra had such strict laws about club fights?"

Ava cast a startled glance in my direction. She opened her mouth, but I frowned and flicked my eyes at Alex.

She closed her mouth, though she didn't look happy about it. She knew as well as I did that if Alex found out some guy had groped her, he would commit murder, and we didn't need that kind of bloodshed two days before Bridget's wedding.

A shadow passed over Josh's face at my reply, but he stayed silent.

"I see." Alex's expression was unreadable, but he smoothed a stray strand of hair out of Ava's eye with more gentleness than I thought him capable of. "How does the other guy look?"

I cracked a smile. "I broke his nose."

A hint of a smirk filled Alex's mouth before it flattened again. "Good. I paid a *significant* sum of money to wipe those police charges off your records, so it better have been worth it."

He pulled Ava closer to him and kissed the top of her head while she curled up against his side. He whispered something in her ear, and she murmured something back that eased the tension in his shoulders.

It was a casual, domestic scene. Nothing extraordinary. Yet it triggered a longing so fierce and unexpected I had to turn away.

I firmly believed people didn't need a significant other to be happy. If someone wanted to be in a relationship, great. If they didn't, also great. The same went for children, marriage, etc. There were no universal barometers for happiness. A person's life could be just as fulfilling without a romantic partner as it was with one.

But there were times, like now, when I yearned to experience that kind of unconditional love. To have someone care for me through the good, the bad, and the inevitable mistakes I made.

What would it be like to be loved so deeply by someone I wouldn't have to worry about every little move possibly driving them away?

*"No, no, no!" My mom ripped the curling iron from my hand. "Look at this mess you made." She gestured at the curls I'd spent the past hour perfecting. "Alastair will be here soon, and I look like I'm wearing a rat's nest on my head. How many times do I have to teach you how to do this? What good is it having a daughter if you can't do one **simple** thing right?"*

My teeth dug into my bottom lip. "But I did it exactly like you—"

"Don't talk back to me." Adeline dropped the still-hot iron on the table and yanked a brush through her hair with sharp, hard strokes, undoing all my work. "You did this on purpose, didn't you? You want me to be ugly." Her eyes welled with tears. "Now I have to fix your mess."

My teeth dug harder into my lip until the coppery taste of blood filled my mouth. She didn't look like a mess at all. She looked beautiful, as always. My mom wasn't as young as in the beauty pageant pictures she displayed all over the house, but her skin was still smooth and unlined. Her hair was a rich auburn, and her body was the envy of every woman in town.

Everyone said I looked like her, especially now that my skin had cleared and I'd **finally** graduated to a real bra. Boys were starting to pay attention to me, including Billy Welch, the cutest boy in my eighth-grade class.

I thought my mom would be happy I looked like her, but every time someone mentioned it, her face darkened, and she'd make an excuse to leave.

"Go. I don't want to look at you anymore." Adeline's eyes raked over me from head to toe. Her anger multiplied until it became a tangible, snarling monster in the room. "Go!"

The tears finally spilled down my cheeks.

I ran out of her room and into mine. I slammed the door behind me and crawled into my bed, where I tried to muffle my cries with my pillows. Our walls were so thin she could probably hear me, and my mom hated when I cried. She said it was unbecoming.

My hiccupping sobs filled the room.

She was right to be mad. She had a big date with the richest man in town, who could take care of all our money troubles if they got married like she wanted.

What if I ruined it by messing up her hair? What if he broke up with her and she hated me forever for it?

My mom and I used to be best friends, but I couldn't do anything right these days, and she kept getting mad at me.

After I ran out of tears to cry, I wiped my eyes with the back of my hand and took a deep, shuddering breath.

It's okay. It'll be okay.

Next time, I'll do her hair right. Then my mom will love me again. I was sure of it.

I blinked back the burn in my eyes at the memory.

My phone buzzed against my thigh as we pulled up to the hotel. My stomach cramped when a candid photo of me arriving in Athenberg popped up. Some dipshit at the airport must've taken it.

Max: Saw this on a gossip blog. Looking good, J.

Max: But we both know you've always looked good on camera

I hated these "casual" texts more than I hated Max's overtly threatening ones. They were a constant reminder of his presence in my life. Every time I relaxed an inch, another one popped up, setting me on edge again.

Of course, that was his intention. Max wanted to torture me with the uncertainty, and he was fucking succeeding.

I wiped my clammy palms against the sides of my thighs as I exited the car and entered the hotel. Alex, Josh, Ava, Stella, and I rode the elevator up to our floor in silence, and my friends had already disappeared into their rooms when Josh's voice stopped me in my tracks.

"I want to talk to you for a second."

I stiffened, my stomach cramping again for an entirely different reason. The last thing I needed was to get yelled at by Josh, of all people.

Still, I stepped into his suite without protest, and the door shut behind us with a soft click.

We were taking a huge risk, considering our close call with Ava earlier that day, but that was the least of my worries right now.

Josh didn't say a word, but he didn't need to. His silent judgment pricked at me, familiar and stinging.

I could guess what he was thinking.

That it was my fault. That I was a bad influence. That I'd dragged Ava into trouble yet again.

It was always my fault.

"Just say it." I stared at the dark flat-screen TV hanging on the wall, taking in my messy hair and tired face. This night turned out to be a total nightmare. My only consolation was that Bridget left before shit went downhill so she didn't have the added stress before her wedding.

My chin wobbled when Josh closed in enough for his body heat to envelop me.

"Are you okay?" he asked quietly. He cupped the back of my neck and rubbed small circles with his thumb.

Pressure ballooned in my chest at his touch. "Yep."

"Jules, look at me."

I pressed my lips together and shook my head, afraid doing so would destroy the flimsy dam holding my tears back.

"Jules." Josh stepped in front of me and grasped my chin between his thumb and forefinger. He tilted it up, forcing me to meet his eyes. Visible concern eroded his granite mask. "What's wrong?"

"Nothing. I'm tired and I want to sleep, so just yell at me like you always do and get it over with."

Surprise coasted through his eyes. "What are you talking about?"

I rubbed my arms, wishing I'd worn something more

substantial than my green silk minidress. "Tonight. Ava got arrested because of me, I'm a bad influence, etc. I'm familiar with the script by now. You've never thought I was good enough."

A muscle ticked along the line of his strong jaw. "I never said that."

"But you were thinking it."

Josh dropped his hand and rubbed it over his face. "I'll admit, when I received Ava's call, I was pissed that you guys had gotten into trouble again, but more than that, I was *worried*. Not only about her..." His voice dropped. "But also about you."

"Why?"

"Why what?"

"Why do you care?"

Silence hummed in the space between us, so taut it threatened to snap at any second.

Josh's Adam's apple bobbed with the force of his swallow, but he didn't reply.

My heart twisted. *Right*. That was what I thought.

"You don't have to pretend to care just because we're having sex."

Fake concern was a thousand times worse than no concern at all, because fake concern gave way to false hope, and false hope destroyed souls. It was one of the biggest lessons I'd learned in my early years. All the times I thought someone cared about me when they only wanted something from me, and when they got it, they tossed me aside without a second thought. Until, of course, they needed something again.

"I heard what you said," I added through the lump in my throat. "To Ava."

A frown creased Josh's brow. "What are you talking about?"

"Freshman year. Our dorm." Part of me was embarrassed,

bringing up something from so long ago, but the moment had clung to me like ivy, its poison slowly eating away at me over the years. "I heard you tell her to stop being friends with me."

I hitched the strap of my bag higher on my shoulder as I walked down the hall toward my room. My professor had an emergency and couldn't make it to campus, so I had an extra hour to kill. Maybe I could check out one of the indie bookstores near campus after I dropped off my textbook.

Outside, gray clouds threatened rain, and there was nothing cozier than browsing a bookstore during a rainstorm. I could already hear the quiet flip of pages and smell the uniquely sweet musk of old books.

I stopped outside my room and fished my key card out of my bag, but before I could open the door, a deep voice floated through the thin wood.

"Why can't you switch roommates? I'm sure the housing office will accommodate you once you explain the situation with Jules."

I froze, my heart suddenly pounding too fast for comfort.

"Because I don't want to switch roommates, Josh." Ava's firm refusal warmed some of the chill on my skin. "She's my friend."

"You've only known her for two months, and she's already getting you into trouble," Josh argued. "Look at what happened with the clock tower."

*Heat prickled my face. Maybe sneaking into Thayer's off-limits clock tower to drink wasn't the **best** idea, but it'd been fun, and Ava had wanted to do something crazy. Plus, campus security released us with a slap on the wrist after they caught us, so we hadn't gotten into huge trouble or anything.*

"She didn't make me go there at gunpoint," Ava said. "What is your problem with Jules? You've been on her case since you met her."

"*Because I look at her and I already know she's trouble waiting to happen. Hell, she's trouble that **already** happened.*" Josh sighed. "*Yes, you're roommates, but you barely know her. You can make other friends, Ava. She's bad news. You don't need someone like that in your life.*"

I'd heard enough.

I spun on my heels and speed-walked toward the exit, hurt blooming in my chest before it gave way to anger.

*Fuck Josh. We'd interacted maybe four times, and he was already passing judgment on me based on **one** incident.*

He didn't know me like he thought he did. But I already knew I hated him.

Josh's tan leached of color. "That was seven years ago," he said in a low voice. "People change. So do opinions."

"Did yours? Because until we started having sex, you treated me the same as you did in college."

He flinched. "Look, I shouldn't have said what I said, but I...I'm protective of Ava, especially after what happened when we were kids. You know as well as I do how trusting she is, and sometimes, she trusts the wrong people. I know now you're not one of them, but I barely knew you back then. I was worried, and I overreacted."

"What about the years after that?" I couldn't shake the sting from the memory. "You've never liked me."

"Because you didn't like *me!*" Josh pushed a hand through his hair. He was close enough I could *feel* the frustration pouring off him. "We got caught in this cycle of insulting and hating each other, and I didn't know how to break it."

"So what changed? Besides sex."

"It's not..." He faltered, and the lump in my throat magnified.

"Exactly." *Don't cry. Don't cry.* "Stop with the fake concern, Josh. It's disingenuous."

His nostrils flared, and for the first time that night, anger glinted in his eyes. "For someone who's so pissed about me making assumptions about her, you're making an awful fuck lotta assumptions about me."

"It doesn't mean they're wrong."

I didn't finish speaking before Josh closed the distance between us and crashed his mouth over mine. I clutched his arms, willing the ache in my chest away even as my body responded to his.

"Is that what you want, then?" he growled against my lips. "Just sex, no feelings?"

"That was always the plan." I injected forced lightness into my tone. "Unless you're not up for it."

"It's like you live to piss me off, Red." His grip turned to steel around my wrists before he released them. "Get on your knees."

By the time my knees hit the carpet, he'd already undid his belt and pants, and heat coiled in my belly.

This. *This* was what I was comfortable with.

Not deep conversations or friendship or hope for some type of future. Just sex. It was all I'd ever given, and all anyone wanted from me.

I closed my eyes when Josh entered me, losing myself to the sensations of his body moving over mine. He played me like the world's most erotic song, and despite the high emotion of the night, I still came with enough force to temporarily wipe my mind blank.

But when the orgasmic bliss floated away, the pressure behind my ribcage returned, stronger than ever.

Josh's harsh breaths sounded deafening in the silence, and a crazy, horrifying part of me wanted to stay here and listen to him breathe forever.

"Get off me."

We were both still on the floor. His body caged mine, and I could feel his every inhale and exhale against my back.

"Jules..." His raw voice scraped against my shredded nerves.

This was a mistake. Everything was a mistake.

"I said *get off me.*" I shoved him off and scrambled to my feet, straightening my clothes with trembling hands.

Josh watched me, his face taut with regret and something else I couldn't identify, but he didn't say a word when I left.

I waited until I returned to my room and stepped into the shower before I collapsed beneath the weight of the night.

The arrest, Max, Josh, *everything.* It all barreled into me until I sank onto the floor and curled my knees up to my chest, letting myself truly cry for the first time in years.

My tears mingled with the water, and I stayed there until the shower ran cold and there was nothing left except for silence.

31

JULES

I ALLOWED MYSELF ONE PITY PARTY A YEAR, SO AFTER MY shower breakdown, I gathered myself together and pushed thoughts of Max and Josh aside until after the wedding.

Luckily, the palace kept us busy with rehearsals, pre-wedding parties, and protocol lessons, and before I knew it, the ceremony was only half an hour away.

Bridget, Ava, Stella, Bridget's sister-in-law Sabrina—her matron of honor as dictated by protocol—and I were gathered in the bridal suite for one last check before we entered the cathedral where the wedding would take place.

Seven thousand guests. Live broadcast to millions of viewers around the world.

Nerves fluttered in my stomach.

"I know I've said it before, but thank you guys so much for being here." Bridget's eyes shimmered with emotion as she looked around at us. "I know the preparations have been crazy, and the scrutiny isn't easy, so I appreciate it."

"We wouldn't miss it for the world." Stella squeezed her

hand, her eyes glowing with a mix of happiness and melancholy.

The same contradictory emotions dripped through me as the clock counted down to the ceremony. I was truly happy for Bridget, especially after everything she and Rhys went through to be together, but her marriage marked the end of an era.

My friends and I were growing up. We were no longer the young, carefree students we once were. We hadn't been in a long time, but somehow, Bridget's wedding drove that fact home harder than her coronation had.

Gone were the days of impromptu weekend trips, late night spa sessions in our dorm, and weekly catchups over coffee and scones at The Morning Roast.

Now, Ava lived with Alex and was constantly traveling for her job. Bridget was a literal *queen* and about to get married. And Stella was so busy with the magazine and her blog I barely saw her, even though we were roommates.

But when we *were* together, it was like old times again, and I would never take that for granted.

"Tell Rhys to treat you right or he'll have to answer to us," Stella added.

Despite her threat, we knew we didn't need to worry. Rhys treated Bridget like a queen even before she ascended to the throne.

Bridget's soft laugh contained a touch of wateriness. "I will."

Someone knocked on the door. Freja, the palace's communications secretary, entered and dipped her head at Bridget.

"Your Majesty. Are you ready?"

Apprehension cascaded across Bridget's face for the first time that day, but she straightened her shoulders and nodded.

We did one last hair and makeup check before we filed

downstairs and across the long hallway connecting the guest-house and ancient cathedral.

The doors opened, and every thought except not tripping during my endless walk down the aisle faded.

Prime ministers. Royalty. Celebrities. *Josh.*

All in the audience staring at me, but of the thousands of pairs of eyes, one in particular seared into me when I passed the pews reserved for the bride and groom's close friends and family.

My heartbeat drummed louder.

I took my place at the altar and trained my eyes on the entrance, determined not to look at a certain friend's brother in the crowd.

*Don't look. Don't look. Do **not** look.*

Bridget entered on the arm of her grandfather, the former King Edvard, and an awed hush blanketed the crowd.

Across the altar, Rhys fell unnaturally still. His eyes locked onto Bridget's, and his face glowed with such love it made my heart squeeze. A meteor could've landed in the cathedral and he wouldn't have been able to tear his eyes away from her.

Bridget's returning smile was visible even beneath her lace veil. The moment stretched between them, so raw and intimate I felt like I was intruding despite the thousands of guests surrounding us.

I blinked away the tears gathering in my eyes. I wasn't crying. I was expelling excess moisture. That was all.

But when the archbishop started the ceremony, I couldn't stop myself from scanning the pews to tamp down my emotion. The last thing I needed was to ugly cry on live television.

My gaze skipped over a handful of recognizable European royals, a world-famous pop singer, and the up-and-coming soccer star Asher Donovan before it snagged on Josh.

So much for not looking at him.

He sat in the second row behind the royal family, devastating in a black tuxedo. He'd tamed his hair into a neat style that emphasized the finely chiseled lines of his cheekbones, and his coal dark eyes burned into mine with an intensity that seeped beneath my skin.

Thud. Thud. Thud.

My heartbeat drowned out the archbishop's voice as Josh's eyes held me captive.

I should look away before my face broadcast to the world what I wasn't ready to admit myself.

And the fact that I couldn't terrified me more than any blackmail or monster from my past could.

32

JOSH

IF REGULAR WEDDING CEREMONIES WERE LONG, ROYAL ceremonies were interminable.

The novelty of being surrounded by the world's richest and most famous faded fast the longer I sat on that ass-numbing wooden pew. I was happy for Bridget and Rhys, but all I could think about was Jules.

The way we left things the other night gnawed at me, and if we didn't clear the air soon, I would fucking lose it.

I stared at her as she stood at the altar. She wore the same purple dress and carried the same bouquet as the other bridesmaids, but she glowed in a way that made it impossible to look away.

I traced her features with my eyes, soaking in the lush curve of her lips and the fine planes of her features. When she smiled at Bridget's entrance, something tripped in my heart.

Some people smiled with their mouths; Jules smiled with her whole face. The sparkle in her eyes, the adorable crinkle of her nose, the small crease in her cheek...watching her smile was like watching the night sky light up with stars.

My muscles tightened when she scanned the pews. If she turned just one more inch...one more centimeter...

Our eyes met. Held.

White hot sparks of awareness blazed down my spine with such force I almost lurched off my seat. I curled my hand around my knee while Jules's smile dimmed and her face flared with equal awareness.

The music drifting through the cathedral faded away, and I was gripped by the sudden urge to storm over to the altar and whisk her away to somewhere we could be alone.

A moment of eye contact wasn't enough. I needed...fuck, I didn't know what I needed. To apologize, to explain, to make her smile at me again the way she did before the other night.

I hadn't spoken to Jules since the night of Bridget's bachelorette. Forty-eight hours, and her absence was already eating me alive.

*When I'm not with her, I wish she were there. When I **am** with her, I want that moment to last forever.*

Sweat coated my palms.

I'd replayed the other night over and over again since it happened.

The unshed tears in her eyes. The hurt in her voice when she told me she overheard me talking to Ava. The way she just *left* after we had sex.

It was the first time we'd truly adhered to the rules of our arrangement. Even our quickies at the beginning ended with some conversation. I thought I would welcome it, but all I'd wanted was to pull her back into my room and kiss away all her hurt.

I made it a point to keep my promises, but my vow to bring our relationship back to sex-only status had died faster than a moth flying into a lamp.

Bridget walked down the aisle and cut off my view of Jules

for a second. By the time she passed, Jules had already looked away. Her eyes were now fixated on the archbishop, so determined I suspected she was making it a point *not* to look at me again.

My hands fisted on the pew next to me.

We were in the same room, but I still missed her so much a moment of broken eye contact sent a deep ache spiraling through my chest.

What the fuck did *that* say about me?

*When I'm not with her, I wish she were there. When I **am** with her, I want that moment to last forever.*

The sweat on my palms intensified.

It couldn't be because...I couldn't possibly...

The past two months raced through my head at warp speed. Everything from Vermont to the other night blurred together into one jumbled stream until cold realization rattled my lungs.

Mother*fucker*.

BY THE TIME THE CEREMONY ENDED AND THE RECEPTION rolled around, I was a coil of raw nerves and tightly wound emotion, and it finally snapped when I saw Jules laughing with Asher Donovan near the dance floor.

I'd tried to talk to her multiple times since we left the cathedral, but she always had some bridesmaid duty to fulfill.

Now that she was finally free, she was flirting with Asher fucking Donovan?

I didn't fucking think so.

I stormed over to them and nearly bowled over the Prime Minister of Denmark in my haste. My heart pounded out a hard, territorial rhythm with each step.

Mine. Mine. Mine.

Up until this moment, Asher had been one of my sports idols, but I wanted to gouge his fucking eyes out for looking at her like that. Like she could possibly be his when she so clearly, irrevocably belonged to *me*.

Asher's eyebrows shot up when he noticed my approach.

"Excuse me." I forced a tight smile. "I'd like to speak with Jules."

Jules's shoulders visibly tensed. Instead of looking at me, she kept her eyes on the other man.

My blood burned.

I'd never been jealous over a woman before, and I hated how it made me feel. Like I was a train barreling toward the side of a mountain, out of control and on the verge of snapping.

"Sure." Asher's green eyes glinted with amusement. "Jules, it was nice meeting you."

"You too." She smiled at him, and the fire in my blood burned hotter. "Let's meet up the next time you're in D.C. You have my number."

Meet up? Number? What the *fuck*?

"I'd love to." Asher kissed her on the cheek. Possessiveness burst, hot and ugly, in my chest. I wanted to yank him off her and deck him in his stupid pretty boy face. "See you around."

Jules waited until he was out of earshot before turning to me. "Yes?"

"What the fuck was that?" I tried and failed to keep the territorial growl out of my voice.

"What was what?"

My jaw locked at her cool, impersonal tone. "*That.*" I gestured in the soccer star's direction. "With Asher. Why the fuck does he have your number?"

"Because I gave it to him." Jules raised her brows. "Is that why you so rudely interrupted us? Because we were in the middle of a conversation, and if you don't have anything substantial to say, I'd like to continue it."

I was tempted to drag her over my lap and spank her for her insolent tone, but there was something more important we needed to discuss besides Asher.

We could deal with him later.

"We need to talk. Alone." I glanced at our friends, but they were too busy on the dance floor to pay attention to us.

"I'm busy, Josh. I have bridesmaid duties to fulfill."

"They're fulfilled."

Bridget and Rhys already had their first dance and cut the cake, and all the guests were busy dancing, getting drunk, or gossiping on the sidelines.

World leaders: they were just like us.

"Oh, of course." Jules placed a hand over her chest. "I defer to your vast experience as a bridesmaid. You clearly know exactly what the role entails."

My knuckles tightened. We were backsliding into our old, bickering selves. Normally, I would've welcomed it as a sign of normality, but right now, it pissed me the hell off.

"Outside in five minutes, Red, or I'll bend you over my lap and spank your ass raw right here in front of every goddamn king, queen, and president in the world," I growled.

A dark pink flush rose on Jules's cheeks. "Don't tell me what to do."

"Then don't test me."

I turned on my heel and stalked out of the ballroom.

Jules must've heard the truth in my threat because she met me outside the party exactly five minutes later, her jaw set in a stubborn line.

We walked down the hall until we reached an unlocked drawing room. I shut the door behind us, and then...silence.

We stared at each other, the air heavy with old hurts and unspoken words.

You've never thought I was good enough.

I heard what you said. To Ava.

So what changed? Besides sex.

My irritation at seeing her with Asher slowly drained away, replaced with guilt and shame. I hadn't known Jules was listening, but I still felt like an asshole for what I said.

"What do you want to talk about?" Jules asked, her tone as stiff as her shoulders.

"I want to..." I hesitated, wishing I had something more sufficient than words. "Apologize."

Once upon a time, delivering an apology to Jules Ambrose would've been as painful as cutting out my own tongue. Now, the words tumbled out with relative ease.

I understood why Jules was upset. She was right. I'd been an asshole.

I should've apologized the other night, but I'd been so taken aback by the revelation I couldn't think of a proper response. Not only to what happened with Ava, but to her follow-up questions.

So what changed? Besides sex.

Everything.

That was what I should've said, had I not been too blind to see it and too chickenshit to say it.

Ours started as a sex-only arrangement, but it'd never been about just sex. Even when I thought I hated her, I was already softening toward her. Every smile, every laugh, and every conversation chipped away at the image I'd constructed of her in my mind until I was left with someone I didn't know but couldn't bear to let go of.

"You already apologized," she said.

"No, I didn't." I took another step toward her. "I'm sorry for asking Ava to end her friendship with you. It was fucked up."

Jules looked away. "It's fine."

"It's not. Even if I didn't mean for you to hear it, you did. I hurt you, and I'm sorry."

She shook her head. A tear cascaded down her cheek, glinting silver in the moonlight, and something in my chest cracked. "Once upon a time, you would've never apologized."

"Once upon a time, I was a dickhead."

"Who says you still aren't?"

A small smile curved my lips, but it disappeared when Jules spoke again.

"What are we doing, Josh? This is supposed to be just sex."

That was what I kept telling myself, too. But I was damn tired of pretending our arrangement hadn't evolved into something that couldn't be constrained by rules, and the thought that Jules believed I was using her for just sex, even if she'd consented to it, made my heart twist into a brutal knot.

I didn't have a problem with no strings attached sex. Hell, that was all I'd indulged in since I started *having* sex. But with Jules, it felt wrong, like a custom-made suit that still didn't fit right.

"There's a difference between what something is supposed to be and what it actually is, Red."

There it was. An admission thinly disguised as ambiguity.

It lingered in the air, which fell so silent I could hear the increased tempo of Jules's breath and every tick of the grandfather clock in the corner.

Tick. Tick. Tick.

I didn't know when I stopped hating Jules and started craving her. All I knew was that I did, and I never wanted to go back.

"Maybe there shouldn't be."

I stilled. "What," I said, my calm voice belying the sudden storm surging through my veins, "is that supposed to mean?"

Jules lifted her chin, but I detected a tiny tremble in her voice. "It means we should date other people. Our arrangement is non-exclusive. It's time we take advantage of that clause."

A dark, ugly beast reared its head and snarled in my chest. "The *fuck* we will."

Who the fuck could she possibly want to date, anyway? Asher Donovan? The fucker was a notorious womanizer, and he didn't even live in D.C.

"Those were the rules," Jules pointed out.

"Rules change."

"No." She inched back, a hint of panic creeping into her eyes. "Not with us."

"You've never had an issue bending the rules before."

I stepped toward her; she stepped back. A simple, ceaseless dance that ended until her back was pressed against the wall and less than an inch separated her mouth from mine.

"What are you so afraid of, Red?" My breath ghosted across her skin.

"I'm not afraid of anything."

"Bullshit."

"This was supposed to be simple."

"It's not."

There'd never been anything *simple* about her.

Jules was the most complicated, fascinating person I'd ever met.

She closed her eyes. "What do you want from me?" she asked, sounding resigned.

Another tear slipped down her cheek. I wiped it away with my thumb, fierce protectiveness rising inside me.

I didn't know what I wanted from her, but I knew I wanted *her*. I knew she haunted my thoughts and invaded my dreams until she was the only thing I could see. And I knew that being with her was one of the few times I truly felt alive.

"I want you." I didn't need to dress the truth up win flowery language; it was powerful enough on its own. "We're not dating other people, Red. I don't give a fuck what the original terms of our arrangement were. Do you want to know why?"

A hard swallow disrupted the delicate lines of her throat. "Why?"

I lowered my head and wound my hand through her hair, pulling her even closer to me.

"Because you're mine," I said against her mouth. "Let another man touch you, Jules, and you'll find out just how easily I can take a man's life as I can save one."

33

JULES

BECAUSE YOU'RE MINE. LET ANOTHER MAN TOUCH YOU, Jules, and you'll find out just how easily I can take a man's life as I can save one.

Josh's words played on a loop in my head like a beautiful, terrifying broken record. Four days later, and I've yet to find the pause button.

Even now, as I tapped away at my computer at LHAC, I sensed the whisper of Josh's declaration against my skin.

Our conversation had ended after that. We'd returned to the wedding, my heart a vigorous drum in my chest, my blood electric in my veins. It was like he'd wanted to engrave his words in my mind, and he'd succeeded.

What are you so afraid of, Red?

Everything.

I'd always been the good-time girl, the one who stuck to casual flings and pushed guys away before they got too close. Scared that if they looked too closely, they would see the real me, and the real me wouldn't be enough.

It hadn't been enough for my mom or Max. Sometimes, it wasn't enough even for me.

But Josh had seen the worst of me, *assumed* the worst of me, and he still wanted to stay. It was enough to induce that most dangerous of emotions: hope.

He's seen **most** *of the worst of you,* a taunting voice whispered in my head.

He didn't know about my past or the things I'd done for money. He never would. Not if I could help it.

"Jules."

I jumped, my heart thundering, before I relaxed. "Hey, Barbs."

The receptionist leaned against my cubicle and tapped the computer screen. "Time to go, hun. The office is closed."

I looked around, shocked to see the office had, in fact, emptied. I hadn't even noticed the others leave.

"Right." I rubbed a hand over my face. God, I was out of it. "Let me just close everything out first."

"No particular rush on my end." She eyed me with a speculative expression. "I was surprised Josh didn't come in today to celebrate the Bower case. It's his day off too."

We'd successfully cleared Terence Bower's criminal record, and we found out that morning that he'd landed a job that would tide the family over while his wife recovered. It was a big win for us, but even though I'd worked on the case since I started at LHAC, I couldn't summon much excitement.

I was too busy worrying over my life to celebrate someone else's, no matter how happy I was for them.

Still, my stomach fluttered at the sound of Josh's name. "Don't know why. You'll have to ask him." I saved the document I was working on and logged off.

"Hmm. I thought you would know, since you're friendly

and all." A mischievous gleam lit up Barbs's eyes. "You two would make a great-looking couple."

"Would we?" My cheeks heated, but I kept my voice even. "I imagine I'd carry most of the weight in that situation."

Her body shook with laughter. "See, you're what that boy needs. He's surrounded by too many *yes* people. All the women fawning over him and not questioning a single thing he says or does." She shook her head. "He needs someone to keep him on his toes. Too bad you're not interested...are you?"

She leaned forward, and I finally understood why the clinic staff called her the office matchmaker.

"Good night, Barbs," I said pointedly, earning myself another laugh.

"G'night, hun. We'll talk later." She winked before returning to her desk.

I packed up my belongings. It *was* odd that Josh didn't come in, but maybe he was catching up on rest. He'd been working overtime at the hospital to make up for the days he'd missed when he was in Eldorra. I hadn't seen him since we returned to D.C., and I'd been hesitant to text him.

After the way we left things, it seemed wrong for our first post-wedding interaction to be anything but face to face.

I also hadn't figured out how to respond to his implicit request to change our arrangement, so there was that.

My phone rang, dragging me out of my chaotic thoughts.

I was so distracted I answered it without checking the caller ID first. "Hello?"

"May I speak with Jules Miller, please?" an unfamiliar female voice asked.

I froze at the use of my old name. I was tempted to tell them they had the wrong number, but curiosity overwhelmed my sense of self-preservation.

"Speaking." I clutched the phone tighter to my ear.

"Ms. Miller, I'm calling from Whittlesburg Hospital. It's about Adeline Miller." Her voice gentled. "I'm afraid I have some sad news."

My stomach spiraled into free fall. *No.*

I knew what she was going to say before she said it.

"I'm sorry to tell you that Mrs. Miller died this afternoon..."

I barely heard the rest of her words through the roar in my ears.

Adeline Miller.

My mom.

My mom was dead.

34

JOSH

THE DOORBELL RANG WHEN I ALMOST WRESTLED MY suitcase closed. The unexpected sound startled me into loosening my hold on the shell, which popped open again with a smug thud.

"*Fuck.*"

I leave for New Zealand in four days. I've refused to check my luggage ever since an airline lost the suitcase containing my signed baseball trading cards when I was twelve, so I'd spent the past hour shoehorning a week's worth of hiking gear into a tiny carry-on.

All that work, down the drain.

"This better be fucking good." Irritation shot through my veins as I marched out of my room and to the front door.

I flung open the door, ready to rip whoever it was a new one, but my foul mood crumbled when I saw who stood on the front step.

"Hey." Jules wrapped her arms around her waist, her skin pale and her eyes suspiciously bright. "I'm sorry for dropping by unannounced, but I...I didn't know where..." Her wobbly smile crumpled. "I didn't want to be alone."

Her voice caught on the last word, and a blade of worry sliced through my insides.

"Fuck being sorry." I opened the door wider and scanned her for injuries as she stepped inside. No bleeding, no bruises, just that lost look on her face. Worry stabbed deeper in my gut. "What happened?"

"It's my mom." Jules swallowed hard. "The hospital called and said she was in a car accident. She—she's..." A small sob slipped out.

She didn't need to finish the sentence for me to guess what happened. But while I'd expected sympathy or even commiserating pain, nothing could've prepared me for the explosion in my chest.

One tiny sob from her, and every hidden explosive detonated, one by one, until pain burned through my lungs and rushed through my blood. It echoed in my head and squeezed my heart so tight I had to force myself to breathe through the ache.

"Come here, Red." The rough crack in my voice sounded foreign to my ears.

I opened my arms. Jules stepped into them, burying her face in my chest to muffle her cries, and it took all my willpower to hold back a visible reaction. I didn't want to heighten the wild emotion rampaging through the air, but *fuck,* seeing her hurting, hurt. More than I thought possible.

"Shhh." I rested my chin on top of her head and rubbed gentle circles on her back, wishing I weren't so damn helpless. I would've done anything, bargained with anyone, to erase her pain, but of all the skills I'd mastered over the years, bringing back the dead wasn't one of them. "It's okay. It'll be okay."

"I'm sorry." Jules hiccupped. "I know this—this i-isn't part of our arrangement, b-but A-Ava's a-at a photoshoot and S-Stella isn't home y-yet and I..."

"Stop saying sorry." I tightened my hold on her. "You have nothing to be sorry about. You can stay here as long as you'd like."

"But w-what about our—"

"Jules." My hand paused on her back for a second. "Shut up and let me hold you."

Her watery laugh lasted for a second before it dissolved into tears again. But fuck it, I'd take a second of her feeling better. I'd take half a second. Anything I could get.

Eventually, her sobs subsided into sniffles, and I guided her to the couch. "I'll be right back."

I didn't have time to grocery shop this week, so I placed a quick delivery order on my phone and fixed a cup of tea in the kitchen. My mom had firmly believed a good cup of tea could solve any problem, and though I rarely drank it myself these days, I always kept some on hand.

Tea and a hot water dispenser—two essentials in a Chinese household.

A pang pierced my chest at the thought of my mom. She'd died when I was a kid, but no one truly gets over the death of a parent.

Jules never talked about her family, so I assumed she had a fraught relationship with her mother, but her mom was still her mom.

I returned to the living room and handed her the drink.

"You didn't poison this, did you?" Her scratchy voice contained a hint of her usual sass.

Relief bloomed behind my ribs, and my lips curved at the callback to one of our earlier conversations.

"Just drink the damn tea, Red."

A shadow of a smile crossed Jules's mouth. She took a small sip while I sank next to her on the couch.

"They called when I was in the clinic," she said, staring into her mug. "The other car ran a red light and crashed into hers. Everyone died on impact. The hospital went through her belongings and found my number...I was the only family she had left."

She lifted her eyes to meet mine, her expression tortured. "I was the only family she had left," she repeated. "And I haven't talked to her in seven years. I had her number. I could've called her, but..." A visible swallow. "I kept telling myself, next year. Next year will be the year I call her and make amends. I never did. And now, I never will."

Jules's voice thickened with a fresh bout of unshed tears.

The ache in my chest hardened into stone.

"You couldn't have known," I said gently. "It was a freak accident."

"But if I hadn't put it off..." Jules shook her head. "The worst part is, I didn't think I would feel like...this." She gestured at herself. "My mom and I didn't part on good terms, to say the least. For years, I was *so angry* at her for what she did. I thought I would be *relieved* when she died, but I..." She sucked in a sharp inhale. "I don't know. I don't know how I feel. Sad. Angry. Ashamed. Regretful. And yes, a little relieved." Her knuckles whitened around her mug. "Is that terrible of me?"

"It sounds like you had a complicated relationship with your mother, and it's normal to feel all those things. Even relief."

I saw it all the time in the hospital. Some patients lingered on the verge of death without truly living or dying. When they finally passed, their families mourned, but they were also relieved that their loved one's suffering had ended. They didn't say it, but I saw it in their eyes.

Grief wasn't one emotion; it was a hundred emotions wrapped in a dark shroud.

Jules's situation wasn't quite the same, but the principle remained.

"Trust me. I'm a doctor," I added with a half smile. "I know everything."

My chest glowed at her soft laugh. Two laughs in less than an hour. I viewed that as a win.

"Were you close to your mom?" she asked. "Before..."

My smile faded. "Yeah. She was the best until the divorce. It got so nasty, and she became erratic. Moody. And when she was framed for trying to kill Ava...well, you know what happened." A lump of emotion lodged itself in my throat. "Like most people, I thought she tried to drown Ava. The doctors and police chalked it up to a mental break, but I still refused to talk to her for weeks after. We'd barely reconciled before she overdosed on antidepressants."

Jules's face softened with sympathy. "Sounds similar to my story. The beginning, at least." She traced the rim of the mug with her finger. "My mom and I were close when I was a kid. My dad left before I was born, so it was only the two of us. She loved dressing me up and parading me around town like I was a doll or an exclusive accessory. I didn't mind—I loved playing dress-up, and it made her happy. But when I got older, I started getting more attention than she did, especially from men, and she *hated* it. She never said it, but I could see it in her eyes every time someone complimented me. She stopped treating me like her daughter and started treating me like I was her competition."

Jesus. "She was jealous of her own daughter?"

I tried to keep the condemnation out of my voice, considering the woman had just died, but my stomach churned at the idea that a mother would compete with her child.

Jules let out a humorless laugh. "That's the thing about my mom. She was used to being the center of attention. Homecoming queen, prom queen, beauty queen. She won a bunch of pageants when she was younger and never got over her glory days. She was beautiful even when she was older, but she couldn't stand not being *the* most beautiful person in the room."

She took a deep breath. "My mom pursued modeling instead of attending college, but she never made it big. After she had me, the jobs dried up, and she became a cocktail waitress. Our town was cheap. We would've had an okay lifestyle, but she had a huge spending problem and racked up a bunch of credit card debt on clothes, makeup, beauty services...basically anything that helped her keep up appearances. Our bills fell by the wayside. There were some days when the only real food I ate was in the school cafeteria, and *many* days when I would come home, terrified that would be the day we got evicted."

I rubbed Jules's back with soothing strokes even as my jaw tensed at the description of her childhood.

Who the fuck would choose makeup and clothing over food for their kid?

But I'd witnessed enough ugliness in the world to know those people existed, and it made me sick that Jules had grown up with one of them.

"When I was thirteen, she got the attention of Alastair, the richest man in town, when he visited the bar where she worked," Jules continued, "They got married a year later. We moved to a big house, I received a generous allowance, and it seemed like all our problems were solved. But Alastair always..." The short pause was long enough for dread to solidify my insides. "...*watched* me and said things that made me wildly uncomfortable, like how nice my legs were or how I should wear skirts more often. But he didn't touch me, and I didn't want people to think I was overreacting to a few compliments, so I didn't say anything. Then one night, when I was seventeen and my mom was out with her friends, he came into my room and..."

I stilled. "And what?" The words vibrated with such eerie calm it was hard to believe they came out of my mouth.

"He said all this stuff about how I should be more grateful for everything he's done for me and my mom, and then he said I could *show* him how grateful I was by...you know."

Rage clouded my vision and painted the world in a film of bloody red. Darkness stirred in my chest, insidious in how slowly it uncoiled, like a monster lulling its prey into a false sense of security before it attacked.

"What happened after that?" Still calm, still flat, though razored tension ran sharp beneath my words.

"Of course, I said no. I yelled at him to get out and threatened to tell my mom what he said. He just laughed and said she'd never believe me. Then he tried to kiss me. I tried pushing him off, but he was too strong. *Luckily*..." Her mouth twisted at the word. "My mom came home early and caught us before he could...do anything else. He spun some story about how I'd tried to seduce him, and she believed him. She called me a whore for trying to seduce her husband and kicked me out that night."

The rage pulsed harder in my gut, expanding and intensifying until it shattered any morals I might've had.

I became a doctor to save lives, but I wanted to slice Alastair's skin off his body, strip by strip, and watch the life bleed from his eyes.

"I was able to withdraw enough money to scrape by for a few weeks before Alastair froze my accounts," Jules said. "I, um, worked odd jobs around town until college. After graduation, I left and haven't gone back since."

"Where's Alastair now?"

God help him if I ever found him, because I had zero compunction about turning my murderous fantasy into reality.

When it came to monsters who preyed on young girls or anyone I cared about, I didn't give a shit about the law. The law wasn't always justice.

"He died my junior year of college," Jules said. "House fire. I was still tracking what was happening back home at the time —call it morbid curiosity—and the news made it into the local papers. There were rumors of arson, but the police couldn't find any hard evidence, so the case went cold."

Alastair's death should've placated me, but it only pissed me off more. I didn't care if he'd burned alive; the bastard got off too fucking easy.

"My mom was out with friends at the time, so she was fine, but it turned out Alastair left her a pittance," Jules continued. "I'm not sure where the rest of his fortune went, but of course, my mom spent her inheritance within a year. She went from having everything to having nothing again." A bitter smile touched her lips. "That was also in the local papers. When you're as rich as Alastair was, in a town as small as Whittlesburg, everything that happens to you and your family is news."

A muscle ticked in my jaw. "And no one questioned the fact that they threw a seventeen-year-old out to fend for herself?"

"No. The townspeople made up their own rumors about how I was stealing from Alastair to fund my drug habit," she said flatly. "How they tried to get me help but it didn't work, they were at their wits' end, so on and so forth."

Jesus fucking Christ.

"The crazy part is, I still wanted to reconcile with my mom, especially after Alastair's death. She was my mom, you know? The only family I had. I called her, got her voicemail, and left my number. Asked her to call me back because I wanted to talk. She never did." Jules wrapped her hands tighter around the mug. "My ego took a huge blow, and that was the last time I reached out to her. But if I hadn't let my pride get in the way..."

"Communication is a two-way street." Some of my anger faded, replaced by a deep ache for the little girl who'd only wanted her mother's love. "She could've contacted you too. Don't be too hard on yourself."

Honestly, her mother sounded like a piece of fucking work, but I kept that to myself. Don't speak ill of the dead and all that.

"I know." Jules sighed. Distress carved tiny grooves in her forehead, but at least she'd stopped crying. "Anyway, enough about the past. It's depressing." She knocked her knee against mine. "You wouldn't make a half-bad therapist."

I almost laughed at the thought. "Trust me, Red. I'd make a terrible therapist." I could barely get my life together, much less advise people on theirs. "I just have experience with dysfunctional families, that's all."

The doorbell rang.

I reluctantly unfolded myself from the couch to answer the door and returned with two large brown paper bags.

"Comfort food," I explained, removing the takeout boxes from the bags.

Macaroni and cheese. Tomato soup. Salted caramel cheese-cake. Her favorites.

"I'm not hungry."

"Eat." I pushed a container of soup toward her. "You'll need the energy later. And drink more water or you'll be dehydrated."

Jules rewarded me with a tiny smile. "You're such a doctor."

"I'll take that as a compliment."

"You take everything as a compliment."

"Of course I do. I can't fathom why anyone would want to insult me." I removed the lid from the macaroni and cheese. "I'm extremely lovable."

"People who are extremely lovable don't have to keep saying it." Jules took a tiny sip of soup before setting it down.

"Most people aren't me." I speared a piece of cheesecake with a fork and handed it to her. After a moment's hesitation, she accepted.

We ate in companionable silence for a while until she said, "I have to fly to Ohio soon. For the funeral. But my graduation is on Saturday, and I have to make the arrangements, and I don't even know how much flights are. They can't be that expensive, right? But it's so last minute. And I have to figure out where I'm going to stay, and I have—"

"Breathe, Red." I placed my hands on her shoulders, steadying her. She was breathing faster again, her eyes taking on the wildness of overwhelm. "Here's what we're going to do. We're going to finish eating, then you're going to take a shower while I look up flights, hotels, and funeral homes. Once we nail those things down, we can focus on the details. And you are not flying to Ohio until after graduation. You went through three years of law school hell, so you're walking across that damn stage. Got it?"

Jules nodded, looking too stunned to argue.

"Good." I handed her the rest of the cheesecake. "Here. That shit's too sweet for me."

After we finished eating, she took a shower while I figured out the logistics of her trip. Luckily, flights to Ohio weren't expensive, and Whittlesburg had a total of two hotels, five bed and breakfasts, and a handful of sketchy-looking motels on the outskirts of town, so it wasn't hard to narrow the choices down.

A quick Google search also turned up a funeral home with good reviews and reasonable prices.

By the time Jules stepped out of the bathroom, I had everything ready to go on my laptop. She gave them a cursory glance before booking.

"Thank you." She sank onto my bed and ran a hand through her hair, still looking a little lost but more animated than before. "You didn't have to do all this." She gestured at my computer.

"I know, but it beats watching some crappy TV rerun for the tenth time."

Jules snorted. Her eyes fell on my open suitcase and widened. "Wait, your New Zealand trip. I forgot that's—"

"Not until next week. I leave Monday." Unease tugged at my gut. I'd been so excited for New Zealand, but my enthusiasm had waned, for some reason.

"That'll be fun." Jules yawned. She wore an old Thayer tee of mine that skimmed her thighs, and her damp hair hung in dark red waves around her shoulders.

Of all my favorite sights in the world—the Washington Monument at sunrise, the autumnal blaze of leaves during a New England fall, the expanse of ocean and jungle laid out before me at the end of a long hike in Brazil—Jules wearing my shirt might just be my number one.

"Get some rest," I said gruffly, discomfited by the strange warmth spiraling through my insides. "It's late, and you've had a long day."

"It's nine, Grandpa." She yawned again.

"Yeah? I'm not the one who looks like I'm trying to catch flies with my mouth." I shut my laptop and turned off all the lights except for my bedside lamp. "Bed. Now."

"You are so bossy. I swear..." *Yawn.* "I don't know how..."

Yawn. "People stand..." Jules's drowsy grumble grew softer with each word until her eyes fluttered closed.

I tucked her beneath the comforter, keeping my touch gentle so I didn't wake her. Her skin was paler than usual, and a touch of red still shaded the tip of her nose and the area around her eyes, but she fell asleep insulting me. If that wasn't proof she was feeling better, I didn't know what was.

I turned off the remaining light and climbed into bed next to her.

Our conversation from Bridget's wedding lingered, unresolved, between us. Did our original arrangement still stand, or had we morphed into something else? I had no clue. I didn't know what the fuck we were or what we were doing. I didn't know what Jules was thinking.

But we could deal with all that another day.

I curled my arm around her waist, tucked her closer to my chest, and, for the first time since our arrangement started, we slept together.

35

JULES

THE DAYS AFTER MY MOTHER'S DEATH PASSED IN A DAZE. When I woke up the next morning, Josh had already left for work, but I found breakfast waiting in the kitchen and a note with step-by-step instructions on what to do next. Which funeral home I should call, what questions I should ask, what I should pack for my trip.

It helped me more than any verbal platitudes could.

I checked off the items one by one, but I was like a robot going through the motions. I didn't *feel* anything. It was like I showed up at Josh's house, depleted every emotion, and now I was running dry.

I didn't know what made me turn to Josh when our relationship was already so complicated, but he was the first person who popped into my mind when I was trying to figure out what to do.

Strong. Comforting. Logical. He was everything I needed when I needed it.

Now, as I listened to the Whittlesburg funeral home director rattle off last-minute details, I wished Josh was still with me. Of course, that was unreasonable. He had work; he couldn't just up and join me in Ohio. Plus, he'd left for New Zealand that morning and wouldn't be back until next week.

A pang pierced my heart at the thought.

"That's everything we need. We should be all set for tomorrow." The funeral home director stood and held out his hand. "Again, I'm deeply sorry for your loss, Ms. Ambrose."

"Thank you." I mustered a smile. I'd used Ambrose instead of Miller since it was my legal name, but it sounded strange coming from his mouth. Ambrose belonged to my life in D.C. Miller belonged here.

Two lives, two different people.

Except here I was, Jules Ambrose in Ohio, and it was even more surreal than I imagined.

I shook his hand and quickly left, my steps eating up the distance between his office and the exit until the sun's golden warmth spilled over me. But once I was outside the dark, dreary confines of the funeral home, I didn't know where to go.

Just two days ago, I'd walked across the stage in D.C.'s Nationals Park, shook my dean's hand, and accepted my law school diploma.

Three years of hard work—seven, if you counted pre-law—distilled into one sheet of paper.

It was both glorious and anticlimactic.

In fact, I barely remembered my graduation. It'd passed in a blur, and I begged off dinner with my friends so I could pack for Ohio. I left the next morning, AKA yesterday, and had spent all my time thus far making funeral arrangements. It was a small, simple ceremony, but every decision exhausted me.

I was scheduled to fly back to D.C. after tomorrow morning's funeral. Until then, I had to figure out how to fill the rest of my afternoon and evening. There wasn't exactly a lot happening in town.

I stared at the lone flyer tumbling down the sidewalk, the used lot of rusted cars across the street, and the brown brick buildings squatting next to each other like weary travelers at a rest stop. Down the street, a group of children played hopscotch, their faint laughter the only signs of life in the stagnant air.

Whittlesburg, Ohio. A speck of a town near the relative behemoth of Columbus, extraordinary only in its utter ordinariness.

Being back was like walking through a dream. I expected to wake up any second, fumbling for the snooze button while the breathy scream of Stella's hair dryer crept beneath my door.

Instead of an alarm clock, a public bus roared past, drenching me in its exhaust and wrenching me out of my trance.

Gross.

I finally moved again. The funeral home sat on the outskirts of downtown, and it didn't take me long to reach Whittlesburg's social and financial center. It consisted of only half a dozen blocks of businesses packed side by side.

Not a dream.

I was actually here. There was the diner where my friends and I hung out after school dances. There was the bowling alley where we took field trips in elementary school, and the little antique shop with the creepy dolls in its window. Everyone was convinced the shop was haunted, and we would run every time we passed it, like the spirits who dwelled inside would reach out and snatch us if we lingered too long.

Returning to Whittlesburg was like entering a time capsule. Other than a shiny new chain restaurant and the cafe that had replaced old Sal's laundromat, it hadn't changed a bit in the past seven years.

I ducked my head and ignored the curious stares of a group

of high school girls clustered on the street corner. By some miracle, I hadn't run into anyone I knew yet, but it would only be a matter of time. I dreaded the questions that would arise once I did.

The thing about small towns was that they had long memories...for better or for worse.

I breathed a silent sigh of relief when I reached my hotel. Forget finding something to do in town. I just wanted to lock myself in my room, order room service, and watch pay-per-view all night long.

I reached into my bag, searching for my—

"Hey, Red."

I froze, my hand still half in my tote. Disbelief twisted my heart and quickened its pace until every beat pounded in my head like a drum.

Thud. Thud. Thud.

It couldn't be him. Maybe the milkshake I'd gulped down at lunch warped my brain and I was currently in the middle of a sugar-induced hallucination.

Because there was *no way* that was him.

But when I lifted my head, I saw his favorite gray sweatshirt. His worn duffel bag slung over his shoulder. His distinctive dimple as his lips curved into a smile so soft it obliterated all the edges of my resistance.

"Surprise." Josh's voice seeped through me like warm honey. "Missed me?"

"I—you..." My mouth opened and closed in what I presumed was a deeply unflattering imitation of a goldfish. "You're supposed to be in New Zealand."

"Change of plans." He shrugged with a casualness people reserved for a change in dinner orders, not international flights. "I'd rather be here."

"Why?"

Thudthudthud. Was it normal for a human heart to beat this fast?

"I want to visit the crochet museum."

Maybe I fell asleep at the funeral home and entered the Twilight Zone, because this was too absurd to be reality. "What?"

"The crochet museum," he repeated. "It's world famous."

Whittlesburg's crochet museum was the town's biggest attraction, but it wasn't world famous by any stretch of the imagination.

The Eiffel Tower, Machu Picchu, Great Wall of China... and the Betty Jones Crochet Museum? Yeah, no.

"World famous, huh?" Something strange and fluttery was happening in my stomach. I never wanted it to stop.

"Yep." Josh's dimple deepened. "Read about it in a magazine in an airport, and I was so inspired I changed flights last minute. I'll take crochet over sailing the Milford Sound any day."

A knot of emotion lodged itself in my throat. "Well, far be it for me to question your love for crochet." *Do not cry in the lobby.* "Are you staying at this hotel?"

"Depends." Josh stuffed his hand in his pocket, his eyes never leaving mine. "Do you want me to stay here?"

A small, scared part of me wanted to say no. It would be so easy to run up to my room and lock myself in there until my mom's funeral, then leave and pretend the trip never happened.

But I was so tired of running. So tired of fighting the world and myself at the same time, of pretending everything was okay when I struggled just to keep my head above water.

It was okay to reach for a life raft, no matter what form it came in.

Mine happened to come in the form of Josh Chen.

I dipped my head in a small nod, not trusting myself to speak.

His face softened. "Come here, Red."

That was all I needed.

I flew to him and buried my face in his chest while his arms closed around me. He smelled like soap and citrus, and his sweatshirt was soft against my cheek.

The curious stares of the receptionist and other hotel guests burned into my side. We would be the subject of town gossip by tomorrow, no doubt, but I didn't care.

For the first time since I landed in Ohio, I could breathe.

36

JOSH

I HADN'T PLANNED TO FLY TO OHIO.

I made it all the way to the airport for my New Zealand flight, but when boarding started, all I could think about was Jules. What she was doing, how she was doing, whether she'd landed safely. The hikes and activities I'd spent months planning held as much interest to me as watching paint dry.

So, instead of flying to my number two bucket list destination (after Antarctica), I'd headed straight to the ticket counter and bought the next flight to Columbus.

Trading New Zealand for Whittlesburg. I was truly fucked in the head, and I couldn't even bring myself to be mad about it.

"Gird your loins," Jules said as we made a left onto a quiet, tree-lined street. "You're about to get your mind blown."

After I dropped off my bag, I'd convinced her to join me on my museum outing. Perhaps I should've chosen a more interesting excuse than a crochet museum, but I read about it on my bus ride from Columbus and it was listed as the town's top attraction. That had to count for something, right?

My eyebrows rose. "Did you just use the phrase *gird your loins?* What are you, eighty?"

"For your information, Stanley Tucci's character uses it in *The Devil Wears Prada,* and both Stanley and the movie are amazing."

"Yeah, and how old is the amazing Stanley?"

Jules cast a sidelong glance in my direction. "I don't appreciate the snark, especially considering the free, in-depth tour I just gave you."

I fought a smile. "It was a fifteen-minute walk, Red."

"During which I pointed out the town's best restaurant, the bowling alley, the shop that had a ten-second cameo in a Bruce Willis movie, *and* the hair salon where I got bangs for a brief, horrifying time in high school," she said. "That's priceless information, Chen. You can't find that anywhere in guidebooks."

"I'm pretty sure I can find the first three in guidebooks." I tugged on a lock of her hair. "Not a fan of bangs?"

"Absolutely not. Bangs and pink eyeshadow. My hard nos."

"Hmm, I think you'd look good with bangs." Jules would look good with anything.

Even now, with purple shadows smudged beneath her eyes and lines of tension bracketing her mouth, she was so fucking beautiful I couldn't stop looking at her.

Her looks hadn't changed drastically over the years, but *something* had changed.

I couldn't put my finger on it.

Before, Jules was beautiful in the way grass was green and oceans were deep. It was a fact of life, but not something that particularly touched me.

Now, she was beautiful in a way that made me want to drown in her, to let her fill every inch of my soul until she fucking consumed me. It didn't matter if it killed me, because in a world where I was surrounded by death, she was the only thing that made me feel alive.

"Trust me, I don't. Anyway, enough about my hair." Jules swept her arm at the building before us. "Behold, the world-famous Betty Jones Crochet Museum."

My gaze lingered on her as we walked toward the entrance. "Looks impressive."

I couldn't have told you the color of the building if you put a gun to my head.

Half an hour and several mind-numbingly boring displays later, I finally yanked myself out of my Jules-induced trance, only to wish I hadn't.

"What the fuck is that?" I pointed at a blue crochet...dog? Wolf? Whatever it was, its face was lopsided, and its beady crystal eyes glinted menacingly at us from its perch on the shelf, like it was pissed we'd invaded its personal space.

This was what I got for being distracted. If I died at the hands of a haunted toy, I was going to be pissed.

Jules squinted at the little gold plaque beneath the wolf/dog. "It was one of Betty's daughter's favorite toys," she said. "Hand crocheted by a famous local artisan and gifted to her for her fifth birthday."

"It looks demonic."

"It does not." She stared at the toy, which glared back at us. I could've sworn its lip curled into a snarl. "But, uh, let's move on."

"You know what, I think I've had enough crochet for the day." I'd paid my dues. It was time to get the fuck out of here before the toys came to life a la *Night at the Museum*. "Unless you want to stare at more quilts and possessed toys."

Jules's mouth twitched. "You sure? You did abandon New Zealand for this *world-famous* museum. You should get your money's worth."

"Oh, I did." My money's *and* my nightmare's worth. I rested my hand on Jules's lower back and guided her toward the exit. "I'm good, trust me. I'd rather see the rest of town."

"We already saw most of it on our walk here. Everything else is residential."

Jesus. "There has to be something we missed. What's your favorite place in town?"

We stepped out into the dying afternoon light. Golden hour was melting into twilight, and long shadows stretched across the sidewalks as we walked toward downtown.

"It closed an hour ago," Jules said.

"I want to see it anyway."

She cast me a strange look but shrugged. "If you insist."

Ten minutes later, we arrived at an ancient-looking bookstore. It was stuffed in between a thrift shop and a Chinese takeout joint, and the words *Crabtree Books* were scrawled across the dark windows in chipped red paint.

"It's the only bookstore in town," Jules said. "I didn't tell any of my friends, because reading wasn't considered cool, but it was my favorite place to hang out, especially on rainy days. I came here so often I memorized all the books on the shelves, but I liked browsing it every weekend anyway. It was comforting." A wry smile touched her lips. "Plus, I knew for a fact I wouldn't run into anyone I knew here."

"It was your haven."

Her face softened with nostalgia. "Yeah."

My mouth curved at the mental image of a young Jules sneaking into a bookstore and hiding from her friends. A few months ago, when the only Jules I knew was the snarky, hard-partying one, I would've called bullshit. But now, I could see it.

Actually, save for Bridget's bachelorette, it had been a while since I saw Jules party the way she had in college. Hell, it'd been a while since *I* partied the way I had in college.

Our first impressions stick with us the longest, but contrary to popular opinion, some people do change. The only problem is, they change faster than our prejudices do.

"Do you have a favorite book?" I wanted to know everything about Jules. What she liked, what she hated, what books she read and what music she listened to. Every crumb of information I could get to fill my insatiable need for her.

"I can't choose *one.*" She sounded appalled. "That's like asking someone to choose a favorite ice cream flavor."

"Easy. Rocky Road for me, salted caramel for you." I grinned at her scowl. "Your favorite flavor for everything is salted caramel."

"Not *everything,*" she muttered. "Fine. If I had to choose one book, just based on how many times I reread it..." Her cheeks colored. "Don't laugh, because I know it's a cliché choice and a children's book, but...*Charlotte's Web.* The family that lived in our house before us left a copy behind, and it was the only book I owned as a kid. I was obsessed to the point I refused to let my mom kill any spiders in case it was Charlotte."

My grin widened. "That's fucking adorable."

The pink on her cheeks deepened. "I was young."

"I wasn't being sarcastic."

A small smile touched Jules's mouth, but she didn't say anything else as we departed from the bookstore.

It was near dinnertime, so we stopped by the diner she dubbed *the best restaurant in town* before heading back to the hotel.

"This place has the best burgers." She flipped through the menu, her face alight with anticipation. "It's one of the few things I missed about Whittlesburg."

"I'll take your word for it." I glanced at the red vinyl booths, black and white checkered floors, and the old jukebox in the corner. "This place reminds me of an eighties movie set."

She laughed. "Probably because the original owner was a big eighties movie fan. We used to hang out here all the time when I was in high school. It was *the* place to see and be seen. One time—"

"Jules? Is that you?"

Jules's face paled.

I turned to the speaker, my muscles already coiled in anticipation of a fight, but my tension melted into confusion when I saw who stood next to our table.

The woman was probably in her mid-twenties, though her makeup and platinum bob made her look older. She wore a tight red top and an expectant expression as she stared at Jules.

"It *is* you!" she exclaimed. "Jules Miller! I can't believe it. I didn't know you were back in town! It's been what, seven years?"

Miller? What the fuck?

I glanced at Jules, who pasted on an obviously fake smile. "Around that time, yeah. How are you, Rita?"

"Oh, you know. Married, two kids, working at my mom's salon. Same as everyone else, 'cept for the salon part." Rita's eyes lit with interest as she looked me over. "Who's *this*?"

"Josh," I said when Jules remained silent. I didn't add a label. I wouldn't know which one to use.

"Nice to meet you, Josh," Rita purred. "We don't see the likes of *you* around here often."

I managed a polite smile.

Rita seemed harmless enough, but the tension emanating from Jules was so thick I could taste it.

"What've you been up to all this time?" Rita shifted her attention back to Jules when I didn't engage further. "You just disappeared. No goodbyes, no nothing."

"College."

Jules didn't elaborate, but the other woman pressed further. "Where at?"

"It's small. You've probably never heard of it."

My eyebrows winged up. Thayer was small, but it was one of the most renowned universities in the country. I bet my medical degree a majority of people *have* heard of it.

"Well, you were lucky to get out when you did." Rita sighed. "This place sucks the soul out of you, ya know? But what can you do?" She shrugged. "By the way, I'm sorry about what happened with your mom and Alastair. That was *crazy*."

"The house fire? That happened years ago," Jules said.

"No. Well, yes, but that's not what I'm talking about." Rita waved a hand in the air. "Didn't you hear? Alastair got caught having sex with one of his business associates' daughters. She was sixteen, so it was *technically* legal under state law, but..." She gave an exaggerated shudder. "Anyway, his business associate went apeshit when he found out. Rumor has it he destroyed half of Alastair's business and Alastair had to take out a bunch of loans to keep it afloat. That's why your mom got such a small inheritance. It was all he had left. Some people say the associate was also the one who set the house on fire, but we'll never know."

Jesus Christ. The whole thing sounded like a daytime soap opera, but one glance at Jules chased away any disbelief I had.

She sat frozen, staring at Rita with wide eyes. Her skin matched the color of the white napkins stuffed into a little metal box on the table. "What—did my mom know? How come this wasn't in the papers?"

"Alastair's family kept it out of the papers," Rita said, obviously delighted she knew something Jules didn't. "Very hush hush, but someone leaked the info. Can you *believe* it? Your poor mom. Though she did know and stayed with him after so..." She trailed off and cleared her throat. "Anyway, what brings you back?"

"I..." Jules finally blinked. "My mom died a few days ago."

A heavy, awkward pause hung in the air.

"Oh." Rita cleared her throat again, her eyes darting around the diner. Crimson colored her face. "I'm so sorry to hear that. Hey, I gotta run, but it was great seeing you again and, uh, condolences."

She rushed off, nearly knocking over a server in her haste.

Good fucking riddance.

"Old friend?" I asked.

"In the sense that she used to copy off my math tests." Jules was starting to regain color, though the shock hadn't fully left her expression. "As you can probably tell, she's the biggest gossip in town."

"Yeah." I eyed her with concern. "How are you feeling about the Alastair news?"

I felt partly vindicated by the man's financial ruin, but Jules had enough going on with her mom's death without dealing with the ghost of her disgusting stepfather.

"Shocked, but not surprised, if that makes sense." She took a deep breath. "I'm glad Rita told me. I know they're just rumors, but when I think about it, it all kind of makes sense— why he left my mom so little money, the mysterious circumstances surrounding the fire. At least Alastair was held somewhat accountable for the things he did."

"And now he's dead."

"And now he's dead," Jules repeated. She huffed out a small laugh. "No need to bring up that asshole again."

"Agreed."

The server arrived to take our orders, and I waited until she left before I switched the subject. "So, Jules Miller, huh?"

She winced. "I changed my last name. Miller was my

mom's name. I wanted a fresh start after I left Ohio, so I applied for a legal name change."

I almost choked on my water. "How the fuck didn't I know this? Ava never mentioned it."

"That's because Ava doesn't know. It's just a name." Jules fiddled with her napkin. "It's not important."

If it wasn't important, she wouldn't have changed it, but I resisted pointing that out. "How'd you come up with Ambrose?"

Some of the tension left her body, and a shadow of mischief crossed her face. "It sounds pretty."

A laugh rose in my throat. "Well, there are worse reasons to choose a name," I said dryly. "Is it weird, being back here?"

Jules paused before answering. "It's funny. Before this trip, I built Whittlesburg up into this monster in my head. I had so many bad memories here—good ones too, but mostly bad. I thought coming back would be a nightmare, but other than the revelation about Alastair, it's been so...normal. Even running into Rita wasn't so bad."

"The monsters in our imagination are often worse than those in reality."

"Yeah," Jules said softly. Her gaze lingered on mine. "And what about your monsters, Josh Chen? Are they worse in your imagination or in reality?"

A silent, charged beat passed between us while I debated my answer.

"Michael sends me letters almost every week," I finally said. The admission tasted sour, like something I'd stored away so long it spoiled before it saw the light of day. "I don't open them. They sit in my desk drawer, collecting dust. Every time a new one arrives, I tell myself I'll toss it. But I never do."

A commiserating spark glowed in her eyes.

If anyone understood the futility of wishing for a redemption arc that would never come, it was Jules.

"You said it yourself. The monsters in our imagination are often worse than those in reality." She curled her hand over mine. "We'll never know for sure until we face them."

My chest squeezed. Her mother's funeral was tomorrow, and she was comforting *me*.

I didn't know how I ever thought Jules was insufferable, because as it turned out, she was pretty damn extraordinary.

37

JOSH

The next day, I accompanied Jules to her mother's funeral. Besides the minister and funeral home staff, we were the only people in attendance, and the service passed without any fanfare.

"Would you like to say any words before we put Adeline to rest?" the minister asked after he delivered the eulogy.

Jules shook her head. "No," she whispered. "I don't want to say anything."

I reached for her hand and gave it a comforting squeeze, wishing I could do more to help. Jules didn't look at me, but she gave me a small squeeze back.

The minister nodded, the staff lowered the casket into the ground, and that was that.

It was, in Jules's words, anticlimactic, but that didn't stop a knot from forming in my stomach when I stared at Adeline's burial plot.

Decades of life, snuffed out just like that, with no one except her daughter and a stranger seeing her off. A lifetime of dreams, fears, accomplishments, and regrets, wiped out by a single freak accident.

It was fucking depressing.

I allowed myself to dwell in melancholy for a moment before I pushed it aside and placed a gentle hand on Jules's elbow. The minister and funeral home staff had already left, but she hadn't moved since the service. "We should head out. Our flight leaves soon."

There was only one evening flight from Columbus to D.C. today, so we were flying together by default.

"Right." Jules sucked in a deep breath and exhaled slowly. "Thanks for being here with me," she said as we walked toward the exit. "You really didn't have to."

"No, but I wanted to." My mouth tugged up in a half smile. "Who knows what trouble you'd get into if I leave you alone?"

"The possibilities are endless," she said solemnly. "You sure you don't want a tour of the Whittlesburg police station before we leave?"

"I'm sure it's fascinating, but I'll pass." I examined her, trying to figure out where her head was at. "How are you feeling?"

"Surprisingly okay." Jules tucked a strand of hair behind her ear. "I think the shock has worn off, and now I'm just...resigned, I guess. I'll never get to say bye to my mom or make amends." She hesitated. "Actually, I know our flight leaves soon, but can we make one stop before we head to the airport? I'll keep it quick."

"Yeah, of course." We were squeezed for time, but I wasn't going to say no to her after her mother's funeral.

Fifteen minutes later, we arrived at a small, dilapidated house near the outskirts of town. Chipped blue paint covered its exterior, and the door was unlocked when Jules twisted the knob.

"The house my mom rented before she died," she said after she caught my questioning stare. "When I notified the landlord of her death, they said I could drop by and pick up any personal items. I wasn't going to, but..."

"I understand." It was Jules's last chance. She was probably never coming back to Ohio.

We stepped into the house. There wasn't much furniture except for a couch, TV, and a dining slash coffee table. Dirty dishes piled high in the sink, and a pot of flowers sat dying on the windowsill.

It was eerie, like the house was patiently waiting for an owner who would never return.

I followed Jules into the bedroom and stayed by the door while she approached the cluster of framed photos on the dresser. They all featured a beautiful older woman with red hair, obviously her mom. In one, she was wearing a gown and smiling at a fancy-looking party; in another, she was being crowned Miss Teen Whittlesburg, according to the sash across her chest.

There were no photos of anyone else, including Jules.

"I thought she would have at least one photo of me," Jules murmured, running her hand over the teen pageant picture. "All these years..." She shook her head and let out a self-deprecating laugh. "It was stupid. I held out hope, but Adeline's never cared much about anyone except herself."

An ache bloomed in my chest. Neither of us had model parents, but I hated seeing her hope vanish. "I'm sorry, Red."

"Don't be." Jules dropped her hand before facing me. "We can leave. We have a flight to catch, and I got what I wanted."

"What's that?"

"Closure."

Closure.

The word echoed in my mind during our ride to the airport.

Maybe that was what I needed with Michael. I'd avoided contacting him for two years, thinking that was the solution to my problem. All it'd done was allow thoughts of him to fester like cancer. Slow, invisible, and gradually bleeding me of life until I was nothing but a shell of myself.

The monsters in our imagination are often worse those in reality.

The sudden, blinding clarity sliced through me like a blade.

"You okay?" Jules asked after we passed through security. Whittlesburg was so close to Columbus it took us less than an hour to arrive at the airport. "You look delirious."

"Yep," I said, still high from my discovery. It was so fucking obvious I felt like an idiot for not thinking of it earlier, but we were the blindest when it came to our own lives.

I didn't look forward to seeing Michael, but it'll be like ripping off a Band-Aid. Once I did it, I could finally move on. I was sure of it.

Closure.

The answer had been there all along.

"We spent two whole days together and didn't kill each other." Jules cocked an eyebrow as we picked up sandwiches and chips from one of the airport's delis and settled at a table in the food court. Our flight didn't leave for another seventy-five minutes, so we had time to kill. "We're making progress."

"It was a day and a half, tops." I smiled, welcoming the shift to a lighter tone after the heaviness of our morning. Sadness lingered in Jules's eyes, but she seemed determined to leave the past behind her. "We still have some time left."

"How reassuring." She bit into her sandwich, chewed, and swallowed before adding hesitantly, "I've been thinking about what you said at Bridget's wedding..."

My pulse quickened. "Yeah?"

"You might be right." She didn't look at me, but pink crept

over her cheeks. "About there being a difference between what something is supposed to be and what it actually is."

The quickening turned into a roar. Warmth glowed in my chest and filled some of the cracks that had formed over the years.

"I'm always right." It was all I could do to suppress a grin.

I'd never wanted an exclusive relationship. It came with too many expectations, and honestly, I'd never *liked* anyone enough to go on more than three dates with them.

Lusted for, sure. Liked? No.

But with Jules...fuck, I didn't even know how it happened. I *liked* her, even when she pissed me off, which was half the time. Our arguments lit me up more than my conversations with anyone else did, and when we actually talked, she was the only person I felt like who got me. The only person who saw past the doctor, the playboy, the adrenaline junkie, and every other mask I wore to hide the messy imperfect pieces underneath.

I swallowed the odd lump in my throat while Jules rolled her eyes and smiled. "Always modest."

"That too."

Her smile widened, and our gazes lingered for a moment before her expression turned serious again. "So, what does that mean for us?"

Good question. I had no experience with the whole relationship thing, but...

"It means we should probably go on a date." My grin exploded at the way her eyes widened. "Don't look so shocked. It's a date, Red. Not a marriage proposal."

"*Obviously,*" she huffed, though the nervous look in her eyes remained. "I've been on dates before."

My smile slipped at the reminder.

Of course Jules had been on dates before. That didn't mean I wanted to think about it.

A ribbon of possessiveness unfurled in my stomach, and it took all my willpower not to grill her for the full name, number, and address of every guy who'd ever fucking touched her.

"Not with me." I rubbed a speck of sauce from the corner of her mouth. My thumb lingered on her bottom lip, and dark satisfaction flared through me when her breath hitched. "*When* I take you out, it'll be the best damn date you've ever had."

"Your ego truly knows no bounds." The breathlessness of her voice erased the sting of her insult.

I leaned forward and replaced my thumb with my lips. "Let's make a bet, Red." My mouth brushed over hers—not in a kiss, but in a promise. "I bet after our date, you won't even be able to *think* about another man."

The last part came out as a low growl.

Jules audibly swallowed. "You're setting very high expectations, Chen."

My smile returned. "Don't worry. I never set expectations I can't meet."

38

JULES

It was strange. I'd left for Ohio, expecting it to be a nightmare, and I returned realizing it was a catharsis.

The trip took the messy, blurred pieces of my life and threw them into sharp relief.

Alastair was dead and couldn't hurt me anymore.

My mom was dead, and no matter how much I agonized over *what ifs,* she was never coming back.

Max remained a threat, but he'd been oddly silent for a while. Until he made his next move, there wasn't much I could do.

And Josh...Josh was one of the few bright spots in my shit-show of a life. Changing our relationship from enemies with benefits to dating was like jumping off a cliff—it could end in the most exhilarating rush of my life or total disaster.

But I already had enough regrets. I didn't want Josh to be one of them.

Sometimes, you had to take a leap or risk getting stuck forever.

"What do you think?" I turned slowly, letting Stella examine my outfit.

Josh and I had our first official date today, but no matter how much I cajoled, threatened, and bribed him, he'd remained tight-lipped about what we were doing, so I was flying blind when it came to the dress code. His only guidance was to dress nice but not *too* nice, which was no freaking help at all.

After much agonizing, I'd settled on a blue sundress with sandals and styled my hair in a high ponytail to stave off the sweltering June heat. It was fun, flirty, and casual enough for a stroll in the park but dressy enough for a nice restaurant.

At least, I hoped so.

Stella assessed me from head to toe before giving me a thumbs up. "Perfect."

Thank God. I didn't have time to change. I was already running late.

Since Josh couldn't pick me up from my house, I met him in Georgetown as requested.

Flutters filled my stomach when I spotted him waiting at our designated meeting spot.

White button down. Dark jeans. Tousled hair. So gorgeous it made my heart hurt.

I kind of wished we still hated each other because our relationship was not great for my cardiac health.

"Hey, Red." Josh looked me over, his eyes heating. "Nice to see you looking presentable for once."

"Nice to see you looking human for once." I gave him an equally deliberate once-over. "How much did you pay for the skin suit to cover up your devil's horns and reptile skin?"

"It was free. I'm just that charming," he drawled.

"I think the seller was just scared you'll suffocate him with your giant ego if you didn't leave soon."

His laugh rolled through me like molten caramel, rich and sweet. "I fucking missed you."

I fell into step beside him as we walked down the street toward our mysterious destination. "It's been three days."

"I know."

The flutters intensified. *Dammit.* When he wasn't being an ass, he could be so...sweet.

"Are you going to tell me where we're going now?" I was too curious not to ask. Why hadn't Josh asked me to meet him at the date spot instead of some random street corner?

He heaved an exaggerated sigh. *"Patience."*

"I don't know what that is, but it sounds boring." I stifled a laugh when he side-eyed me.

"You're insufferable."

"So you keep saying, yet you missed me and you're on a date with me. What does that say about *you*?"

"That I'm a glutton for a beautiful punishment."

I bit my lip to contain a burgeoning smile. "You should look into that. Doesn't sound healthy."

"I did. There's no cure, I'm afraid."

I stumbled on a loose cobblestone and would've face planted on the sidewalk had Josh not caught me by the wrist.

"Careful," he said, his eyes aglow with amusement. He knew exactly what he was doing, the bastard. "Don't want you to fall."

"I won't." I mustered a haughty tone and smoothed down my skirt, my cheeks red.

After another five minutes or so, we finally stopped in front of a tiny shop with a striped awning and the words *Apollo Hill Books* stamped in gold on the windows. Piles of books filled the display, obstructing my view of the shop's interior, and two royal blue carts groaned beneath the weight of discounted tomes on the sidewalk.

Now I knew why Josh hadn't asked me to meet him here—the street was only wide enough for pedestrians and bicycles. A car didn't have a chance of squeezing through it. The same went for the surrounding streets.

"Welcome to the best bookstore in the city." Josh swept a dramatic arm at the building and grinned at my stunned expression.

"How have I never heard of this place?" My heart beat fast at the prospect of what lay beyond the white wood door. Discovering a new bookstore was like discovering a new type of precious gem: exhilarating, wondrous, and a touch surreal. "I've lived here for years."

"It opened a few months ago and flies under the radar. I found out about it from another resident whose cousin's friend owns it." Josh opened the door.

The minute I stepped inside, I fell in love. No, not fell. I *crashed* into love, hard and fast, seduced by the floor-to-ceiling bookcases, the charmingly haphazard piles crowding the oval table in the middle of the store, and the sweet, musky scent of old books. The bold emerald carpet contrasted with the understated cream walls, and several wrought-iron chandeliers cast a warm glow over the space.

It was the bookstore of my dreams, manifested into reality.

"What did I tell you?" Josh's voice rolled down my spine in a velvety caress. "Best bookstore in the city."

Other than the store owner, we were the only people present. It was hard to believe the hustle and bustle of the city lay on the other side of the door. It was so hushed, I felt like we'd entered a secret world created just for us.

"This is the only time I'll admit you're right." I ran a reverent hand over a nearby pile of books. The store contained a mix of new releases and used books, and I wanted to explore them all. "Are we spending our date browsing? Because I'm fully onboard with that."

"Sort of." Josh leaned against the side of a bookcase and slid one hand into his pocket, the picture of gorgeous insouciance. "I would start with your favorite childhood book."

"Why?"

"Trust me." He angled his chin toward the nearby children's section.

The heat from Josh's gaze warmed my skin as I scanned the shelves until I found what I was looking for. There were only three copies of *Charlotte's Web,* and I assumed there was a note or something similar in one of them.

The fact he'd remembered such a small detail from our conversation in Ohio sent a burst of tingles shooting through me.

Focus, Jules.

I plucked one of the copies off the shelf and flipped through the pages. Nothing out of the ordinary.

I tried a second copy. Nothing.

But when I opened the third book, a slip of paper fluttered to the ground. I picked it up, and a smile burst onto my mouth when I read the words scribbled in Josh's neat scrawl.

Your favorite food, but you have to make it.

B3, S4, #10.

"Is this a bookstore scavenger hunt?" I bounced on my feet, unable to contain my delight.

"Scavenger hunt and puzzle." Josh's cheek dimpled. "Have to make sure your brainpower meets my standards, Red. I don't date dummies."

"Understandable. *Someone* has to be the brains in the relationship."

Josh's soft laugh settled inside me. "Solve the clue before

you get cocky, sweetheart. There's a prize waiting for you if you do."

I perked up. I *loved* prizes. I had a whole box of certificates, trophies, and medals I won in high school and college. "What is it?"

"You'll find out. Or maybe not." He shrugged. "Let's see."

My skin buzzed from both our exchange and the thrill of the hunt, but I tamped down my desire to continue our verbal sparring session and refocused on the clue.

Your favorite food, but you have to make it obviously referred to an Italian cookbook.

As for *B3 S4 #10*...my brain scrambled to untangle its meaning. It was a scavenger hunt, so the clue likely led to a specific cookbook. All the books were organized in alphabetical order by the author's last name, so what could the numbers stand for?

I scanned the bookcases, trying—

My attention jerked back to a sign printed with the number one. It was displayed on the side of the nearest bookcase.

The *books* weren't numbered, but the bookcases were, and every bookcase comprised of multiple shelves. Bookcase, shelf. *B3 S4*.

Cookbook section, bookcase three, shelf four...#10. Tenth book on the shelf?

It was worth a try.

My chest thumped with anticipation as I beelined to the shelf in question and counted the books from left to right. *One, two, three, four...*

Number ten was an Italian cookbook.

Giddiness surged through my veins. I shot a triumphant glance at Josh, who tried and failed to hold back a smile, before I flipped through the book and found a second note.

Now that I'd cracked the code, this one was easier to solve.

It guided me to the travel section for a thick guidebook to Italy. That, in turn, led me to the art section for a biography about Michelangelo, which funneled me to a romance about a painter falling in love with his neighbor turned muse.

The note in the romance novel didn't contain a clue. Instead, it contained one sentence.

Jules, will you go out with me?

Was it possible for a human being to literally melt? Because that was the only explanation I could think of for the way my knees weakened and my insides liquefied. I was a ball of nothing except emotion, held together by a roaring heartbeat and a string of butterflies.

"We're already on a date, idiot." My cheeks ached from smiling so hard.

Josh's mischievous expression melted into something warmer. "Figured I should formally ask before we head to the next stop."

"Where's that?"

"You'll see. Thanks, Luna." He nodded at the grinning bookstore owner, who handed him a shopping bag packed with books.

I'd been so caught up in the scavenger hunt I hadn't realized she'd been following me, picking up every book with a clue after I moved on to the next section.

"The books are yours. You're welcome for diversifying your reading," Josh said.

I was too stunned to come up with a good retort. "How did you organize this?"

"Like I said, Luna is a coworker's cousin's friend. I worked it out with her. Plus, I bought a shit ton of books in exchange, so it was a win-win."

"That's..." *Don't cry.* That would be humiliating, but the fact that Josh had gone to so much trouble for our date...

A lump lodged itself in my throat as we said goodbye to Luna and exited the bookshop.

"Jules Ambrose, speechless. I should've done this earlier," Josh joked. "Would've saved me a lot of headaches in the past."

"Hilarious." I found my words again. "So, where's the prize you promised me?"

"You'll get it later."

I narrowed my eyes. "Are you scamming me, Josh Chen?"

A smile played on his mouth. "Maybe." We stopped in front of Giorgio's, an intimate Italian restaurant tucked on a side street. Its windows glowed with candlelight, and the soft strains of jazz music floated into my ears when he opened the door. "Guess you'll have to trust me."

Three months ago, I wouldn't have trusted Josh Chen if I was drowning and he was my only lifeline. Now, I didn't think twice before I followed him and the hostess to a table in the back corner.

"I wouldn't make you cook," Josh said, referencing the first scavenger hunt clue. "I don't want to die from food poisoning."

"Quick, quit your job at the hospital. You should be a comedian." I paged through the menu. "Since we're here, I assume I meet your intellectual standards and am officially the brains in the relationship."

"Among other things," Josh said softly.

My menu flips slowed. I raised my head, and my stomach flipped at the intensity in his eyes. "Other things?"

A slow smile spread across his mouth. "No fishing for compliments, Red."

"I'm not fishing. I hate fishing." *What are you even saying?* Still, I rambled on, too nervous to sit still or stay quiet. "Speaking of, why do guys always put fishing pictures in their dating profile? It's a turnoff, honestly."

"I don't, and you don't have to worry about that."

"Why not?"

"Because neither of us are dating anyone else, Red," Josh said, so calm and matter of fact the words etched themselves into my skin as truth.

Our server arrived, saving me from coming up with an eloquent response. It would've been a futile effort, anyway. I couldn't even focus on my food, much less piece the thousands of words in my vocabulary into a coherent sentence.

All I could focus on was the man across the table. The fullness of his lower lip, the shadow of his dimple, the rough caress of his voice and the bronze glow of his skin in the dim light.

I didn't know how I ever thought Josh was annoying, because I could stay here and listen to him talk forever.

"Remember what you told me in Eldorra? About forgiving, even if I don't forget?" Josh rubbed his jaw. "Alex and I are going to a game next week."

Pleasant surprise rushed through me. "That's great."

"We'll see. He's such an asshole, it could hurt more than it helps."

I laughed. "True. But he's always been an asshole, and you guys were friends for years."

"Also true. It's weird, because he was so fucking hard to crack, especially when we first met. And that was him *trying* to be personable. Normally, I would've written someone like that off, but..." A frown touched Josh's brow. "I don't know. I guess I thought he needed a friend. No matter how rich you are, you still need someone to have your back. Someone who doesn't do it for the money."

I softened at his words. "You're a good person, Josh Chen."

"Only sometimes." He let out an embarrassed laugh. "You were right, you know. What you said after the Black Fox about me holding onto my grudge because that's all I have left to hold onto."

The Black Fox. That night seemed like a lifetime ago. We'd been so *angry, a*nd we'd said so many hurtful things, but if I had to do it over, I wouldn't change a thing. That night led us to where we were now. And even with the freshness of my mother's death and the specter of Max hanging over me, I was happy with where I was, because for once in my life, I didn't feel alone.

"I wouldn't say that's the *only* thing you have left to hold onto," I said.

The rest of the restaurant fell away as the moment stretched between us, taut and brimming with a million unspoken words. The answering flare of emotion in Josh's eyes arrowed into my chest and pierced a shield I hadn't known existed.

The result was utter chaos—heart bared, pulse wild, stomach fluttering with a swarm of escaped butterflies.

"Careful, Red." Pleasurable goosebumps dotted my skin at Josh's soft warning. "Keep saying things like that, and I might never let you go."

Heat blazed over my face. I was getting lightheaded from the lack of oxygen, but no matter how hard I tried to breathe, it wasn't enough. Every ounce of air vibrated with an electric charge that lit me up from the inside.

I might've collapsed right there at the corner table in Giorgio's had the jangle of bells over the entrance not loosened the stranglehold on me. It was followed by a cool, clear voice.

"Alex Volkov. Table for two."

Josh and I tore our eyes from each other and turned to the front of the restaurant in mutual horror.

Alex and Ava stood near the hostess's stand. They hadn't noticed us yet. Alex was busy looking at Ava, and Ava was busy chatting with the hostess, but it was only a matter of time. The restaurant was *tiny*.

"Oh my God." I averted my eyes and shielded the side of my face with my hand. "What do we do?"

As far as Alex and Ava knew, Josh and I still hated each other. If we were somewhere more casual, we could play it off as having accidentally run into each other, but there was nothing accidental about sitting at the same candlelit table in a romantic restaurant on a Friday night.

"We have two options." Josh's voice was so low it was almost inaudible. "One, we stay and face the music with courage. Two, we sneak out through the back before they see us like cowards."

We stared at each other.

"Option two," we mouthed in unison.

Luckily, we'd already paid. The challenge was getting to the kitchen without Alex and Ava seeing us.

We kept our backs to the rest of the restaurant as we edged toward the swinging double doors. We didn't want to attract attention by running, but my heart felt like it would fall out of my chest with each passing second.

By some miracle, we snuck into the kitchen before our friends spotted us. Once we did, we broke into a run, earning ourselves started glances from the staff.

"Hey!" one of the line cooks yelled. "You're not supposed to be in here!"

"Sorry!" I yelled back over my shoulder. "We wanted to pay our compliments to the chef!"

"The pappardelle al ragu was excellent," Josh added. "Five out of five stars."

"I'm calling the manager." The line cook raised his voice. "Sergio!"

Shit.

"Go, go, go!" Josh grabbed my hand and pulled me toward the exit. We spilled out into the alleyway behind the restaurant right as a man whom I assumed was Sergio shouted something incomprehensible at us. We didn't stop running until we were several blocks away, and I bent over to catch my breath.

"Shit," I wheezed. Cardio wasn't my strong suit, and it showed. "I can't believe we just did that."

"At least we left a big tip." Josh wasn't even out of breath, the bastard. "We'll throw a Yelp review on top of that. Good food, clean kitchen. We saw it with our own eyes."

For some reason, the suggestion struck me as absurd. I doubled over again, this time from laughter. A second passed before Josh joined me.

Maybe it was the food, the adrenaline from our near run-in with our friends, or the crisp evening air, but exhilaration whipped through me until the world tilted.

I had never felt so incredibly, indescribably *alive*.

Our laughter gradually faded, but the balloon of pleasure in my chest lingered.

"So, tell me, Red." A smile lingered at the corners of Josh's mouth. "On a scale of one to ten, how great was the date?"

"Hmm." I tapped my chin. "Seven point five, rounded up to eight for the scavenger hunt."

"Eight, huh?" He took a step toward me.

My heart beat a little faster. "Uh-huh."

"What do I have to do to make it a ten?" His gaze dropped to my mouth.

"Well, you do owe me a prize." Was that breathless, giddy voice mine? "Keep your promises, Chen."

"You're right." Josh cupped my face with one hand and brushed his thumb over my lip. Electric sparks formed over my skin. "How rude of me to keep you waiting."

He leaned down and kissed me. The touch was featherlight, but it traveled from the top of my head to the tips of my toes.

"How about that? Are we at ten yet?" he whispered against my lips.

"Um." My head swam with pleasure. "Maybe a nine."

"Hmm. That won't do." He kissed me again, firmer this time. His tongue swept along the seam of my lips and nudged inside when I parted for him. A fog of lust clouded my brain while he explored my mouth, his hand a possessive weight on my hip. When he finally pulled back, I could barely remember my name. "What about now?"

"Nine point five," I rasped after a long, dizzy pause.

"Nine point five." Josh wrapped my ponytail around his other hand and gave it a light yank that shot straight to my core. "Are you playing with me, Red?" he asked silkily.

"Are you complaining?"

His eyes glowed with amusement and something else that sent warm tendrils spiraling through my insides. "Not even a little bit."

This time, the kiss was harder, more urgent.

I sank into it, letting Josh's touch and taste sweep me away to a place where we were the only people who existed.

I once read somewhere that the opposite of love wasn't hate, it was indifference. The flames of hate and passion burned in equal measure.

I couldn't pinpoint the specific moment my feelings toward Josh changed. I didn't even know what my current feelings toward him were, exactly.

All I knew was, he set me ablaze, and I never wanted the fire to go out.

39

JOSH

"Man, I missed this." I stretched my legs in front of me and reached for a beer. "Nothing beats the VIP suite."

"Obviously. That's why it's called the VIP suite." Alex sat next to me, his eyes tracking the game. The Nationals were playing the Dodgers, and they were down by three runs in the fifth inning. Not too bad.

I was more of a basketball guy, but Nats games were more fun to attend. Alex and I turned them into a tradition when we were in college. Whenever we wanted to talk about something we didn't want people on campus to hear, we headed for Nationals Field and let the game play in the background while we hashed our shit out.

Well, I hashed shit out while Alex sighed and reminded me how stupid other people were. It was like therapy, except with sports, beer, and a grumpy best friend.

I hadn't realized how much those sessions helped until they ended.

Of course, that was assuming said best friend wasn't the *cause* of my problems.

"Dude, you're still on probation," I said. "No sarcasm until you're out of the woods."

"That wasn't part of our deal."

"We didn't have a deal."

"Exactly."

I glared at Alex. "You want me to forgive you or not?"

"I bribed you with VIP seats to the game, and you accepted. That means you've already forgiven me." He smiled. "It's called a shadow contract."

I maintained my frown for another minute before I caved and snorted out a laugh. "Touché."

I took a swig of my drink. I thought it would feel weird, slipping back into one of our old traditions after so long, but it was like time never passed.

My phone buzzed with a new text, and my lips curled into a smile when I read it.

Jules: How's the bro date going? Should I be worried?

Me: TBD. Alex knows how to treat a guy right, but you're prettier

Jules: Are you saying I don't know how to treat you right??

Me: You spend half your time insulting me, Red

Jules: It's not my fault you're a masochist

Jules: Excuse me for catering to your kink *eye roll emoji*

Another laugh rose in my throat.

Me: That's not my kink, sweetheart

Me: Maybe you need a reminder on what my kink IS

My hand around her throat. Her nails clawing at my skin.

Her whimpers and pleas as I edged her toward insanity before I fucked the fight right out of her.

I sent the last message as a tease, but heat surged through my blood at the thought.

Jules and I hadn't had sex since Ohio. Now that we were dating, I wanted to do it properly, and in a fit of sheer idiocy, I'd implemented a no-sex-until-our-third-date rule.

It was backwards as fuck, considering we'd already slept together, but it felt right. Or maybe I *was* a masochist. I was blue balling myself, and Jules wasn't having a great time with the sexual deprivation either.

The third date rule wouldn't be so bad if we had *time* to date. Unfortunately, neither my hospital schedule nor her job at the clinic gave two shits about our sex life, so we hadn't even had our second date yet.

I wouldn't be surprised if my dick mutinied before then. Just up and jumped ship due to sheer neglect.

The three dots indicating Jules was typing popped up, disappeared, then popped up again.

Jules: Yes, I do ;)

Jules: Better make that multiple reminders so I don't forget

I suppressed a tortured groan.

Josh: You're fucking killing me

Josh: Ending this before I have to sit through the rest of the game with a goddamn boner

Though it might be too late for that.

Jules: Coward

Josh: Tease all you want, Red

Josh: I'll remember every word next time I'm fucking you

I shoved the phone in my pocket before I did something

stupid, like bail on the game, drive to her house, and make good on my threat.

On second thought...

"Who's the girl?" Alex's words threw a bucket of cold water over my X-rated fantasies.

Baseball game. VIP suite. Reconciliation with Alex.

Right.

I cleared my throat and shifted in my seat, trying to hide the lingering effects of my texts with Jules. "How the hell did you know it was a girl?"

"Your face gives it away." Below us, a collective groan erupted in the stadium when the Dodgers scored another run. "So, who is it?" Alex faced me, a touch of curiosity warming his cool green eyes. "You looked disgustingly besotted while texting."

"I did not look *besotted*." I finished my beer and reached for another one. Was it my fifth or sixth? I wasn't sure. My tolerance had jumped, and it took a lot to even get me buzzed these days. "Besides, you're one to talk. Next time Ava texts you, I'll take a picture of your face so you know what *you* look like."

Instead of taking the bait, Alex tipped his head to the side. The curiosity sharpened into knowing. "It's not just sex. You're dating her."

Motherfucker. "I never said that."

"You implied it."

"No, I didn't."

"Yes, you did."

I released an aggravated sigh.

Man, fuck having a best friend. They were overrated know-it-alls.

"Fine. I *may* be dating someone." Trying to outargue Alex was like trying to nail jelly to a wall—futile and a waste of time. "You don't know her."

"Don't be too sure. I know a lot of people."

"You don't know *her*." If I told him, he would tell Ava, and I would rather guzzle a gallon of filthy Potomac River water than have *that* conversation with my sister.

Now I understood how she'd felt when she'd been dating Alex behind my back.

"Hmm." He leaned back in his seat, his eyes piercing through my skin. "Josh Chen dating seriously. Never thought I'd see the day."

"I could say the same about you."

"Sometimes, people change. And sometimes, they meet people who make them want to change."

"And *sometimes,* people sound like a human fortune cookie."

Except for a few rare gems, Alex's advice swung from wildly disturbing—like the time he suggested I blackmail a professor who had it out for me because I'd corrected him in class—to irritatingly vague.

"Speaking of change..." I hesitated before continuing. "Michael's been sending me letters. I haven't opened any yet, but I might visit him soon. In prison."

I hadn't even told Ava yet, and I wasn't sure I ever would. She'd finally moved on from what Michael did; I didn't want to drag her back into that mess.

However, that meant Alex was the only other person who might understand the significance of what I was saying.

He stilled, his features hardening until they appeared carved from stone. Michael may not have murdered his family, but he *had* tried to murder Ava. It was an equal offense in his eyes.

"I see." Zero inflection. "When are you visiting him?"

"I don't know." I stared at the field without really seeing it.

"Next day I have off, maybe. Don't even know what I'll say to him."

So, how's the food in prison?

Hey, Dad. Did you always want to grow up to be an attempted murderer, or were you inspired by the true crime shows Mom liked to watch?

You're a piece of shit and I wished I hated you as much as I should.

I rubbed a hand over my face, exhausted just thinking about it.

I needed to talk to him, but that didn't mean I wanted to.

Alex was quiet for a long moment before he surprised the fuck out of me by saying, "Maybe you should open his letters."

A startled laugh escaped my throat. "Are you shitting me? I thought you would try to discourage me from seeing him."

"He's a piece of shit, and I would happily watch him bleed if I could," Alex said coldly. "But he's your father, and as long as you avoid confronting him, he'll always have a hold on you. The bastard doesn't deserve it."

It sounded disturbingly close to Jules's advice.

Intellectually, I already knew I needed closure, but hearing Alex lay it out in such stark, unsentimental terms hit hard.

"Yeah." I tilted my head back and stared at the ceiling, giving up any pretense of watching the game. "Is it bad that part of me wishes he had a good excuse for doing what he did? I know nothing can excuse it, but...fuck. I don't know." I rubbed my hand over my face again, wishing I could articulate the turmoil eating away at my insides.

"Ava had complicated feelings toward him, and she was the one he tried to kill." Alex's eyes darkened. "When someone raises you, it's hard to let that go."

"That apply to you too?"

Alex's uncle had been the one behind his family's hit, and

he'd died in a mysterious fire soon after that revelation came to light.

I never asked about the fire, because I was sure I didn't want to know the answer. When it came to Alex, ignorance was bliss. For the most part.

"No."

I shook my head, exasperated but unsurprised by the curt answer. "You think I *should* visit Michael?"

"I think you should do whatever you need to do to put him behind you." Alex shifted his attention back to the game. The Nats had closed the score when we weren't looking; they were now down by only one. "Don't let him ruin your life any more than he already has."

Alex's words ran through my mind for the rest of the game.

They were still echoing in my head when I returned home and opened the desk drawer. A thick pile of letters nestled against the dark wood, waiting for me to pick them up.

I think you should do whatever you need to do to put him behind you.

It was ironic how quickly I'd jump off a literal cliff, bridge, or plane, but when it came to the personal moments, the ones that mattered, I was a child standing at the edge of a pool for the first time.

Scared. Hesitant. Anticipatory.

After another minute's pause, I sat in my chair, opened the first envelope, and started reading.

THE HAZELBURG CORRECTIONAL FACILITY'S VISITATION room resembled a high school cafeteria more than a prison facility. A dozen white tables scattered across the stark gray floor, and other than a handful of generic landscape paintings, the walls were bare of decoration. Security cameras whirred in the ceiling, silent voyeurs to the reunions playing out between prisoners and their families.

My knee bounced with nervous tension until I closed my hand around it and forced it to still.

The tables were close enough I could pick up other people's conversations, but they were drowned out by snippets from Michael's letters in my mind. I'd read them so many times in the week since I opened them that their words had seared into my brain.

How's your residency going? Is it anything like Grey's Anatomy? You used to joke about keeping a journal listing all the show's inaccuracies once you were a resident. If you actually have one, I'd love to see it...

I just saw Groundhog Day. Life in prison feels like that sometimes...living the same day over and over again...

Merry Christmas. Are you doing anything for the holidays this year? I know doctors have to work through the holidays, but hopefully you're taking some time off. Maybe go see the Northern Lights in Finland like you've always wanted...

The letters were generic and innocuous, but they contained just enough inside jokes and shared memories to keep me up at night.

Reading the letters, I could almost believe Michael was a normal father writing to his son and not a psycho bastard.

The door opened, and a man in an orange jumpsuit walked in.

Speak of the devil...

My stomach twisted.

His hair was a little grayer, his wrinkles a little more pronounced, but otherwise, Michael Chen looked the same as he always had.

Stern. Cerebral. Solemn.

He sat across from me, and heavy silence stretched taut between us like a rubber band on the verge of snapping.

Prison guards watched us with hawk eyes from the edge of the room, their heavy scrutiny a third participant in our nonexistent conversation.

Finally, Michael spoke. "Thank you for coming."

It was my first time hearing his voice in two years.

I flinched, unprepared for the nostalgia it triggered.

That was the same voice that had soothed me when I was sick, encouraged me after I lost a basketball game, and yelled at me when I snuck out clubbing with a fake ID in high school and got caught.

It was my childhood—the good, the bad, and the ugly, all wrapped up in one deep, rumbling tone.

"I didn't come for you." I pressed my hand harder against my thigh.

"So why did you come?" Except for the brief shadow that crossed his face, Michael betrayed no emotion at my unsentimental response.

"I..." My answer stuck in my throat, and Michael's mouth curved into a knowing smile.

"Since you're here, I assume you've read my letters. You know what's happened with me over the years, which isn't much." He let out a self-deprecating laugh. "Tell me about you. How's work?"

It was surreal, sitting here and talking to my father like we were on a fucking coffee date. But my brain had blanked, and I couldn't think of another course of action except to play along.

"It's fine."

"Josh." Michael laughed again. "You have to give me more than that. You've wanted to be a doctor since high school."

"Residency is residency. Lots of long hours. Lots of sickness and death." I flashed a hard smile. "You know a lot about that."

Michael winced. "And your love life? Are you seeing anyone?" He skipped over my last statement. "You're getting to that age. It's time to settle down and start a family soon."

"I'm not even thirty yet." Honestly, I didn't know if I wanted children. If I did, it wouldn't be until *way* down the road. I needed to experience more of the world before I settled into the white picket fence and suburban house life.

"Yes, but you have to allot a few years to dating first," Michael reasoned. "Unless you're already dating someone." His eyebrows rose when I remained silent. "*Are* you dating someone?"

"No," I lied, partly to spite him, and partly because he didn't deserve to know about Jules.

"Ah, well, a father can hope."

We continued our small talk, using mundane topics such as the weather and upcoming football season to sidestep the elephant in the room. Other than punching him in the face, I'd never confronted him about what he did to Ava.

The knowledge sat in my stomach like a concrete block. Ignoring it felt wrong, but I also couldn't bring myself to shatter the light, if somewhat forced, conversation between us.

I'm sorry, Ava.

After floating adrift for the past two years, I could pretend I had a father again. As fucked up and selfish as it was, I wanted to savor the feeling for a while longer.

"How's prison?" I almost laughed at my inane question, but I was genuinely curious. Michael's letters detailed the minutiae of his days, but they hadn't revealed how he was dealing with his incarceration.

Was he sad? Ashamed? Angry? Did he get along with the other inmates, or did he keep to himself?"

"Prison is prison." Michael sounded almost cheerful. "It's boring, uncomfortable, and the food is terrible, but it could be worse. Luckily…" A dark gleam lit up his eyes. "I've made some friends who've been able to help me out."

Of course he had. I didn't know the ins and outs of inmate politics, but Michael had always been a survivor.

I wasn't sure whether I was relieved or pissed that he wasn't suffering more.

"Speaking of which…" Michael lowered his voice further until it was nearly inaudible. "They've asked for a favor in exchange for their, ah, friendship."

Icy suspicion welled in my chest. "What kind of favor?"

I assumed *friendship* was code for *protection*, but who knew? Crazy shit happened in the prison system.

"Prison politics is…complicated," Michael said. "Lots of bartering, lots of invisible lines you don't want to cross. But one thing everyone can agree on is how valuable certain items are. Cigarettes, chocolate, instant ramen." A small pause. "Prescription pills."

Prescription pills were valuable even in the real world; on the prison black market, they must be gold.

And who had easy access to pills? Doctors.

A fist grabbed hold of my guts and twisted.

Once upon a time, I would've given my father the benefit of the doubt, but I knew better now. Perhaps he did miss me and wanted to make amends. He had, after all, written to me for two years.

But at the end of the day, Michael Chen only looked out for himself.

"I see." I forced my expression to remain neutral. "I'm not surprised."

"You've always been smart." Michael smiled. "Smart enough to be a doctor, obviously. I mentioned that to my friends, and they asked if you wouldn't mind helping us out."

He had some balls to ask me to smuggle him pills in the

middle of the visitation room. His voice was too low for the guards to hear, but maybe the guards were in on it. In some prisons, the inmates ran the show, and the system as a whole was corrupt as fuck.

"You haven't changed at all, have you?" I didn't bother to pretend I didn't know what he was talking about.

"I *have* changed," Michael said. "Like I said, what I did to Ava was wrong, but the only way I can make amends is if I stay alive. And the only way for me to stay alive is to play the game." His jaw tensed. "You don't know what it's like in here. How hard it is to survive. I'm *depending* on you."

"Maybe you should've thought of that before you tried to *murder my sister*." My pent-up anger didn't explode; it seeped out of me, slow and steady, like toxic fumes poisoning the air.

For the first time since he showed up, Michael's "remorseful father" mask slipped. His eyes pierced me like twin daggers. "I raised you. I fed you. I paid for your schooling." He bit out each word like a bullet. "No matter how wrong I was, it doesn't change the fact that I'm *your father*."

The principle of filial piety had been ingrained in me since I was a child. Perhaps it even played a part in why it was so hard for me to cut ties with Michael, because a part of me *did* feel like I owed him for everything he'd given me growing up. We had a nice house and went on fancy family vacations. He bought me the latest gadgets for Christmas every year and paid for Thayer, one of the most expensive schools in the country.

However, there was a line to the blind obedience, and he'd crossed it a thousand times over.

"I appreciate all you did for me as a kid." My hands formed white-knuckled fists under the table. "But being a parent is about more than providing basic necessities. It's about trust and love. I heard your confession to Ava, *Dad*. What I didn't hear was a fucking apology—"

"Don't curse. It's unbecoming."

"Or a good explanation for why you did what you did, and I will fucking curse if I fucking want to, because, again, you *tried to murder my sister*!"

My pulse crescendoed into a deafening roar while my heart battered against my ribs. *There* was the explosion I'd been waiting for. Two years of pent-up emotion gushed out at once, erasing our brief moment of bonding.

The other inmates fell silent. One of the guards moved toward me in warning but stopped short of interrupting us.

Michael's eye twitched. "You're my son. You can't leave me here to rot."

He sounded like a broken record.

Our shared genes were the only bargaining chip he had left, and we both knew it.

"You've survived two years. I'm sure you'll survive another twenty more." I stood, my chest hollow now that I'd expelled all my emotion. Numbness set in and turned my skin cold.

I'd hoped against all hopes that my father could somehow redeem the unredeemable. That he could give a good reason for why he did what he did, or at least show genuine remorse. But it was suddenly, blindingly clear that while he could mimic love, he couldn't actually *feel* it.

Perhaps he loved me in his own way, but that didn't stop him from using me. If I were of no use to him—if I didn't have access to the pills he craved, and if I weren't his one remaining tie to the outside world—he would cast me aside without a second thought.

"Josh." Michael let out a forced laugh. "You can't be serious."

"You're my father by blood, but you're not my family. You never will be. I'm sure your *friends* will understand." I stood, a bitter taste coating my tongue. "I won't be visiting again, but I wish you all the best."

"*Josh.*" Panic crept into his eyes, followed by stunned hurt. It might be the first real emotion I'd seen from him in a long time, but it was too late.

At some point, we had to let go of who a person used to be or who they *could* be and see them for who they really were. And the person Michael Chen had become wasn't someone I wanted to call my father.

"Sit down," he said. "We don't have to talk about the pills. Tell me about your travels. You always liked traveling. Where are you going next?"

My eyes burned as I walked away.

"Josh." The panic bled into his voice. "*Josh!*"

I didn't answer or say goodbye.

I signed out and kept walking until I hit the blazing heat outside the prison.

I had closure, but no one told me closure was such a bitch. It clawed at my bones and ripped a bloody gash through my heart until every breath became a battle.

But instead of trying to assuage it, I embraced it. Because even though pain hurt like a motherfucker, it proved you were still alive, and it was only after it faded that you could finally heal.

40

JULES

The doorbell rang less than a minute after I finished my online bar review lesson.

The exam was in less than a month, which meant I lived and breathed prep until it was over. No going out, no coffee catchups with my friends, no big dates with Josh. When we *did* see each other, Josh and I kept it low key; sometimes, our hangouts consisted of me studying while he made coffee and ordered takeout.

But when I answered the door and saw him standing in the hall, his face a mask of granite, all thoughts of the bar vanished.

"I visited Michael." His hollow voice told me all I needed to know about how the visit went.

Shit.

"How are you feeling?" I didn't ask for details about the visit; they weren't important. What *was* important was how Josh was handling the aftermath.

I opened the door wider so he could enter. Stella was at work, and I had the place to myself for the next few hours.

"Like how you'd expect." Josh shot me a lopsided smile, but

his muscles were visibly tense. His eyes fell on my open laptop and textbooks. "Sorry, I didn't mean to barge into your study time. I know you're busy…"

"Don't worry about it. I was due for a study break anyway." I'd been studying for six hours straight, and my eyes were blurry from staring at the screen so long.

I welcomed the distraction, though I wish it were a happier one.

I sank onto the couch next to Josh. "Do you want to talk about it?" I asked. "Usually, I charge for my therapeutic services, but you're hot, so I'll give you a complimentary fifteen-minute session."

"I *am* hot." He nodded. "I like you. We're off to a good start."

"Well, I have a lot of experience with delusional narcissists. I live in D.C., after all."

Josh's rough laugh wrapped around my heart. "That's a valid point."

My smile lingered for another moment before I sobered. "Seriously, how are you?"

He leaned his head against the backrest. "Sad. Pissed. Resigned to the fact my father and I will never reconcile. And…" His throat flexed with a hard swallow. "Relieved that I can finally put it all behind me. I read his letters. It was just bullshit emotional manipulation. Michael will never change, and seeing him and cutting ties was fucking painful. But I got what I needed."

"Closure," I said softly.

"Yeah." He turned to face me, his eyes dark with self-depre-cation. "I realize how stupid it was to put off confronting him for so long. I put my life on hold for two years when I could've just gotten it over with and moved on."

"It's not stupid." I curled my hand around his and

squeezed. "You weren't ready. It's not just about the confrontation. It's about giving yourself time to prepare. Figure out what you want."

"Yeah." He knocked his knee against mine. "You're not as shitty a therapist as I thought you'd be."

I placed a hand over my chest in mock outrage. "I give you a free session, and that's how you repay me? By insulting me?"

"You love it when I insult you."

"Newsflash, genius. *No one* likes getting insulted."

"You want to test that theory?" Josh's voice lowered.

Just like that, the air shifted. Heavy emotion gave way to a crackling electricity that buzzed over my skin and surged through my blood. It'd been way too long since I'd had sex, and every look, every word, kindled another spark of arousal.

But it wasn't just about sex. Sometimes, the only way to purge the emotional was through the physical. Catharsis in its rawest form.

If this was what Josh needed after his visit with Michael, I would give it to him.

"What did you have in mind?" Josh had been there for me when I needed a distraction from Max. It was time for me to return the favor...not that that was a hardship in any way.

A shadow of tension remained in his eyes, but his smile was all silk and wickedness. "Take off your clothes, Red."

An insistent beat pulsed between my legs at his soft command.

I stood and kept my gaze on his as I slowly slid the top button of my shirt out of its hole. Banked heat incinerated the shadows in his eyes and engulfed me in its flames.

"What kind of man makes the woman do all the work?" I unbuttoned the second button. "I didn't realize you were such a slacker, Chen." *Third button.* "Or is it performance anxiety that's holding you back?"

I cast a pointed glance at his groin, but my mouth dried at the size of his arousal.

I'd forgotten how big he was. How rough he liked it.

Fourth button.

Nervous anticipation rolled through me like a rising tide.

"It's interesting how you keep insulting me like I won't take every word out on you later," Josh said calmly when I shrugged out of my shirt and let it flutter to the ground. "Or maybe you *want* me to take it on you later?"

Fire blazed on my cheeks.

I shimmied out of my pants, my fingers shaking.

"That's what I thought." His smile turned knowing. "Underwear, too. Take it off, then walk to your room."

The air conditioning was on full blast, but the heat of his stare on my naked body warmed me from head to toe.

He walked behind me, his steps near silent, like a predator stalking willing prey.

My anticipation crescendoed when we reached my room, but it devolved into confusion when Josh opened my closet and flicked through the hangers until he pulled something off one of them.

"What..." I trailed off at the sight of the silk scarves in his hands.

My stomach tumbled over itself. *Oh God.*

He wrapped the scarves around his fist so they didn't trail on the ground. "Get on the bed, Jules."

Normally, I would put up more of a fight, but I was too wet and aching to do anything except what he said.

The mattress dipped beneath my weight. Josh joined me less than two seconds later, and I sucked in a sharp breath when he pushed me down on the bed and tied my hands to the headboard posts.

"What are you doing?" I could barely hear myself over the

roar in my ears. My nipples were so hard it was almost painful, and my juices slicked my thighs at the gallery of X-rated images playing in my head.

"Since you think I'm so lazy..." He moved down my body, and I let out a small yelp when he yanked my legs apart and tied my ankles to the remaining posts. "I might as well prove you right."

Josh stepped off the bed to admire his handiwork. I was tied spread eagle on the bed, and a hot flush stole over my face when I realized he had an unimpeded view of how turned on I was—my clit swollen and throbbing, my thighs wet with my arousal.

But when he turned and opened my nightstand drawer, dread trickled into my veins.

He wouldn't.

"Josh, don't you fucking dare."

"Dare what?" His voice was all innocence, but a dark gleam entered his eyes when he found what he was looking for.

A bead of sweat formed on my forehead at the sight of lube and one of my favorite toys—a double-ended vibrator with clitoral suction. It was expensive as hell, and for good reason. It could bring me to a mind-blowing orgasm in less than thirty seconds.

It could also keep me on edge for hours, depending on the speed and intensity.

"This isn't funny." I tugged at my ties, but he'd knotted them so expertly they didn't budge.

"If you want me to untie you, just say so." Josh leaned his hip against the dresser, infuriatingly casual. "I'll do it and leave you in peace. Is that what you want?"

I set my jaw but remained silent.

"That's what I thought." He approached me again and dragged the tip of the vibrator over my clit, just light enough to send a bolt of sensation rocketing through my body but not enough to provide the friction I desperately needed.

My hands curled into fists. I wouldn't give him the satisfaction of responding.

His soft laugh drifted over my body and spiked my already raw nerve endings. "You can fight it all you want, but your pussy gives you away every time. You're fucking *dripping*, Red." He slid a finger inside me, and my nails carved grooves in my palms from the effort it took to hold back a moan.

"So stubborn." He tsked. "Let's see what we can do about that."

He removed his hand. A second later, the cool silkiness of the lube dripped onto me, making me jerk.

I wasn't an anal sex virgin, but it'd been a while since I'd gone there, so I was grateful when Josh used more gel than usual to prep me.

"You look so beautiful, tied up and waiting for my cock." His breath skated over my neck before he followed it with his tongue. He kissed and teased the sensitive spot on my nape while he pushed the vibrator inside me with agonizing slowness. "But we're going to have some fun first. Since I'm so *lazy* and all."

"Josh..." My whimper hitched into a gasp when he shoved the last inch of the toy into me, filling me to the point of discomfort on both ends. "Just fuck me, dammit."

"I would, but I'm a slacker, remember? Better to let something else do the work."

The vibrator switched on. and finally wrenched a strangled cry out of me. My earlier discomfort gradually faded, replaced by intense, searing pleasure.

Oh God.

I couldn't think. Couldn't breathe. All I could focus on were the sensations zinging through my body as the vibrations ricocheted through me. I ground against the bed, desperate for relief, but Josh had tied me in a way that rendered me near immobile.

All I could do was lay there, a slave to his whims while he played me like the world's most exquisitely torturous song.

Fast. Slow. Fast. Slow. Bringing me to the edge again and again until I was a puddle of pure, unrelenting need.

"You're right." Lust strained his voice, and I would've taken greater pleasure in the fact this was as torturous for him as it was for me had I not been near the edge of insanity. "Sometimes, it pays to just sit back and watch."

He sat in the corner and palmed his cock, his eyes like burning flames against my naked flesh while I squirmed against my ties.

"Please," I sobbed. "I can't...Josh...I need you inside me. *Please.*"

I couldn't take it anymore. If I didn't come soon, I would die. I was sure of it.

The vibrator stopped, and I tensed with anticipation when he rose and walked toward me. The mattress dipped beneath his weight as he straddled me, but instead of pulling the toy out and entering me, Josh set the remote down and palmed my breasts with both hands.

"I don't think you've learned your lesson yet, Red." His velvet voice contrasted with the roughness with which he pinched my nipples.

I sucked in a sharp breath when he pushed my breasts together and slid his cock in between them. Pre-cum dripped onto my skin, allowing him to thrust more easily.

I'd never let a guy do this before, but...*God.*

The hardness of his arousal against the softness of my breasts stoked the flames in my body so high I thought I might combust.

My breaths came out in soft pants when Josh picked up the pace, fucking my tits faster until the head of his cock grazed my chin with each upward thrust.

"*Fuck*, your tits are perfect," he groaned. He gave another few pumps before thick ropes of cum painted my face and chest.

I barely had a chance to catch my breath before he wiped some of the cum off my chin with his cock and pushed it inside my mouth. I swallowed eagerly, too mindless with lust to do anything except what he wanted me to do.

He'd just buried himself all the way down my throat when the vibrator buzzed to life again.

My body instinctively jerked. I strained against my ties, my earlier desperation returning in full force as pleasure pulsed through me.

I was going to die like this—tied up, covered in cum, and craving orgasm. My brain was already short-circuiting, and if the explosion building inside me didn't find a release soon, it would incinerate me from the inside out.

"You said you wanted me inside you." Josh pulled out and wiped more cum off my face before shoving his cock back in my mouth. "You should've been more specific, sweetheart."

I let out a muffled protest before he cleaned me up, again and again, until I'd swallowed all his cum and he was fully hard again.

"You like this, don't you?" he growled. He stared down at me, his face taut with desire as he pumped in and out of my throat. "Getting face fucked and filled in every hole like a good little slut."

"Mmmphf." My answering moan was drowned out by the buzz of the toy and the roar in my ears.

I was on fire—every nerve ending aflame, every second an eternity of exquisite torture.

It was heaven, hell, and everything in between.

Josh let out another groan before he pulled out of me again. He slowly slid the toy out of me, and I whimpered at the resulting emptiness. After being so full for so long, it seemed wrong not to have something inside me.

The silk scarves went next, one by one, until I was finally free.

"Such a good girl." Josh rubbed a tear of frustration from my cheek. "You swallowed every drop of cum. That deserves a reward, don't you think?" He pushed his thumb into my mouth, letting me taste the saltiness of my need.

"Please—" A gasp cut off my words when he entered me and buried himself to the hilt in one smooth thrust.

"*Fuck.*" He cursed, his voice turning guttural as he thrust in and out of me. "You take my cock so well, Red. Like your pussy was made for me."

Despite his filthy words, his touch was gentle as he kissed me and settled into a slow, leisurely rhythm. Unlike the previous times we had sex, this didn't feel like fucking; it felt like something sweeter, more intimate.

It felt like making love.

The ball of tingles at the base of my spine climbed higher at the thought.

I closed my eyes, my breaths coming out in staccato bursts. It was too much. Josh's kiss, the way he stretched me out, the sensitivity from the edging session...

My orgasm slammed into me, both unexpected and inevitable. I bowed off the bed with a sharp cry, and I didn't get a chance to recover before Josh picked up the pace and pounded into me hard enough for a second orgasm to roll right into the first one.

"That's it. Scream for me, Red. Let it all out." Josh reached between us and pressed his thumb against my needy, swollen clit. "You come so beautifully around my cock."

I did, again and again until I was limp with exhaustion and couldn't scream anymore.

It was only when I collapsed against the bed, my body sore from multiple blinding, toe-curling orgasms, that he slowed his pace again and came with a heavy groan.

"Good girl." He smoothed my hair back from my forehead and gave me a lingering kiss. "You did so well."

It was embarrassing how much pride glowed in my chest at his words.

He rolled to the side of me and curled an arm around my shoulders, drawing me close. Goosebumps of pleasure dotted my skin when he brushed the back of his hand down my arm in a lazy pattern.

"You know, you're the first guy I've been with in my room." Drowsy content pulled the admission out of me as I snuggled deeper into his side.

I'd never truly cuddled after sex. I thought I would despise it, but clearly, I'd been missing out.

Josh's hand stilled before he resumed caressing my arm. "First *and last,* Red."

I laughed at his soft growl. "Possessive much?"

"Damn right I am." He moved his hand up to cup my neck. The firm, territorial touch sent another thrill down my spine. "I don't like sharing."

"Sharing is a virtue, Josh."

"I don't give a flying fuck. I don't share. Not when it comes to you."

My breath hitched. Golden warmth spread through my chest and lit me up from the inside out.

I didn't know how to respond, so I kissed his shoulder and basked in the moment instead.

I should get out of bed. Stella was coming home soon, and my clothes were still scattered in the living room, but I couldn't tear myself away just yet.

One more minute. Then I'll get up.

I buried my face in Josh's chest, soaking in his warmth and scent. Between Michael and Max, our lives were storms of chaos, but at least we could find temporary peace in moments like this.

"Thank you," he said quietly, breaking the silence. "For being here. I needed this."

"Anytime." I lifted my head, my chest pinching at the touch of vulnerability in his eyes. "But if you pull another edging stunt, I'll chop your dick off."

Josh's face broke out into a dazzling grin. "I'd believe you more if you hadn't come so hard around it multiple times, Red."

I turned my nose up, my cheeks heating. "I was faking it."

"Hmmm." He leaned down and nuzzled my neck. "I can tell when something is real or fake. Your orgasms were real." He grazed his nose over the line of my jaw before capturing my mouth in a soft kiss. "And so is this."

The ache spread from my chest to behind my eyes and nose.

I didn't trust myself to speak, so I turned my head away until I gathered my emotions.

I didn't make a habit of trusting many people. I could count the number of people I *truly* trusted on one hand, and I never thought Josh would be one of them. But life had a way of blindsiding us, and for once, I didn't mind.

Josh and I stayed entwined in comfortable silence until the clock ticked toward the half hour and he reluctantly pulled away.

"I'm gonna hop in the shower," he said. "Stella's coming home soon, right?"

"Yeah." I sighed. I loved Stella, but in that moment, I wished I lived alone.

Josh gave me one last kiss before he climbed out of the bed and slipped out of the room. A minute later, the faint sound of the shower running filtered through the door.

His scent lingered even in his absence, and I wished I could bottle it up so I could carry it around with me all day.

If past me saw present me, she would've slapped me for being so sappy. But it felt *good* to trust someone enough to rely on them, and to have them trust *you* enough to turn to you when they were having a bad day.

I stared at the ceiling, unable to suppress a goofy smile.

I might've lain there all afternoon, or at least until Josh got out of the shower, had an incoming call not interrupted my cheesy inner ramblings.

"Hello, Jules."

It was amazing how quickly two simple words could turn the mood.

A lead spike punctured the balloon of giddiness in my chest, and cold sweat slicked my palms at the sound of Max's voice.

"What do you want?" The shower was still running, but I snuck a peek at the half-open bedroom door anyway in case Josh magically popped up again.

"It's funny you should ask," Max said. "I've *just* decided on the favor I need from you. Isn't that wonderful? You've been so...eager to find out what it is."

Dread formed a lead weight in my stomach. "Spit it out, Max," I growled. "I don't have time for your games."

He sighed. "Where's the patience, J? But fine, since you want to know so bad, I'll tell you. I need you to retrieve something for me. I have some...friends in Ohio who are *very* interested in this item."

Retrieve, AKA steal.

The lead weights multiplied. "And what is this *something*?"

"I'll text you the picture and address." I could practically see Max's smug smile. "It took me a while to track it down. You're welcome, by the way, for doing the hard work. All *you* have to do is what you do best. Lie and steal."

Max hung up before I could reply.

That goddamn *asshole*. If I ever had the chance, I would chop off his dick and feed it to him.

Unfortunately, I couldn't do a damn thing as long as he had that video of me, so I stared at my phone and waited for his text to pop up.

Once it did, I had to blink twice to make sure I was seeing correctly.

It can't be. But no matter how much I stared, the image remained the same.

My blood iced over.

It was a picture of a painting. Brown and green splashed across the canvas in a way that was reminiscent of vomit, and tiny yellow spots added nonsensical detail on the edges.

The art was hideous, but that didn't bother me as much as where I'd seen it before.

The item Max wanted me to steal was the painting in Josh's room.

41

JULES

"You okay, hun?" Barbs eyed me with concern. "You've been unusually quiet all day."

"Yep. Just stressed about the bar." I forced a smile and refilled my coffee mug. I shouldn't be drinking caffeine this late in the day, but I wouldn't be able to sleep regardless. Max's directive to steal Josh's painting had kept me up every night since I received his text three days ago.

"I'm sure you'll do great." Barbs opened the fridge and handed me a Saran-wrapped plate of apple pie. "Here. Pie always makes things better."

My smile was more genuine this time. "Thanks, Barbs."

"Anytime, hun." Barbs winked and left, her mug of beloved Earl Grey tea in hand.

I sipped my coffee and grimaced at the bitter taste. I loved a lot of things about the clinic, but its coffee wasn't one of them.

While I choked down the drink, I stared at my dark phone and waited for it to light up with another text from Max. It never did.

He'd been clear. I had one week to steal Josh's painting or it was game over for me.

Three days had already passed, which meant I had four days left.

My next sip went down the wrong pipe. I erupted into a fit of coughs, shaking so hard some of the liquid splashed out of my cup and scalded my hand.

"Fuck!" I wheezed. I placed the remaining coffee on the counter and ran my hand under cold water, all while coughing my lungs out.

"Everything okay?"

I jumped at the sound of Josh's voice behind me. I knocked over the mug in the process and spilled the rest of my drink down the front of my dress.

"Fuck!" I repeated, more emphatically this time.

I reached for the paper towels, but Josh beat me to it. He yanked a handful off the dispenser and mopped up the coffee running down my leg while I tried to salvage my ruined outfit.

It wasn't happening. The stain had already settled deep into the fibers and turned a substantial portion of the blue skirt a deep, ugly shade of brown. I finally gave up and tossed the paper towel into the trash with a small scream of frustration.

"I guess that answered my question." Josh eyed me with concern and the tiniest hint of amusement. "Bad day?"

"How'd you guess?"

"My deductive powers are one of my many impressive talents," he quipped. "Coffee spill aside, you've been distracted all day."

"Stressed about the bar." I mumbled my go-to excuse. To be fair, I *was* stressed about the exam. It just wasn't my main stressor.

My stomach cramped with guilt.

I'd spent the past three days brainstorming over how to

extricate myself from my Max dilemma, but I couldn't think of a feasible solution that didn't involve revealing the truth about my past.

Perhaps my friends wouldn't judge me, but I was terrified of how Josh would react. For years, he'd thought I was a horrible person, or at least a horrible influence. The last thing I wanted was to prove his initial impressions of me right when we were finally making progress in our relationship.

"Well, if you need a study partner, I happen to know a devastatingly handsome and intelligent one." Josh paused. "I'm talking about myself, by the way."

Despite my tension, a small laugh rustled my throat. "Of course you are. I appreciate the offer, but you'll distract more than you help."

"Understandable. My looks have distracted many a student. It's one of the pitfalls of having this, I'm afraid." He waved a hand in front of his admittedly spectacular face.

"It *is* uniquely hideous." I patted his shoulder. "Don't worry, I'm sure they weren't judging. People are much more open-minded these days."

His chuckle settled on my skin like a rich velvet blanket. "God, I want to fuck you so bad right now."

I wasn't a prude by any means, but heat cascaded down my neck at hearing him state that so directly in the middle of the clinic kitchen.

"*Josh.*"

"Yes?" He lifted one eyebrow. "You need to get out of that dress soon anyway. What better—"

"Am I interrupting something?" Ellie's voice cut into our conversation.

We hadn't even noticed her arrival.

I immediately stepped back and winced when the hard kitchen counter dug into my lower spine.

"I was helping Jules with her spill." He gestured at my dress without missing a beat. His features were a mask of professional civility, but the devilish gleam in his eyes remained.

"Oh, wow, that sucks." Ellie wrinkled her nose. "I hope it's not a new dress."

"It's not. Hot date?" I quickly switched subjects.

The office closed in ten minutes, and Ellie had already changed out of her business-appropriate blazer and pants into a dress and heels.

Pink stained her cheeks. "I'm, ah, going to the movies with Marshall."

I hid a smile. She'd finally gotten over her crush on Josh and switched her attention to Marshall. I wasn't sure whether my and Marshall's kiss spurred that along—we always found people more desirable when other people found them desirable —but I was happy to see she'd moved on.

For entirely unselfish reasons, of course.

"Speaking of which, I should head out. I just came to grab my charger. Left it here during lunch. Good night!" Ellie plucked her phone charger from the outlet near the microwave and rushed off.

"We should head out too, but at different times so people don't get suspicious." Josh's eyes sparkled with playfulness. "Meet you on our corner in twenty."

"We don't have a corner," I pointed out.

"We do now." Josh's dimple made a glorious appearance. "Twenty-third and Mayberry. Twenty minutes, Red. Be there."

He left before I could argue.

I shook my head, but I closed out my desk with deliberate slowness until the office emptied and Barbs and I were the only people left.

"C'mon, hun, I'm not getting any younger." She motioned

me out the door with an impatient hand. "And you're too young to spend a minute longer in the office than you have to."

"You always tell me what I want to hear."

"That's what I'm here for." She waved. "Good night."

"Night."

It took me only five minutes to walk to Twenty-Third and Mayberry. As promised, Josh waited for me on the corner. He leaned against the light pole with his hands tucked in his pockets, but he tapped his watch when he saw me.

"Nineteen minutes. Almost late, Red."

"Good thing I wasn't," I said, too distracted to come up with a witty response. All I could focus on was how to bring up his painting without arousing suspicion.

Maybe I could convince him to get rid of it? It was still deception, because I knew the painting was valuable and he didn't, but it was better than stealing from him.

"So, I was shopping online the other day and came across some nice art," I said casually. "Better than that monstrosity you have in your bedroom."

"Monstrosity?" Josh placed a hand over his heart. "Red, I'm offended. That painting is the epitome of taste. I bet it would fetch a pretty penny if I put it up for auction."

If only he knew how right he was.

"And yet, you bought it for cheap at an estate sale." I forced myself to inject lighthearted snark into my tone. "So excuse me if I don't believe you."

"Not everyone knows the value of what they throw away." Josh wrapped an arm around my waist. "One day, you'll grow to love it as much as I do."

My heartbeat drowned out the echo of our footsteps. "You don't really love it, do you?"

He gave me a strange look. "Not in the sense that I'll run

into a burning building to save it, but I have a soft spot for it. Reminds me of art camp."

Surprise coasted through me. "You went to art camp?"

"Yeah, for one summer when I was eight." Josh winced. "Figured out that art is, uh, not my strongest suit, so I switched to basketball."

"Wow." Suddenly, it all made sense. "No wonder you love terrible art. It reminds you of you!"

I laughed when Josh slapped my ass in retaliation.

"I can't believe you admitted you're not the best at something," I said as we arrived at his house. "Remind me to mark it down in my calendar. It's truly a historic moment."

"Funny." He unlocked the front door and waited for me to enter first before following me inside. "Don't spread it around because I don't let just anyone see my weaknesses. My lack of artistic talent is a very sensitive topic."

"Is that so?" I smiled despite myself. "I feel special."

"You should. Even though you can be fucking exasperating and a pain in my ass—"

My smile disappeared. "Hey!"

"You're one of the few people I trust." His face softened as he looped his arms around my waist and pulled me closer. "Never thought I'd say that, considering our history. But even when we couldn't stand each other, I could always count on you to be honest with me. After what happened with Michael and Alex..." His throat bobbed with a hard swallow. "That means more than you know."

Our earlier lightheartedness grew heavy with poignance.

Oh God.

"I..." Guilt rocked my stomach like storm-tossed waves. *Tell him.* "Josh, I..."

I'm being blackmailed by my ex. I have a sex tape where I let some random guy do obscene things to me so that said ex could steal from him. I'm a thief and a liar and you were right about me all along.

The words sat on the tip of my tongue but refused to leave. I wasn't hiding some small secret. I used to be a *criminal*, and I had a sex tape with a virtual stranger.

I wouldn't blame Josh if he walked away after finding out.

My chest cramped at the thought.

"You know me," I finally managed. "Honest to a fault." I summoned what I hoped was a passable imitation of a smile.

"Emphasis on fault," Josh teased. "It's okay. We can't all be as perfect as I am."

He brushed his mouth over mine before he cupped the back of my neck and deepened the kiss.

I kissed him back, trying to engrave every detail in my mind.

The warm whiskey taste of his lips. The firmness of his touch. His clean, intoxicating scent and the way his muscles molded against my body.

I cherished the kiss like it was our last, because depending on how the next few days played out, it might just be.

42

JULES

I broke into Josh's house four days later.

Okay, *break in* might be too strong a phrase, since I knew where he kept his spare key, but he didn't know I was entering his house while he was at work. Plus, I had to make it *look* like a break-in.

After a week of tossing, turning and agonizing, I finally had a plan. Not a great one, since it depended on luck and someone I barely knew to help me, but I'd cross those bridges when I got there.

First, I had to steal the painting and get Max off my back before his deadline. Then, I could work on removing the hold he had on me, AKA get rid of the sex tape.

My pulse drummed in my ears as I sifted through the potted plant on Josh's porch. He had a night shift and wouldn't be home until morning, but that didn't stop me from freezing every time a twig snapped or a car passed.

After several minutes of searching in the dark—I didn't want to alert his neighbors by turning on my phone's flashlight —I spotted the pale silver gleam of his spare key. I loosely repotted the soil before I unlocked the front door and slipped into the silent house.

It was more menacing in the absence of Josh's warmth. Every shadow was a hiding place for monsters, each creak a gunshot that flayed my already shredded nerves.

Sweat stuck my knit cap against my forehead as I walked through the living room and into his bedroom. Luckily, his room wasn't The Louvre and the painting wasn't the Mona Lisa. All I had to do was unhook the art from its peg and slide it into my oversize portfolio bag.

No wailing alarms, no security bursting through the door with their guns drawn.

It was so easy it was almost sickening.

When someone trusted you, you didn't have to work that hard to slip past their defenses.

Guilt swirled in my chest as I searched Josh's room for other items to pilfer. It would be too suspicious if I stole only the painting.

I couldn't bring myself to take his laptop, but I snatched one of his spare watches, the small wad of emergency cash he stashed in the back of his sock drawer, and his iPad. I'd keep them safe until I returned them after my plan, hopefully, worked.

I was in the process of messing up his room and opening all the drawers when my phone buzzed with a new text.

I banged my hip against the sharp edge of the dresser in surprise. "*Shit*."

I should've silenced my phone. It was a sloppy, amateur mistake, and I silently cursed myself as I opened the message.

Stella: Kangaroo or koala?

It was the code question we used to make sure the other was okay. We were the only ones who knew the nonsensical answer, so no one could pretend to be us over text in case we were kidnapped or something.

I typed out a quick reply.

Jules: Pink Starburst.

Stella and I always informed each other if we were staying out later than usual. Screw waiting until your roommate was missing for twenty-four hours before raising the alarm; if someone fucked with one of us, the other would know almost immediately.

I just hadn't expected Stella to be home so early. She told me she had a work event, and those usually ran until midnight.

Stella: :) Hot date?

Stella: One of these days, you'll tell me who Mystery Guy is

She knew I was dating someone; she just didn't know who.

I stared at her texts for a second before I shoved my phone back into my pocket. I didn't have time to get into a conversation about Josh. If I didn't pull off my plan, there wouldn't *be* anything to tell, because we would be over.

Familiar nausea twisted my stomach.

"Stop it," I whispered. "The plan will work."

The plan will work. The plan will work.

I chanted the silent mantra as I finished setting up the fake-but-not-really-fake burglary. I left the front door unlocked, replanted the spare key in the pot, and hoped like hell real burglars wouldn't show up before Josh came home.

Since he lived near Thayer, his neighborhood was eerily quiet during the summer. No raucous house parties, no chatter from students heading to and from one of the campus bars, no one to stop me as I strolled down the street with my loot.

The logical part of me knew there was nothing overtly suspicious about a woman walking around at night with a portfolio bag. The paranoid part of me was convinced the bag served as a neon sign announcing to the world what a terrible person I was.

Liar! Thief! Do not trust her! it screamed.

Great. Now I was hearing voices from inanimate objects.

I tightened my hold on my bag and quickened my pace until I reached the metro station, where I pulled out my phone again to update Max.

Me: I have it.

Me: I'll drop it off now.

I didn't want to hold onto the painting any longer than I had to.

Max: It's almost eleven at night. Where's your sense of propriety?

Max: Unless, of course, you'd like to give me something else...

I gagged at the suggestion. I was already grossed out by the fact I used to have sex with him. I would rather set myself on fire than let him touch me again.

Me: Give me an address, Max.

Me: Or I'm throwing the painting in the Potomac.

Obviously, I wouldn't, but I'd take any chance to fuck with him.

Max: You're no fun anymore, J.

Despite his complaint, he followed up with an address. A quick Google search told me it was a hotel near NoMa.

He considered me such a negligible threat he didn't bother to hide where he was staying. I wasn't sure whether to be relieved or offended.

When I arrived at the hotel, the receptionist didn't spare

me a glance as I walked through the lobby and took the elevator up to the ninth floor.

I wasn't surprised by the lack of security. The place wasn't exactly the Ritz-Carlton. Sections of wallpaper curled away from the plaster in yellowing stripes, the carpet was so thin I could feel the wooden floors beneath, and the hall stank of cigarette smoke.

My steps faltered outside Max's room. Meeting him in the middle of the night in some sketchy hotel wasn't the smartest idea. He'd always disdained physical violence and deemed it a "lower" form of manipulation, but it'd been seven years. A person could change a lot in seven years, especially if they'd spent most of it in prison.

Right as I was about to leave and text him an excuse for why I couldn't make it tonight after all, his door opened.

"Jules." Max smiled, looking freakishly normal in a white cotton T-shirt and jeans. "I thought that was you." He rapped his knuckles against the wall. "Thin walls. I heard your footsteps from a mile away."

"Congratulations." I shoved the portfolio bag at him. I'd stored the rest of Josh's items in a separate purse, which I kept tucked inside my jacket. "Here's your stupid painting."

"Right here in the hall?" He clucked his tongue. "No manners. What if someone sees us?"

"I'm pretty sure we could do a drug deal in the lobby and no one would blink an eye."

"There are benefits to staying in a hotel such as this one." Nevertheless, Max stepped back into his room, out of the line of sight of anyone walking down the hall, before he pulled out the painting. He examined it with a small grimace. "This is truly hideous."

"Then give it back." It was worth a try.

Max chuckled. "Glad to see you've kept your sense of

humor. No." He tucked the art back into the bag. "This baby is worth a lot of money."

"Fine. Now you have it," I said curtly. "I assume you'll be leaving soon."

I held my breath while he stared at me, hoping he'd take the bait and tell me when he planned to leave. I needed to know how much time I had to implement the second part of my plan.

"Don't worry. I'll be out of your hair by this weekend," he drawled. "Which isn't to say I won't contact you again in the future if I miss you. We had such fun times together."

I bit back a scathing retort. The longer I stayed, the more likely I'd slip up. Besides, I didn't want to give Max the satisfaction of getting a rise out of me.

I turned on my heel and stalked to the elevator without replying. I made it back to the metro without incident, and relief cooled my veins as the train whooshed through the tunnel toward Logan Circle.

Phase one, complete.

It was too late to initiate phase two, so I went straight to my room when I returned home. Thankfully, Stella was already asleep, so I didn't have to answer any questions about where I'd been.

I stripped off my clothes and jumped into the shower, letting the hot water wash away the sticky film of guilt on my skin.

It was past midnight. Max had the painting, and Josh would be home in less than seven hours.

There was no going back.

Thick, steamy air clogged my nostrils with each shallow breath when I pictured Josh's reaction to the "break-in."

No. It's fine. I'm going to return the items, including the painting.

Maybe. Hopefully. .

My mind raced as I ran through my scripts tomorrow, both for Josh when he inevitably tells me about the burglary and for the person whose help I needed.

My plan was simple, but it hinged half on reality and half on hope.

It would work, though. It had to work.

There was no other option.

43

JOSH

SOMETHING WAS WRONG.

My house looked the same as it had when I left last night—curtains drawn, the row of plants on the porch lined up neatly against the wall—but the hairs on the back of my neck pricked up nonetheless.

I scanned the surrounding area, my senses on high alert. I didn't spy anyone lurking in the bushes or pointing a sniper rifle at me through a neighbor's window, so I inched toward the porch with caution.

Instead of using my key, I twisted the doorknob and was only half surprised when it opened without resistance.

It confirmed what my gut already knew: someone broke into my fucking house.

I pushed the door open all the way. My heart banged against my chest, more out of anger than alarm. I doubted the burglar was still here. Most thieves broke in during the day when people were at work. If they came at night, they must've been watching me. They knew I worked the night shift sometimes.

My skin crawled at the violation. The idea that someone had been watching me and planning for the right moment to break into my house made me sick, but this wasn't the time to dwell on that.

First, I needed to figure out what the hell they stole.

Logic took over, and I called 911 before I did a quick search for missing high-value items. My TV was still there, as were my PlayStation and the signed Michael Jordan basketball Ava gifted me for my twenty-third birthday. The house appeared untouched.

I'd almost convinced myself I was being paranoid and merely forgot to lock the front door...until I entered my room.

"Mother*fucker.*"

Clothes spilled out of my ransacked drawers, bottles scattered half-cracked on the dresser, and there was a glaringly empty spot on the wall where my painting once hung. The burglar had destroyed my room.

Hazelburg was one of the safest towns in the country, which was why I hadn't bothered to install a security system. Which cosmic force did I piss off for this shit to happen?

Anger rushed back in a blinding wave as I took another inventory of my belongings. Surprisingly, my laptop was still there, but my painting, emergency cash, iPad, and watch were gone. Nothing too valuable, but still.

The fact that someone had come into my room and rifled through my belongings without my consent made my pulse spike.

I needed a strong drink and a nice, long session with a punching bag to alleviate my fury, but I had to wait for the police to arrive first.

When they did, one of them swept the room for evidence while another took my statement. A frown creased his face after I listed the missing items.

"So the burglar stole four items worth a couple hundred dollars combined and left your laptop?" His words weighed heavy with skepticism.

I didn't blame him. I didn't fucking understand it either.

"Maybe something spooked them and they left before they could grab it." It was the only explanation I could think of.

"Hmmm." The officer's frown deepened. "Okay. We'll do our best to find the perpetrator and recover your items, but I want to set the right expectations. Only thirteen percent of burglary cases are ever solved."

That was what I figured, but it sounded like he'd given up on the case before he started.

"I understand." I forced a tight smile. "I appreciate any help you can give, Officer."

The police left soon after with no leads, taking my hopes of recovering the items with them. In a week, my case would be sitting at the bottom of their to-do list, collecting dust.

Somehow, the day got shittier and shittier.

I walked into the kitchen and cracked open a bottle of vodka while I dialed Jules. There was nothing she could do, but I needed someone to talk to, and she was the first person that popped into my mind.

"Hey, what's up?"

My muscles loosened a smidge at the sound of her voice.

"Someone broke into my fucking house." I poured the vodka into a glass and tossed the drink back. Its cold burn doused some of the flames of my anger. "Stole a bunch of shit. The police just left and said they'll look into it, but the fucker who did this is probably in another state by now."

Jules's audible inhale cut across the line. "Oh my God."

"Yeah." I placed the empty glass in the sink and put her on speaker while I returned to my room. Now that the police had cleared the scene, I needed to clean up the mess the burglar left. "Lucky you, they took the painting you hated so much." I tried to lighten the mood. "You hire someone to break into my place, Red? Because if you really wanted to get rid of the art, you could've just asked. I would've thrown it away for you."

"Funny." Her laugh sounded forced, or maybe that was my lack of sleep talking. "Do you want me to come over?"

"Nah." I wanted to see her, but she had enough going on without dealing with my shit. "Finish studying. I'll swing by later if you need a break."

I didn't have to clock in for my next shift until late afternoon.

"Sounds good." There was a strange catch in her voice. "Josh, I...I'm sorry this happened to you."

"It's fine. I mean, it sucks, but in the grand scheme of things, it could've been worse. At least I'm alive."

"Yeah," Jules said quietly. "My prep lesson starts soon, but we'll talk later?"

"Yep. I l—" I froze at the word that almost slipped out of my mouth. "Let's do that," I finished lamely.

I hung up, my heart rattling with panic.

What. The. Fuck?

Maybe it was the alcohol, but I almost said the three words I'd avoided saying my entire life. Words I never thought I'd say to Jules. But in the moment, they'd felt so natural they almost escaped without me realizing it.

They weren't the result of sudden, blinding clarity the way they were in movies. There'd been no meaningful eye contact at the end of a deep conversation, no special kiss at the end of a magical date.

Instead, they were the culmination of a million small moments—the way Jules tried to distract me with her fish propaganda declaration during *Finding Nemo*, her quiet sympathy when I told her about my patient's death, the way she tasted and fit against me like she was the last piece in the jigsaw puzzle of my life.

Somehow, she'd gone from the last person I wanted to be around to the first person I turned to when I needed comfort or just someone to talk to.

I wished I could say I didn't know how I ended up here, but I'd been on a slow, steady march toward this moment since our first kiss. Hell, maybe even before that, with Vermont and our clinic truce.

I'd just been too blind to notice the destination in my GPS had changed.

Ten minutes ago, the burglary had consumed my thoughts; now, it was barely a blip on my radar.

I had a much bigger problem to deal with.

This is a strictly physical arrangement.

No falling in love.

Red, you'll fall in love with me before I ever fall in love with you.

The banging in my chest intensified.

"Oh, *fuck.*"

44

JULES

My breakfast rose in my throat, and I had to make a conscious effort to force it back down when I hung up Josh's call.

I felt faker than a *Mona Lisa* print hanging in the lobby of a seedy motel.

You hire someone to break into my place, Red? Because if you'd really wanted to get rid of the art, you could've just asked. I would've thrown it away for you.

I wiped a clammy palm against my thigh.

Stella had already left for work, so it was just me and my screaming conscience.

You're a liar and a terrible person. Josh was right about you all along, the insidious voice in my head taunted. *You're the worst thing that's ever happened to him.*

"Shut up."

This is why everyone always leaves you. Why no one loves you. You don't deserve—

"Shut. *Up.*"

I paced the living room, trying to drown out the insecurities rearing their ugly heads.

I *wasn't* a bad person. Sometimes, I made bad decisions, but that didn't make me a bad person. Right?

Sweat stuck my shirt to my skin.

"It's fine. I have a plan. I'm going to return everything to him, and I'll get rid of Max." Saying the words out loud eased some of my nausea.

I didn't have the luxury of wallowing if I wanted to carry out the rest of my plan, so I allowed myself five more seconds of self-loathing before I straightened my shoulders, exited my apartment, and took the elevator up one floor.

It was time for phase two.

As long as Max had the tape, he had leverage over me. I wasn't naive enough to trust he'd go away no matter how much I "repaid" him. The only way to get rid of him for good was to get rid of the tape. I didn't know if it was possible to destroy every copy of a digital file for good, but I was desperate enough to try.

The only reason I hadn't tried before was because I had no clue how to go about doing it, and I didn't want to risk failing and pissing him off.

But the other night, as I lay awake staring at the ceiling of my fancy new apartment, I realized there was *one* person who might have the computer skills to pull off my plan: Christian Harper, AKA my landlord, AKA Rhys's old boss.

I remembered Bridget saying he'd tracked down the person who leaked photos of her and Rhys to the press last year. That wasn't quite the same as deleting a video that could have dozens of copies floating around in cyberspace, but it was worth a shot.

The elevator doors pinged open.

I walked down the hall to Christian's fortress-like front

door and rang the bell, praying like hell he was home. I'd only seen him twice since Stella and I signed the lease—once at Bridget's wedding, which he'd attended thanks to his connection with Rhys, and once in passing in the lobby.

I dropped by Pam's office yesterday and harangued her until she confirmed he was in town. She'd made some snarky remark along the lines of how "Mr. Harper isn't interested in the likes of *you*," but I didn't care if she thought I wanted to seduce Christian. She was irrelevant.

I rang the doorbell again. Max left this weekend. If Christian wasn't here, I was screwed.

I had a plan, but that didn't mean it was a *good* plan. It relied heavily on good luck, and I could only hope the gods took pity on me and threw a bone my way.

I even borrowed one of Stella's manifestation crystals, just in case it helped.

I stared at the closed door. *Come on, come on...*

Just as I was about to accept defeat, it opened, revealing glittering amber eyes and sculpted cheekbones.

It was only eight in the morning, but Christian was already dressed in an exquisitely tailored suit. Between that, his perfectly styled dark hair, and his clean-shaven face, he looked like he'd already been at work for hours and closed several multimillion-dollar deals in that time.

"Ms. Ambrose." His smooth, decadent voice filled the air with its richness. "To what do I owe this pleasure?" He flicked his gaze over my shoulder like he expected to see someone behind me.

When he didn't, a shadow of what looked like disappointment crossed his face before it disappeared as quickly as it came.

"Good morning. I'd like to ask a favor." I got straight to the point. Every second counted, and Christian Harper didn't seem like the type of man who enjoyed beating around the bush, anyway.

"A favor." Amusement shimmered in his eyes like whiskey shot through with firelight.

"Yes." I lifted my chin, trying to contain my nerves. I realized the irony of asking for a favor when a favor was what landed me in my current predicament, but the universe had always had a crappy sense of humor. "You helped Bridget and Rhys with their...problem last year, and I would be grateful if you could assist me as well. It's a, um, digital problem, and you're supposed to be the best of the best when it comes to those things."

A little flattery never hurt, right?

"I was returning a favor for Rhys, not granting one." Christian seemed unmoved by my compliment. "The question now, of course, is why I would assist you." His smile, though polite, only sharpened the razor edge of his question.

I faltered. "Because...you're a nice person?"

He *had* reduced my monthly rent to a fraction of its price with no strings attached. At least, none that we could see.

Maybe I should've fleshed out my plan more.

Christian's smile faded. "Your biggest mistake, Ms. Ambrose, would be assuming I'm a nice person," he said softly.

A shiver of unease slithered down my spine. Still, I forged ahead. I had no choice. "You don't need to be a nice person to help me. I'll owe you one."

It was a reckless promise, considering I knew next to nothing about him. I could end up as beholden to him as I was to Max. But he was friends with Rhys, and Rhys was a stand-up guy, so that had to count for something. Right?

"Rhys was my top employee, a former Navy SEAL, and the future Prince Consort of Eldorra," Christian said. "What can you offer me?"

"Professional legal advice?"

"I have a team of lawyers on retainer."

"A custom-made thank you cake from Crumble & Bake?"

"I don't eat dessert."

That was just wrong. What kind of monster didn't eat dessert?

I chewed on my bottom lip, trying to think of something else. "My eternal gratitude? I'll sing your praises to all my friends."

Christian tipped his head to the side, his gaze assessing.

You've got to be kidding me. I'd meant that as a *joke.*

"One favor from you in exchange for a favor from me," he said. "To be decided upon on a future date of my choosing."

Wariness crawled into my stomach. It sounded suspiciously like what Max had asked of me, minus the whole creep factor. "What kind of favor?"

I swear to God, if Christian asked me to sleep with him—

"Nothing sexual or illegal." His reassurance didn't ease my anxiety. I had a shitty history with the *F* word. "That's my offer. Take it or leave it."

Agreeing to an open-ended favor was a dumb idea, but I didn't have the luxury of long-term planning when faced with a short-term emergency. Besides, Christian was the CEO of a reputable organization, not some low-life criminal like Max.

I hope I don't regret this.

"I'll take it."

A satisfied gleam entered Christian's eyes.

I couldn't shake the eerie sense I'd just struck a deal with the devil. But whatever favor he wanted in the future would be worth dispelling the black cloud of the sex tapes once and for all.

Right?

"Excellent." He opened the door wider. "My next meeting isn't until eight-thirty. You have eleven minutes."

I followed him through his penthouse and explained my situation—the tapes, Max's blackmail threats, my desire to erase the recordings once and for all. I omitted the part where I used to steal for money; Christian didn't need to know, and I didn't have time to get into it anyway.

"I see." He sounded almost bored by my dilemma.

I was half annoyed that he didn't appreciate the gravity of the situation and half hopeful that his calm response meant he had a solution.

Christian didn't speak again until we reached his private library. Colorful books filled two walls of floor-to-ceiling shelves, and windows carved massive nooks on the remaining walls and bathed the room in piercing morning light.

A man stood in the middle of the room, dressed in a suit as expensive-looking as Christian's. Annoyance etched deep lines in his face as he spoke rapid-fire Italian into his phone, but he hung up abruptly when he saw us.

"Dante, I trust everything is all right," Christian said, like the other man hadn't sounded like he was ready to murder someone in broad daylight.

Dante flashed a tight smile. "Yes, of course." He slid his eyes toward me, his curiosity a warm weight against my skin.

He looked a little older than Christian, maybe mid to late thirties, but that only added to his physical appeal. He wasn't as classically good-looking as Christian, but he exuded a rugged masculinity that would make most women swoon. The thick dark hair and muscled frame didn't hurt, either.

"I didn't realize you had company," I said to Christian. It seemed too early for a business meeting, but what did I know? I wasn't a CEO.

"I was just leaving." Dante held out his hand. Silver cufflinks engraved with tiny *V*'s glinted on his shirtsleeves. "Dante Russo."

"Jules Ambrose."

He gave me a curt nod and slid an indecipherable look at Christian. "We'll finish our conversation later. My grandfather just died." He delivered the news like he was announcing a trip to the grocery store.

My eyes rounded with shock, but Christian didn't even blink. "Of course."

After Dante left, Christian walked to the computer in the corner and typed something. A minute later, the printer spit out a sheet of paper, which he handed to me along with a pen.

His cufflinks flashed in the light, and I realized they were engraved with the same *V*'s as the ones Dante wore.

"Sign this, and I'll take care of the tape."

I scanned the text. "You have a contract for *favors?*" It was a standard agreement listing the terms of our deal, but if I reneged on it, I would be held liable for...I blinked to make sure I read it correctly. "Two *million* dollars? You've got to be joking."

"I don't joke about business, and anything that involves my time and skills is business." Christian nodded at the paper. "As I'm sure you're aware, Ms. Ambrose, contracts protect both parties. If I'm unable to fulfill my end of the agreement, the contract is void. If I renege on the deal, I am also liable for two million dollars. It's only fair."

Yeah, except two mil was a drop in the bucket for him whereas it was an impossibility for me.

"Those are my terms. We haven't signed anything yet, so you can still walk away." He gave an elegant shrug. "Your choice."

A favor of his choosing or I would owe him two million dollars...

My head pounded with indecision.

What were the chances he would ask me to do something *really* awful? He said anything sexual or illegal was off the table.

There was a fifty-fifty percent chance I would regret this, but my desire to get rid of Max overrode everything else.

I scribbled my signature on the designated line and handed it back to him. Christian signed after me, and that was that.

We were officially in business.

"It's quite difficult to erase something forever once it's in the digital realm, but it's not impossible," Christian said.

Not for me.

I heard his implication loud and clear.

Some of the anxiety in my stomach loosened. I didn't know him well, but I knew Christian Harper was damn good at what he did. He hadn't built the world's most elite security company from the ground up by slacking.

"I will, however, require your assistance with one part of the plan. I can have my men do it, but it's much easier this way." Christian smiled. "Here's what you need to do..."

45
___

JULES

I RETURNED TO MAX'S HOTEL THE NEXT AFTERNOON.

Christian's instructions were simple, if not easy, and there was no point dragging the inevitable out.

Either the plan would work, or it wouldn't.

I knocked on Max's hotel door, intensely aware of the man hidden in an alcove at the end of the hall. Christian had sent one of his men to accompany me. Kage would wait out of sight until I entered Max's room, after which he could monitor what was happening through the nifty camera disguised as a necklace pendant. Apparently, he had some sort of device that could disable the door's key card scanner in case the situation with Max turned nasty.

"Jules." Max gave me a genial smile, but suspicion lurked in his eyes. "I didn't expect to see you here again. Come back to collect on your...benefits?" His gaze dipped to my chest.

My skin crawled beneath his leering scrutiny, but I forced myself to remain semi-civil so I could get inside his room. "No, but I have something important to tell you about the painting."

I glanced around the hall like I was paranoid someone would hear us. "Let's talk about it inside."

Max narrowed his eyes. For a second, I was afraid he'd deny my request, but after several long, agonizing beats, he opened the door wider for me to enter.

I stepped inside and scanned the room, searching for his computer. If he packed it away...

Relief settled into my bones when I spotted the open laptop on his desk. *Thank God.* If I didn't see it, Kage would've had to distract him so I could search for it, but this made my job much easier.

"So, what do you want to tell me?" Impatience threaded Max's voice when I remained silent.

I turned to face him while I edged backward toward his desk. "I think the painting I gave you is a fraud." I stuffed my hands in my sweatshirt pocket as casually as possible.

My fingers closed around the tiny gadget Christian gave me, and I let out a small cough to hide the soft beep it made when I pressed the power button.

The device was a wireless hacking tool Christian had developed himself. He'd explained how it worked, but the technical terms had gone way over my head. All I knew was, it had to be within five feet of the hacking target, and it couldn't be turned on until it was or it would attach to a different network. Or something like that.

I trusted Christian knew what he was doing, so I followed his instructions to a tee despite understanding only half of what he said.

"The one you stole from your boyfriend's place? It's not." Max smiled at my jerk of surprise. "You thought I didn't know you were fucking your little doctor boy toy? I had to case his place after I tracked the painting down. I saw you going in and out of his house at all hours of the day. Doesn't take a genius to figure out what you two were doing." His smile turned nasty. "Once a whore, always a whore."

Blooms of outrage colored my cheeks. "Is that the best you can come up with? The name-calling is getting old, Max. Find a new insult or don't use one at all, especially since I came here to *help* you."

Come on, Christian.

He said it would take two minutes for the device to connect to the computer, then an additional five to ten minutes to find the video, depending on how many files Max had. In hindsight, I was lucky Max sent me screenshots to fuck with me the past few weeks—Christian could use them as a basis for his search. Otherwise, it would take his software far longer to scan every video if it didn't know what it was looking for.

We agreed he would text me only after he found and destroyed all copies of the video. I'd personalized his alert tone, so I would know it was done without having to check my phone.

"Help me?" Max stared at me, his suspicion mounting. "Why would you do that?"

"Because I don't want you to come back later and pin the blame on me. I want this"—I gestured between us—"to be over with as soon as possible." I snuck a peek at the clock. *Shit.* It'd been less than five minutes. I needed to drag the conversation out longer. "How do you know for sure the painting's not a fraud?"

"My friends confirmed it," he said coldly. "Besides, everyone thinks it's junk. No one would copy junk, Jules." He walked toward me, his steps heavy against the paper-thin blue carpet.

I forced myself to hold my ground. Kage was right outside, but being trapped in a hotel room with Max made my heart lurch with panic.

"What's so special about the painting anyway? It's hideous." I should've worn something other than a sweatshirt. It clung to my skin, suffocating me. The heat rose from my torso to my face, and I felt like I was burning alive in an incinerator of my own making.

"Value doesn't always equate to beauty." Max looked me over from head to toe, his implication clear. "The painting is one of a limited number that belonged to a famous European collector. It's worth a lot of money in certain circles, but it was sold at an estate sale by mistake and switched from owner to owner until we tracked it down to your boyfriend's house. Took a lot of paperwork tracing and bribes to get to that point, but we did it." His eyes glinted with malicious amusement. "Imagine my delight when I learned about your connection to the current owner. It was like fate dropped you into my lap."

Yeah, no kidding. Fate liked to fuck me over as a hobby.

"Did you tell him about the painting?" Max asked. "Or did you suck his cock so good he handed it over without complaint?"

"At least he knows what to do with his cock, unlike some other people I know." My voice dripped with poisonous honey. "Sucking it is no hardship at all."

Max's words still poked at old insecurities, but I refused to let him shame me for enjoying sex, dammit.

Guys slept with multiple partners and were lauded for being players; girls did the same and were decried as whores. It was a double standard as old as time, and I was fucking sick of it.

Satisfaction flared in my stomach when his face turned a mottled red. One universal truth about men: nothing dented their ego and pissed them off more than questioning their manhood.

"Careful, Jules." Icy rage flowed beneath Max's words, but

his mask was slipping. I could see it in his eye twitch and the vein pulsing in his forehead. Beneath all that fake "niceness" was a fragile little shit who was one insult away from exploding.

I swallowed a ball of trepidation. *It's fine. Kage is right outside.*

"One press of the button. That's all it'll take before everyone knows what a whore you are. I wonder what your boyfriend will say when he sees another guy fucking you in the ass and coming all over your face. Or what Silver & Klein will say when they see what their potential employee likes to do in her spare time." He cocked his head, his eyes glittering with malice. "Maybe I'll upload it to a porn site. Get paid. It's hard for prior felons to get a job these days. Gotta do what I gotta do to put food on the table."

The metal gadget dug into my palms. Oxygen ran thin at the prospect of the video being uploaded online for the world to see. Of strange men jerking off to one of the worst moments of my life.

I shouldn't have provoked Max so early. What if Christian couldn't erase the video? What if he missed a copy? What if—

The soft notes of Christian's personalized alert tone burst from my phone.

The one we set so I would know once the job was done.

My heart rattled harder against my ribcage. Now that the moment was here, I couldn't untie my tongue. How much did I *really* trust Christian to get the job done? It would be so easy to miss a file. Nothing truly died in cyberspace. And what if Max made a *physical* copy?

The walls pressed in, caging me in yellowing floral wallpaper and the scent of mildew.

Can't breathe can't breathe cantbreathecantbreathe...

Another, more impatient burst of music sliced through the

silence. Christian was probably monitoring the situation via the camera and wondering why I hadn't made my next move yet.

I sucked in a shallow lungful of air.

I'd come this far. There was no backing out now.

"Actually," I said. "You might want to check your phone. See if that video is still there. Things disappear in cyberspace all the time."

Beads of sweat dotted my forehead as Max stared at me. I could practically see him piecing the puzzle together—my unannounced arrival, the way I'd stretched out our conversation, why I was suddenly so willing to talk back.

Once it clicked, he jabbed at his phone, his eyes moving back and forth over the screen with frenzied speed.

Air flowed to my lungs again when he snarled.

It was gone. From his phone, at least.

Max didn't say a word as he pushed past me toward his laptop. Each frantic tap on the keyboard sounded like a gunshot in the silence.

I inched toward the door but kept my eye on him. His reaction would tell me everything—whether Christian had destroyed every copy, or whether he had another copy of the video stashed somewhere.

When Max finally looked up, his features contorted into a mask of rage, my knees weakened with relief.

After years of the tape hanging over my head, it was finally gone.

I was home free.

"What did you do?" he hissed.

"I took back what belonged to me. Control over my body." A thick pressure inside me eased, so suddenly and completely I would've floated off the ground had I not been terrified any movement would shatter this delicate dream. The pressure had been a part of me for so long I hadn't realized it was there until it was gone. "I also want the painting back. It doesn't belong to you *or* your friends."

Max moved so fast I didn't get a chance to blink before his hand closed around my wrist in a crushing grip. A small cry fell out at the pain lancing up my arm.

"You fucking bitch—" He only got half his sentence out before tattooed hands yanked him off me and tossed him aside like he was nothing more than a rag doll.

Kage.

Somehow, he'd entered the room without either of us noticing.

"Hands off the lady," Kage growled.

Max sputtered in shock as he took in the other man's bulky, six-foot-two frame. "Who the fuck are you?"

Kage crossed his arms over his chest. He didn't answer.

"The painting, Max." My wrist still throbbed from where he'd grabbed me, but I ignored it. "Where is it?"

His jaw flexed with anger, but he wasn't dumb enough to test Kage's capability for violence. "The closet," he ground out. "In the portfolio bag."

I glanced at Kage, who nodded. He kept an eye on Max while I retrieved the bag from the closet and unzipped it. The painting was nestled inside the black material, safe and sound and hideous as ever.

Thank God.

"This isn't over," Max said as I walked to the door. He'd wrestled his outward fury under control, but his eyes shone with anger and panic. I assumed his "friends" wouldn't be too happy about him losing the painting. "You think you solved all your problems just because you got rid of the tape and took back the painting? You're still a liar and a whore. Eventually, your boyfriend will figure it out and toss you aside the way everyone does. The way I'd planned to do before you snuck off in the middle of the night like a coward."

I stopped in the doorway. Max was pushing every button he could find. Some of it I brushed off; others peeled the scabs off healing wounds until they bled again.

Sweat dampened my palms at the prospect of Josh finding out what happened.

"Maybe I'll nudge the process along. Give the good doctor a heads up on who, exactly, broke into his house. I'm sure he'll appreciate the truth." The poison from Max's words dripped into my veins.

Kage's low growl rumbled through the air. He stepped toward the other man, but I held out my arm to stop him.

This wasn't his fight.

"Actually, Max it *is* over." The bag strap slipped against my palms. "You don't have the tape. You don't have evidence of anything that happened in Ohio. If you did, you would've used it already. And you can *try* to tell Josh, but he's not going to believe you over me. You have nothing."

Max paled. He curled his hands into fists, his chest rising and falling with shallow breaths.

Without the armor of blackmail, he looked small. Weak, like the Wizard of Oz after the curtain was pulled back.

A strange, unexpected seed of sympathy sprouted in my stomach. For all the terrible things he'd done, Max had saved me when my mom kicked me out. Granted, he'd pulled me into a life I was less than proud of, but without him, I might've ended up homeless.

I would still cut his balls off if I had the chance, but he was right. I did owe him. Not money or my body, but some acknowledgment of our shared history that would allow me to walk away for good with a clear conscience.

"I'm sorry you spent all those years in jail," I said. "Seven years is a long time, and I understand why you're angry. But you're out now, and it's a chance for a fresh start. Don't get sucked into your old life any more than you already have." I swallowed hard. "It's easy to get caught up in old habits and hurts, but you'll never be happy chasing things that no longer exist. It's time to move on from the past. I did."

I walked out, leaving Max red-faced and alone in his hotel room.

My mind tumbled with a thousand thoughts as Kage and I rode the elevator down to the lobby.

It's time to move on from the past. I did.

Except I hadn't, not really.

I'd planned to plant the stolen items back in Josh's house and leave him to figure out why the burglar would do such a thing. But if I did that, my lies would *always* be an albatross around my neck. Even if Josh never found out what happened, I would know. Every time he kissed me, every time he smiled at me, I would know I was keeping something from him, and it would eat me, and eventually us, alive.

How could you build a relationship on a foundation of lies?

The answer: you couldn't.

The elevator doors opened. I walked through the lobby, barely noticing the ugly orange carpet and threadbare sofas.

Moving on from the past didn't mean burying it beneath a new foundation and hoping no one found it; it meant exposing the ugliness to the light and taking responsibility.

You couldn't heal from something if you didn't acknowledge it.

As Kage and I stepped out of the hotel, my thoughts crystallized into clarity.

I knew what I had to do.

I had to tell Josh the truth.

46

JOSH

"You're in a remarkably good mood." Clara cocked an amused eyebrow as I signed out from my shift. "Does the reason begin with a *J* and rhyme with *rules?*"

"Cannot confirm or deny," I said, practically whistling.

Last week's burglary aside, I'd had a damn good week. I'd put Michael behind me, Alex and I were on our way to being real friends again, and work had been relatively easy. For the ER, that meant no patient deaths and no mass casualty incidents, though there had been a nasty case involving an idiot with a blowtorch.

Plus, Jules's bar exam was next week, which meant we could finally go on real dates again soon.

I already had our first post-bar date planned: a weekend trip to New York to see a special limited-time revival of *Legally Blonde: The Musical*, sandwiched between lots of good food and even more sex.

I'd have to trade shifts again to make the weekend happen, and it was expensive as hell on a resident's salary, but Jules deserved it. Getting through the bar was a big deal.

"Fine. Don't tell me, but I can guess." Clara rolled her eyes good-naturedly. "One of these days, you'll have to confirm your relationship, or the other nurses won't stop hounding you about dating."

"I'll confirm after you admit *your* relationship with Tinsley is serious." I smiled at her scowl. She'd been dating Tinsley for months and still refused to make it official. And people said *I* had commitment problems. "That's what I thought."

"Goodbye, Dr. Chen," she said pointedly.

I laughed and waved before I left.

I'd scheduled drinks with Alex for tonight, but that wasn't for another four hours. I had time for a shower and a quick nap, maybe a bit of New York research. I read about a dessert place there that reportedly served incredible salted caramel ice cream.

I typed in the security code when I arrived at my house and pushed the door open. One of the first things I did after the break-in was install a home security system. Alex recommended it, so I assumed it was good.

Well, it was the tenth one he recommended. The first nine were expensive as shit, but at least this one cracked his top ten.

I was already half asleep by the time I finished my shower, but the sound of the doorbell jolted me awake.

I threw on a pair of sweatpants and answered the door. Pleasant surprise filtered through me when I saw Jules standing on the front step.

"Hey, Red." I greeted her with a cocky grin. "Can't stay away from me, huh? Don't blame you." I gestured at myself. "Look at all this."

I was still shirtless from the shower, and I didn't want to brag or anything, but my abs were a fucking work of art.

"If I knew you had company, I would've waited," she said dryly. She was carrying a large portfolio bag, which was strange, since she didn't draw. Maybe she went shopping earlier. "Wouldn't want to interrupt your weekly lovefest with your ego."

"*Daily*," I corrected. "Self-love is critical to maintaining one's self-esteem. But you're hot, so you're allowed to interrupt." I drew her inside and kicked the door closed behind us before planting a kiss on her lips. "Here for a study break?"

"Um, sort of." Jules tucked a strand of hair behind her ear, looking unusually nervous.

"Well, don't take too long of a break. As happy as I am to see you, I want you to kick ass on this exam." Anticipation zipped down my spine. "I have a surprise for you after it's over."

"Can't wait."

I frowned at her subdued response. Normally, she'd be hounding me about what the surprise was until I caved. "You okay?"

"Yes. No. I mean, I have something to tell you." She drew in a long breath without meeting my eyes. "It's about the painting the burglar stole."

"Okay..." I narrowed my eyes. "You're not making me buy that painting we saw online the other day, are you? The one of the dogs playing poker? Because it's cool and all, but there must be a thousand other people who own it."

"No." Her laugh sounded forced. "Actually, it's a funny story. I have the painting. The one you're missing."

Confusion drew my brows together. "You found a print of it?"

"No." Jules fiddled with her bag. "The real thing. The one stolen from your room."

My smile slipped, and foreboding settled over my skin like a layer of frost. How the *fuck* did she get the painting when the police couldn't even find a lead?

"What are you talking about?"

Instead of answering, Jules slowly unzipped the portfolio bag and withdrew the painting.

I stared at it blankly.

There it was, in all its brown and green glory. I'd never realized how condescending it was. The painting smirked at me, its taunt a singsong voice in my head.

I know something you don't. And you're not going to like it when you find out...

"That's not all." Jules's voice shook so violently she sounded like a distorted version of herself.

My foreboding hardened into icy disbelief when she reached into her purse and retrieved three additional items.

My watch. My iPad. My rolled-up wad of emergency cash.

No.

She set them on the coffee table, the tremble in her hands matching the one in her voice.

No, no, no.

"Tell me you hunted down the thief and recovered those items." I barely heard myself over the roar in my ears. "Tell me the burglar had a crisis of conscience and dropped those items on my porch when I was in the shower and you found them. Dammit, Jules, tell me *something*!"

Something other than the suspicion winding its way around my throat and choking off my air.

"I stole the items." Jules's confession hit me like a bullet in the chest. Pain pierced my flesh, making me flinch. "I'm so sorry. I didn't want to do it. He was blackmailing me, and I didn't know what else to do except go along with it, and I..."

Her rambled explanation faded as the roar grew louder. Her words ran together into a murky stream that painted the world in ugly grays and vicious reds.

She was the artist, and I was trapped in a surrealist nightmare of her making.

"Who?" I latched onto the last thing I remembered hearing.

My brain was sluggish, and it took more effort than usual to get the word out.

Jules wrapped her arms around her waist. "Max."

Max. The guy I met at Hyacinth.

Liquid dark rage seeped through my veins and into my voice at the mention of that smug-faced fucker. "Start from the beginning."

I listened, numb, as Jules explained everything more clearly this time—the jobs she pulled in Ohio, her relationship with Max, her sex tape, his blackmail, how she broke into my house and how she finally got rid of the video and recovered the painting.

When she finished, the ensuing silence was loud enough to deafen me.

"I'm sorry." Jules swallowed. "I should've told you all this earlier, but I didn't want to ruin what we had when we were just starting to get along. I wasn't sure how you would react, and I thought..."

"You thought?"

"That if I told you about my past, it would confirm everything horrible you'd ever thought about me." Her voice grew smaller with each word, like she was realizing how fucking stupid they were.

My rage pulsed harder. It leaked from my veins and spread into my chest, hollowing it out until nothing else remained.

Half of it was directed at Max for what he did to Jules.

The other half...

Breathe.

"I see." No matter how hard I tried, I couldn't summon an

ounce of warmth. My blood had iced into one solid, painful pool, and I was afraid any movement would crack it. Splinter it into a thousand icicles that would shred me open from the inside out. "So why are you telling me now?"

"I didn't want to lie to you anymore. I *never* wanted to lie to you, but I..." Jules took a deep breath and straightened her shoulders. "I wanted us to have a fresh start. No more secrets or lies."

"I see," I repeated. The cold in my chest intensified. "I forgive you."

She faltered, her face twisting with confusion at the contrast between my words and my chilly tone. "You do?"

"Yes." I smiled. The movement felt strange, like I was contorting my mouth into a position it was no longer capable of. "Come here, Red."

The nickname tasted bitter on my tongue.

After a moment's hesitation, she stepped toward me.

Even with ashen skin and dark circles shadowing her eyes, she was the most beautiful, treacherous thing I'd ever seen.

I curled my hand around the back of her neck and rubbed a gentle thumb over her skin before I yanked her toward me and kissed her hard enough to draw a whimper of pain.

"That hurt?"

Jules shook her head, her muscles taut beneath my touch.

"Good." I softened the kiss, soothing her lips with my tongue. "You shouldn't have lied, Red," I whispered. "You know I hate liars."

I detected a soft tremble in her shoulders. "I know."

"But you..." I dragged my mouth over the line of her jaw and down her neck. "You are so beautiful. So sweet beneath that prickly armor you wear. You know things about me no one else ever will." I sank my teeth into the curve between her neck and shoulder. "How can I stay mad at you?"

Jules let out another whimper when my hand inched beneath her skirt and brushed over her pussy. For once, she wasn't wet for me.

But we would change that.

I slipped my hand inside her underwear and caressed her until she flooded my fingers and her body melted into mine.

My movements were cold. Mechanical. I'd done them a million times, and I watched her mouth part in little moaning gasps with apathy.

My cock strained against my zipper, hard and angry. It was a physical reaction more than anything else, but it was the only part of me that still felt alive.

Jules was teetering on the edge of orgasm when I yanked my hand away.

"Get on your fucking knees."

She jerked at my harsh tone, but after a second's hesitation, she slowly sank to her knees without argument.

"Do you want this?" I tilted her chin up, forcing her eyes to meet mine. "Tell me if you don't, Red. This is your last chance."

Jules's throat bobbed with a swallow. "I want this."

I released her chin and tugged her head back with one hand while freeing my cock with the other. "Tap my thigh if you want me to stop."

That was the only warning I gave her before I shoved myself down her throat. She gagged at the brutal invasion, her eyes welling with tears, but her hands remained planted in her lap.

I gripped her hair with both hands and fucked her mouth, deeper and deeper until the obscene sound of my balls slapping against her chin mixed with her choked gurgling.

My jaw clenched as I stared down at her. The sight of her kneeling before me, tears and mascara running down her cheeks while she choked on my cock, sent an irrational wave of fury through me.

I closed my eyes and tipped my head back. That turned out to be a mistake, because the minute I did, unwanted memories banged through my brain.

Vermont. The clinic. Hyacinth. The picnic. Ohio.

Every puzzle piece that shaped our relationship into what it was now, tainted.

It wasn't about the size of Jules's lies. I didn't give two fucks about a stupid painting and some gadgets. It was about trust.

All I'd ever wanted was honesty, and all I'd ever gotten was deception.

Tension knifed through my gut.

I opened my eyes and yanked my cock out of Jules's mouth. Sweat coated my skin, and my heart drummed a painful rhythm in my chest.

She was a mess—hair tousled, mouth swollen, cheeks streaked with tears. She stared up at me, those huge hazel eyes saying words I didn't want to hear.

"Get on all fours."

I couldn't bring myself to look at her, but even when I fucked her from behind, images of her seared through my brain.

The glint of her hair in the sunlight. The fire that sparked in her eyes when she insulted me. The softness of her palm against mine and the way her mouth tilted up just a fraction higher on the right when she smiled.

Pressure suffocated my chest.

Jules was close to coming. I could hear it in the way she breathed and feel it in the way she squeezed around me.

It was funny how sometimes, I was attuned to her every movement, and other times, I didn't know her at all.

I leaned down until my mouth hovered next to her ear.

"Remember when I said I forgive you?" I reached around to pinch her clit. "I lied."

Jules's orgasm hit her at the same time my words did. She gasped out a half sob, half moan while I came right after her.

The empty release did nothing to ease the pressure behind my ribcage.

I disentangled myself from her and stood. She slumped forward on the ground, her dress bunched around her waist, her shoulders shaking with soft cries.

"How does it feel to be lied to, Jules?" The raw, angry words sounded like they came from someone else. Someone crueler than I ever thought I could be. "Doesn't feel good, does it?"

The ice in my veins had melted. I was drowning from the inside out, and part of me wanted to give in, sink beneath the surface, and never come back up.

Michael. Alex. Jules.

Three of the people I trusted most all stabbed me in the back. Michael and Alex's betrayals hurt, but Jules...she *knew* how fucked up I was from what happened with the others.

Intellectually, I understood her reasoning for not telling me earlier. Emotionally, I couldn't stop the hurt from poisoning every memory of us.

Careful, Red. Keep saying things like that, and I might never let you go.

You're one of the few people I trust...even when we couldn't stand each other, I could always count on you to be honest with me.

Heat blazed across my cheeks.

I was a fucking idiot.

Jules pushed herself off the ground and faced me. Giant blotches of red bloomed across her face and neck. She'd stopped crying, but her breaths sounded abnormally loud and shallow in the silence.

"It seems only fitting for us to end things with a goodbye fuck." A cruel smile slashed across my mouth. The unyielding pressure had crawled up my throat, and it took twice as much effort to get my words out. "At least you got an orgasm out of it, so don't say I never gave you anything. I'll miss that tight pussy of yours though. No one takes my cock better than you do. It's your best quality."

Vicious hurt slashed across her face and speared me in the chest like a hot poker.

The only person I hated more than her in that moment was myself.

"What I did was wrong, and I'm sorry." Her small voice contained the barest hint of her usual fire. "But you're being cruel."

"Am I?" I mocked. "Well, I'm fucking sorry. As you can see, being a nice guy hasn't served me all that well in the past." My eyes burned.

Looking at her hurt. Hearing her hurt. *Everything* hurt.

"You could've fucking told me, Jules. Did you really think so little of me that you thought I'd judge you for things you were manipulated into doing? That I wouldn't have been on your side and took that fucker down with you? I understand why you didn't tell me the truth at Hyacinth, but after Ohio..." My jaw clenched. "That's what fucking hurts the most. That I considered you worthy of trust but you didn't think the same of me."

Jules's chin wobbled. She pressed a fist to her mouth, her eyes glistening in the dim light.

"If you'd asked for the painting, I would've given it to you." My voice cracked. "I would've given you anything you wanted."

A sharp sob bled through her fist, followed by another, and another, until her gasping breaths soaked every molecule of air.

I watched, unmoving, as she hyperventilated, but my muscles strained with the effort to hold still.

I loathed the part of me that still wanted to comfort her. It was the part with no self-preservation, that needed her so much it would willingly hand her the knife to stab me in the chest just so she could be the last thing I saw before I died.

She was right. I *was* a masochist.

"Get out."

Jules flinched at my quiet command. "Josh, please. I swear I didn't—"

"Get. Out."

"I lo—"

"Don't you *dare* say it." My pulse spiked with another burst of adrenaline. *Breathe. Just fucking breathe.* "I said, get out, Jules. *Get the fuck out!*"

She finally moved, her soft sobs growing fainter as she stumbled toward the door. It closed behind her, and then...silence.

The tension holding me upright collapsed.

I doubled over, hands on my knees, silent shudders wracking my body. The pressure inside me strangled every vital organ, but no matter how much it built and built, it refused to explode. It just sat there, suffocating me from the inside out.

Jules was gone, but I still *felt* her. She was everywhere—in every inch of the room, every fragment of my thoughts, every beat of my heart.

The visceral urge to destroy everything that reminded me of her propelled me off the couch and into my room. I rifled through my desk drawer for the *Legally Blonde* musical tickets and tore them into shreds, taking perverse satisfaction in the confetti of destroyed paper fluttering into my trash can.

Next went the shirt I let her borrow the first night she slept over; the receipt from Giorgio's, which I'd kept as a stupid secret memento of our first date, and the pillow with her scent lingering on it. Every little thing that contained even the sparsest memory of us, destroyed and tossed.

By the time I finished, my room looked like how I felt: empty and hollow.

Unable to stand the sight of the stripped room, I walked to the kitchen and grabbed the nearest bottle of whiskey.

I would've been concerned about how much I'd been drinking lately if I gave a shit about anything except drowning out Jules's lingering presence. It wasn't like I was fucking blacking out every night.

I didn't bother pouring the whiskey in a glass; I tipped my head back and chugged straight from the bottle.

I don't know how much I drank, nor did I care.

I just drank and drank until I sank into the darkness of oblivion and thoughts of Jules finally faded from my mind.

47

JULES

Remember when I said I forgive you? I lied.

I stumbled toward the metro, Josh's words echoing in my brain like an endless taunt.

Remember when I said I forgive you? I lied.

When I said I forgive you? I lied.

Forgive you? I lied.

I lied.

I lied.

Tears blurred my vision, and I wasn't sure if I was going in the right direction, but I didn't care. I just needed to get away.

From Josh's cruel words, his cold eyes, and his vindictive touch.

From the knowledge that I'd fucked up and had no one to blame except myself.

People said to have loved and lost was better than never having loved at all.

They never said a damn thing about what it was like to have the person you loved and lost look at you like they utterly loathed you. Josh had never looked at me like that, not even when I *thought* he hated me.

I swiped at my cheeks with the back of my hand, but it was like trying to sweep water back into the ocean. Utterly futile.

I knew there was a chance Josh would react badly to the truth. I just hadn't expected him to react *that* badly.

The worst part was, he was right. I hadn't trusted him to take my side after learning the truth. I'd been so blinded by my insecurities, so terrified of destroying one of the few beautiful things in my life, that I turned its destruction into a self-fulfilling prophecy.

Josh hadn't cared about the sex tape or the stupid painting. He'd only cared that I lied to him.

I was such a fucking idiot.

If you'd asked for the painting, I would've given it to you. I would've given you anything you wanted.

Fresh needles of pain pierced my chest. My heart burned like someone had raked it over hot coals, and I couldn't drag enough air into my lungs. Maybe it was because every breath hurt.

Every breath, every heartbeat, every blink. Normal bodily functions that all just *hurt*.

Even my body hated me.

I wiped my face again as the metro came into view. I'd made it, sort of.

Six stops until I reached the station near my apartment, then a five-minute walk to my building.

Six stops. Five minutes.

I could survive for that long.

"Get yourself together," I hiccupped. "Before people call the cops on you."

I was already attracting a mix of alarmed and concerned looks from passersby. Talking to myself probably didn't help.

Luckily, the train arrived right as I entered the platform, so I didn't have to wait. I chose the emptiest car and curled up in the corner, watching the dark tunnels rush by outside. My crazed reflection stared back at me from the opposite window— hair wild, black tracks of mascara running down my face, skin covered with blotches of bright red like I had a nasty case of hives.

Did you really think so little of me that you thought I'd judge you for things you were manipulated into doing? That I wouldn't have been on your side and took that fucker down with you?

I closed my eyes, wishing with everything in me that I could turn back time and redo all my decisions regarding Max.

I was supposed to be a lawyer. Logical, reasonable, strategic. But when it came to Max and Josh, I'd been anything but.

How had I fucked up my own life so badly?

I opened my eyes again, not wanting to spend too long in my thoughts. They would just torture me.

Instead, I watched the metro stops pass by with a detached awareness.

Tenleytown. Van Ness. Cleveland Park. Adams Morgan/Woodley Park.

By the time I reached my stop and made the short trek from the station to The Mirage, my sobs had given way to a cold numbness.

I walked through the dark, silent apartment, my steps unnaturally loud against the hardwood floors. Stella wasn't home, so I didn't have to field questions about why I looked like such a hot mess.

All I wanted was to sleep the night away, but I managed to take a quick shower before I climbed into bed. My movements were stiff and mechanical, like I wasn't truly there.

I wish I weren't.

Despite the exhaustion pulling at my eyes, I couldn't fall asleep, so I just stared at the ceiling and listened to the silence.

Maybe it was my imagination, but a whiff of Josh's cologne from the last time he slept over lingered. If I closed my eyes, I could almost pretend he was there, his face buried in my neck and his strong body cradling mine.

You know, you're the first guy I've been with in my room.

First and last, Red.

Possessive much?

Damn right I am. I don't like sharing.

Sharing is a virtue, Josh.

I don't give a flying fuck. I don't share. Not when it comes to you.

Something warm and wet trickled down my cheek. Its saltiness teased my lips, and I realized I was crying again.

Unlike my earlier sobs, these tears didn't make a sound. They were quiet screams trapped in my chest, burrowing into my bones and suffocating me.

I didn't bother wiping them away. I just lay there, staring into the darkness and letting it eat me alive.

48

JULES

THE ONLY GOOD THING ABOUT MY BREAKUP WITH JOSH was that it gave me more time and motivation to study for the bar. I was motivated before, but there was no push greater than the need to distract from a broken heart.

I took the next week off from the clinic and used it for one last prep marathon.

Wake up at seven a.m.

Eat breakfast and shower.

Video lectures and notes until noon.

Lunch and a short break.

Assignments and practice essays.

Dinner and another break.

Practice MBE (Multistate Bar Examination) questions.

Sleep.

I stuck to the same schedule every day, afraid that if I deviated, I would fall into a dark hole I couldn't claw my way out of.

Structure was good. Structure kept me from having to make decisions or think about anything other than what the next item in my to-do list was.

Of course, that only lasted until I actually *took* the bar exam. After that...

I stared at the sheet of paper before me.

A husband and wife decided to start a bike shop with the wife's brother. They filed a certificate of organization to form a limited liability company...rented a storefront commercial space...signed contract to purchase 150 bike tires...

I blinked and shook my head before re-reading the setup more carefully. A migraine crept behind my temples, but I was almost at the finish line.

After six hours of testing, this was my last question—for the first day, anyway. I still had the multiple-choice exam tomorrow, but I'd worry about that then.

The scratch of my pencil filled my ears as I scribbled my notes down before typing my final responses into the computer.

What type of LLC was created—member-managed or manager-managed? Explain.

Is the LLC bound under the tire contract? Explain.

And so on and so forth.

I finished literally a minute before time was up. I submitted the test electronically and exited the testing site, waiting for a rush of relief or excitement. After so many years of school and months of studying, I was half finished with the exam that would determine the future of my career.

But the rush never came.

I just felt...empty.

"I think I did okay," a woman near me said into her phone. I recognized her as another attorney hopeful from the testing site. She laughed at whatever the person on the other end said. "Stop...yes, of course. Dinner tonight. I love you."

A lump of emotion clogged my throat.

In an alternate universe, I would be on the phone with Josh, making plans to celebrate. Something low key, since tomorrow was still a test day, but knowing him, he'd turn it into a whole production.

Dinner at my favorite restaurant, an at-home massage, sex to help me "relieve stress"...

"You'll use any excuse for sex, won't you?" I teased. I took off my jacket and tossed it on the couch right before Josh grabbed my waist and spun me around.

"Who says I need an excuse?" His cheek dimpled. "You want to fuck me all the time, Red. Admit it. But, since you mention it..." My breath hitched as he slid a palm up my thigh. "Completing half the bar exam is a big deal. It deserves to be celebrated."

"Does it?" I tried to maintain a poker face, but it was difficult when his thumb was rubbing circles over my skin like that.

Heat burned low in my belly.

"Mmmhmm." Josh's eyes sparkled with mischief. "You know what they say. All test and no reward makes Jules a very dull girl."

"Literally no one says that."

"I do, and I'm one of only two people who matter." He brushed his lips over mine. "Now, about your reward..."

The ding of the elevator shattered the fantasy into a million jagged pieces.

I wasn't in Josh's living room after a romantic night out; I was in the cold hallway of a nondescript building downtown, my stomach cramping and my chest tight as I lost him.

Again.

Some stupid, naive part of me hoped Josh would magically show up and surprise me like we were starring in a cheesy rom com, but of course, he didn't.

My breaths picked up speed. The chill of the air conditioning burrowed into my bones, and the echo of footsteps against the marble floors took on a menacing note.

I need to get out of here.

Unfortunately, the open elevator was going up, not down, and the other elevator seemed to be stuck on the sixth floor.

Instead of waiting, I pushed open the door to the stairwell. I was only on the third floor, so it was an easy enough walk down to the lobby.

It seems only fitting for us to end things with a goodbye fuck.

I'll miss that tight pussy of yours, though. No one takes my cock better than you do. It's your best quality.

Fresh hurt sliced through me at the memory of his parting shot. Josh always knew which buttons to push, good or bad.

But still, I missed him so much it hurt to breathe.

Come here, baby.

You're supposed to be in New Zealand.

I'd rather be here.

I hadn't seen him since our breakup. He hadn't swung by the clinic, and he'd ignored all my calls and texts. But if—

"I need the painting back, Jules."

My head jerked up just in time to catch a glimpse of blue eyes and light brown hair before Max pinned me to the wall.

I let out a small cry when my head banged against the concrete. My vision blurred at the impact, but I could still make out the harsh lines of Max's expression.

"I don't have it," I gasped. "I threw it away."

I didn't want him going after Josh. Christian had promised to keep an eye on Josh in case Max's "friends" tried to steal the painting again, but it wasn't a sustainable solution.

I hadn't wanted to throw it away without returning it to Josh first. He deserved to know. But I told him the danger when I explained the situation the other night, and I hoped he was smart enough to get rid of the art before Max's friends showed up at his doorstep.

"Don't lie, Jules. I always know when you're lying."

Whiskey coated Max's breath. There was no trace of the clean-cut, gentlemanly mask he liked to wear. Wild panic ran through his bloodshot eyes, and his lip was curled into an ugly sneer. A thin sheen of sweat coated his face and glistened beneath the stairwell's fluorescent lights.

He was near feral. Unhinged.

My heart jackhammered in my chest, and a thick, pungent taste filled my mouth.

It was the taste of fear.

"They're going to kill me if I don't find it." A bead of sweat dripped down his forehead. "I *need* the painting back. You're going to help me."

"I told you, I threw it away." My heart raced so fast I might pass out.

I could hear people's footsteps outside the door—so close, yet so far away.

Why is no one using the stairs, dammit?

A scream of frustration trapped in my chest. Of all the days for me to take the stairs, which I *never* did, I had to choose today.

I should've lied and gone along with Max's plan until I could get help, but my oxygen supply ran scarce, and I couldn't think properly.

Besides, what if he hurt Josh? What if—

"You stupid, fucking *whore.*" Max pressed his forearm against my throat until I gasped for air. I clawed at his hold, but he was too strong. "This is all your fault. You ruined my life. I asked you for *one* favor, Jules. One favor in exchange for seven years, and you couldn't even do that." His harsh breaths clouded my face in a haze of alcohol.

Drunk and desperate. The most dangerous combination.

"Maybe I should take my payment another way," he said, his voice so nasty it made the hairs on the back of my neck stand up. Max reached between my legs. "See if your pussy is still tight enough to make me come."

Dots danced before my vision. My limbs were growing heavier, my struggles for breath weaker, so I did the only thing I could do—I kneed him in the balls with every ounce of strength I had left.

His howl of pain ripped through the stairwell. He released me and doubled over.

I allowed myself one second to bask in the sweet air flowing through my lungs again before I stumbled toward the exit, but I only made it two steps before a hand shoved against my back. I didn't even get a chance to scream before I plummeted down the stairs. My head slammed against something cold and hard, and I caught only the briefest glimpse of the stairwell door opening before everything went dark.

49

JOSH

"You forgot to ask about their allergies," I snapped. "How am I supposed to treat a patient properly if I don't have all the relevant information? This is the ER, Lucy. We can't afford *any* kind of fuckups."

Lucy shrank back from my harsh tone.

I usually had a great working relationship with the nurses, but I was too irritated by the sting of antiseptic in the air, the clicks of the keyboard at the nurses' station, the squeak of shoes against the linoleum floors...basically everything.

I ignored the heat of Clara's glare from several feet away. It wasn't my fault if people were incompetent.

"I'm sorry," Lucy said, her face pale. "I'll make sure to remember next time."

"Good." I turned on my heel and left, not bothering to say goodbye.

"Don't stress about it," I heard Clara say behind me. "It was your first mistake since you started working here. You've been doing a great job."

She caught up with me a minute later, her irritation as

sharp as the one running through my veins. "Doctor, can I speak with you? *Alone*."

"I'm busy."

"You can make time." Clara yanked me into the nearest side hallway. Doctors and nurses rushed past us, too caught up in their own work to pay us much attention. "What the hell is wrong with you?"

Her eyes bore into mine, equal parts concerned and annoyed.

"Nothing is wrong with me. I'm doing my job. Or I would be, if *someone* wasn't holding me up." I leveled her with a pointed stare.

"Does your *job* include alienating every person in the ER? If so, you're the Employee of the Month," Clara said coolly. "I don't know what's wrong, but you've been acting like a boor for the past week. So here's my advice, both as a nurse *and* your friend. Cut that shit out, or you'll ruin everything you've worked for the past three years. No one likes an asshole doctor." She jabbed her finger at my chest. "Next patient. Room four. We don't have time for your moodiness right now, so I suggest you set whatever the fuck is bothering you aside and stop making it harder on everyone else around you. You want to do your job? Then *do your job*."

She stalked off and disappeared around the corner.

I stood there for several stunned seconds before I released a sharp exhale.

Clara was right. I'd been acting like a grade-A ass. What happened last week had messed me up, and I'd been taking it out on everyone around me.

My jaw flexed when I remembered my breakup with Jules, but I didn't have time to dwell on that right now.

I had a job to do, and I'd already wasted valuable time.

I checked the patient's information in the hospital's online system before entering the room. She was female, aged twenty-four, named…

My skin chilled right as the words sharpened onscreen.

Jules Ambrose.

You've gotta be shitting me.

It had to be another Jules Ambrose. The universe wouldn't have that fucked up of a sense of humor.

But when I pushed open the door to room four with a shaking hand, there she was, looking like she'd stepped right out of my most beautiful nightmare.

She stared back at me, her eyes wide with shock. A nasty cut slashed across the corner of her forehead and hit me like a punch in the gut.

Jules. Hurt.

Time slowed into one endless, painful beat. It was so quiet I could count each individual thud of my pulse.

One. Two. Three.

You'd think a week would be long enough to blunt the serrated edges of my pain, but you'd be wrong. They raked against my insides, making me bleed all over again, but they were nothing compared to the worry raging in my gut.

How the *hell* did Jules get that cut? What if it was infected? What if she—

Jules shifted, and the soft squeak of leather finally dragged me out of my trance.

In this room, we weren't exes.

She was a patient; I was her doctor. This wasn't the time to wallow in our personal history or freak out over one small cut… no matter how much the sight of her blood made my heart twist.

"I'm Dr. Chen." I spoke in a clipped, professional tone, thankful none of my inner turmoil bled through.

I would treat Jules like I would any other patient—one I didn't know.

The more distance I placed between us, the better.

"Hi, Dr. Chen. I'm Jules." The tiniest of tentative smiles played on her mouth and stole the breath right out of my fucking lungs.

Focus.

Thank God my attending physician wasn't here. As a third-year resident, I usually started the patient encounter before telling my attending, who'll see the patient on his own after I gave him the pertinent information.

If my attending *were* here, he would *not* have approved of how distracted I was. He could always tell when my head wasn't in the game.

Clara had already checked Jules's ABC's—airway, breathing, and circulation—so I jumped straight into the questions, hoping they'd ground me.

"What happened?" I stared at my clipboard like it was the most fascinating thing I'd ever seen. The less I looked at her, the less likely I was to cave like a cheap umbrella during a thunderstorm. I was still pissed at her. One injury didn't change that.

She's fine. It's just a cut.

"I fell down the stairs," she said quietly.

My hand stilled for a fraction of a second before I continued my notes. My heart thumped so loud it almost drowned out my next words. "How many stairs were there?"

"Maybe a dozen? I'm not sure."

Fuck. Sweat coated my skin at the mental image of Jules crumpled at the bottom of a flight of stairs. I almost reached for her the way I would've had we still been dating, but I forced my personal feelings aside and examined her extremities for injuries.

I couldn't find any physical wounds except for the cut on her forehead and a couple of bruises, but that didn't mean she was in the clear.

The sweat intensified as the worst-case scenarios for all possible internal injuries flashed through my mind.

Stop. She's your patient. That's it.

"Did you hit your head?" It was an obvious question, given the cut, but I had to ask.

Jules nodded.

"Did you pass out?"

"Yes."

I swallowed the lump in my throat and ran through the rest of my questions.

Are you taking any blood thinners? No.

Is there any chance you're pregnant? No.

"Are you hurting anywhere in particular right now?"

My question hung between us, thick with unspoken meaning.

Despite everything that happened between us, the thought of Jules hurt made it so fucking hard to breathe.

"My head, shoulder, and lower back."

"What about your neck?" I felt along her C-spine and breathed a silent sigh of relief when she didn't flinch. "Does it hurt?"

Jules shook her head. "No. It's just the places I mentioned. Physically, anyway," she added softly.

The air thinned while the ache in my chest intensified.

She was so close I could hear her breathing.

I'd forgotten how much I loved that sound—the sound of her just existing, reminding me that no matter how fucked up the world got, there was at least one good thing in it.

At least, there used to be.

I set my jaw and finished the physical examination as

quickly as possible. "Right. I'll order a CT scan, just in case." My crisp words bounced through the fluorescent-lit room, erasing any hint of softness. "How did you fall down the stairs?"

A long silence passed before she answered. "Someone pushed me."

I stared at her, sure I'd heard wrong. "Someone pushed you."

Jules nodded, her lips tight. "I was walking down the stairs after my bar exam. I was distracted, so I wasn't paying much attention to my surroundings. The person...surprised me, and they pushed me when I tried to get away. I hit my head and passed out. When I woke up, I was in the back of a taxi with a woman, someone I recognized from the testing site. She said she'd just entered the stairwell when she heard me fall, but she didn't see anyone else. She dropped me off at the hospital and, well, here I am."

She relayed what happened in a matter-of-fact manner, but the slight shake in her voice told me the incident freaked her out more than she let on.

Slow, poisonous rage oozed into my bloodstream.

I wasn't a stranger to anger, but I'd never felt like this before.

Like I wanted to hunt down the person responsible and rip them apart with my bare fucking hands.

"Who?" My calm voice belied the violence brewing in my stomach. "Who did this to you?"

She said the person surprised her. Judging from her tone, it was someone she knew.

I guessed the answer before she told me.

"Max." Apprehension crept into Jules's eyes, like she was afraid of how I'd react to the name, and for good fucking reason.

Max. The guy who had a sex tape of her. Who blackmailed

her into stealing from me. Who put his fucking hands on her and destroyed the only beautiful thing in my life...*us*.

My rage deepened, tinting my world a bloody crimson.

"I see." I betrayed none of the emotion roaring through my chest. "I'm going to make some arrangements for your CT scan. I'll be right back."

I left the room and pulled out my phone. It took me less than two seconds to shoot Alex a text.

Me: I need you to find someone for me.

_____

50

JOSH

The great thing about having a morally questionable best friend was that they didn't question you when you did morally questionable things.

Alex didn't ask why I wanted to track Max down; he just did it. It took him less than an hour because, according to him, Max left a trail of digital crumbs so obvious a blind Luddite could've followed it.

When we found him hoovering drinks at a dive bar like an alcoholic Dyson, Max was already three sheets to the wind, and it took only the promise of more booze, drugs, and girls to lure him with us.

I let Alex do the talking and took a separate car in case Max recognized me, but he was so drunk he didn't notice anything was wrong until we entered a silent, secluded house on the city's outskirts.

By then, it was too late.

"He must've really pissed you off." Alex examined Max's bound form the way a scientist would examine a particularly interesting specimen beneath a microscope. "This isn't your usual style."

I flexed my hands into fists.

Max sat tied to a chair in the middle of the basement, his mouth duct-taped shut and his body twisting in a futile struggle against his ties. His alcohol-induced haze had cleared, and I saw the stark reality of his situation reflected in his eyes.

Good.

I wanted him to feel every second of this.

"My usual style isn't working for me." The rage I'd suppressed during my work shift roared back, drowning out any reservations I might've had.

I was a doctor, not a fighter. I'd pledged to do no harm. But the Josh that made that pledge was different than the one in this room. Even memories of him were hazy, buried beneath the weight of the past week's events.

I walked over to Max and ripped the tape off his mouth. I wasn't worried about anyone hearing us. The house was Alex's secret city hideaway, the place where he went when he needed to be alone but didn't have time for a longer trip, and it was soundproofed and secured enough to make The Pentagon weep with envy.

"You recognize me." It wasn't a question.

Max's awareness of my identity was obvious in the pinch of his mouth and the burning flame of panicked resentment in his eyes.

"Jules told me what you did. Ohio, the painting, the blackmail, everything." I bent until we were at eye level. "You should've skipped town when you had the chance. Staying here was a stupid move. Pushing Jules down the stairs was even stupider."

I saw Alex arch an eyebrow out of the corner of my eye.

Otherwise, he didn't react to the new information or mention of Jules.

"She deserved it." Max didn't deny my accusation like I'd expected. He must've known it wouldn't do him any good. "The people who wanted the painting are pissed I lost it. They're out for blood." A bead of sweat trickled down his forehead. "She fucked me over and thought she could walk away with no consequences. After everything I did for her when we were young. She had no job, no home, and *I* took her in. You think I want to stay in this fucking city? I can't go back to Ohio, not without the painting. She *deserved it!*"

His voice rose with each word until spittle frothed at his mouth. His sour, whiskey-tinted breath clouded the air between us and made my stomach twist with disgust.

"That sounds like a personal problem. You get in bed with the wrong people, you pay the consequences. The only thing I care about..." I gripped his shoulder and dug my fingers into the pressure points until he squeaked with pain. "...is the fact you hurt her. That was a big mistake, Max."

"Surprised you're still taking her side after what she did," Max panted. Malice mingled with the resentment in his eyes. "She hurt more than she helped by returning that painting to you. My friends will be coming for you next, and they're not as nice as I am."

I wasn't a fucking idiot. I'd already took steps to mitigate that possibility, but Max didn't need to know that.

"I wasn't going to kill her. I just wanted to give her a scare. Rough her up a little, scare her into helping me again." Max's eyes darted around the room, searching for help that didn't exist. "It's not fair that she keeps getting away with what she did. I went to jail for something we *both* did while she went to a fancy school and made fancy friends. It's *not fair.* She owes me!"

He sounded like a petulant child throwing a temper tantrum.

"She only got into that life because of *you*." I clamped down harder on his shoulder. "Don't act like you're an innocent martyr."

"So protective of her even after she lied and stole from you." Max's lip curled, his desire for a cheap shot outweighing any sense of self-preservation. "What is it? Is it the pussy? I remember it was pretty good, especially her first time when she bled all over my cock. There's nothing like breaking in a virgin. But it's probably worn out—"

His sentence cut off with a choked cry when I slammed my fist into his face.

Fury darkened the edges of my vision. The world narrowed until the only thing I could focus on was my fierce, all-consuming need to cause the man in front of me as much pain as possible.

But I wanted this to be a fair fight. That way, I could let loose without any guilt.

I held out a hand. Alex slid a knife into my open palm, and I slashed the ropes binding Max.

He lurched out of his chair, but he didn't make it two steps before I hauled him back by his collar and punched him again.

The satisfying crunch of bone ripped through the air, followed by a howl of pain.

Max clutched his broken nose with one hand and swung at me with the other. I dodged his clumsy attempt with little effort, and I heard another crunch when my fist connected with his jaw.

My blood sang with exhilaration as the storm inside me finally found its release. Every punch, every spray of blood on my face loosened an inch of pressure in my chest.

The air crackled with unleashed violence, and soon, the snap of bone gave way to the wet sound of bloodied flesh.

Sweat and blood blurred my vision, but I kept going, fueled by mental images of Jules's injuries and Max's earlier taunts.

I didn't want to do it. He was blackmailing me...

They pushed me when I tried to get away...

Is it the pussy? I remember it was pretty good, especially her first time when she bled all over my cock.

A fresh wave of rage swept through me, and I punched Max hard enough that he collapsed onto the ground. His hands scrabbled against the floor as he tried to crawl away, but there was nowhere for him to escape.

"Please." He gasped out a wet, gurgling plea. "Stop. Please..."

I barely heard him.

It wasn't just Jules. It was Michael and Alex and every patient I lost in the ER. Every bottled-up hurt, disappointment, and frustration from the past few years. I unleashed it all on Max until his pleas died off and his body turned limp.

My heart thundered with adrenaline. I should've done this sooner. *This* was the outlet I needed.

I hauled my arm back for another blow, but firm hands closed around my biceps and pulled me back.

"Josh." Alex's voice splashed a cold bucket of water on the flames consuming me. "That's enough."

"Get off me," I bit out. I strained against his hold, desperate for another fix. For more relief. "I'm not done."

"Yes, you are. Keep going, and you'll kill him." Alex turned me around without releasing my arms and pinned me with a glare. "If that's what you want, fine. But it's not."

"You don't know that." My ragged breaths echoed in the empty space.

The basement contained no furniture save for the chair, a

table, an industrial sink, and a fridge. I didn't want to think about what activities Alex usually conducted down here. Probably something similar to what I just did.

"I know you're not the type of person who wants another's death on your hands," he said calmly. "You're not a killer, Josh. Besides, look at him. You've made your point."

I stared at the unconscious heap on the ground. Max's face was a mangled mess of blood and pulp. Sticky dark liquid pooled around his body, and if it weren't for the faint rise and fall of his chest, I would've thought he was already dead.

I did that. Me.

Alex hadn't laid a finger on him.

My heart rate slowed the longer I stared at Max. The soft drip of the sink in the corner reminded me of the drip of blood, and I was suddenly hyperaware of the coppery liquid coating my face and clothes.

I'd beaten him half to death.

Bile rose in my throat.

I wrenched myself out of Alex's grasp and stumbled to the sink, where I dry heaved until my throat was raw and moisture burned my eyes.

I hadn't eaten since before my shift, so nothing came out, but that didn't stop nausea from roiling my stomach.

What the fuck had I done?

Kidnapping. Assault and battery. Probably a dozen other crimes that would end my career if anyone found out.

I started off wanting to make Max pay for what he did to Jules and ended up using him as my human punching bag.

Fuck.

I turned on the tap and splashed water on my face, hoping to wash off the blood, but its stain remained even after the pinkish water ran clear in the steel basin.

When I finally lifted my head, my skin numb from the

chill of the water, I saw Alex next to me. He leaned his hip against the counter with an unreadable expression. "Feel better?"

"Yes. No. I don't know." I rubbed a hand over my damp face and glanced at the still unconscious Max. My stomach lurched again. "What are we going to do about him?"

"Don't worry. He won't go to the police." Alex walked over to him and nudged his prone form with disdain. "It's more trouble than it's worth."

True. Max was only a few months out of jail, and he'd already committed aggravated assault and was involved in a conspiracy to commit grand larceny. If the police looked into his background, he was fucked.

"And if he comes after us later?" I asked.

"Please. He's a common thief trying to play in a league above his own." Alex sounded unimpressed. "Plus, if what he said was true, he has enough problems to worry about without trying to take revenge on us. Whoever wants your hideous painting will keep him busy."

"It's not hideous," I growled. "It's *unusual,* and it's worth a lot of money."

I'd shopped the painting around after Jules's confession. It was tainted with bad memories, and like Max said, the people after it would come after *me* if I held onto it. I was lucky they hadn't already. I guess they didn't trust Max enough to finish the job Jules started.

The only way to get Max's mysterious "friends" off my back and not screw over the next owner was to sell it to someone no one would dare steal from.

I finally found a suitable buyer yesterday, and we were scheduled to sign the contract in two days, after he returned from a business trip.

I assumed whoever was tracking the piece would know I'd

sold it, but just in case they didn't, the buyer promised to publicize the sale.

"Enough about the painting. Even if Max won't call the police, we can't just leave him here." If we did, he might very well die of blood loss, and Alex was right. I wasn't a murderer. I wouldn't be able to live with myself if anyone died at my hands.

The urge to vomit returned. "He needs medical attention."

Alex's sigh contained multitudes of exasperation. "You and Ava. So driven by your consciences. No wonder you're siblings," he muttered. "Fine. I'll send someone to take care of him."

"Take care of him as in..."

Another, deeper sigh. "As in medical attention, Josh. I'm not going to kill him. I barely know him."

"Right." With Alex, it was always best to double check.

At his suggestion, I rinsed off in the upstairs shower and changed into one of his spare outfits while he took care of the situation.

By the time I emerged, Max was already gone and Alex sat in the living room, scrolling through his phone.

"What the fuck? Do you have magical house elves or something?" I sank next to him on the couch.

I felt better after the shower. Not *good*, but better, though images of Max's bloodied form would haunt me for a long while.

I swallowed the lump of guilt in my throat.

"No. I have a highly competent, highly paid team." Alex didn't look up from his phone. "Besides, you were in the shower for an hour. A geriatric grandmother could've taken care of Max in that time."

"Bullshit. I was in there ten minutes, tops."

"That's not what the clock says."

I glanced at the grandfather clock in the corner. He was right. It'd been *over* an hour since I jumped into the shower.

I mentally added loss of time awareness to the long list of shit I needed to worry about.

"I'm going crazy." I closed my eyes and pressed a fist to my forehead. "What the fuck is happening to me?"

I felt like a passenger who didn't know their train had flown off the rails until they looked out the window and saw the ground rushing toward them.

One minute, I lived a charmed life—popular and accomplished, with a great family and great friends. The next, it all burst into flames until only ashes were left.

"If it's about Max, don't feel too bad. He's a piece of shit, and he had it coming. But he'll survive." Alex slid a glance in my direction. "You never answered my question earlier. Do you feel better?"

I hated to admit it, but... "Yeah."

The dark cloud that had stalked me for two years was still present, but it was lighter. More manageable.

"Good. Now explain Jules to me."

"Jesus Christ." I cracked my eyes open and glared at Alex. Renewed tension zipped down my spine and turned my muscles into stone. "There's nothing to explain, but if you're curious, she's five-six with red hair, hazel eyes—"

"You almost beat a man to death because he hurt her," Alex said. "Don't insult me by pretending she doesn't mean anything to you."

I pinched the bridge of my nose, regretting, not for the first time, my eighteen-year-old self's decision to befriend the man sitting next to me.

Still, after keeping my relationship—my *former* relationship—with Jules secret for so long, it would be nice to talk about it with someone...even if said someone had the emotional range of a teaspoon.

"You promise not to tell Ava?" I wasn't ready for that conversation yet.

"I promise not to bring it up, but if she asks me about it directly, I'll tell her the truth." Alex lifted his shoulder in a shrug. "Sorry."

I've never heard anyone sound less sorry in my life. But the chances of Ava asking about me and Jules were low; she still thought we hated each other.

After a long moment of deliberation, I explained the whole saga to Alex, starting with my and Jules's clinic truce and ending with her visit to the ER.

When I finished, the pressure had resettled in my chest, and Alex stared at me with an uncharacteristic glint of disbelief in his eyes.

"What?"

"Ninety-nine percent of people in this world are idiots," he said. "I regret to inform you that you're one of them."

My brows snapped together. "I'm convinced you don't actually want to be my friend again."

Where was the ass kissing? The flattery? He gave up his company and flew to fucking London for Ava, but I couldn't get so much as a sympathetic *that sucks, man*? Talk about getting the short end of the grovel stick.

"I'll send you flowers later if you're that upset about it," Alex said dryly. "But first, listen to yourself. You're in love with Jules, for God knows what reason, and you're upset she lied after she told you the truth?"

My shoulders tensed. "I'm not in love with her."

"You almost killed someone for her."

"So? You almost kill someone every day. It's nothing special."

"Don't try to change the subject. You're bad at it." Alex flicked a piece of lint off his pants. "You say I don't actually want to be your friend again? Then I'll give you something you say you want so much. The truth."

"Which is?"

"That you're a stubborn fuck who's too blind to see what's right in front of you."

My tension hardened into a migraine. "I changed my mind. I don't want the truth."

Alex continued like I hadn't spoken. "Jules may have lied to you, but she also *willingly* told you the truth. If she kept her mouth shut, you probably would've never found out what she did. The only reason someone would make an unprompted confession like that is because they want a fresh start, and the only reason they'd want a fresh start when the relationship is already going well is because they realized something."

Get. Out.

I lo—

*Don't you **dare** say it. I said, get out, Jules. **Get the fuck out!***

My heart slammed against my chest and bruised my ribcage with each painful thud.

"I don't have to tell you what the realization is," Alex said. "You're smart enough to figure it out. But according to you, she didn't tell you earlier because she was afraid of how you'd react. She didn't think you'd take her side. Now, tell me. How *did* you react when she finally told you?"

The oxygen in the room thinned.

Forget painful. Every breath was downright excruciating.

"I'm not a big fan of Jules, but you are my best friend. I want you to be happy." Alex's face softened a smidge, but that didn't blunt the harshness of his words. "You can't be happy if you have your head buried so far in the sand you think you can just walk away and forget her. Take it from someone who tried to do the same once with someone I love. You'll be miserable until you resolve the situation."

I'd never heard Alex utter so many words in such a short time. I would've been more stunned had I not been busy replaying them in my mind.

*She didn't tell you earlier because she was afraid of how you'd react. Now, tell me. How **did** you react?*

I tilted my head back and squeezed my eyes shut again. "Oh, *fuck.*"

What the hell have I done?

51

JULES

My hospital visit was a blur of tests and examinations. I had a cut on my head, several nasty bruises, a shoulder sprain, and a mild concussion, but otherwise, I was pretty lucky. It could've been so much worse.

Despite my concussion, I opted to finish the bar exam the next day. I just wanted to get it over with. Plus, it was multiple choice; if worse came to worse, I could bubble something in and pray for the best.

I handed in my test and returned the administrator's smile with a tired one of my own.

It was done. The results were out of my hands now.

I wouldn't know whether or not I'd passed until October, so I might as well celebrate by sleeping for the next, oh, seventy-two hours.

Exhaustion weighed down my limbs as I exited the exam room, but now that the test was over, I couldn't stop replaying yesterday's hospital visit in my head.

Obviously, I knew Josh worked in the ER, but I hadn't expected him to see him for some reason.

My heart twisted at the memory of his cold, clinical examination. I didn't think he would rush to my side and forgive me just because I was injured, but I'd expected a little more... warmth? Empathy? Instead, he'd treated me like I was just another patient he didn't personally know.

Polite and competent, but emotionally detached.

Don't think about it. Not now.

Getting too caught up in my head was what screwed me over yesterday; if I hadn't been so distracted, Max wouldn't have been able to surprise me like that.

Cold sweat broke out on my skin. I didn't think he'd be stupid enough to come back a second day in a row, but desperate people did desperate things. I imagined his "friends" weren't happy he'd lost the painting, and he wanted revenge for what happened in his hotel.

I'd underestimated his capability for physical violence.

Then again, if there was one recurring theme in my life, it was that people were never who I thought they were.

I quickened my steps so I could squeeze into the elevator before the doors closed. It was packed shoulder-to-shoulder and smelled faintly of tuna and body odor, but it was still better than the stairwell. You couldn't pay me enough money to take the stairs again.

I hitched my bag higher on my shoulder, taking solace in the pepper spray and taser sitting inside it. I'd borrowed them from Stella, who'd kept them on hand since her short-lived but terrifying episode with a stalker last year.

As a well-known influencer, she dealt with her fair share of creeps, but that guy had crossed the line. He'd sent her disgusting letters detailing what he wanted to do to her and messaged her candid photos of herself around town, which freaked her out so much she'd gone to the police. They hadn't been any help at all, but luckily, the stalker stopped contacting her after a few weeks and she hadn't heard from him since.

I was the only person who knew about it since we lived together. If Stella hadn't been concerned about the guy showing up at our house, she wouldn't have even told me. She had a bad habit of keeping all her problems to herself.

The elevator doors slid open.

Thank God.

I liked tuna; I did *not* like the smell of it mixed with B.O. and half a dozen different perfumes.

I walked across the lobby, eager to return home and binge another pint of ice cream. I'd inhaled so much Ben & Jerry's over the past week I was surprised I hadn't ballooned out of my clothes.

I'd almost reached the exit when two words stopped me in my tracks.

"Hey, Red."

My pulse spiked at the sound of that nickname, in that voice, *here...*

No. It can't be.

My mind was playing tricks on me again. There was no way Josh was here after the way he'd treated me yesterday.

A messy knot of emotion tangled in my throat.

Several people brushed past me and shot me strange looks. I was rooted to my spot on the marble floor, and I wanted to move. I really did. But my body refused to comply, and all I could do was stare at the exit, both longing to reach it and happy to stay in my bubble of delusion forever.

What if it was him? What if he was here? What if...

A shadow sliced across the sun-drenched floor before a body moved in front of me and blocked the exit from view.

I slowly raised my eyes, skimming over the T-shirt-clad chest, broad shoulders, and tense jaw before I met Josh's eyes.

My heart whimpered like a wounded animal eager for comfort from the only person capable of providing it.

"I wasn't sure if you heard me." He stuffed his hands in his pockets. His brows were drawn tight over worried eyes, but a tentative smile played on his mouth. "How did the test go?"

"I—fine." I couldn't wrap my head around what was happening. It was too surreal.

Josh might as well be a different person from yesterday, and I wasn't just talking about the one-eighty in his attitude. Gone was the clean-cut doctor; in its place was someone gruffer, more world-weary. Stubble shadowed his cheeks and jaw, his skin had taken on a pallid case, and his hair looked like he'd raked his fingers through it a thousand times. Regret filled his eyes and sent my stomach tumbling off a cliff.

There was only one thing he could be regretting, and—

Don't go there.

I bit the inside of my cheek until a coppery taste filled my mouth. I refused to get my hopes up only for him to crush them again.

"Can we go somewhere to talk?" Josh stepped to the side to let another person pass. "I have..." He paused, his throat flexing with a hard swallow. "I have something I need to tell you."

"You can tell me here." I discreetly wiped my palms against the sides of my thighs. My shirt stuck to my skin despite the icy blasts of air conditioning, and my skin alternated between hot and cold each second.

"Okay." Instead of arguing, Josh tilted his chin toward a side hallway. "At least let's get out of the way before someone mows us down. Lawyers are an aggressive bunch, aspiring lawyers even more so."

A shadow of his dimple appeared.

I puddled at the sight of it. Of the top three things I missed most, his dimple sat squarely at number two, after his kiss and before his playful insults.

But whereas my insides were a mess of emotions, my exterior remained frozen. I couldn't summon a smile for the life of me.

Josh's dimple disappeared, and he swallowed hard again.

Somehow, I got my legs to work. We walked to the hallway in silence, and Josh twisted the doorknobs until one opened. It revealed an empty office. No furniture, just a whiteboard and a blue carpet. It was so hushed I could hear every thump of my pulse.

I stepped inside and rubbed the sleeve of my silk blouse between my fingers, taking solace in the mindless, familiar motion. "What are you doing here? Don't you have work?"

"I traded shifts so I could take today off." Josh locked the door behind us and raked his gaze over my face. Warmth buzzed beneath my skin at his slow, thorough perusal. "I wanted to make sure you were okay."

Delirium, exhaustion, or both pulled a rusty laugh from my throat. It sounded strange, like a car engine sputtering back to life after a week of non-use.

"I'm fine, but you didn't take the day off and show up to my bar exam just to make sure I was okay." A familiar ache crept into my chest. "You were the one who treated me yesterday. You know how I'm doing."

"About that." There was no hint of a smile on Josh's face anymore. "I'm sorry if I came off...unconcerned."

I shrugged as casually as I could. "You're a doctor. You were professional and did your job. That's all anyone could ask for."

"I'm not just your doctor, Jules."

The air suffocated my lungs. "You're also my best friend's brother."

"More than that." He took a tiny step toward me, and I took an instinctive step back.

I raised my chin, willing myself not to cry. I'd already shed too many tears over him. "Not anymore."

No one takes my cock better than you do. It's your best quality.

No matter how many times I replayed his words, they slashed deep every time.

That was the thing about someone who'd seen the best and worst of you—they knew exactly which buttons to push, which words would sting the hardest.

Josh's jaw ticked, but instead of arguing, he switched the subject so suddenly it nearly gave me whiplash. "I found Max yesterday."

"You *what?*" This encounter was growing more surreal by the minute.

"I found Max," he repeated. "He won't be bothering you anymore. Alex and I made sure of it."

"What...how..." Nothing made sense. "You told *Alex?* What did you guys do? You didn't kill him, did you?"

I was only half joking. I wouldn't be devastated if Max died, but I also didn't want Josh putting himself in jeopardy for me. Alex was a coin toss, but Josh? He wasn't a killer, and if he did something in a fit of rage, it would haunt him for the rest of his life.

The prospect of him suffering like that was worse than any blackmail or hurtful words.

"No. But I wanted to." A hard smile cut across Josh's face. "Alex, of all people, talked me down. I won't bore you with the details, but I promise, our point came across loud and clear. Max won't contact you again."

"Why would you do that?" Hope reared its treacherous head, and I shoved it back down. My hopes always led to disappointments. "You didn't care when I came into the hospital yesterday."

Josh's eyes darkened from rich chocolate to endless, unnerving obsidian.

"I don't care?" Another step toward me, another step back.

Our dance played to the rapid beats of my heart, and it didn't end until my back pressed again the cool wall and Josh crowded me with his warmth. When he spoke again, the low, dangerous timbre of his voice sent shivers rippling down my spine.

"I walked into that room and almost lost my shit when I saw you were hurt, my job be damned. I wanted to kill Max for laying a hand on you. That's not hyperbole, Jules. If you saw what he looked like after I was done with him..." His breath skated over my skin. "Luck saved him. But if he so much as breathes in your direction again, I will rip his entrails out and strangle him with them. So yes, Red, I fucking care. So much so it terrifies me."

I was falling down another helpless spiral where his words were my only cushion and the air sang sweetly even as I plummeted toward potential death.

His quiet promise of violence should've frightened me; instead, it sizzled through my veins like an electric current.

"You hate me." I was breathless and aching, wishing so hard for what he said to be true and utterly terrified it wasn't.

"I've never hated you."

"Liar."

His soft laugh filled every molecule of air between us. "Okay, once upon a time, I hated you a little bit." His smile faded, his eyes growing serious. "I don't know what you did to me, Red. But somehow, I went from wanting to kill you...to willing to kill for you."

My stomach tumbled further into free fall. A thousand

golden bubbles filled me until I felt like a balloon being carried away by the wind.

I didn't know what changed since last week, when Josh—

Remember when I said I forgive you? I lied.

The balloon popped with the swiftness of an assassin's blade.

Josh wasn't cruel. He didn't manipulate people's feelings for fun. But last week, he could've given Alex a run for his money in the cruelty department.

What if this was another one of his twisted games? He *said* everything I wanted to hear, but I didn't trust his sudden one-eighty. A week wasn't long enough for someone to get over the fury he'd displayed.

"For me, or for my *tight pussy*?" I asked, quoting him. My chin wobbled. "That's my best quality, right?"

Pain slashed across his face. "Jules…"

"It's not fair for you to do this." My vow not to cry splintered as a tear scalded my cheek. "Just because I just fucked up doesn't mean you can keep torturing me. We have to move on."

A low growl rumbled from his chest.

Josh rubbed the tear away with his thumb, his touch infinitely gentle, but his eyes blazed with intensity. "There's no fucking moving on," he growled. "Not for me. Not for us."

"You kicked me out of your house last week." Fresh hurt strangled my lungs. "You fucked me, then you tossed me aside just like everyone else."

He'd been angry, and rightfully so. But the memory of his words…the look in his eyes…

He weaponized the biggest insecurity I had and turned it against me.

Josh blanched, and the pain on his face sharpened into something so visceral it would've broken down my resistance had I not been so terrified.

As much as I wanted Josh back, I couldn't put myself in a situation to be used or manipulated again.

"It's been one week. What changed?" Another tear slipped down my cheek. "Do you miss the sex? Is that it?"

"No! That's not..." Josh pushed a hand through his hair. "I admit, I reacted poorly when you told me the truth. *More* than poorly. I was blindsided, and I was so fucked in the head from everything that happened the past few years that I lashed out in the cruelest way I think of." His Adam's apple bobbed from the force of his swallow.

"Everyone I trusted has lied to me. But you...I told you things I've never told anyone. Things that hurt to admit even to myself. Your betrayal hit harder than any of the others combined, but that was my mistake. Thinking it was a betrayal when you were also the only person who's ever told me the truth of your own accord. You didn't wait until you were caught, even though you probably could've kept it a secret forever and I would've never found out. And I..." His voice cracked. "I was an idiot. And I'm sorry. And I lo—"

"Stop." I couldn't breathe. "Let me go. Please."

I needed to think. To process. There was too much going on, and I couldn't...I couldn't...

I sucked in another shallow inhale. It did nothing to clear my light-headedness.

"I can't." Agony scraped his voice raw. "I'll do anything you want except that." Josh lowered his mouth, his heart a wild drum against mine. I turned before he made contact, terrified that if I gave even an inch, he'd take all of me and break the few whole parts I had left.

He froze, his breaths heavy with regret. "There's no letting you go, Red. It would be easier if you asked me to tear my heart out with my own fucking hands." He rubbed another tear from my face. "Yes, you made a mistake, but I was cruel, and I said things I never should've said."

Josh buried his face in my neck. Dampness touched my skin, and I realized I wasn't the only one crying.

"I'm sorry," he said hoarsely. "For reacting the way I did. For lashing out at you when you tried to do the right thing. For not choosing you the way you deserve when you're the only thing I've ever wanted."

A small sob rose in my throat.

"I'm sorry, I'm sorry, I'm sorry..." He whispered the mantra as he trailed soft kisses up my neck and over my jaw. "I'm so fucking sorry."

Josh reached my mouth and hovered there, seeking permission. Seeking forgiveness.

I stared at the floor, my eyes burning with the effort to hold back hope.

"Please." His ragged plea shredded my resistance. "Tell me what to do, Red. I'll do anything."

"I..." Between yesterday's incident with Max, sitting for the bar exam, and the way Josh scrambled my brains every time he was near, I couldn't think properly. A dull ache formed behind my temples and blurred my vision. "I need space. I just need to...I need..."

Every breath brought in less and less oxygen.

I *wanted* to believe Josh, and I certainly wasn't blame-free in our mess. Wasn't I the one who wanted him to forgive me for lying?

But now that the moment had come, some infuriating, intangible *thing* prevented me from fully embracing the situation.

What if he was lying again?

What if I made another mistake and he walked away for good?

What if he woke up one day and decided *he* made a mistake?

Remember when I said I forgive you? I lied.

What good is it having a daughter if you can't do one **simple** *thing right?*

Once a whore, always a whore.

No one takes my cock better than you do. It's your best quality.

The jumble of voices in my head sharpened the ache into a piercing pain. The walls pressed in until the phantom scrape of white plaster against my skin roiled my stomach.

I wasn't claustrophobic, but sometimes my thoughts trapped me in a cage so small I suffocated with each breath.

"I can't do this right now." I blinked, trying to clear my vision. "Give me...give me some time. I just need to think."

The past forty-eight hours had tossed my life into chaos, and I needed to get my bearings before I could move forward.

Josh exhaled a shuddering breath. "Jules..."

"Please." My voice broke.

He closed his eyes for a brief moment before he pressed a kiss to my forehead. "Okay." His raw whisper clawed at my heart. "Take however much time you need. I'll wait."

For some reason, his words sent a fresh ache through my chest. "Why?"

No one had ever waited for me. I couldn't fathom why they would.

"Because you're it for me. Whether it's today, tomorrow, a year, or decades from now, that'll never change." Josh's lips brushed against my skin before he pulled back, his face taut with emotion. "I'm human, Red. I've made mistakes in the past, and I'll make many more in the future. But one mistake I'll never make is letting you go, not when there's even a sliver of a chance left for us. Because the possibility of you is better than the reality of anyone else."

Saltiness trickled down my cheeks.

"So, like I said..." Josh brushed away my tear. "I'll wait. For as long as it takes."

52

JULES

I took that Friday and Monday off from the clinic and returned to the office Tuesday morning, more confused than ever. I'd spent the past few days agonizing over Josh, but I still didn't know what to do about us. The more I thought it, the more my head hurt, so it was nice to settle into the mindless rhythm of work again. At least it took my mind off my utter mess of a personal life.

Luckily, there'd been an influx of new cases while I was out, and they kept me busy well into the afternoon until the bells over the front door chimed.

We were closed for lunch, so it had to be a staff member...or a volunteer.

My heart jumped in my throat when I turned and saw Josh walk in, still wearing his scrubs and sneakers from the hospital.

Everyone else was eating out or in the kitchen, so it was just the two of us.

"Hi." Somehow, the word made it past the parched desert of my throat.

"Hi." Josh stopped next to my desk, his eyes drifting to the bandaged cut on my forehead. A visible swallow worked its way down his throat. "How's the cut?"

"Better. I'll survive." I mustered a smile. "Shouldn't you be resting right now?"

Now that he was closer, I could see the faint purple smudges beneath his eyes and the lines of exhaustion bracketing his mouth.

"I should. But I wanted to see you."

A swarm of butterflies soared through my stomach and left a trail of tingles in their wake. "Oh."

Oh? God, I sounded like an idiot, but I'd lost all ability to function properly.

Josh's lips curved with a faint hint of bitterness. He'd kept his promise to give me space to think, but the air between us hummed with so many unspoken words I was drowning in them.

Frustration welled in my stomach. What was *wrong* with me? Why couldn't I let go and get back together with him the way I wanted? I wasn't upset about his hurtful words. I understood why he lashed out the way he had, but something held me back.

Josh opened his mouth like he wanted to say something else, but after a beat, he closed it and walked to his desk. We worked in tense silence until my phone rang and interrupted my pitiful attempt to focus on the clinic's latest case.

Surprise coasted through me when I checked the caller ID and saw who was calling. We'd exchanged numbers at Bridget's wedding, but I hadn't expected to actually hear from him again.

"Hi, Asher," I said after I picked up.

The sound of Josh typing fell silent.

"Hey, Jules." Asher Donovan's smooth drawl flowed over the line. "Sorry for calling out of nowhere, but I'll be in town tomorrow for a last-minute trip and wanted to see if you're free for drinks. I'd love to catch up."

"I..." Asher was gorgeous, charming, and a world-famous athlete. I should be all over his invitation, especially considering how much I'd enjoyed our brief bonding over a certain British royal's drunken shenanigans at Bridget's wedding.

But in that moment, I wasn't thinking about drinks with the man *People* magazine deemed The Most Eligible Bachelor in Sports. Instead, I was trying my damn hardest not to look at the man sitting less than ten feet away.

The heat from Josh's stare seared into my skin and distracted me so much I wasn't even starstruck by the fact I was on the phone with *the* Asher Donovan.

The universe really was throwing everything at me at once, good and bad.

"It's not a date," Asher added. "Just two friends hanging out. And...okay, you're the only person I know in the city. But I'd hang out with you regardless."

"Good to know." I laughed. "But tomorrow..." Honestly, all I wanted was to sleep my nights away like I'd had the past week, but maybe going out would do me some good. It'd make me feel more human and less like a sad shell trudging through the motions of life. "Okay. Let's do it. The Bronze Gear at six? It's a bar downtown."

The heat consuming my left side erupted into an inferno. Despite the frigid air conditioning and my flimsy silk blouse, sweat trickled between my breasts, and it took every ounce of willpower not to sneak a peek at Josh.

"Perfect," Asher said. "I'll be in disguise. Baseball cap, blue shirt."

"Does that actually work?" I doubted a mere baseball cap could disguise him. His face wasn't one people forgot.

"You'd be surprised. People see what they expect to see,

and no one expects to see me hanging out at a D.C. bar on a Wednesday night. See you soon, Jules."

"See you."

When I hung up, the silence was so oppressive I swore I could hear the rush of my blood through my veins.

"Asher Donovan?" Josh's casual question was at odds with his tight voice.

"Yes. He'll be in town and wants to grab drinks."

More silence.

Why was it so freaking hot in here? I lifted my hair off my shoulders and finally glanced to my left. Josh's jaw clenched so tight I was surprised it didn't crack.

My heart skipped a beat. "It's not a date," I added softly.

I didn't know why I felt the need to clarify that. Josh and I weren't dating anymore, and my meetup with Asher was platonic. Still, a frisson of guilt snaked through me at his granite expression.

"Maybe you don't think it's a date." A grim smile touched Josh's mouth before he turned back to his computer. "But trust me, Jules. Any man would be an idiot to let you go if there was even a chance with you."

"I figured I'd drop by D.C., pick some poisonous mushrooms, and use them to concoct a special pre-game brew," Asher said. "What do you think?"

"Sounds great." I fiddled with my straw.

As promised, Asher and I met up the next night for drinks at The Bronze Gear. Normally, I'd want to hear all about his latest feud with another major soccer star, but I was too distracted to pay much attention to our conversation.

What was Josh doing right now? Sleeping, probably. He'd showed up again at the clinic that day after another long shift, despite Barbs's insistence he go home. He'd looked ready to collapse at his desk.

Shouldn't you be resting right now?

I should. But I wanted to see you.

Asher's laugh dragged me out of my thoughts. "Part of me is offended you're so blatantly ignoring me." His tone was drier than the gin in his glass. "Another part is intrigued."

Heat warmed my cheeks. Admittedly, I was awful company right now.

I also bet Asher didn't get ignored often, and not only because he was a Ballon d'Or winner. If he weren't such a talented soccer player, he'd make a killing as a male supermodel.

Sculpted cheekbones, green eyes, dark hair...and I felt nothing except my earlier frustration over my situation with Josh.

I pissed myself off sometimes for more reasons than I could count.

"Your ego can take it," I said lightly, trying to shake off my melancholy. "Though I'm surprised the cap is actually working."

Asher had pulled his baseball cap so low it shadowed half his face, and his plain T-shirt and jeans were a far cry from the stylish outfits he usually wore. Thick stubble covered his usually clean-shaven cheeks and jaw. Still, I was surprised by how many people passed by us without sparing him a second glance.

He was right. People saw what they expected to see.

"Why are you in D.C., anyway?" I asked, switching subjects. "You said you were in town for a last-minute trip?"

"Can't say, or my agent will kill me." Asher finished his drink. "But I have several meetings in the U.S., and one of them is in D.C."

I was surprised his U.S. trip wasn't all over the news. Then again, I didn't follow sports updates, so maybe it was, and I just didn't know.

"Does it feel weird, being so famous?" I asked. I couldn't imagine having my every move dissected.

"It was, but I got used to it." He flashed a sardonic smile. "Can I tell you a secret?" When I nodded, he said, "I never wanted to be famous."

My eyebrows shot up. "Come on."

Some celebrities shied away from the spotlight, but Asher seemed to thrive in it. He was always dating the latest super-model, driving the fastest car, and attending the hottest party.

"It's true." He leaned back in his chair. "There's a certain liberation to being a so-called nobody. No expectations, no pressure, just me and my love for the game. For the longest time, I held myself back because I was afraid of hitting the big time. Me, a nobody from Berkshire, playing for the biggest clubs and against the best players in the world? I didn't deserve it. But I love football—or soccer, as you Americans call it—and that mindset affected my game. I didn't even realize until my old coach called me out on it. And now..." Asher shrugged. "Like I said, I got used to the fame. But more importantly, I can play to my potential. I just had to get out of my own way."

I didn't deserve it.

The words echoed in my head and filled my lungs with sudden, icy realization. *Oh God.* Maybe the reason why I—

"Enough about me," Asher said. "Let's talk about why that guy is staring at me like he wants to rip my head off for the past fifteen minutes." He tilted his chin toward someone over my shoulder.

Had someone finally recognized him?

I turned, and my realization gave way to shock when I saw Josh sitting a few tables over. I had my back to the door, so I hadn't noticed him arrive..

Instead of looking away, Josh held my gaze, his eyes dark and his jaw lined with tension. The air suddenly crackled with an electricity that lit up my nerves.

"He's the guy from the wedding, right?" Asher drew my attention back to him. Amusement glowed in his eyes. "Boyfriend?"

"Not really." *Not anymore.*

The amusement deepened. "It's complicated, then."

"You could say that." Complicated, messy, and one of the few beautiful things I'd experienced in my life.

Even though I was no longer looking at Josh, the sparks from our two seconds of eye contact remained.

I didn't deserve it.

I just had to get out of my own way.

Any interest I had in continuing drinks with Asher dissipated into dust. "I'm so sorry, but—"

"Go." He waved me off. "I had a feeling our night would be cut short. And I'm ninety percent sure my cover is blown, so save yourself while you can."

I followed his gaze and spotted two men beelining toward us, their eyes fixed on Asher with the enthusiasm of overzealous fans.

Yikes. "Good luck."

Asher laughed. "Thanks for that, and for keeping me company for a few hours. If you're ever in Manchester, let me know."

"I will."

I got out of there right as the men reached our table.

"Are you Asher Donovan?" one of them asked. "I'm a huge fan! That goal you scored against Barcelona last year..."

I shook my head, hoping Asher didn't get mobbed once *everyone* figured out who he was. But like he said, he was used to it. I had a feeling he could take care of myself.

I, on the other hand, had a bigger issue to deal with.

Instead of approaching Josh, I exited the bar and lingered on corner of the sidewalk outside. The Bronze Gear was getting more crowded, and I didn't want to hold a conversation in there.

As expected, Josh appeared less than a minute later.

"You're not very subtle," I said. Despite the thick summer heat, goosebumps peppered my skin.

"I'm not here to be subtle, Red." He stopped in front of me.

Warmth dripped from the air and into my veins. "What are you here for, then?" I attempted to sound lighthearted despite the flutters in my chest. "Are you stalking me, Josh Chen?"

"Are you trying to forget me, Jules Ambrose?"

I gulped at his dark tone.

"Because if you are..." Josh took another step toward me. "It's not going to work."

The flutters went wild. "You have an awfully high opinion of yourself."

A hard smile cut across his face. "I promised I'd give you all the time you needed, and I will. But I'm not going to sit back while you date other guys, Red."

"I told you it wasn't a date."

"And I told you I don't share. Not when it comes to you." Josh's eyes burned into mine. "I don't give a fuck if he's a multi-millionaire and plastered on every magazine in the world. He could be the King of fucking England, but he'll never give you what I'm willing to give you."

The goosebumps multiplied. "What's that?"

"Everything." He'd closed the distance between us until our mouths were only centimeters apart. I stood my ground, but the electricity from earlier returned in full force and buzzed through my veins. There were a handful of other people on the sidewalk. They weren't close enough to hear us, but it didn't matter anyway. The rest of the world didn't exist when Josh was near me. "My heart. My soul. My *dignity*. What do you want me to do, Jules?" His voice splintered into something jagged and painful. "Do you want me to fucking beg? Say the word, and I'll be on my knees."

Moisture gathered behind my eyes. I shook my head, my chest aching.

What are you so afraid of?

I didn't deserve it.

I just had to get out of my own way.

Josh's question from Bridget's wedding echoed in my head. I didn't have the answer then, but I had it now.

I was afraid of me.

Even when I started falling for Josh, part of me knew we wouldn't work out as long as I was keeping a secret from him. But now that nothing stood in our way, I was terrified—of being hurt, of not being enough, and of actually being loved when I didn't deserve it.

I wasn't the little girl from Ohio anymore, but some things were so ingrained from childhood that they became a part of us without us even knowing. After a lifetime of being unwanted, I had no clue how to handle someone who wasn't willing to walk away.

Maybe it was time I learned.

"Promise me we're real," I whispered.

I could drag this out, make triple sure he wouldn't break my heart again. But I was so *tired* of resisting and sabotaging myself. After years of swimming against the current, it was time to sink into something I wanted for once, no matter where it took me.

And at the end of the day, no grand gesture matched that of making a promise...and keeping it.

Josh cupped my face with his hands. "I promise." A tiny smile tipped his lips, and his eyes searched mine with cautious hope. "You're stuck with me forever, I'm afraid."

His words sank into my skin and filled every inch of me with their warmth.

Just let go, Jules.

After one last beat of hesitation, my lips parted in tentative invitation.

Relief exploded across Josh's face before he took it, his mouth moving over mine in a deep, almost desperate kiss that made my toes curl. I melted against him, savoring the taste and feel of him again.

My chest loosened, and every nerve ending sparked with awareness.

Some kisses you felt in your bones. This one I felt in my soul.

"Twelve days, eight hours, and nine minutes. I spent every second thinking of you." Josh's lips brushed against mine as he spoke. "I thought I knew what I wanted before. Becoming a doctor, chasing the next high. Being the most popular, most liked person in the room. I thought those things would make me happy, and they did. Temporarily. But you..." He rested his forehead against mine. "You're the only thing that could make me happy forever."

I choked out a half laugh, half sob. "Careful, Chen. Keep saying things like that, and I might never let you go," I said, mirroring his words from our first date.

That beautiful dimple of his appeared in all its glory. "I'm counting on it." He curled his hand around the back of my neck and pressed another, softer kiss to my lips. "In case it's not clear, I fucking love you, Jules Ambrose, even when you drive me crazy. *Especially* when you drive me crazy."

"That's because you're a masochist." I couldn't contain my smile. "It's okay. I love you anyway."

It was my first time saying those words to a guy, but they didn't feel strange. They felt like they'd always been there, just waiting for the right time and right person before they revealed themselves.

Josh's hand stilled. "Say that again."

"I love you," I breathed, body thrumming, heart so full it could burst at any second.

A small grin blossomed on his face. "Damn right. I'm pretty fucking lovable, unless I'm being an ass...which I was for the week after you told me about the painting." He glanced at the group of teenagers staring at us, and I realized we were starting to attract attention from passersby. "But maybe we should continue this somewhere more private."

My apartment was only two blocks away. Stella wasn't home, and we barely made it into my bedroom before Josh kissed me again and sank to his knees before me.

"Twelve days, twelve orgasms." He pushed up my skirt, his breath warm against the sensitive skin of my thighs. "That seems fair, don't you think?"

A small fire kindled in my lower belly. "What—"

My question died an ignoble death when he pushed my panties aside and ran his tongue over my clit.

Oh God.

I fisted Josh's hair as he licked and sucked until my orgasm ricocheted through me. I didn't get a chance to come down from my high before he delved in again, and soon, I was little more than a gasping, boneless mess. If it weren't for his strong hands bracing my hips and holding me up, I would've already collapsed.

But despite the orgasms rocking through me and the thick scent of sex in the air, what we were doing didn't feel like sex.

It felt like love.

53

JOSH

"This wasn't what I had in mind when you said we'll continue things at your house." Jules's soft grumble was muffled by my pillow.

I suppressed a laugh as I iced her shoulder with a towel-wrapped ice pack. "I never said what the *things* would be."

After I *thoroughly* apologized at her apartment, we took the train to my house before Stella came home. The minute we did, I had Jules lie down in my bed so I could tend to her injuries.

She'll fully heal in a few weeks, but the thought of her in any sort of pain, even if it was temporary, made my heart twist.

"It was implied. I feel misled. Bamboozled. Falsely advertised to." Jules lifted her head to glare at me. "Where's my makeup sex, Chen?"

My laugh broke free. "Were your earlier orgasms not enough?"

I skimmed my fingers up her neck to her face, where I pushed a strand of hair out of her eye. The entire train ride home, I couldn't stop staring at her, afraid she would disappear if I looked away for too long.

There'd been every chance Jules wouldn't forgive me for how I treated her, and I wouldn't have blamed her if she hadn't.

But thank the fucking Lord she had.

You fucked me, then you tossed me aside just like everyone else.

An ache pierced my chest at the memory of her words.

God, I was such an ass.

"Oral sex isn't the same." Jules's words morphed into a soft sigh when I kissed her neck and gently stroked her wetness.

"You want me inside you, Red?"

A shudder rolled through her body. "*Yes.*"

My already-stiff cock hardened further at the breathy hope in her voice, but I held strong. "You have a shoulder sprain, Jules, not to mention bruises all over. You could exacerbate your injuries."

She let out another, less pleasurable sigh. "This is what I get for dating a doctor, isn't it?"

"Hmm." The corner of my mouth tipped at her exasperation. "There are benefits to dating a doctor, though. For example..." I pushed one finger inside her while I kept my thumb on her clit. "I'm *very* good with anatomy."

Jules's grumble melted into a string of moans as she arched into my hand. I kissed my way down her chest and bare stomach, and her moan turned into a cry when I spread her open and delved in with my tongue. Stroking, sucking, licking. Worshiping her like it was penance and she was my salvation.

"Josh...I'm going to..." Jules's soft gasp arrowed straight into my heart. "Inside me. *Please.* I want to come when you're inside me."

I paused and groaned. My heart hammered so hard I felt it in every inch of my body, and my cock was close to exploding. "You're killing me, Red."

We shouldn't. She was injured. They were mild injuries, but still. The smart thing would be to wait until she was fully healed.

But God help me, I couldn't deny her anything when she was pleading like that.

Against my better judgment, I lifted my head and rose until we were eye level again.

"It's going to be a little softer today, okay?" I brushed another strand of hair out of her eyes.

Jules nodded with such enthusiasm I almost laughed again, but any humor died when I rolled on a condom and pushed inside her, inch by inch, until I filled her completely.

Her moan mingled with mine.

She felt so fucking good. Tight and wet and made for me, like she was the jigsaw puzzle I'd been missing all my life.

My skin misted with sweat from the effort of holding back an orgasm, and I let out a soft warning growl when Jules tightened around me.

"Can't help it." Her breaths came out in short pants. "You're too big."

Whenever we went even a few days without sex, she had to adjust to my size all over again.

"And you take every inch beautifully." I pulled out, then slid back in with a slow, smooth glide. Jules squirmed a little, but her muscles gradually relaxed, and pride lit my chest. "That's it. Just like that. You're doing so well."

Jules's face flushed with pleasure. "Josh..."

"Your pussy was made for me, Red. Every part of you, made for me." My own breaths harshened as I increased the pace. The sensual, languorous rhythm was a one eighty from our usual rough, furious fucking, but in a way, it was even hotter.

I could savor every glide of my cock into her and every one of her whimpers and moans as I fucked away every bad memory from our last time together.

"Don't hold back," I growled when her teeth sank into her bottom lip. I could tell from the tenseness of her muscles that she was about to come. "I want to hear your sweet screams."

I reached down to rub her clit, pressing with just enough pressure to tip her over the edge while I picked up the pace. A cry of pleasure ripped from Jules's throat. Her back arched, and I grunted at the sensation of her tight pussy walls pulsing around me.

My chest expanded at the sight of her like this—completely undone and so beautiful I couldn't look away if my life depended on it.

"That's it." I rubbed my thumb over her cheek and leaned down to kiss her. Hard. "Good girl," I whispered. "I love hearing you scream for me."

Jules's whimpers shot straight to my cock, and it didn't take long before I came with a loud groan.

I rolled off her, not wanting to jostle her shoulder, and we lay there in contented silence until we caught our breath.

Sex was great, but this part? The one where we basked in the glow and each other's presence? It was even better.

I turned on my side and wrapped an arm around Jules's waist, drawing her closer. I never gave a fuck about cuddling before her, but I loved having her in my arms. It just felt…right.

"How's your shoulder?"

"Still attached." Jules laughed at my scowl. "It's *fine*. See? We had sex, and I didn't die."

"Not funny." I didn't even want to joke about her dying. "I'm checking your shoulder again later, just in case."

"Yes, Dr. Chen," she teased. "Do you offer these kinds of hands-on checkups to everybody, or am I special?"

"I only offer them to my most stubborn, infuriating, pain in the ass patients. The ones I can't stop thinking about. Luckily..." I smoothed my palm over the curve of her ass. "I only have one of those."

Jules's breath hitched. "Lucky me."

"Lucky you," I drawled, a cocky smile forming on my lips.

"Arrogant ass." She laughed before her face turned serious. "Do you still have the painting? Max's associates will come looking for it, and I don't—"

"I took care of it."

"How?"

"You'll see."

She winkled her nose. "Cryptic much?"

"It's a surprise, Red. You'll see," I repeated.

Jules huffed and dropped the subject, but I could tell she was intrigued. Nothing piqued her interest like a surprise.

Now, all I had to do was figure out how to reveal it...*after* I figured out how to retrieve those musical tickets I destroyed last week. I could fold both things into one.

I grazed my knuckles over her back in lazy strokes, content just to listen to her breathe, while she yawned and buried her face in my chest. Now that the high from sex was wearing off, exhaustion lined her face and shadowed her eyes.

"We're going to have to tell Ava, you know," she mumbled. "Eventually. Someday."

"Don't remind me." I grimaced at the thought of Ava's reaction. "How long do you think we should wait? A year? A decade?"

"A decade, or maybe a century. A century sounds good. She'll be so..." Jules's voice slowly drifted off.

I peeked down at her. Out cold, just like that.

Between what happened with Max, her bar exam, and our makeup, she must be worn out.

I kissed the top of her head and tucked her closer to me.

We could worry about Ava later.

For now, I wanted to enjoy the moments that belonged only to us.

54

JOSH

I RUBBED A REASSURING HAND OVER JULES'S BACK AS WE stepped off the elevator and straight into an apartment that looked like it'd been lifted from the pages of *Architectural Digest*.

Light gray walls, black marble floors, gold fixtures. It screamed *bachelor pad*, but unlike two years ago, feminine accents now added a softer touch: a bouquet of white lilies here, a watercolor painting there.

"We'll be fine," I whispered to Jules.

We'd both fucked up in our own ways, but we could finally move on from the past together...after we cleared our last hurdle.

"Easy for you to say," she whispered back. "You're a blood relation. I'm not."

"She loves you more than me."

"Hmm. That's true."

My laugh died when Ava met us at the private elevator entrance to the apartment she shared with Alex. I quickly dropped my hand from Jules's back.

We'd finally scrounged up the courage to tell Ava the truth a week after we made up, but all that courage died in the face of my sister's expectant smile, which melted into suspicion when she saw Jules standing by my side.

I'd called to tell her I was coming, but I'd left out the part about bringing Jules. I didn't want her piecing two and two together before we told her ourselves.

Then again, that might've been a smarter move. Let her get the shock out of her system before we saw her.

Dammit, Chen.

Well, it was too late now. We had to face the music as it came.

I pasted on my most charming grin. "Hey, sis. You look absolutely *ravishing* today. Here." I shoved a box containing her favorite Crumble & Bake red velvet cake at her. "I brought you a gift."

Ava didn't take the cake. Instead, her eyes roved between me and Jules, who stood next to me with an overly bright smile of her own.

"What are you doing here together?" Her suspicion visibly deepened. "You're not going to ask me to mediate another argument, are you? Because you're both grown adults."

Jules and I exchanged a quick look.

Maybe we should've come up with a better plan than *bring Ava cake to butter her up.*

Alex came up behind Ava and notched an eyebrow when he saw the Crumble & Bake box.

Really? That's your plan? He didn't have to say the words for me to hear them, loud and clear.

I glared at him. *Shut up.*

He replied with a smirk.

Asshole.

He seemed to have forgotten that *he* once snuck around my back to date my sister.

"Let's talk about this over cake," Jules chirped. "Nothing like red velvet to start the night right."

Ava crossed her arms over her chest. "I need to sit down for whatever you're about to tell me, don't I?"

"Maybe. Probably." I cleared my throat. "Definitely."

The four of us settled in the living room—Ava and Alex on one couch, me and Jules opposite them. It was near sunset, and the dying rays of light streaming through the windows spliced the room into half shadow, half golden warmth.

The cake box sat on the coffee table between us, unopened.

"So, the reason we're here together is because, uh, we came together," Jules said.

Alex sighed and rubbed a hand over his face.

"And the reason we came together is be*cause...*" *C'mon man, it's a Band-Aid. Rip that fucker off and deal with the consequences later.* "We're dating," I finished.

Ava stared at us with a blank expression.

"Romantically," Jules clarified.

"Boyfriend and girlfriend," I added.

More silence.

Ava hadn't moved since we started talking, which wasn't good.

A bead of sweat trickled down my spine.

It was crazy. I shouldn't be scared of my *little* sister. But chatty Ava was normal; silent Ava was kinda terrifying.

Then, she did the last thing I expected. She burst into laughter. She covered her face, her shoulders shaking, while Jules and I exchanged another, worried glance.

Fuck, did we break my sister?

"Good one," Ava gasped in between breaths. "You almost

had me." She tried to straighten her face only to collapse into laughter again a second later.

"Uh..." Of all the ways I pictured this conversation going, Ava losing her marbles wasn't one of them.

Jules knocked her knee against mine. "She thinks we're joking," she hissed.

"I *know*." I cleared my throat. "Ave..."

"Honestly, I'm impressed you guys put aside your differences long enough to come up with this plan." Some of Ava's mirth had finally subsided, though her grin remained.

"Ave..."

"Is this payback for Vermont? Because that was months ago, and I had no idea there'd only be one bed."

"Ava, we're not joking!"

My declaration rang through the room, followed by thick, stunned silence.

My sister's grin disappeared. "You're not..." Her eyes darted between us again, taking in our tense expressions and the way our thighs touched. Horror dawned on her face. "You're *actually dating*? How is that possible? You hate each other!"

"Welllll..." I dragged the word out. "Not anymore."

Jules chimed in. "We've been working together at the clinic—"

"It started as a no strings attached kinda thing—"

"We didn't plan for this to happen—"

Our voices overlapped in a rushed explanation before Ava held up a hand and cut us off. "How long have you been dating?"

I winced. "Er, a week this time around."

"What do you mean, *this time around*?"

Goddammit. We *definitely* should've come up with a script for this.

Since it was too late, Jules and I forged ahead and told Ava everything, starting with our sex-only arrangement and ending with our reconciliation last week. We left out the ugly details about Max and chalked our breakup up to a misunderstanding, but otherwise, it was a pretty comprehensive summary.

By the time we finished, Ava's skin had taken on a faint green tint. She glared at me. "You're telling me you've been sleeping with my best friend *for months*?" She pointed at Jules. "And you've been sleeping with my *brother* for months? I can't believe you didn't tell me earlier!"

Jules gave a helpless shrug. "I never found the right time to tell you I was banging your brother."

The green tint on Ava's skin deepened.

"You did the same with him!" I gestured toward Alex, who watched the scene unfold with a bored expression. He didn't even *try* to help. *Traitor.* "You guys were dating for months before I found out. Don't be a hypocrite."

"That was different," Ava growled. "We didn't loathe each other with a burning passion, then turn around and start making out."

"I know this is a shock, considering my past...differences with Josh." Jules's bottom lip disappeared between her teeth. "But with us working together at the clinic and seeing each other so much, it just sort of happened. We really hadn't planned to keep it from you for so long. We just weren't sure it was even going anywhere, and we didn't want to tell you until we were. It would make things too awkward."

"Right." Ava closed her eyes and took a deep breath. "Alex, bring me a knife."

I paled. "Whoa, whoa, whoa!" I held up one hand and drew Jules closer to me with the other. "I'm your only brother. You love me. Remember when I gave you the last of my Milk Duds at the movie theater? Good times."

Ava ignored me until Alex returned with the requested knife.

I scowled at him. So this was how I was going to die. Betrayed by my best friend *again* and stabbed to death by my sister. Julius Caesar had nothing on me in terms of a shitty death.

My heart pounded as Ava grasped the knife, leaned forward...and opened the dessert box. She sliced off a piece of cake and took a bite.

Silence descended.

"Should we say something else?" Jules whispered.

"She still has a knife in her hand," I whispered back. "Let's wait."

We watched while Ava finished eating with an unreadable expression. But when she spoke again, her voice had lost some of its hard edge. "How serious is this?"

Relief loosened the knot of anxiety in my chest. I recognized that voice. She was coming around.

I wasn't worried about her cutting us off forever because we snuck around behind her back, but I also didn't want to spend weeks on the outs with my sister.

"I no longer want to kill her every time I set eyes on her, so pretty serious," I joked before sobering. "Listen, I know this must be weird as fuck for you, but I promise, we wouldn't be here if it *wasn't* serious. You know what I asked you when I found out about you and Alex? What you said?" I flicked my gaze to Alex, whose bored expression gave way to one with more interest. "I feel the same about Jules."

"Ava." I stared at her in shock, trying to make sense of a world that had turned upside down. My sister and my best friend. My best friend and my sister. Together. "Do you...love him?"

There was a short pause.

When Ava finally answered, her voice was soft but steady.
"Yes. I do."

Present Ava stared at me a second longer before she stood and tilted her head toward the kitchen. "Let's talk. Alone."

Jules gave me a semi-nervous glance as I stood. I responded with what I hoped was a reassuring smile before I joined my sister in the kitchen.

"Did you mean what you said?" Ava asked once we were out of the others' earshot. "About what you feel for her?"

"Yeah." My face softened. "I love her, Ave. We may still fight and argue sometimes, but at the end of the day...she's it."

I would take a thousand fights with Jules over a thousand easy days with anyone else.

Because I didn't want easy. I wanted her.

"Right." Ava sighed. Her shoulders finally relaxed, and a smidge of guilt passed over her face. "I didn't mean to give you such a hard time, especially since you were so understanding when I told you about Alex. But I *know* how you are with women, and I know how Jules is with guys. You both hate commitment. I just don't want you breaking each other's hearts. I love you both, and I can't choose a side if that happens. That being said..." She jabbed the blunt edge of her knife into my chest. "If you hurt her, I will murder you."

"What makes you think I'd be the one doing the hurting? I could very easily be the hurtee."

Was that a word? If it wasn't, it was now.

"Murder. You," Ava emphasized with additional jabs.

"Fine." I grinned. "So, does that mean you're okay with us dating?"

"I guess," she grumbled through a burgeoning smile. "My brother brought to his knees by my best friend. Good job, Jules."

Another scowl replaced my grin. "She did not *bring me to my knees*. At least, not figuratively."

This time, Ava's smile was the one that disappeared. "Okay, one rule. Don't talk or make innuendos about your sex life. *Ever*." She mimed gagging.

I laughed and pulled her into my chest for a hug. I ruffled her hair the way I did when we were kids, earning myself a muffled protest. "I won't, but the rule applies to you, too."

"Fine." Ava batted my hand away and smoothed her hair with another grumble, but her annoyed expression soon melted into something softer. "Seriously, I'm happy you're happy. I know things have been hard with...everything. I'll always be here for you, but I'm glad you have someone like Jules by your side. She can be a bit...*dramatic* sometimes"—we both let out knowing laughs—"but she has one of the biggest hearts I know."

A ball of emotion formed in my throat. "I know." I squeezed Ava tighter and dropped a small kiss on the top of her head. "Thanks, sis."

Even though we annoyed the hell out of each other sometimes, I was lucky to have her as my sister. Before I met Alex, she was my sounding board for all my problems and vice versa. We didn't confide in each other as often now that we were all grown up with our own lives, but there would never be a day when we didn't have each other's backs.

55

JOSH

AFTER WE RETURNED TO THE LIVING ROOM, AVA WHISKED Jules away for what I assumed was a similar conversation to the one we had, minus the sibling stuff. However, instead of staying in the apartment, they decamped to a nearby bar so Ava could quote unquote try and forget she ever heard the phrase *banging your brother*.

Personally, I thought they left the apartment so they could secretly plan how to gang up on me in the future—I *know* how they work—but I was so relieved by Ava's acceptance of my and Jules's relationship, I didn't care.

After the girls left, I joined Alex by the wall of windows, where he stood with a pensive expression.

"I'm surprised you didn't go with them." I came up beside him and stared down at the city laid out before us. Dusk transformed the skies into a palette of soft pinks and purples, and lights flickered on in the sea of buildings until they resembled a carpet of tiny jewels. "You're usually glued to Ava's side."

Alex had been paranoid about Ava's safety since his uncle kidnapped her; he even hired a bodyguard for her until she chafed at the constant shadow. They got into a huge fight over it before Alex caved and dialed back on the protection detail.

"We're working on that." A hint of disgruntlement colored his voice. "She says I'm too paranoid."

"You *are*. And I say this as her brother, someone who's very invested in her well-being."

He let out a small rumble of irritation but let the issue drop. "There is another reason I stayed behind. I need...I want to tell you something."

My eyebrows climbed at his uncharacteristic stumble. "Okay. As long as it's not another confession about a seven-year lie, because I swear to God..."

"Now who's the paranoid one?" Alex rubbed a hand over his jaw, his brow knitting in a frown.

The longer he hesitated, the more my curiosity spiked. Alex rarely struggled for words. Except for Ava, he didn't give enough of a shit about anyone to care how his statements were received.

"I've never had much of a family," he finally said. "As you know, my parents and sisters were murdered when I was a child, and my uncle was a psychopath."

Only Alex could deliver such brutal facts with such unflinching honesty.

"I didn't have many friends growing up either, and that was fine. I dislike a majority of people I meet. I had my business and side projects, and that was enough." His throat bobbed with a hard swallow. "Then I met you and Ava. You were both quite irritating in the beginning, with your insistence on adhering to social niceties and your determination to see the best in people, no matter how foolish an endeavor that is."

I snorted, but a strange tightness gripped my chest.

"But..." Alex hesitated again. "You also saw the best in me. You're the only people who've ever seen more in me than a bank account, a status symbol, or a business connection. We may have different views on life and the way we approach things, but you and Ava..." His voice softened. "You're the closest thing I have to a family."

Ah, fuck. If I teared up over something Alex said, he'd never let me live it down.

But I knew how hard it must've been for him to admit that. Alex was as sentimental as a porcupine was cuddly, but for all his faults, he was a good friend in the only way he knew how— loyal, unquestioning, and willing to burn the world down for the people he loved.

"Fuck, man, you should've warned me you were going to get all sentimental and shit. I would've brought more Kleenex."

The words came out more choked than I would've liked.

A small smile graced his mouth. "It's facts, not sentimentality. On that note..." He reached into his pocket and retrieved a small velvet box. "I'd like to formalize the relationship."

Were my ears deceiving me, or I did detect a touch of nervousness?

I stared at Alex blankly. Part of me knew what he was hinting at, but my sluggish brain couldn't catch up in time. "Formalize what relationship?"

"The family one." He snapped the box open and nearly blinded me.

Holy fucking crap.

The ring nestled against the velvet cushion gave the Wollman Rink a run for its money in terms of size. I didn't know much about diamonds, but I knew this one had to cost *at least* five figures.

It blazed like a fallen star in the dying late afternoon light. Smaller diamonds dotted its platinum band and threw rainbow prisms across the room, and the silver letters stamped on either side of the ring cushion read *Harry Winston*.

"I wanted to tell you before I proposed." Alex closed the box again, saving my retinas from being seared right off. "You know how I feel about Ava, so I won't bore you with a regurgitation of the facts. I also despise the outdated tradition of asking permission to marry. That being said, I know how much she values your opinion. I do too, and while I don't *need* your permission..." He swallowed hard. "I would very much like to have it."

Silence rang in the wake of his words.

Alex. Proposing to Ava. So he would be my brother-in-law.

The disjointed yet connected thoughts tumbled through my head. *Holy fuck.* I'd known Alex and my sister would be endgame since the day I learned he gave up his company for her. He got it back after she forgave him, but for him to even *consider* doing something so drastic, he had to be in deep.

Yet I never could've imagined the proposal would come so early, or that he would ask for my permission.

Alex never asked for permission from anyone.

"I didn't want to propose until after you and I...sorted through some of our issues." Alex watched me with sharp eyes, his features taut with tension. "I didn't want to put either of you in that position."

I finally found my words through the well of emotion in my chest. "My sister's rubbing off on you. You actually sound human."

"I'm good at imitations."

There was a moment of stunned silence before a laugh burst from my mouth. "Shit, Volkov, don't kill me with shock before the wedding. Ava will be pissed."

Alex's lips curved. "Is that an implicit blessing?"

"Don't get ahead of yourself." I sobered. "You're right. We have very different worldviews, and we hit a bit of a, ah, rough patch over the years. I still think you're an asshole eighty percent of the time. But you...you walked my sister home every day for a year like a psycho Romeo. You always put her safety and well-being ahead of yourself, which for you is saying a fucking lot." I swallowed hard. "Ava is my only sister. My only real *family*. I've always taken care of her growing up, and I don't trust her with just anyone. But I trust her with you."

If there was one thing I was certain of, it was that Alex would lay his life down on the line for her. He may be an asshole to everyone else, but I could always trust him to take care of Ava.

I clapped him on the back as the tightness in my chest intensified. "So yeah, you have my fucking permission. Just don't kill her with the ring, because that shit is bright as fuck."

A suspicious brightness glowed in Alex's eyes before he blinked and it disappeared. He let out a relieved-sounding laugh. "She'll be okay. She's tougher than you."

"That's true." Despite her sunny optimism and what some would call naïveté, Ava had always been a survivor. I shook my head in my disbelief. "Can't believe I'll be stuck with you forever as my brother-in-law."

I didn't doubt Ava would say yes, but having Alex Volkov as my brother-in-law...Lord help me.

"Lucky you." A small smile remained on Alex's mouth, but his eyes turned serious again. "Speaking of which, I also have a proposal for you."

"Alex." I clutched my chest. "Ava's not gonna like it if you propose to me too. Bigamy is illegal in D.C."

"Funny." He walked to the bar and poured two glasses of whiskey, one of which he handed to me. "If Ava says yes..."

"She'll say yes."

An uncharacteristic hint of nerves coasted through Alex's eyes before it vanished beneath cool green ice.

"*When* she says yes, I'll need a best man." He rubbed his

thumb over his glass, his tense shoulders at odds with his casual tone. "Since you're my best friend, and one of the few people I can stand to be around for more than five minutes at a time, consider this my official ask to you."

Ah, fuck. Emotion rushed back into my chest and swelled until it formed a lump in my throat.

Before our falling out, Alex had been there for every game, every crisis, and every emergency I had. He was the only person outside my family I trusted, and I was the only one he uttered more than a dozen words to at a time.

We'd been best friends, but he'd never called me that, at least not in my presence. Today was the first time.

"That depends." My voice came out scratchy before I cleared my throat. That fucker would *not* make me cry. *Not today, Satan.* "One, do I have full authority to plan your bachelor party in any way I see fit? Two, do I get box seats for life to any sports game I want? Three, can I take your Aston for a spin?"

Alex released a sigh so weary I half expected him to collapse beneath its weight. "Within reason, yes, and no."

One and a half out of three. Not bad. I hadn't expected him to say yes to the Aston thing anyway. He never let anyone drive his precious car.

"I'll take it." I raised my glass. "You've got yourself a best man."

"I'm thrilled."

"I can't wait until our Vegas blowout," I said, ignoring his dry response. "Actually, shit, let's level up. You're a billionaire with a *b*, as you always remind me. Let's go to Macau. No, Monaco. No, Ibi—"

"You're getting ahead of yourself. I haven't proposed yet."

"But you *will*, and it's best to be prepared." My grin faded at the sight of Alex's tight jaw. "She'll say yes," I repeated in a softer voice. "Don't worry."

Another hint of nerves flickered in his eyes. "I don't worry." He rubbed his thumb over his whiskey tumbler again until some of the tension drained from his shoulders. "But no Ibiza. I can't stand island parties."

"Deal." Monaco sounded more fun, anyway. "Here's to an epic proposal and even more epic bachelor weekend."

I lifted my glass again. Alex clinked his against mine, and I waited until we'd both drained our drinks before I added, "I'd be your best man even without the box seats, you know."

The ice in his eyes cracked, revealing a sliver of softness. "I know."

A poignant beat passed before we coughed at the same time and let out awkward laughs. Alex might petrify into stone if we dwelled too much on the sentimentality of the moment, and I didn't want my sister to marry a literal statue.

"Now that that's out of the way..." I threw an arm around his shoulders and steered him toward the couch. "Let's talk about how we'll make this a stag party you'll never forget. I'm thinking tigers, tattoos..."

"No."

I brushed off the buzzkill. "Actually, how do you feel about cage diving with sharks? We can fly to South Africa for the weekend..."

Alex rubbed an exasperated hand over his face while I rambled off ideas and tried to hold back a grin.

Me annoying the shit out of him while he feigned irritation?

It was like old times, only better, because this time, there were no lies or secrets between us.

Every great friendship had chapters.

This was the start of our new one.

56

JULES

"I'm here! I'm here!" Stella rushed through the door, her hair flying around her in a dark cloud. "What did I miss?"

I pinned the brunette across from me with an exasperated glare. "*Ava*."

"It wasn't my fault." Her eyes sparkled with laughter. "Stel asked what we were doing, I told her, and...well, I might've spilled the beans."

We'd been drinking at a bar near her apartment for two hours, during which she grilled me about my feelings toward Josh, our relationship, and our plans for the future. She was mostly joking, I think, but that didn't stop me from sweating like I just finished the New York Marathon.

"Nothing except an interrogation worthy of the CIA." I finished the rest of my cranberry vodka while Stella slid into the seat next to mine.

She must've come straight from work, but instead of a boring business suit, she wore a gorgeous white linen dress and turquoise necklace that set off her bronze skin. The perks of working at a fashion magazine, I supposed.

"I highly doubt that." Stella brushed a stray curl out of her eye. "I can't believe you didn't tell me. All this time, you've been dating *Josh*? He's the Mystery Guy?"

Heat rushed over my face. "Can you blame me? Look at the way you're reacting. Personally, I don't think it's *that* big a deal." So what if Josh and I had hated each other for almost the entire time Stella knew us? People changed. "It's not like I'm dating the Pope."

"You dating the Pope would be more believable," Stella quipped.

"Funny. You're all hilarious." Despite my grumbles, my cheeks ached from smiling.

For all their good-natured teasing, my friends seemed genuinely happy for me—well, after Ava recovered from her initial shock—and now that Josh and I were out in the open, a huge weight had lifted off my shoulders.

There was a certain thrill to sneaking around, but I hated lying to my friends.

"At least you didn't tell Bridget yet." I knocked my foot against Ava's foot under the table. I didn't need to be accosted by all my friends at once.

Her cheeks pinked. "Erm, about that..."

As if on cue, my phone lit up with an incoming FaceTime call from a certain European royal.

"*Ava*."

"You can't expect me to keep the news to myself. I'm never the first to get a good scoop." She held up her hands. "Besides, Bridge was in the group chat."

I sighed, but since it was too late to put the news back in the box, I answered the call.

Bridget's face filled the screen. "You're dating *Josh Chen*?" she asked without preamble. "What? How? Why?"

"Hello, Your Majesty. Good evening to you, too," I said pointedly. "How are you doing?"

"Don't *how are you doing* me." Bridget pushed her green cloth headband higher up on her head. She must've turned in for the night, because her face was scrubbed free of makeup and I caught a glimpse of her silk pajama top at the bottom of the screen. "Tell me everything. Don't leave out any details. I always miss the good stuff over here in Europe."

"Don't you have royal duties to attend to or something?"

"It's midnight, Jules, and my royal duties consist of wrangling ministers who insist on acting like grade schoolers. Please, let me have some fun." A masculine rumble murmured something offscreen. Bridget turned her head to whisper something back before she faced me again. "Rhys says hi."

She panned the camera so I could see Rhys, who waved at me from his spot next to her in bed. His gray eyes glowed with bemusement.

I let out another sigh, but I recounted the story again, starting with the clinic truce. When I finished, Bridget and Stella stared at me with open mouths.

"Wow. That's..." Bridget shook her head. I'd propped my phone up against a glass so we could all see her. "Somehow you and Josh together make zero sense and all the sense in the world."

"Does this mean you guys have stopped bickering?" Stella asked with a hopeful expression.

"Nope. We bicker more," I said cheerfully. "It leads to great ha—" *Hate sex.* I cut off abruptly when Ava's eyes widened with alarm. "You know."

Stella wrinkled her nose. "I don't, and I don't *want* to know. I'll never be able to look at Josh the same."

"You will one day." Stella didn't date much, but it wasn't for lack of interest from guys—she fielded suitors every day. Romance simply wasn't a priority. "Enough about me. What about you?"

"What about me?" Wariness touched her features.

"You're the last woman left standing." Mischief lit up my face. "Who's going to be the guy who sweeps you off your feet?"

"When you find him, let me know," she said dryly. "In the meantime, I'm just trying to survive Anya."

Anya was her boss and the editor-in-chief of D.C. *Style* magazine.

While Stella told us about her latest photoshoot, which apparently involved a hungover supermodel, a live python, and a gallon of baby oil, a familiar photo drew my attention to the TV hanging over the bar.

Shock stole my breath from my lungs. Brown hair, blue eyes, stubbled jaw, unsmiling face.

Max.

The volume was off, but the closed captions were on, so I could read what happened.

"...body was found in a hotel room in Baltimore. The victim, Max Renner, was stabbed multiple times and died at the scene. Renner was recently released from prison for grand larceny and is believed to be involved in an Ohio-based crime ring. Police suspect other members of the crime ring are responsible for his murder, and the FBI..."

Max was dead.

All those years, all that heartache, *he was dead.*

I guess his associates finally caught up with him.

Other than a trickle of relief, I felt...nothing. Not even vindication after what he did in the stairwell.

I'd truly put him in the past.

I dragged my attention back to my friends in time to see Stella's face pale at something on her phone while Ava and Bridget chatted about Bridget's upcoming diplomatic trip to Argentina.

A seed of concern sprouted in my chest. "Is everything okay?" Stella rarely looked that rattled.

"Yes." She slid her phone into her bag and smiled, but it looked more forced than usual. "Something came up at work, but I'll deal with it later."

"You should find a job that treats you better," I said gently. "You're talented enough. You can even go full-time with your blog."

Stella made a ton of money from brand sponsorships.

"Maybe one day."

I took the hint from her subdued response and dropped the issue, though my concern remained. Stella kept all her feelings and troubles bottled up. It wasn't healthy in the long run, but now wasn't the time to get into it.

We rejoined Bridget and Ava's conversation and eventually shifted topics to Ava's promotion at work. It was past midnight in Eldorra, but Bridget stayed up with us to talk.

My chest glowed with warmth.

It felt like old times, when we would order pizza and talk into the early hours of the morning in our dorm room.

We weren't eighteen anymore, but we were still *us*. Even if one of us lived on a different continent now, and we didn't see each other as much as we used to at school, our friendship was a steady rock.

It was comforting to know that no matter how much some things changed, others will always stay the same.

57

JULES

"WHAT'S THE SURPRISE?" I BOUNCED ON THE BALLS OF MY feet, unable to contain my curiosity as we stepped into the elevator of a luxury Upper East Side apartment building. "Tell me, *please*. I'm dying here."

Josh had surprised me with a trip to New York to catch the last showing of the *Legally Blonde* musical revival earlier that night, and he said he had another surprise for me before we left tomorrow. I'd tried to pry the secret from him during our entire cab ride here, but he'd refused to budge.

"Red, we will literally be there in a few minutes." He pressed the button for the penthouse, and my curiosity ramped up another notch. "Haven't you ever heard the term *patience*?"

"Patience?" I pretended to think. "Nope, never heard of it."

I laughed when he swatted my ass in playful punishment.

I'd been floating on a high since Josh and I got back together. I caught myself humming at the oddest times, like when I was loading the dishwasher or waiting for the metro, and my cheeks ached from smiling so much. Even stress over my looming bar results couldn't dampen the weightlessness in my chest.

Nothing turned a person into a bigger cheeseball than being in love, and I wasn't even mad about it. There were worse things than being cheesy. Besides, cheese was a top tier food group.

When we arrived at the penthouse, a woman in a stunning white dress checked our names off a list and waved us in with a smile. "Welcome to the exhibition, Mr. Chen, Ms. Ambrose. The gallery is to your right."

"Exhibition?" I took in the sleek, modern furniture and glass walls overlooking Central Park. The place looked like a private residence, not a museum.

"Private collector. He's hosting a party displaying his newly acquired works." Josh guided me to a long marble hall lit by a domed glass skylight. Dozens of paintings hung on the wall in gilded frames, and well-dressed guests circulated with champagne in hand.

I squeezed Josh's hand again when his eyes lingered on a glass of the bubbly golden liquid.

"And how did you score an invite to this exhibition?" I asked suspiciously. Who could Josh possibly know in New York?

His smug grin rang a dozen alarms. "You're looking at it." He pulled me further down the hall until we reached one painting in particular.

My jaw unhinged. "You're *joking*. How is this possible?"

It was the *atrocious* painting from Josh's room, the one that brought me so much grief last month. Except now, instead of a Hazelburg bedroom, it hung in a multimillion-dollar apartment between a Monet and a de Kooning.

"I sold it. I didn't want whoever is after the painting to come after me again, so I made the sale as high profile as possible. If they want to fuck with the new owner..." Josh shrugged. "It's on them."

"Jesus." I admit, it *was* a genius move, though I still couldn't fathom the idea anyone this rich would pay to have such an ugly painting in their house.

Max was gone, but I was curious about who was intimidating enough that it would deter whatever criminals he'd been running around with.

"Who's the new owner?" I asked.

"I am."

I turned at the rich, somewhat familiar voice, and my eyebrows flew up when I saw who it belonged to. I'd only met him once, but I'd recognize that glossy dark hair and beautiful olive skin anywhere.

Dante Russo smiled. "It's nice to see you both again. I hope you're enjoying the party."

So I wasn't the only one who remembered our encounter in Christian's library.

"We are, thanks. Your gallery is beautiful," I said graciously.

I made a mental note to Google Dante later. I'd heard his name somewhere before, but I couldn't pinpoint it.

He inclined his head in acknowledgment. "Appreciation for beauty is part of my family business. Luxury goods," he said when my brow knit in confusion. "Fashion, jewelry, wines and spirits, beauty and cosmetics. All part of the Russo empire." A self-deprecating note crept into his tone.

Of course.

It suddenly clicked. I read a recent magazine profile of The Russo Group, the world's largest luxury goods conglomerate.

Dante was the CEO. According to the profile, he was also rumored to have one of the most ruthless security teams in the corporate world. There was an urban legend that his head of security once caught someone trying to sneak into his house while he was away for business. The unlucky thief ended up in a month-long coma with two broken kneecaps, a mangled face, and every rib shattered.

The thief had refused to name names, and there was no hard evidence tracing it back to Dante, but his reputation stuck.

No wonder Josh was so confident Max's associates wouldn't fuck with him.

We made more chitchat for a few minutes before I hesitated and said, "I'm sorry to hear about your grandfather."

Enzo Russo founded the Russo Group sixty-five years ago. He was a bona fide business legend, and his funeral had dominated the headlines a few weeks ago.

Dante didn't seem distraught over his grandfather's death, but it felt like the polite thing to say considering how recent the funeral was. Plus, I'd been there when he received the news in Christian's library.

An iron blanket fell over his sculpted features. "Thank you. I appreciate it." He glanced over my shoulder. "Apologies for cutting our conversation short, but my *fiancée* has finally arrived." He sounded less than thrilled. Was there anyone in this man's life he *did* like? "Please, enjoy the rest of the party." He nodded at us and strode off, his tall, muscled frame cutting a striking figure in the crowd. At the end of hall, a beautiful Asian woman watched him approach with a half nervous, half defiant expression. His fiancée, I assumed.

"I would pay to see someone try to steal from him," I said. "Good job."

Josh smirked. "I try. How do you know him?" He sounded more curious than concerned.

"We met at Christian's house when I asked for his help with Max." I spotted a server bearing down on us with a tray of champagne and quickly shook my head.

"Right. Is it just me, or do all rich people know each other?" he asked.

"I wouldn't be surprised. They live in a small world." I eyed the painting again. Unlike the others, it lacked a plaque engraved with its name, artist, and origins. "So, does this oh-so-precious piece have a name?"

"Apparently. Dante was already familiar with it when he bought it." Josh took my hand again as we walked to the next painting. "It's called *Magda*."

58

JOSH

THERE WAS ONE BRIGHT SPOT TO THE WHOLE MESS WITH the painting: I sold it to Dante for a shit ton of money. It wasn't enough for me to retire on, but it was enough to pay off my med school loans, splurge on nice dates with Jules, and build a comfortable nest egg for the future.

I was pretty sure Dante had undervalued the art during our negotiations, but fuck it. I was just happy to be rid of the damn thing.

I pushed open the door to the clinic, my steps lighter than it had been in months. I'd just finished a nine-hour shift, but Jules only had a few weeks left at LHAC, and I wanted to spend as much time with her as possible before she started her job at Silver & Klein.

The first thing I noticed when I stepped inside was the group clustered around Jules's desk, oohing and aahing over something.

"Is this a workplace or is this a party?" I quipped, coming up behind them. "What's going on?"

"It's lunchtime, Josh." Ellie tossed her hair over her shoulder. "We deserve a break. Right, Marsh?"

Marshall stared at her with a besotted expression. "Absolutely."

Poor guy. He was so smitten with her he would've jumped off a bridge had she asked him to.

Then again, I felt the same way about Jules, so I wasn't one to talk.

"Hey, Red." I placed a gentle hand on her shoulder and resisted the urge to kiss her.

Everyone at the clinic knew we were dating now, but we still kept things professional when we were in front of our coworkers. No PDA, though I couldn't resist sneaking a kiss every now and then when we were alone.

"Hi." She smiled up at me, and it should be fucking illegal how that one tiny thing made my chest swell.

"Hi." I smiled back.

The air between us thrummed with electricity, and I wished, not for the first time, that we were alone instead of surrounded by a half dozen coworkers.

Everyone around us sighed—some with dreaminess, some with mock exasperation.

"I knew you would make a good-looking couple." Barbs beamed, her eyes glinting with smugness. "No one believed me."

When we broke the news of our relationship two weeks ago, she'd been so ecstatic she baked a giant blueberry pie and brought it in the next day. According to her, it was to celebrate her first love match at LHAC, even though she wasn't responsible for us getting together.

Then again, she was the one who pushed me to see Jules in the kitchen during Jules's first day here, so maybe she did deserve a little credit. If I'd found out about Jules working here another day, another way, I might've never offered a truce, and we wouldn't be where we were now.

Plus, Barbs had been less insufferable than Clara, who gave me the world's biggest shit-eating, *I told you so* grin when she found out.

"In that regard, I carry all the weight in the relationship," I drawled, earning myself an elbow jab from Jules.

Barbs's grin widened. "Funny, she said the same thing."

"I'm not surprised." I smoothed a hand over Jules's hair. "Poor thing can be delusional."

"Look in the mirror, Chen." Jules sniffed. "That is, if it hasn't already cracked from facing you every day."

My laugh joined everyone else's. "Touché, Red. Touché." I leaned over her shoulder and looked at her phone. "What are you guys all staring at, anyway?"

"She's showing us pictures from her friend's proposal." Barbs's gray curls quivered with excitement. "Look at that ring! I'm surprised the poor girl didn't topple over from the size of it."

I shook my head as Jules scrolled through pictures of Alex and Ava's proposal on her phone.

Alex had officially proposed over the weekend. The bastard couldn't do anything halfway, so he flew Ava to London for a "special photography exhibit" and popped the question at the gallery where they reconciled.

Their wedding was scheduled for next summer, but preparations were already in full swing, with Jules, Stella, and Bridget as bridesmaids. Ava couldn't decide who she wanted as her maid of honor, so she chose to forego one altogether.

"Now this one should be framed and hung." Barbs leaned over and tapped on the screen when Jules reached the last picture.

In it, Alex knelt on one knee while Ava had one hand clapped over her mouth. Her eyes were glossy with tears. The entire gallery had been stripped and redecorated for the proposal—twinkling strings of lights clipped with Polaroids Ava had taken of the two of them together, a table set with candles and flowers in the middle of the room, and blue rose petals scattered over the floor. The blaze from the open ring box was blinding even in two-dimensional form.

It was also the only photo I'd ever seen of Alex where he looked visibly, wildly nervous.

I rubbed my hands together. Man, I couldn't wait to hold this over his head the next time I saw him. A nervous Alex, immortalized for all eternity.

The universe loved me.

Everyone oohed and aahed over the picture a while longer before they finally dispersed to their desks, and Jules and I entered the empty kitchen to "get more coffee."

The minute the door closed, I cupped the back of her neck and drew her to me for a proper greeting. She tasted like caramel and coffee, and I savored her sweetness for a minute before I pulled back.

"Hi." My lips brushed hers with the word.

"Hi." Jules's smile settled in my chest like a ray of warmth. "Is this how you greet all your coworkers, Dr. Chen? Because it's highly inappropriate."

"Only the infuriating, pain-in-my ass ones." I nipped her bottom lip lightly in punishment for her sass. "A kiss is the only way to shut them up."

"Don't let the nurses know, or you'll have a mutiny on your hands. They'll be pissing you off left and right."

"It's a good thing I'm not interested in any nurses. Besides..." I rubbed my thumb over the nape of her neck in small circles. "No one pisses me off like you do."

Jules melted into my touch. "You're such a charmer."

"It's one of my many excellent qualities," I drawled. "Anyway, how's the wedding planning going? Ava turn into Bridezilla yet?"

"Josh, she literally got engaged four days ago. She's still in Europe."

Alex had extended their trip so they could visit France and Spain after London.

"Hey, I've never been a bride. I don't know how these time-lines work."

Jules let out a good-natured sigh. "It'll be a while before we get into the swing of things, but..." A blanket of hesitation fell over her face. "Speaking of brides, we're getting to that time in our lives. Bridget's married. Ava is engaged."

"Yep."

"Do you...want to get married anytime soon?"

My thumb stilled on her skin. "Do you?" I watched her carefully for a reaction.

We'd only been dating for a few months, but now was as good a time as any to discuss our expectations for the future.

We stared at each other for a second before we blurted out our answers.

"No, I'm not financially ready yet—"

"I still have to finish my residency and take my boards—"

"There's so much I want to do before—"

"So many places to travel—"

Our words jumbled together in our haste.

Jules laughed, covering her face with her hands. "Oh, thank God. Not that I don't want to get married and have kids eventually, but now..."

"...Is not the right time," I finished. "Totally agree."

I already knew she was the one I wanted to spend my life with, but marriage came with financial responsibilities neither of us was equipped to handle at the moment.

Besides, when we did have our wedding, I wanted it to be

her ultimate dream wedding. I wanted our honeymoon to be fucking epic. Those things weren't possible when I was constrained by my residency, and Jules was navigating her first years as an attorney.

"There's too much of the world to see first." I rubbed my thumb over her hand. "And I want to see it all with you."

A blush of pleasure climbed up her neck and over her face. "Is that a promise, Chen? Because I'll hold you to it."

I smiled, wondering how the fuck I ever thought Jules was anything other than my perfect match.

"It's more than a promise, Red. It's a guarantee."

EPILOGUE

JULES

One month later

"Open it."

"No."

"Jules." Josh placed his hands on my shoulders. "No matter what's on that screen, you'll be fine. I'll be here. The anticipation will kill you more than the results."

"Easy for you to say." I cast a nervous glance at my laptop, where the login page for my bar exam results stared back at me. "You're not the one whose entire future is riding on one measly score."

I'd waited for so long, and now that the results were here, I wanted to chuck my computer across the room and pretend they didn't exist. Ignorance was bliss and all that.

My stomach churned when I remembered everything I had going against me. I'd taken the bar fresh off my breakup with Josh and injured after my psychotic ex pushed me down the stairs.

The outlook did not look good for a passing score.

"It's not your entire future." Josh's calm voice loosened some of the knots in my muscles. "If you don't pass, you'll take it again until you *do* pass. You're going to be a kickass attorney one day, Red. Don't doubt yourself. Besides..." He kissed my forehead. "It's better to rip the Band-Aid off than let the uncertainty fester."

"Right. You're right." I took a deep breath.

It was fine. I'll be fine. Not passing the bar wouldn't be the end of the world.

I mean, it would be the end of *my* world, but not the end of *the* world.

I walked to my laptop and typed in my username and password with shaking fingers. My breakfast swirled in my stomach, and I regretted wolfing down the blueberry waffles Josh made.

When the score report loaded, I closed my eyes, my heart a frantic steel drum in my chest.

Just get it over with. You'll be fine.

Behind me, Josh rested his hands on my shoulders again, his presence strong and comforting.

I finally cracked my eyes open and zeroed in on the total score at the bottom of the page.

295.

It took a second for the numbers to process. Once they did, I let out a loud squeal.

"I passed!" I jumped up and banged my knee against the underside of the table, but I didn't even feel the pain. I turned and threw my arms around Josh's neck, smiling so wide my cheeks ached. "I passed, I passed, I *passed*!"

He laughed and spun me around. "What did I tell you? Congrats, Red." Pride seeped into his voice, rich and warm. "Now you can support me on your big-time lawyer salary while I toil away in my residency."

I was scheduled to start my job at Silver & Klein next week. Part of me was sad to leave the clinic, but I hoped I would still be able to work with LHAC in some capacity. Lisa mentioned she was interested in partnering with a corporate law firm to expand the clinic's services, and after I established myself at Silver & Klein, I planned to propose a partnership between my new company and my old one.

Meanwhile, Josh had entered his fourth and final year of residency, after which he'd take his board exams and become a fully licensed doctor.

We were well on our way to achieving our dream careers, but honestly, I was happier about the fact I had Josh by my side through it all. It made every achievement sweeter and every failure less bitter.

"I knew you were a gold digger." Even after paying off his med school loans, he had enough money from selling the painting to be financially comfortable for decades, but that didn't stop me from teasing him. "Using me for money. I am shocked. Appalled. Scandalized—"

Josh cut me off with a kiss. "Don't worry." His voice lowered as he ran one large, warm palm up my thigh. "I can repay you in non-monetary ways."

My heart rate picked up, and I bit back a moan when he reached the cleft between my legs. I was already soaked for him, as confirmed by the satisfied gleam in Josh's eyes. He was always such a smug bastard about sex.

I hated how much I loved it.

"I don't believe you," I breathed. "I need a demonstration first."

"You drive a hard bargain." He slipped my underwear to the side and rubbed his thumb over my clit. "What kind of demonstration would you like? You want me to fuck your pussy till you forget your own name? Eat that sweet little cunt out until you come all over my face? Or maybe..." He pushed a finger inside me and curled it until he hit a spot that made my limbs tremble. "You want me to fill every hole like the needy little slut you are."

A whimper escaped at the mental picture he painted. My toys weren't strangers in our sex life, and the last time he'd used them on me while fucking my mouth...

A pleasurable shudder wracked my body.

"Which is it, Red?" Josh worked another finger inside me. "Use your words."

"I..." I struggled to form a coherent response, but I was too distracted by the slow pump of his fingers in and out of me.

A bundle of electricity pooled between my legs.

"Your verbal skills could use work." He tsked in mock disappointment. "But since I'm feeling generous and we need to celebrate you passing the bar, I'll provide a sample demonstration of all three..."

Josh was right about my verbal skills needing work, because by the time he finished his "demonstrations" three hours later, my body was limp and it was a struggle to even remember my own name.

"Mmph." I made a contented noise as drowsiness settled over me like a warm blanket and pulled heavy on my eyelids. We'd moved from the living room to his bed, and I just wanted to sink into his pillows and never leave. "Good sample."

Josh's soft laugh tickled my skin as he pressed a kiss to my shoulder. "How do you feel about a full demonstration, then?" He caressed the curve of my ass, and the butterflies in my stomach went crazy again.

"Stop," I moaned, half horrified, half aroused. "I will die if I have one more orgasm."

The chances of me walking properly tomorrow were already close to zero.

"Okay, okay. I'll give you a reprieve." Josh laughed again before he rolled over and reached for his phone. "I actually bought you a proper gift in anticipation of you passing the bar." His dimple deepened. "Well, I bought *us* a gift."

I perked up, my curiosity overpowering my drowsiness. "Is it a toy? Lingerie? The *Kama Sutra*?"

"No, Red." He tapped my nose, his eyes sparkling with exasperated amusement. "Get your mind out of the gutter."

I made a face while he pulled something up on his screen. "Look who's talking. Your mind *lives* in the gutter."

Josh swatted my ass in light punishment before he handed me his phone. "Careful, or that reprieve is going to be more temporary than you thought."

I ignored my prickle of anticipation at his words and squinted at the document onscreen. It looked like...a plane ticket?

When the tiny words finally came into focus, I sucked in a sharp breath. "New Zealand? We're going to *New Zealand*?"

"Early next year when I have vacation days again. But I bought flexible tickets so we can change the dates in case you can't take that week off at your new job." Josh's grin nearly blinded me. "Excited?"

"Are you freaking kidding? It's *New Zealand!*" My stomach flipped as images of snow-capped mountains and pristine blue waters filled my mind. Outside of the US, I'd only been to Eldorra, Canada, Mexico, and a few Caribbean islands. New Zealand was one of the top destinations on my bucket list.

"What if I hadn't passed?" I asked, staring at the e-ticket again to make sure it was real.

Yep, there they were. My name, the travel dates, and the destination. All real.

He shrugged. "Then it would've been a comfort gift."

Emotion clogged my throat and crawled into my chest.

"Josh Chen, sometimes you are..." I set the phone aside and kissed him. Forget salted caramel. Nothing tasted as good as him—like mint and sex. "Tolerable."

"Tolerable?" He hitched an eyebrow. "That's not good. I'm supposed to be insufferable, and you..." He threaded his fingers through my hair and gave it a gentle yank. "You're supposed to hate me."

I dug my nails into his thigh until I heard his sharp inhale. "I do."

A slow smile spread across his face. "Show me."

I dug my nails harder in his skin before I trailed them over his chest and climbed on top of him. I tugged hard on his hair and flinched when he spanked my ass again, this time so hard the sting reverberated through my body.

Wetness coated my thighs, and I moaned, all traces of drowsiness gone.

Screw walking properly. It was overrated anyway.

JOSH

Four months later

"If I die, I will drag you to hell and torment you for eternity." Jules wrapped an arm around my waist, her face several shades paler than usual as we shuffled toward the edge of the platform.

Behind us, the bungee jump operator checked our harnesses one last time.

"If you die, I die, Red." I grinned and kissed her cheek. "Hell with you sounds like heaven to me."

Her tense expression cracked. "That was corny as fuck, Josh."

"Yeah, so? I'm hot enough to pull it off." I peered down at

the river below us. "Besides, you may want to be nice to me. You don't want our last words to be insults, do you?"

It was our last full day in New Zealand, and we were at Queenstown's Kawarau Bridge for a tandem bungee jump. Jules had taken all our previous activities in stride—skydiving, paragliding, whooshing across a canyon with the Shotover Canyon Swing. But she'd never looked as nervous as she did now.

Her face paled further. *"Don't say that."*

"I'm kidding, I'm kidding." I tightened my arm around her waist. "We'll be fine. Trust me."

"We better be, or I promise, I'll let Cerberus bite your genitals off."

I grinned. I loved when she got violent.

"Are you ready?" The operator asked, keeping a hold on the backs of our harnesses.

I looked at Jules, who took a deep breath and nodded.

"We're good," I said.

My heart crashed against my ribcage in anticipation.

The operator gave us a small push, and...

We jumped. Fast and hard, the wind whistling in our ears as we plummeted toward the deep turquoise waters of the Kawarau River.

Jules's scream mingled with my exhilarated laugh.

Fuck, I missed this. The adrenaline. The rush. The feeling of being so *alive* that the entire world lit up around you.

But it wasn't just the bungee jump. It was the fact I was experiencing it with Jules. No one and nothing could make me feel as alive as she did.

I captured her mouth in a kiss, distracting her from the rope's recoil. For most people, the recoil was the most terrifying part of bungee jumping, and she was already nervous enough.

Her muscles tensed, but they relaxed again when I deepened the kiss and tightened a protective arm around her waist. She didn't scream again on our way down.

Pride bloomed in my chest. *That's my girl.*

A raft waited for us at the end of our last free fall. The two staff members unhooked us from our harnesses, and we collapsed, face up, on the mattress-like cushion.

"Holy. Shit," Jules wheezed after she caught her breath.

I turned my head to look at her. "Told you that was going to be amazing."

"I don't know if *amazing* is the right word. I saw my life flash before my eyes." She turned as well so we faced each other. Her cheeks were tinged pink from the wind, and her hair fanned out around her in a silky red cloud. She was so fucking beautiful it made my chest hurt. "But it was worth it for that kiss alone."

"Spiderman and Mary Jane have nothing on us."

"Absolutely not."

We grinned at each other and lapsed into a comfortable silence as the raft glided toward shore.

After a whirlwind week of activities, we could finally share a moment of peace.

Part of me wanted to stay here and explore New Zealand with her forever. Another part couldn't wait to live out the rest of our lives together back home.

I was in my last year of residency; Jules was thriving at Silver & Klein and had already been tapped to work on a huge case with a senior partner. We also moved in together last month so we could maximize our time together between our crazy schedules. We compromised on the commute by choosing a house halfway between her office and the hospital.

That meant Stella was now living in The Mirage alone. She'd worked out a deal with the landlord so she didn't have to pay Jules's portion of the rent for the remainder of her lease.

That alleviated some of Jules's guilt over leaving her friend high and dry in their old apartment, though Stella insisted it was fine.

New Zealand was a fantasy; D.C. was reality. Both were pretty damn amazing.

"Still hate me?" I whispered, lacing my fingers with Jules's.

Her eyes sparkled with mischief as she squeezed my hand. "Always."

I smiled. "Good."

THE END

Thank you for reading *Twisted Hate!* If you enjoyed this book, I would be grateful if you could leave a review on the platform(s) of your choice.

Reviews are like tips for author, and every one helps!

Much love,
Ana

P.S. Want to discuss my books and other fun shenanigans with like-minded readers? Join my exclusive reader group, Ana's Star Squad!

For TWO steamy/sweet bonus scenes of Josh and Jules, visit this link: BookHip.com/QSZFJKM

Keep in touch with Ana Huang

Join my Facebook reader group, Ana's Star Squad, to get the latest updates and talk about books, Netflix, and more!

facebook.com/groups/anasstarsquad

You can also find Ana at these places:

Website:
anahuang.com

Bookbub:
bookbub.com/profile/ana-huang

Instagram:
@authoranahuang

Goodreads
goodreads.com/anahuang

ACKNOWLEDGMENTS

First, a HUGE shout out to my alpha and beta readers Brittney, Sarah, Rebecca, Aishah, Allisyn, Salma, and Kimberly and my specialty alphas Logan, Aya, Alexa, and Ashley for your amazing, honest feedback and medical and legal expertise, You saw the story in its rawest form, typos and all, and your feedback turned a rough draft into something I'm proud to share with the world.

To Amber, for always being there when I'm overthinking (AKA 99% of the time) and being a rockstar PA.

To my editor Amy Briggs and proofreader Krista Burdine for working your magic as only you can do.

To Quirah at Temptation Creations for the beautiful cover and the teams at Give Me Books and Wildfire Marketing for keeping me sane during the chaos of release month.

Finally, to my readers, bloggers, bookstagrammers, and bookmakers, I LOVE YOU! I will never get over how supportive and incredible you all are and I'm so grateful for each and every one of you.

xo, Ana

He'll do anything to have her . . . including lie.

Order *Twisted Lies* now for Christian and Stella's story.

Available from

PIATKUS

Don't miss the other books in Ana Huang's addictive Twisted series . . .

Available now from

PIATKUS